Michael Jecks began his series of me[dieval] West Country mysteries after thirteen 'interesting' [year]s in the computer industry. He finds writing consi[derabl]y more secure, and much more fun as well, leav[ing him] plenty of time to indulge his fascination w[ith medie]val history, local legends and the folklore o[f Dartmo]or.

His thirteen previo[us novels] featuring Sir Baldwin Furnshill and Baili[ff Simon] Puttock, most recently *The Tournament of Bl[ood], Th[e] Sticklepath Strangler* and *The Devil's Acolyte*, ar[e a]ll available from Headline.

Michael and his wife and daughter live in northern Dartmoor.

Acclaim for Michael Jecks' previous mysteries:

'Brisk medieval whodunnit'   *Literary Review*

'Michael Jecks has a way of dipping into the past and giving it the immediacy of a present-day newspaper article . . . He writes . . . with such convincing charm that you expect to walk round a corner in Tavistock and meet some of the characters'   *Oxford Times*

'A tortuous and exciting plot . . . The construction of the story and the sense of period are excellent'   *Shots*

'Jecks' knowledge of medieval history is impressive and is used here to great effect'   *Crime Time*

'A gem of historical storytelling'   *Northern Echo*

'Really difficult to put down'   *Historical Novels Review*

The Mad Monk of Gidleigh

Michael Jecks

headline

First published in 2002
by HEADLINE BOOK PUBLISHING

First published in paperback in 2003
by HEADLINE BOOK PUBLISHING

10 9 8 7 6 5 4 3 2

ISBN 0 7553 0169 2

Printed and bound in Great Britain by
Clays Ltd, St Ives plc

HEADLINE BOOK PUBLISHING
A division of Hodder Headline
338 Euston Road
LONDON NW1 3BH

www.headline.co.uk
www.hodderheadline.com

For all at Caterham & District Rifle Club,
but especially my good friend
Hugh Keitch.

Good shooting!

Acknowledgements

There are too many people to whom I am indebted for me to mention them all, but I am especially grateful to Mike, a great countryman and local historian in his own right, for introducing me to his friend, the late Dickie Narracott, last hereditary Warden of the Bradford Leat. From them came the plot, and I am hugely grateful.

There is another person who must be thanked. In the week that my copy-editor asked where we could find a vocabulary of medieval curses and insults, along came an email with thirty-odd. Max, thanks!

Finally I have to thank those who have helped, advised, guided and slapped me down occasionally: first my wife Jane, then my agent Jane; Marion, Andi and Shona, the world's three best commissioning editors (I would say that, wouldn't I), and Joan Deitch, for copy editing with courage, conviction and courtesy.

Having said all that, of course, I have to point out that all errors are *their* fault and not mine.

Glossary

Benefit of Clergy If a priest or monk was accused of a crime, he could claim the 'benefit' of being tried only by his peers in an ecclesiastical court. This meant that he was safe from penalties of life and limb – he couldn't be hanged. To prove his eligibility, he had to recite, usually, the *pater noster* in Latin or a similar sequence that only a cleric would be expected to know.

Chevauchée A small band of warriors on a raiding party; the name was given to the raid or campaign as well as the group itself.

Frankpledge All the male inhabitants of a vill were automatically members of the Frankpledge. At the age of twelve they had to swear to keep the peace and to restrain anyone who did not. All members were answerable for any infringements and for damages caused by others. This system was imposed by the Franks (the Normans) after the invasion.

Grace In the 1300s Grace could be said either before or after the meal, unlike today when it is invariably spoken before the meal.

Leyrwyte A fine imposed on women for sexual incontinence.

Pater Noster The 'Our Father' prayer; at the time of Baldwin and Simon, it was known only by priests and recited in Latin.

Petty Treason (*petit treason*) The term given to simple treachery. It was the treason of a serf to his master, or even a wife to her husband, as opposed to high treason, which was treachery against the Crown.

Placebo This was the evensong of the dead, known from the first word of the service.

Seven Interrogations The seven questions asked by a priest to confirm that a dying person believed in God, the scriptures, Jesus, and that God would forgive those who sincerely regretted their sins and offences.

Seyney Many monks lived in conditions of extreme hardship, and there were times when they had to be sent away for a short period to recover. At such times, they would be rested and given better food, including good cuts of meat. This re-creational period was known as a 'seyney'.

Stannaries The Stannaries of Devon were any locations in which miners claimed to have found tin to mine. These sometimes lay beyond the bounds of Dartmoor, which at the time was a relatively small area.

Vill A basic administrative area. It could mean a single farm, a hamlet, a small town, borough or city. Every part of England belonged to a vill. In later years, the vill or group of vills grew to become a 'parish', but this did not happen until the Tudor period.

Cast of Characters

Sir Baldwin de Furnshill	Once a Knight Templar, he has returned to his old family home in Devon where he is now Keeper of the King's Peace. He's known to be an astute investigator of violent crime.
Lady Jeanne	His wife, to whom he has been married for two years. Jeanne is a widow whose first husband abused her. She has now learned to enjoy married life.
Edgar	Baldwin's servant and Steward.
Simon Puttock	Bailiff of the Stannaries, and Baldwin's closest friend and trusted companion. Based at the administrative and legal centre of the Stannaries, Lydford Castle, Simon is responsible for keeping the peace wherever miners work under the Warden of the Stannaries, Abbot Robert Champeaux of Tavistock.
Margaret Puttock (Meg)	Simon's wife, the daughter of a farmer, whom he married many years ago.
Edith	Simon and Meg's daughter, some fifteen years old.
Hugh	Simon's servant of many years.
Elias	A sad, widowed ploughman.
Sir Richard Prouse	Terribly wounded in a tournament in 1316, he is the impecunious owner of Gidleigh Castle until his death in 1322 aged thirty.
Mark	On the death of the previous incumbent, he was given the chapel

at Gidleigh. The monk is not happy in the rural backwater.

Piers
An intelligent and hardworking peasant, now Reeve in the vill.

Henry
Piers's young, somewhat feckless son.

Huward
The miller, living near to the castle.

Gilda
Tall, attractive wife to Huward.

Mary
Eldest daughter of Huward and Gilda, she is known for her kindness and beauty.

Flora
The younger of Huward's two daughters, and perhaps not so attractive as Mary.

Ben
The miller's spoiled and precocious son.

Osbert
A local freeman who adores Mary, but whose affection is not reciprocated.

Sir Ralph de Wonson
Master of Wonson Manor, he acquires Gidleigh on Sir Richard's death.

Esmon
Son of Sir Ralph, he is an experienced warrior and successful raider.

Lady Annicia
Wife of Sir Ralph and mother to Esmon.

Surval
The hermit who tends to Chagford Bridge, maintaining the small chapel at which he prays for travellers and pleads for forgiveness.

Roger Scut
A cleric at the canonical church of Crediton, he makes notes during Baldwin's inquests.

Thomas
One of the new Constables at Crediton; a surly but loyal servant of the Law.

Godwen
The second Constable at Crediton; he hates Thomas because of a dispute over a woman from many years before.

Wylkyn
Once Sir Richard Prouse's servant, and an essential part of Gidleigh's household because of his skills with salves and potions, Wylkyn has run away from the castle to live with his brother and become a miner.

Sampson
The vill's fool, poor Sampson is dependent upon alms which he collects at the castle's door.

Brian of Doncaster
The leader of the garrison at Gidleigh, Brian is ambitious and has tied his future to Esmon thinking that the son of Sir Ralph will have a glorious career which must offer opportunities for profit.

Saul
A carter who makes his money by transporting food and goods from one town to another.

Alan
Apprentice to Saul, Alan often joins him on his travels.

Author's Note

There are some aspects of medieval life which often give rise to confusion, and it's probably a good idea to clear up some of them before launching into another story.

Even the most basic concepts of medieval law can give us difficulties. Nowadays we think of the 'parish' as being the smallest political and administrative unit. The parish, though, was a Tudor invention, largely designed to deal with problems with the poor. It didn't exist in the early 1300s, when the smallest unit was the 'vill'. A Norman term, it could mean anything from a tiny hamlet to a borough, or even areas lumped together to form a city.

Every man who was not a magnate, knight or his kinsman, cleric or some other form of freeman, had to be in a 'tithing'. Basically this meant that every man was part of a group of ten, twelve, or maybe more men. (A 'tithe' literally means one tenth.) In the less populated rural south and west of England, a vill tended to be a tithing. When a man became 'outlaw', he lost his place within a tithing. This was crucial to medieval life because he was now without any protection. Not even the tithingman, the leader of the tithing, would speak up for him.

Each boy, on reaching adulthood at the age of twelve years, must join his frankpledge and swear to keep the law. On making the oath, he immediately became liable for keeping the peace himself, and liable for damages – both for his own actions and the actions of other members of his tithing. Frankpledge, or frank pledge, as the words suggest, were an imposition of the Normans after the invasion, but based upon a mistranslation of the Old English *frithborh*, which meant 'peace-pledge'. Under the Normans, this became a tool for control of the peasants.

Every peasant was responsible for keeping the peace in his tithing and was legally responsible to, amongst others, all his neighbours. That was why onlookers would pile in to calm fights, stop robbers, even soothe bickering between a husband and wife. It was an effective means of self-policing.

Here I should point out that women were not included in tithings, nor did they have to join a frankpledge. Women and children couldn't be 'outlawed' for the excellent reason that they were never 'inlawed'. However, they could be 'waived', which had the same unpleasant implications.

There are far too many books on the history of British law for me to list them all here, but Pollock & Maitland's *History of English Law* is an excellent start.

The Keeper of the King's Peace had a unique role to play within the legal machinery of England.

In each county, a number of courts would each month record offences that should be considered by the King's own judges. Some men were imprisoned ready to be hauled before the judges, others would be set loose, after a payment to guarantee their appearance in court. Then, once a year, the Sheriff would come on his 'Tourn' to consider all the cases. Finally, the King's Justices would arrive, usually once every ten years or so, and would listen to all cases outstanding, issuing swift justice. If you doubt this, consider that during the Eyre of 1238, the Justices disposed of some thirty pleas each day. And a losing petitioner in a matter of felony would have been taken out immediately to be hanged!

The point here is that the Sheriff and the Justices were turning up a long while after many of the offences had been committed. The primary purpose of the Coroners and Keepers was thus to 'Keep' – that is, maintain a record – of the offences. In the case of the Coroners, they had the task of investigating every sudden death; they also had to visit wrecks, and record discoveries of treasure trove.

We have, from Kent, several copies of the Keepers' Rolls, which were investigated in 1933 by B. Putnam PhD for the Kent Archaeological Society. She discovered that in the terrible years of King Edward II's reign, the job of Keeper changed quite dramatically.

Initially, in December 1307, their duties were: to enforce the peace and the statute of Westminster; to arrest those who resisted and keep them in custody until the King commanded otherwise;

to maintain the coinage and prices; and attach coiners and fore-stallers. This is a good series of duties, along with maintaining the records, but in 1314 the job had expanded to: enforcing the peace and the statute; inquiry by sworn inquest of trespasses and crimes; arrest of those indicted by the inquests; pursuit, if necessary, with the *posse comitatus* from vill to vill, hundred to hundred, shire to shire, and imprisonment until lawful delivery by the command of the King; to submit a monthly report to the King's Council of names of malefactors; mandate to the Sheriff to assist and empanel jurors. There was also a promise of 'supervisors' to 'determine' their indictments.

Thus, in the space of seven years, the job had grown to give Keepers the job of catching and arresting crooks and seeing them in court. By 1316 these duties had expanded again to include holding formal inquests into felons and felonies. Probably these developments were nothing more than a proof of the disastrous early years of the century, with famine, disease and war leading to an inevitable increase in crime as the poor struggled to survive.

There is another fascinating insight which we glean from the Kent records. Putnam looked at the records of Gaol Delivery for the same period, and then correlated the names. Interestingly, she found that many of the Justices of Gaol Delivery were the Keepers who had originally tried a man and sent him to gaol in the first place (Gaol Delivery meant that the suspect was delivered from gaol to the judge to have his case decided). In the same way, it was not uncommon for a juror who had decided upon a man's guilt during the original inquest, to then sit on the jury of Gaol Delivery.

We know very little, sadly, about how the inquests would have been conducted since there are no extant records written by an independent viewer; however, by looking at the set-up of other courts, it is clear that the same general procedures appear to have prevailed, and thus we may extrapolate from them to see how Baldwin might have run his court.

While looking at Baldwin's role, it would be unfair not to briefly mention Simon's, because the Bailiff's duties were as extensive in many ways.

The Bailiff of Lydford was the servant of the Stannaries, the ancient tin mining areas of Devon (Cornwall had its own system and its own Stannary). Key areas of responsibility were situated in the centre of Dartmoor, but I believe that his territory was much wider than this. He was responsible for preventing fights and arguments between miners and local landowners, and mining didn't stop with the old forest of Dartmoor. As a proof of this, one need only consider that the stannary towns of Tavistock, Ashburton and Chagford, were *all* outside the known extent of the forest of Dartmoor.

These towns were all administrative centres. Each Stannary town controlled its own territory from the perspective of collecting tolls and taxes. However, the Warden of the Stannaries was in overall charge, and it was his duty to present any criminals who had committed felonies before the King's Justices.

The Warden delegated his responsibilities widely, especially during the wardenship of Abbot Champeaux of Tavistock, because the good Abbot had far too many other things on his plate to be able to watch over every transaction. Thus many tasks were given to his bailiffs. We know that in the 1300s his bailiff was fined for failing to arrest suspects and bring them to Lydford to the castle purpose-built as the Stannary Gaol. The bailiff would have been a man used to working on his own, a negotiator, someone capable of calming fights between miners or disputes between landowners and miners; he himself sometimes had to resort to violence. He would have been a local man, someone who knew the moors reasonably well, but who understood men and could assess them swiftly.

This is the sort of man Simon was – rugged, determined, sure of his own authority in the name of the Abbot, and committed to serving his master.

For more information on the Stannaries, look at H.P.R. Finberg's *Tavistock Abbey* (Cambridge University Press) and Sandy Gerrard's *The Early British Tin Industry* (Tempus Publishing).

Michael Jecks
Northern Dartmoour
April 2002

Prologue

In the darkened room, the man's shattered body gave a final convulsive jerk. A curious reflex caused his good arm to fly skywards as his body tensed, his back arching like a bow. The weird posture was emphasised by the guttering candles. Their thick, yellow flames gave off a greasy, black smoke that rose to the rafters, giving the chamber a grim, lowering atmosphere, as though the ceiling itself was moving closer to witness this last act in a life which had been so filled with pain and despair. As he died his shadow seemed to blacken, as though his entire soul was transformed into a larger figure looking down on the people in there, especially upon his hated neighbour, Sir Ralph de Wonson.

Sir Richard had never liked him or his brother, Sir Ralph thought to himself. At least Surval the hermit had gone after sitting up and praying for Sir Richard all night – not that it would have given the poor sick knight much comfort to see him there. Involuntarily, Sir Ralph's eyes went to the shadow's hand, showing in stark relief against the painted wall, raised high over Sir Ralph's head, the fingers curled like talons about to strike him down.

Over the muttered prayers of the monk, Brother Mark, Sir Ralph could hear the rattling breath as Sir Richard's soul fled. And then, as the arm collapsed and Sir Richard's oldest servant, Wylkyn, sprang forward with a concerned frown on his face, Sir Ralph smiled with the relief of the winner in a long race.

'Rest in peace, Sir Richard,' he murmured, crossing himself and standing a moment.

This was the one man who could have become a brake on his ambitions: Sir Richard Prouse, lately the master of Gidleigh in the Hundred of South Tawton, once a powerful, handsome knight, tall, muscular and with a mind as keen as his sword; now a mere shell. A bad fall at a tournament in 1316 had devastated his body, leaving him lame and crooked, needing a stick to walk even a small distance, unable to mount a horse or wield a weapon. He had been only twenty-four when he was wounded; he was thirty the day he died.

However, a man didn't need the strength and power of a Hector to stand in another man's way. Sir Richard Prouse had successfully managed to thwart Sir Ralph's every ambition. Now he was gone – and it was Sir Ralph's time. He could do all he desired.

That was the thought that filled him as he left that foul little room in the castle's gatehouse. He felt his contemplative mood falling away even as he stepped under the lintel and found himself out in the open air again. He glanced about him at the castle's fine walls, at the good-sized stables and huge hall, and smiled to himself. Gidleigh Castle was a prize worth winning. It was all he could do not to shout his delight aloud.

He pulled up his belt and wriggled: his heavy tunic of bright green wool was a little too tightly cut about his shoulders. Any other day, this would have put him in a bad mood, but not today. His boots leaked, his shoulders were pinched, and he had noticed a stain on his hose, but he didn't care *because the castle was his at last*.

A horse whinnied, but he took no notice. Nothing mattered, today of all days. He was freed, he was come into his new wealth. This fine Tuesday in the early summer of 1322 was the first day of Sir Ralph's new life.

The horse neighed again, more loudly this time, and Sir Ralph looked at the gateway in time to see a glistening black stallion pelt in, skidding to a halt on the cobbles as the laughing rider hauled on the reins, only to stand panting and blowing, shaking his great head. Froth marked his flanks, and sweat, but the rider looked as fresh as when he had set off an hour earlier. Now he kicked his feet free of the stirrups and sprang down, a young man wearing a grey tunic and parti-coloured hose of red and blue. Simply dressed, he nonetheless gave the impression of money.

'Well?'

'He's dead, Esmon,' Sir Ralph said with quiet satisfaction.

His son gave a harsh laugh. 'About time! I feared the clod was going to drag it out another week!'

A haggard-faced servant was walking past the court, and Sir Ralph called to him. 'You! Fetch us wine and bring it to the hall.'

'Sir.'

'And hurry!'

Sir Ralph, a tall, trim figure, with a strong, square face and dimpled chin, turned and marched to his new home. Although his fair hair had faded a little, he was in the prime of his life; he had been tested in many combats, and had never been the loser. That knowledge gave him the confident swagger, but it was his position in the world that gave his grey eyes their steadiness. He was Lord of Gidleigh now, the owner of this land, the ruler of his villeins and all their families, the unopposed master of all the farms and moors about here, from Throwleigh all the way to Chagford.

'You're sure there's nothing can take it from us?' his son asked.

A momentary irritation crossed Sir Ralph's features. 'What could happen?'

Esmon's face was longer than his father's, but he had the same light hair. Barely seventeen years old, his occasional lack of confidence was displayed by either belligerence or a propensity to redden when he was unsure or embarrassed. Now he made an effort to shrug as though unconcerned. 'The law . . . a clerk might find a reason.'

'Not with us, not with our Lord Hugh Despenser returned to the country and in power. They say that no one can be presented to the King without his approval – nor without paying him! You think anyone would dare to say a word against us? Nay, boy. We have our wealth now. We've increased our demesne to double its previous size.'

'All because a usurer was murdered.'

'Yes,' Sir Ralph chuckled.

It had been so easy, he told himself, marching into the hall and sitting in Sir Richard's own chair. The damn thing was uncomfortable, he discovered: he'd have cushions made, or get the chair destroyed and order a new one. That might be better – a proof that the old lord was gone and the new one installed. It would do for now, though.

The wine arrived, and he noticed the peasant bringing it cast a look at him sitting in the chair. So! The villeins here weren't happy that he had their manor, eh? They would just have to learn to accept it, or suffer the consequences!

Sir Ralph took up a mazer of wine and watched the man's departing back. There were rumours of dissatisfaction. It was lucky that they had Esmon's friends here, a group of men-at-arms who had served the Despensers with Esmon during the brief rebellion in Wales the previous year, 1321. Having Brian of Doncaster with his men meant a little additional security, and that was all to the good. Sir Ralph had even heard someone mutter that it was suspicious, the way Sir Richard had suddenly fallen victim to illness after six years of moderate health – but Ralph himself had known strong men collapse suddenly after a tiny pin-prick, their limbs swelling appallingly until they expired. True, there was no obvious mark on Sir Richard, but he had been feeble in body since the tournament, with one side crippled, a badly dragging leg, a thin and weakly arm that must be tied into his belt, and only one eye. The other had been cut out and blinded.

It was the gout had made him take to his bed, but then delirium and fever had set in. Sir Ralph shrugged. It was common enough for men to contract diseases which took them away quickly. There was no mystery as far as he was concerned, and no doubt the rumours would soon fade.

'It's good land, Father. I've been over the whole estate,' Esmon said.

'What is the mood of the peasants?'

'Surly, but they'll obey. They are scared.'

'Good.'

It was ironic that he should have won this castle. In the past he had learned to win money and land in battles, but this, his most prized possession, had been won by his political contacts. Sir Richard had been in debt to a banker who had died and whose possessions had subsequently reverted to the Crown. There all the unpaid debts would have been foreclosed instantly, the King demanding immediate repayment, if things had run their normal course. Sir Richard would have been forced to take on a new loan or leave his castle, and the estate would have been absorbed by the King if it hadn't been for my Lord Hugh Despenser, who wanted to reward Sir Ralph for past favours, especially his support during the Despenser Wars.

When Lord Hugh realised that Sir Ralph coveted this little manor, he spoke to the King and the property was conveyed to Sir Ralph, in exchange for oaths of loyalty to death. Sir Ralph lost no time in advising his neighbour that he expected to take possession of his new property.

Sir Richard had fought, of course, and tried to have the King listen to his pleas, but soon after beginning his actions, he sickened and took to his bed. It was the last straw, people said. His feeble constitution couldn't bear the prospect of losing his home and lands. So instead of being evicted, he would leave the place in a winding-sheet. Ah well. No matter. It was all Sir Ralph's now.

All the land, all the rents, all the taxes. And all the villeins, he reminded himself with a wolfish grin, thinking of the girl with the sunny smile and long dark hair who lived at the mill.

Wylkyn was struck by a faint odour as he stood over the body of his master, but it didn't register immediately. All his attention was taken up by the ravaged corpse before him, by the twisted body and the lunatic smile that showed the agony of his last contortions.

Wylkyn sniffed back the tears as he washed his master and laid him out. He had been the loyal servant of this man for many years, and this last service was his way of respecting Sir Richard. Smoothing away the signs of pain and distress, he wondered what could have caused the death. Gout was the reason why Sir Richard had been installed here in his bed, because his one good foot had grown so painful that even to touch the base of the big toe caused the knight to cry out. Even having a blanket over it was intolerable. And then he had begun to complain that his sight was disordered

– a curious affliction that made him feel giddy and nauseous. That was a matter of two or three days ago now, and suddenly he was gone!

His had been a miserable existence, Wylkyn knew, and he sighed as he gently manipulated the body, easing the tortured features into a more relaxed expression, closing the staring eyes and crossing Sir Richard's arms over his breast.

As he worked, the priest murmured his doggerel in the corner in that low, sing-song voice that he always used, as though it added to the significance of words which Wylkyn couldn't understand anyway. The servant felt his sadness increasing as he acknowledged each wound and mark on his dead master. There was the appalling group of scars at the base of his neck, stretching over his shoulders, where the mace that had taken away the use of his right arm and leg had struck him, leaving Sir Richard a cripple and figure of fun among the less honourable nobles in the area. Although those were the wounds that did him the most harm, it was the other scar that people noticed first, the one on his face.

It stretched from above his temple, past the ruined eye-socket, and down to his jaw, where the blade had sliced cleanly through. The bones had healed, but Sir Richard never again saw from that eye, and the hideous mark had made him hide away, fearful of the attention it always attracted. Pretty women shuddered and turned from him, children sometimes screamed and bolted.

There were other problems. Some, like the gout, were as painful as anything Sir Richard had sustained in the tournament. Thanks to Wylkyn's fascination with herbs and potions, the knight had made good progress, for Wylkyn had learned how to treat Sir Richard as a patient as well as a master.

When he had finished setting out his master's body, Wylkyn collected the cup and jug of wine from beside the bed, and made his way back to his little room beside the gatehouse. It was only a lean-to affair, two thin walls making a room in the angle between the gatehouse itself and the castle's outer wall, which here was stone, unlike the fencing at the rear. Sir Richard had never had enough money to complete the defences of his home.

It was sad that he'd gone. Especially now, Wylkyn reckoned, looking out at the men in the yard. Sir Ralph of Wonson had brought his own guards with him, as though seeking to stake his claim to the place. Everyone knew he had always wanted Gidleigh for his own. With its fertile land and abundance of farms, it was a good place for a lord who wanted to fleece more peasants.

Wylkyn was a free man and had been since 1318, when Sir Richard had given him a signed letter of manumission, in grateful thanks for his medical knowledge, and on the express under-standing that Wylkyn would not leave him. With the death of his master, Wylkyn felt his debt had been fully repaid. He had done all he could to ease Sir Richard's pain, but now he had no patient, he could leave at any time he wanted.

From the look of the new master and his men, the time to go was soon. He didn't want to remain here and see the place converted into the home of brigands and bullies.

Setting the jug and cup neatly on their shelf, he gave a deep sigh. He was exhausted after four days and nights spent sitting up and tending his master. Poor Sir Richard! His passing had been every bit as painful as his life. He'd started fading, but then suddenly he had become delirious, which was when the priest had been called; however, he had stayed less than a day, saying that his own congregation needed him more. He and Sir Richard had never been very friendly. That was why Mark, the monk, had been summoned instead. His little chapel had no congregation, so he could come and sit with the dying man.

Sir Richard had complained, in his lucid moments, of losing his sight. It was the one thing which terrified him, losing the sight in his one good eye. Wylkyn did all he could, but nothing worked; Wylkyn knew his poor master was dying.

Wylkyn considered his future. His brother lived on Dartmoor, and he could always go up there to live for a while. With his stock of potions and salves, he might even be able to earn some sort of a living from the miners.

At the thought, his eyes went to his pots and jars, lined up neatly on the shelves where he had left them. *All bar one*. With a slight frown, he stared at his second highest shelf, where the potions were out of alignment.

Wylkyn was careful, always, to obey the instructions of his tutor and keep all pots in their place, precisely positioned. A clean and tidy room showed a clean and tidy mind, his tutor always said, and Wylkyn believed he was correct. That one particular pot had been moved, he had no doubt, and now he understood why his master had suddenly failed and died.

Reaching up, he took down the jar. The lid was loose. Some apothecaries and physicians might be careless, but not Wylkyn. His tutor had explained that the vitality of many herbs lay in their freshness. All jars should be properly sealed after use. Someone had jammed this one on in a hurry.

Wylkyn had bought this herb only recently in order to prepare some slaves and medicines for Sir Richard's gout. Failing eyesight, giddiness, sleepiness and delirium, he reminded himself. The very same symptoms that this herb would produce in excess.

He went to the cup and jug he had brought from the gatehouse and sniffed. Now he could smell it – an unmistakable narcotic odour, sweet and heavy, slightly acrid. He tasted the wine gingerly. The bitterness seemed to almost bite through the flesh of his tongue. This wine had been adulterated with poison. And he knew which one: henbane.

Mark, priest of the nearby chapel of Gidleigh, remained kneeling in the death chamber, his head bowed, running the beads of his rosary through his fingers as he prayed. He felt a genuine sadness to be present at the passing of this soul. Others who had witnessed the death gradually slipped away, following Sir Ralph's lead, leaving Mark to maintain the vigil on his own.

The cleric was a young man, scarcely twenty, with clear, large, dark eyes. His face was pleasingly proportioned, with high cheeks and a wide brow, and his chin bore a small dimple. Women liked his slim build and narrow, delicate hands, and if he had not worn the cloth, he would have been snatched up as a husband long ago.

Now, although he tried to keep his mind focused on Sir Richard, he found his concentration wandering. Even a monk could only keep his mind on one topic for so long, and he had been here for more than three days.

Sir Richard had never been a generous or particularly friendly man. Piers, one of the local peasants and the Reeve of the vill, had once joked to Mark that the knight was so mean, he'd sell the steam off his piss if he could, but that mattered little to the priest. All he knew was that the knight had shown him some grudging respect, and in any case, a man who died deserved prayers, even if he was a miserable devil most of the year. Not that Mark could criticise a man for that. He had often felt low in spirits himself, since he was moved here to this wet, miserable land, and *he* was hale and healthy. How much worse it would be if you were born here and tied to the land, or if you were crippled and in constant pain, like Sir Richard.

He looked up as Wylkyn returned to the room, grim-faced. He stood a moment, staring down at Sir Richard's face, then bent forward and kissed his forehead gently, before walking from the room, leaving Mark alone with the body.

Mark was about to continue with his murmurings when he felt a gentle breeze sough against his cheek, as soft as a woman's sigh. There, at the opposite side of the room was a figure, clad in tatters of some heavy grey cloth and surrounded by light from the bright sun outside. It was Surval the Hermit.

Mark felt a shiver run down his spine. The creature – he hardly deserved to be called a man – was unwholesome. Mark could *smell* him almost before he could see him. Last night, when the two were here praying for Sir Richard, the stench had been enough to guarantee that Mark would not fall asleep. There was an odour of filth and something else quite repellent – not at all the aura of sanctity which a religious man should have carried.

Surval appeared to be gazing about him, and Mark realised he could see scarcely anything in this gloom after the sunlight outside, not that he would have found it easy to see Mark in his corner, kneeling near the head of the bed. Something about the hermit made Mark's tongue cleave to the roof of his mouth. He couldn't have continued praying if he'd wanted.

The old hermit clumped his staff on the ground and shuffled through the thin scattering of rushes, slowly approaching the palliasse on which the dead knight lay. Mark could see the hermit's eyes glittering as he bent down to Sir Richard's dead face and studied it. Suddenly Mark was certain that the hermit knew he was there.

'Rest easy, Sir Richard. You were weak, but that was no surprise. Your father was weaker. Fear not but that others will protect your folk. Boy – where's your tongue? Pray for him! All we sinners need prayer.'

Mark cleared his throat, but before he could speak, the hermit spoke again, more softly. 'And you more than many, eh?'

Chapter One

Mark knew what Surval meant. It was late in the year 1321, before the death of Sir Richard, when Mark first met her. Before that, he had only ever seen Mary as an occasional visitor to his chapel, and it was some months before he came to know the miller's daughter not as a priest should know his flock, but as a man knows his wife.

Not that he had any premonition of disaster at the time. Until then, the young monk had lived a life of quiet desperation here on the moors, with little or no prospects. If he had spent any time considering his future, he would have hoped for a short period of service here in the chapel at Gidleigh, followed possibly by the gift of patronage from the knight. That dream was shattered when Sir Ralph had seen Mary at Mark's home. Afterwards, there was nothing here for him but his prayers and work, and the struggle to avoid the devil's temptations. In this desolate place, Satan's efforts seemed to have redoubled.

Mark's mind flew back to the past, and the first time he met her. *She* was surely the devil's best effort.

He had to keep working. That thought was uppermost in his mind when he slowly brought himself upright, his knee-bones grinding against each other as the weight made itself felt, the leather straps that bound the strong wicker basket to his shoulders squeaking in protest. Grunting with the effort, he began lurching up the short hill to the chapel, unaware that his every move was being closely watched.

His task wasn't easy. Winter had set in weeks ago, and the water about his feet was near to freezing. He couldn't feel his toes, and although there was no ice, every step he took fell upon the leaves that lay rotting thickly on the stream's floor, making him slip and curse through gritted teeth, using words which he had heard often enough among the peasants, but which he knew he shouldn't use himself.

The basket of stones was an unbearable weight, but he had set himself the task of enclosing the chapel in a wall, and he would go to the devil rather than fail. The only thing that made sense of his life in this foul backwater was the effort he spent each day, collecting rocks and bringing them up the incline to the chapel, tipping the basket on top of the heap. When he had a big enough pile, he would grade the stones, using the largest for the bottom of the wall, graduating them with smaller and smaller rocks until he reached the topmost layer. The tiniest would be used to fit the interstices, gravel and chips blocking the cracks so that no wind could pass through.

He toiled on. Sweat was prickling at his forehead now and along his spine, forming a chilly barrier between his flesh and the coarse linen shirt. Over that he wore a habit of *strait*, a thick mix of short wool, lamb's wool and flocks, the usual stuff that the moors produced from their weak, suffering sheep. Nothing like the soft cloth produced in the warmer, drier land about Axminster, where Mark's family lived. The material from his home would never itch and scratch like this. He fancied he could feel every hair, each one tickling or stabbing him through his shirt. It was all but intolerable.

As was the pain in his thighs, the strain in his groin, the tautness in his shoulders and neck. It felt as though his muscles had solidified, as though they had been forged and hammered and were now as inflexible as iron. It was hard to imagine that they could ever relax again, and Mark's breath came in shallow gasps as he struggled with his burden.

The path here was well-trodden, for he had been working on this project for two months now, ever since he had realised that he must fight the mind-destroying tedium of his existence or go mad.

When the Bishop had sent him here, it had not been intended as a punishment, Mark knew. Bishop Walter had always appeared pleased with Mark's progress. Whenever they met, he was polite – a bit distant, maybe, but that was not surprising, since he was one of the most powerful men in the whole country. How else was a great magnate to respond to a lowly priest?

Mark had been with Exeter Cathedral for some years, and he had learned his lessons well. He had anticipated travelling, perhaps visiting the college at Oxford which Bishop Walter was so fond of, and then going on to Paris, or even Rome itself, but then one priest had died, another had run off with a woman, a third had been accused of murder . . . and suddenly Mark had been asked to serve the small community here, at the small chapel near Gidleigh. It was only until a replacement was found, he was told, but that was in 1320, a year ago last August, and no one had yet been found. Mark was beginning to think he'd be stuck here for ever.

Certainly Bishop Walter had no idea of Mark's secret motive in wanting to come here: it stemmed from his desire to see his real father at long last.

He finally reached the mound of stones, and slowly bent his knees, then allowed his body to tilt backwards until the basket sat on the ground behind him. Letting the thick leather straps fall from his shoulders, he was suddenly struck with the feeling that he had become weightless, as though he could float upwards by simply raising his arms. It was a curious sensation, one which he had noticed before, and he wondered what caused it. There seemed no logical reason. Perhaps the stones weighed down his soul, because the reason he was carrying them was to protect himself, keeping his mind and thoughts pure.

No one else would have volunteered to come here, he thought as he eyed the view sombrely, rubbing at his shoulders where the straps had chafed. A sudden noise made him spin round and stare up the valley's side. There was a roadway up there, a narrow track that led from the moors down to Gidleigh itself. It must have been someone on that path, he told himself. This place was terrible. He spent much of his time jumping at the slightest sound. It was so desolate, so lonely.

This land was fierce: it fought all who lived on it, in his opinion. It sucked the vivacity from them, leaving deadened husks – whey-faced youths or chestnut-brown men who looked as though they were forty years old when they were only twenty. And the women were worse. Either they were worn out from too many birthings, or they were ruddy-faced and as incontinent as bitches in heat. They terrified the chaste young scholar, but there was another part of his soul, a very human part, which jealously watched the young bucks flirting with them. On more than one occasion, he had stumbled across naked buttocks hammering between parted thighs, and had rushed away, horrified; yet he also knew that the pounding in his chest wasn't only from disgust.

There were times when, if he had been offered the solace of feminine company, he would have taken it, and that knowledge scared him. It was against his training and vocation to lie with a woman. Other priests might have sunk to that sin, but he had thought himself immune to such lust, that he had more willpower. It was to distract himself from his dreams of voluptuous female flesh that he had immersed himself in this building.

It was hateful, this place. Stories abounded of the devil, how he had tempted men and women into sin, how he and his hounds hunted for lost souls across the moors. When he still lived with his mother, Mark had known men who had laboured all their lives, but somehow they seemed less ancient than the shrivelled folk of Dartmoor. The people here had no sense of humour. Their existence was harsh, unleavened with laughter or pleasure. One survived, and that was all, in their world.

Mark gazed before him, thrusting his chilly hands beneath his armpits for warmth; he could feel the fingers like individual twigs of ice.

From here the land sloped down to the river. There, at the bottom, was the narrow track that led from Gidleigh to Throwleigh, a dangerous place in summer, when outlaws lurked, but safer now in the depths of winter when even the fiercest felon must be settled in his hovel. From here, at the door of his chapel, the priest could see the hills rising to the south. Bleak, they were, as though they had been blasted by God's fury.

Glancing up, he saw that the clouds were heavy with threatening storms, lowering over the moors. They suited his mood, and he grabbed his basket and made his way through the ankle-deep black mud to his door. His legs were quickly caked up to his knees, and his habit was sodden and bespattered with it before he reached the small lean-to cob and thatch room that was his home.

It was tiny, but sufficient for his needs. There was a palliasse to sleep on, a few strands of hay – all he could afford – spread over the floor to keep in the warmth, and a good-sized hearth in the middle of the floor. At the wall which the room shared with the chapel stood his chest, a simple, plain box which contained his spare shirt, vestments and some parchment. It was little enough, and he found it a depressing sight. The fire was all but out, and the chamber was dingy and damp.

At least he could throw a faggot of sticks on his fire and enjoy the quick rush of heat. It might just bring the feeling back into his blue fingers and toes. The thought of flames was at once delicious and terrible: he knew that his chilblains would complain and the pain would be worse as the feeling returned to numbed toes and fingers. It was only at night, when he went to bed, lying beneath his rough blanket, that he knew peace. There, with the thick sheepskin pelts keeping him warm, he felt a kind of contentment. With his eyes closed, the room could have been anywhere. The dying fire at his side could have been the embers on the hearth of a great lord's hall, the palliasse beneath his back a herb-filled mattress in a king's solar and the thick skins and blanket the richly decorated bedclothes from an abbot's private chamber. In his imagination, Brother Mark slept in magnificent halls.

In the morning, though, he always returned to real life and awoke shivering, huddled into a ball, arms wrapped about his breast and legs drawn up to his chin against the overwhelming chill.

Now, as the storm broke outside, he kicked his fire into life, poking the embers with a stick and then throwing a faggot on top.

Almost instantly there was a crackling, a thin wisping of smoke, and then a sharp sound, like ripping cloth, as the dried twigs caught fire. He stood for a moment, holding his hands to the warmth and wincing as the first tingling began in his fingers. It was blissful, and he offered up a prayer of thanks to God.

He must put more logs on while the faggot burned. At the side of his door was a stack of thick branches which he had collected during the summer. He went to them and dragged the nearest over. At the door a projection caught on the doorframe, and he grimaced at a shooting twinge in his lower back as he pulled. It was like having a bowstring fail, a sudden explosion in his muscle, then a tearing upwards. He bit at his lip, but grunted and carried on, and dropped the bundle onto the fire. Nobody could come to help him. More logs he hauled slowly across the floor and set near his fire. One he positioned carefully over the flames where it might take light. It was over this that he would warm his supper.

Sitting on his stool, he shivered as the flames licked upwards, then grabbed his trivet and set it over the heat to warm some milk. He must have something to take away the chill from his bones. As the milk began to steam in his old pot, there came a knocking at his door. He rose stiffly and opened it with a scowl on his face. Interruptions always happened when a man was about to eat, he found.

Later, when he sat in irons in Sir Ralph's gaol and had time to reflect, he realised that this was the moment when the whole future course of his life was decided.

As Mark had entered his home, Sampson had wriggled back along the edge of the trees, giggling. He pushed his way though the cold leaves and twigs until he came to the hole in the hedge. Made by a fox, it smelled rank, but bad smells didn't worry Sammy, never had.

He stuck his head out and rolled his eyes from side to side. Someone might be there, might see him. Didn't want that, no. Better to look, better to see them before they saw you. You see someone, you hide quick. Don't let them find you, that was best.

Don't show yourself. Don't give them something to throw stones at. Everyone throws stones at him. It's hard. Sad.

No noise. No people. He glanced both ways. Safe. With a great shove, he squeezed out, shooting down the muddy slide and landing on his hands on the icy stones and frozen mud, grazing both palms.

'Poor Sammy!' he whimpered, his mood changing instantly. Sniffing at them, he licked at the blood like a hound, wincing at the stinging. He cradled his scraped flesh against his breast. 'It hurts, it does. It hurts . . .'

He was so engrossed in his misery that he didn't hear the horse walking towards him from the west.

'Sampson, fool, get out of the road.'

The voice cut into his thoughts like a hatchet through an apple. Glancing up, he saw the great dappled palfrey approaching and threw himself from its path, kneeling, his hands clasped before him, keeping his eyes from the rider.

'You contemptible little whore's whelp. I've told you before about blocking my path, haven't I?'

Sampson shivered. 'Please, Master, don't hit 'un! I hurt my hands, Master, hurt bad. I'll not be in your way again, Master. Not again.'

Sir Ralph listened to him with his head cocked. His clear grey eyes were slightly narrowed as though he was listening to Sampson's pleas, but in reality Sir Ralph de Wonson didn't care what the lad might say. Sampson was the vill's idiot. He had been born stupid so many years ago, it seemed as though he had always been there in Sir Ralph's memory, a drooling figure on the edge of all the vill's events. Always near, but never a part. There was something about Sampson that offended Sir Ralph. The imperfection of the imbecile, probably. Or perhaps it was the knowledge that such an awful affliction could only be the proof of an especial evil in his soul or in that of his father, which was demonstrated in this way, like a leper whose malady reflected the sexual sins of his parents. Whatever the reason, Sir Ralph detested him; indeed he had more than once thought about executing him, because a cretin like him was an embarrassment to the community, and probably wasn't particularly happy in himself either. Assuredly no man could be content without a brain.

That he had not killed Sampson was not the result of any foolish sentimentality. Glancing down at Sampson, he thought how easy it would be, to draw his sword and thrust it down into that skull. The bone was so thin, it would offer no resistance to a sharp blade like his. End of Sampson. Sir Ralph could not help but glance up and down the road. There were no witnesses, and he was sorely tempted. Sampson's mind was that of a child. His cheap tunic, given to him by the last priest at the chapel, was faded and worn, and permanently smeared with mucus and dribble, for Sampson slobbered worse than a mastiff. The sooner he died, the better for everyone.

His hand moved towards his sword hilt – and then he saw the figure up ahead, a spare, stooped man leaning on a staff, keen eyes peering ahead above a thick beard.

'God's blood, but there's never any peace!' Sir Ralph muttered. 'Am I to be stopped by that damned hermit now?'

As he watched, Surval appeared to nod to himself, then slowly turned and walked through a gate and into a field.

It was better, Sir Ralph told himself as his ardour cooled again. He had given his oath and he wouldn't be foresworn. Many years ago his father had made him promise that he would never harm Sampson. Father was long dead now, but that didn't affect Sir Ralph's oath. He had given his word and as an honourable man he couldn't break it. A knight without honour was nothing.

He shrugged. There it was: a noble had duties, and that was that. Sir Ralph pulled his rich red woollen cloak aside and reached for the whip that dangled from his saddle's crupper. Idly, he slashed with it, twice, and the weighted leather cut through the thin tunic and flesh of Sampson like a razor.

'Next time you block my way,' he murmured, 'I'll take off one of your ears. You obviously don't need them because you don't deign to use them.'

With a last short swipe he cut open Sampson's forehead, and then patted his horse's neck. 'Come, Bayard, let's get you home and fed.'

Sampson lay in the road weeping, the blood trickling from the slashes in his back and brow, and it was only after some little while that he could raise himself and stare after the knight. The freezing mizzle had stopped for a while, but now it was coming down thicker. Sampson slowly rose to his feet, sobbing, and stood with his hands thrust under his armpits to protect them before setting off homewards, hobbling on his bad leg.

'I hate you, Master. Hate you!' he moaned pathetically. He had never hurt the master, never meant to upset him, but Sir Ralph treated him like a dog. All Sampson wanted was to be liked, and he did all he could to please people, but they hated him and whipped him or punched him for no reason. He couldn't understand. It wasn't fair.

'I hate you,' he repeated, but his voice was almost a sigh, without passion. No point being sad. People just didn't like him. He was stupid. They could live normally, but no one trusted him. Others would marry and have children, but he was doomed to a life apart. Alone.

The mizzle stopped and the clouds parted. Suddenly the land was warmed by a thin sun, pale and wintry, but better than the freezing rain. He could feel it on his back.

Only one man was like him. The priest. He was lonely, too. That was why Sampson liked to watch him. The priest made him feel whole, as if he wasn't completely alone in the world.

He heard steps, and caught his breath. There was no hole in which to hide here; the walls and hedges were solid. He cast about for an escape but there was nothing, not even a rabbit hole, and the noise of voices and laughter came more loudly on the calm air. He threw himself to the edge of the roadway, hoping that whoever it was would leave him alone if he withdrew from their path.

It was three lads from the vill, all of them adults, at sixteen years or so. Spotting Sampson, they hurried to him with a whoop, one boy kicking at him, then grabbing a stick and thrashing him with it, while two others threw stones and mud at him with gay abandon, as though they were taunting a cock in the pit or a bear at the stake.

'Leave me!' Sampson screamed in terror. He covered his face – if he couldn't see them, maybe they'd leave him alone. Pebbles stung him, balls of mud smacked into his upper arms and back, making him cry out and whimper. A larger lump of stone cracked his finger where it protected his temple, and he shrieked with the pain, but the missiles still flew, flung with the concentrated malice of men attacking another who was weaker than them.

Trying to flee, he clambered to his feet and began to limp away, but a lump struck him above his ear and stunned him, setting his head ringing. He felt himself stumble and his bad leg snagged a rock, tripping him; he fell flat, both bony elbows striking the ground together. Winded, he burst into paroxysms of tears at the fresh pain, weeping with utter dejection. He hated his life – he hated himself.

Gradually he became aware that the missiles had ceased. Then, to his amazement, he realised that a soft voice was speaking to him. Looking up, he saw that the three boys had gone, and that only Mary, the miller's daughter, was with him. He was too astonished to speak as she crouched beside him. And then something burst inside him, and he was overwhelmed. All tears forgotten, he knew only that he adored this girl, he worshipped her.

Even when she had helped him to his feet and continued on her way down the road, he stood gazing after her, occasionally sniffing, shoulders hunched like a child's. It was the first time since his mother had died that anyone had shown him kindness.

He would do anything for her, he thought, his heart swelling with love. If he had known then that she had only a year to live, he would have offered to die in her place, and done so gladly. But he didn't know, and for the next few months his adoration grew.

Until more than a year later, in early 1323, when he saw her corpse lying at the side of the road.

Chapter Two

After his chance encounter with Sampson, Sir Ralph rode on up the hill. At the top, he continued south-east, making a circuit back towards his manor at Wonson.

He felt out of sorts; at a time of hardship like this, a drooling idiot like Sampson was a luxury the vill could scarce afford. The Church always said that men must support those who were unable to support themselves. That was all very well for churchmen, who took food and money from others to fill their bellies and their purses, but it was different when you were responsible for keeping your people fed, like Sir Ralph.

Entering the copse that bounded the stream, he jogged along, until something made him glance up. Looking through the trees, he saw Surval again. The old hermit was staring straight at him.

Unsettled, Sir Ralph tried to put the man from his mind. His path led him back down the lower lane beneath the chapel. There was no sign of the priest when he glanced that way, but he noticed Mary entering the field above Mark's home and heading towards the monk's door. Sir Ralph ran his eyes over her figure with interest. She was a fine-looking girl – *very* fine. When she'd been younger, she'd looked a little ungainly with her long, coltish legs and clumsy gait, but she had filled out well. She would adorn any man's bedchamber, and Sir Ralph wondered whether she had already been rattled. He doubted it somehow. Huward was a stern parent.

Then he grew thoughtful. There was no reason for the girl to be visiting the chapel. If she wanted a word with a priest, there was a perfectly good man at Gidleigh, or the one at Throwleigh. So what was she up to? No matter how many times he told himself that she could be quite innocently taking a message for her mother, or offering some charity to a poor monk in the form of victuals, his mind kept turning to the normal reasons for a girl to visit a boy. The monk might look weakly, but Sir Ralph knew there was a certain charm in his features, a regularity about his face, an attractiveness to the large eyes.

'Damn him, I'll speak and make sure!' he swore.

A scant half-mile north of him as he rode, Lady Annicia was in the yard of their manor, watching the servants. An elegant, slender woman in her mid-thirties, with pale features and chestnut hair, Sir Ralph's wife was fortunate enough to know her place in the world and to be perfectly satisfied with it. Her sparkling amber eyes held a contentment and calm certainty. She had given birth to a son, Esmon, so her life could be called a success. Her husband was now a wealthy magnate and could expect still more advantages, especially now he had allied himself with the Despenser family, the King's own favourites, once they were allowed to return from their exile, as the rumours indicated they soon might.

If there was one aspect of life with her husband that was less than pleasing, it was his womanising. Not only was it an insult to Lady Annicia, it was a malign influence on their child. Esmon had grown up considering all the local girls to be little more than exciting toys with which he could play. Sometimes a toy was damaged. When it was, he threw it away and found a replacement. The same was true of the women with whom he played. There were always more.

It was no surprise. Esmon was a terribly good-looking boy. As soon as one girl was thrown over, there were always three more ready to replace her in his affections. It was undoubtedly foolish, but most of these females seemed to think that by ensnaring Esmon, they would win his heart and wind up living here in the castle as his wife. The idiots!

In the case of her husband, she knew that Sir Ralph had enjoyed some of the women in the area. He had been doing so for years, ever since before their wedding, but that didn't mean Lady Annicia had to understand his behaviour, nor that she had to approve. It was demeaning and embarrassing for her to know that he sought out other women occasionally, but he was at least discreet. She didn't have to suffer the shame of having women with squalling brats turning up periodically and demanding help.

She could only hope that Esmon would be the same. While all the stales in the vill were throwing themselves at him, it would be a miracle if he didn't enjoy himself with more than a few. There was one only a short way from the manor house – that little strumpet Margery. She had certainly fluttered her eyes at him often enough. Still, Esmon was capable of taking her without getting emotionally involved, Annicia reckoned. He was brighter than that. And to be fair, at least Margery wasn't trying to win him as a husband. From all Annicia had heard, she was little better than a prostitute.

This was a good manor. Not as large, perhaps, as poor Richard Prouse's castle, which bounded the manor on three sides, but even so, it was comfortable, and that was something Richard hadn't known in the five years or more since that terrible fight during which he was crippled. It was terrible to see a man so ruined when he had been so virile and masculine before, and it was partly that which made her determined that Esmon would never hazard his life in tournaments if she could prevent it.

With that thought in her mind, she found herself glancing at the men in the yard, and doing so, she caught the eye of Brian of Doncaster. Arrogant puppy! He stood there with his thumbs stuck in his belt as though he owned the place. All because her son had brought him and some other men-at-arms back with him after his time in Wales last year, helping guard a Despenser castle.

Brian met her gaze without flinching or looking away, and she felt her face freeze. The look on his face was much like the expression Sir Ralph wore when he drank in the looks of another young woman, a territory waiting to be conquered. That Brian of Doncaster should dare to look upon her so openly was a disgrace. Stories of ladies falling for the blandishments of men-at-arms and esquires among their households were all too common, but Lady

Annicia had no intention of behaving in so lewd a manner. Especially with a man who was little better than a peasant.

She only broke off her cold stare when Brian was called away by one of his men.

'That man!' she hissed to herself.

It didn't matter what Esmon said, that this Brian may have been valiant and a lion in battle. Lady Annicia felt that he was only in the castle because he wanted to lift her skirts and possess her.

Mary hated seeing Sampson so mistreated, and she banged on the priest's door with an urgency born of anger at witnessing such mindless cruelty.

'Who is it?' snapped the priest's voice before he opened the door.

Mary was in no mood to be spoken to like a child found tormenting a man's cat, and was prepared to be as curt with Mark himself. 'I often pray in your chapel, Father. Have you forgotten my name?'

Mark stood back from the door. Of course he hadn't forgotten her name, or anything else about her. Mary had appeared in his more exciting dreams since he had first noticed her figure, and now he often found himself surreptitiously observing her well-filled bodice when he should have been concentrating on his offices. She was the most attractive woman for miles, in his view, and that was one very good reason for him to maintain a certain aloof distance. He daren't risk compromising himself with her. As a priest he had to be constantly on guard against women and their wiles.

Mark threw a look over his shoulder at his milk. It was not overboiling yet, but he didn't want to leave it too long. He needed that warming drink, just as he needed a rest before he celebrated the next service in the chapel. With his sore fingers and feet, he was not in the mood to be polite. Mary was very pretty, but Mark felt that it was more important that he should get that warm drink inside him than that he should stand here gossiping. 'What do you want?' he asked more politely.

Mary bit back her first sarcastic rejoinder. 'It is cold out here, Father. Can't we talk inside?'

'Why, what do you want to discuss that shall take so long?'

'Father, I am *freezing*. Won't you let me in?'

With a bad grace, he reluctantly grunted assent and pulled the door a little wider. She slipped in past him, and as she did so, he felt her hip brush against his groin. It was fleeting, the merest touch, but it set his heart beating a little faster, especially when he caught a whiff of her fresh, sweet scent, as though she had rolled in new-cut grass infused with lavender.

'What is the matter?' he asked gruffly.

'It is that poor dunderwhelp Sampson. He's been beaten again. I saw three boys attack him just now, up on the high road.'

'So what?' he demanded. The sweetness of her smell was overpowering. It seemed to fill the room, and he took a pace away from her, but mere distance gave him no relief, and he could feel his blood coursing, being this close to a woman in his own room.

'Can't you stop them? Preach a sermon about how they should leave the feeble-minded alone?' she said.

'Who were they?'

'Just boys,' she said hurriedly, for she did not want to have to reveal that one was her brother Ben. 'You don't have to talk to them yourself, just make it plain that those who bully Sampson will have to answer to God in the future, and maybe even to the Lord of the Manor for breaking the King's Peace.'

'I shall try,' he said. For some reason he found he was eager to agree to anything that might please her.

'I thank you,' she said.

Now she was so close, he could see that she was quite beautiful. Her calm demeanour reminded him of a statue of the Madonna in Exeter. Both had the same deep blue eyes, small, pointed chins, slender noses and broad brows. The statue also had delightful breasts which seemed scarcely decent on the religious figure, and which attracted the ribald attention of many of the younger choristers, but Mark was keen to avert his eyes from Mary's own breasts. To look, he thought, would be to lose himself, to see the earthly pleasures he was missing. This girl, this young woman, appeared so soft, caring, gentle . . . He felt like a knight who, seeing a woman for the first time, wanted to go and slay a dragon to attract her attention.

Mary had noticed his confusion, and assumed that he was simply eager to be rid of her. She was preparing to flounce to the door, for she saw no reason for his being so dismissive, when she noticed the pot on the fire. A thick crust of creamy bubbles was swiftly rising to the brim, and she tutted to herself. Taking a thick fold of her skirt in her hand, she reached to the handle, to rescue the pot from the fire, but before she could take hold of it, Mark saw what she was doing.

Afterwards, he could only think that the devil put the idea into his mind, but so chilled was he from his day's exertions, that he could only think that the girl was going to steal his hot milk. All thoughts of her attractiveness fled, and he leaped forward, reaching for the pot. Grabbing the handle, he lifted it, but then he realised how hot it was. His palm was seared by the heat, and it was all he could do not to hurl the thing from him. He cautiously set the pot down, before biting his lip in anguish and letting go of it, blowing on his hand, refraining, just, from the oaths that threatened to shower from his mouth.

'Is your hand all right?' she asked solicitously. 'Let me see it.'

'No. It is fine.'

'It can't be! The pot was boiling. Why didn't you let me take it from the flames? Oh!' Her face softened as she approached him. 'You were trying to save me from burning myself, weren't you?'

To deny it and confess his true motive would have reduced him to her ridicule, and he wasn't going to have that. And then the pain seemed to subside as he felt her hand on his forearm. She took his hand gently in her own cool, slightly callused ones, studying the raw, painful mark. 'Oh Father, it's badly burned, isn't it?' She met his eyes. 'Thank you for trying to protect me.'

As he opened his mouth to speak, he saw her own mouth drop to his hand, and as her lips touched the wound, as light as feather-down, he forgot the burn entirely. When she brought her face back up again, he couldn't help himself leaning down a little, and in response she lifted herself to him, and their lips met briefly.

She left a short time afterwards, and he sat alone in the gloom of his home, but now he was less aware of his loneliness. In its place was a terrible certainty that although he hadn't touched her body, in his mind he knew he had wanted to. If she had allowed him, he would have taken her.

He must reject any further advances from her. His difficulty was, he was certain that he would be unable to refuse, should she offer him her lips again. The idea that she might offer him more was too terrible to consider, and yet that was precisely what he did consider for the whole of that long, sleepless night. Especially after Sir Ralph's visit.

On a whim, Sir Ralph took the lane from the ford up to the castle. It climbed up around a hillside smothered in trees, to join with the mud-filled track that led the short way down to the Castle of Gidleigh and the small church at its side. Usually he would have spurred his mount here past the castle gate, for he disliked Sir Richard, but today he ambled along the way and hesitated at the entrance before turning eastwards. It was that fleeting sight of Mary that had made him change his route. He would go to Huward's mill.

Although he and all the villagers referred to it as 'Huward's', in fact it was Ralph's own. Every manor had at least one mill, and each of the villeins would pay the miller one tenth or a twelfth of their grain for the privilege of having it ground into usable flour. The miller must pay the lord to fleece the peasants, and all too often was tempted to take more than his agreed share, leading to disputes and fights, but Huward was too wise to try anything like that. He knew when he was on to a good thing and so far appeared to have been fair in his dealings. Either that, Sir Ralph told himself, or he was simply too clever to be caught. Sir Ralph liked to drop in occasionally, unannounced, to check on the place. It was the best way of seeing whether he should increase the miller's rent, and it was always enjoyable to see his family.

Huward was a heavy-set man in his early forties, with a sparse reddish moustache and beard. His hair was pale brown, and was receding to expose an angled forehead that raked back sharply from his nose. His eyes were small and close-set, but kindly, and surrounded by cracks in his weatherbeaten face.

'Huward.'

'Godspeed, my Lord.'

Sir Ralph glanced about him, then dropped from his horse and threw the reins to the miller. Without speaking, the knight marched to Huward's door and entered, ducking below the low doorway.

Inside, Huward's youngest daughter, Flora, sat teasing lambs-wool out into a long, ragged snake while her mother, Gilda, spun it using a weight until it had become a long cord. Sir Ralph smiled at them, and Gilda glanced out through the door, nervously looking for her husband, who was peering in, still holding onto the horse, before giving him a sombre nod of her head.

Sir Ralph grinned to himself as he studied the workings of the mill. The woman was attractive still, even after six babies, three of which had survived. She was full-breasted, with a sturdy frame and long legs. Her eyes were green, a peculiar colour, and her dark hair had bright copper-coloured tints. She had a strange look to her. When she spoke or looked at a man, her oval face was turned to him entirely, as though giving him her full attention. Her slim eyebrows made her look almost severe, but the lie was told by her lips. The lower was quite narrow, the upper wider and more plump, which gave her the appearance of smiling. Sir Ralph had always liked that upper lip.

Her well-preserved looks were probably due to Sir Ralph's own careful treatment of Huward. The miller had a better time of it than most others in the vill. This mill had been a part of Sir Ralph's inheritance from his father.

Having taken note of the number of sacks waiting to be ground, Sir Ralph strode out and took his reins back. 'It looks well. I'll have the gather-reeve visit you to assess your rents.'

Huward said nothing, merely nodded solemnly and watched as the knight mounted, then, pulling his horse's head about, raked his spurs down the animal's flanks and cantered off.

'What did he want?'

Flora had left her mother and now stood at Huward's side. He put an arm about her shoulders and gave his youngest daughter a hug. 'I don't know, my love. He says he likes to keep a tab on us, but I wonder if there's more to it. It's always easy for a lord to get more money by seeing how much we grind.'

He shot a look inside as he spoke. His wife sat on her little stool as though she had not seen Sir Ralph's arrival, but then she looked up as if she could feel her husband's eyes upon her, and when she stared past him after the clattering hooves, he could see she was pale.

His little hut looked dilapidated, and as Surval stood outside, he nodded to himself in approval. For him, it was comfort and peace, but others saw only the ruination and wouldn't bother him here. The place had nothing to offer anyone. It was only when he stepped inside that the heat blasted at him from the roaring fire. Surval hated the thought of dying from the cold, and the older he grew, the more he appreciated a good fire. It made him feel guilty, because with his sins, he should have allowed himself to suffer, but if he were to freeze himself to death, that would be no better than intentionally starving himself, a form of suicide. Far better that he should keep himself alive to pray and beg forgiveness.

He set his staff by the door and inspected his boots. They were worn and soggy, and he knew he would soon have to take them in to the cobbler's in Chagford. In years gone by there had been a wandering cobbler who had mended his shoes on his way to the Chagford market, in exchange for a blessing from the Hermit of the Bridge, but he had apparently changed his route in order to avoid the expense of supporting the hermit. Many people did that, Surval knew. Strangers were happy to offer him alms – a bundle of firewood or a loaf of bread – but locals who passed him every day grew resentful and changed their routes.

No matter. Sitting on his old three-legged stool, he pulled his boots off and held his thick, horny feet towards the glowing embers, drawing a large horn of ale from the little barrel at his side. A farmer's wife in Murchington gave him five gallons a week. It wasn't much compared with a monk's allocation of a gallon a day, but it sufficed.

At one end of his room was a cross, and he knelt on the damp soil before it, then lay face down, his arms widespread in imitation of Christ on the cross. This was his manner of praying, the old way, showing proper respect for Christ and His sufferings. When a man had committed such a foul and heinous sin as Surval, he must show all the respect he could. As a murderer should.

Later, when he had stacked logs on the hearth and set his tripod over them, his pot filled with peas and leaves, the water beginning to swirl as the heat got to it, he sat back and stared at the flames. He knew Sir Ralph of Wonson perfectly well. A nasty piece of work, in Surval's view, although better than Sir Richard Prouse. *He* had wanted to evict Surval from here, just because he didn't like the hermit.

Sir Ralph had been lord of the neighbouring manor of Wonson ever since inheriting it from his father fifteen years ago. He had grown up there, had learned the arts of warfare and had taken on his knighthood, all while living only a scant mile from Gidleigh. Easy enough for a man like him to ride about the countryside on a great charger, as Surval told himself, nodding.

There were many reasons for a knight to wander about the land, and few were honourable. Especially now, at a time of trouble. The famine was scarcely over, and many stooped to robbery to help fill their empty bellies; even knights.

He sipped his ale, stirring his potage. Many things worried him: Sampson, Sir Ralph and his foul son, Esmon. Surval knew what the knight and his son were guilty of, but Surval had no right to point out their evil. He was a sinner himself; he had killed. How could a miserable soul like him try to show a man of Sir Ralph's stature the error of his ways? Surval was a sinner, yes, but he wasn't a hypocrite.

In any case, what could a poor hermit do? He gave a cynical grin, but there was no humour in it, only self-knowledge and disgust. Looking over at the cross, he shook his head slowly, and then fell to the floor again, sobbing.

'Oh, God! Please let me find peace!'

The banging on the door had stirred Mark from his delicious reverie about Mary, and he shot to the present with a start.

'Sir Ralph!' he cried as the door opened.

It was a miracle. Today he had felt the first urgent desire to remain here. Whereas the place had appeared dismal before, now it was blessed with the angelic presence of Mary. He could not dream of going elsewhere. Why live in Exeter when there was such a heavenly influence on this delightful vill? And now his father had arrived. Perhaps this was a message from God, that Mark should broach the subject of his paternity while he had the chance?

'Sir Ralph, I am so glad you have—'

'Be silent, boy! I'm not here to exchange pleasantries. What was *she* doing here?'

Mark gaped. 'Who?'

'Don't piss about with me!' Sir Ralph said, ominously taking a step forward. 'What was Mary doing here?'

'Mary? She came by to talk about—'

Sir Ralph grabbed a handful of his robe, pulling him close. 'Well she won't do so again. I know about clerics, about what you get up to with women! I've heard of monks getting their women pregnant by telling them it's a penance they have to undergo – all sorts of crap! I won't have it here. You touch her – or any other peasant woman here – and I'll make you regret it! Understand?'

Long after he had gone, Mark sat shaking his head in disbelief. All this time he had hoped for a reconciliation with his father, an opportunity to explain who he was, and now, before he could open his mouth, Sir Ralph had already formed the opinion that he was a callow, womanising clerk like so many others. It was unfair!

He must find the right moment to speak to Sir Ralph again, explain that he wasn't trying to molest Mary.

Sir Ralph could help him, if he accepted his paternity, and make Mark's future considerably more rosy. Surely he must accept his responsibility!

For a moment he fell to wondering whether Sir Ralph would object to his own son seeing Mary. With that, he found a picture of her face appearing in his mind, and soon he was lost in a romantic dream about her. A dream that would indirectly lead not to one death, but to many.

Chapter Three

Unaware of the fears – and hopes – that her impulsive kiss had stirred in the young priest's breast, Mary hurried home.

The mill was a large building, thatched, and with the great wheel turning slowly on its bearings. It was old, and the walls were cracked and pitted, the cob weakened by a thousand burrowing insects and creatures. In fact, as she glanced about her at the comforting little homestead, she realised that animals seemed to be everywhere. The cockerel stood arrogantly on the log store at the side of the house, the fuel already sadly depleted, while his hens scrabbled in the soggy dirt below him. Nearby, in the shelter of the store, was the old grey cat, cleaning a paw elegantly. He was a vicious brute: he'd scratch or bite as soon as look at Mary, and she left him well alone, for all that he always had this apparent inner calmness, as though he was still a playful little kitten. He paused and turned his evil yellow eyes towards the copse, and soon she heard what had distracted him. In among the trees was the scuffling and grunting of the family's old sow. The cat returned to his preening and Mary went on to the house.

It was a happy place, and Mary herself had been content through her childhood. Her father was comfortably off, her mother was attentive and loving, and Mary had been appreciated as intelligent and pretty. The idea that before too long she must leave was alarming. Not that she had decided upon a husband yet, but soon she must think of a man. She was of an age where the longer she dallied, the more her looks would begin to fade, and if she wasn't careful, she would be unmarriageable.

At the door she saw Osbert waiting. Os was an ox-like young man, a little older than her, built like a great bullock, with his stout legs and chest, his thick arms and shoulders, surmounted by a square face under a messy thatch of sandy hair. He was kind and generous, always polite to her, as he should be. A freeman, he was invariably poverty-struck, always grateful for the offer of a cup of ale or loaf of bread, so although Mary was a serf and he was free, her status as daughter of a miller meant Os was deferential.

Poor Os. Wherever she went, he followed her with a hound's eyes, and what made his affection for her more difficult to bear was the way that he ignored Flora, Mary's sister, who treated him with a reverence she usually reserved for the figure of Jesus in the church. Flora was utterly besotted with Os, a ridiculous passion in Mary's mind, but there it was. Other girls often had these grand loves. At least Os was better than some.

It was dreadfully difficult. Life was always confusing, but love she found the most distressing emotion of all, because she didn't feel that way towards any of the men in the vill. Here was Os, a good, kind man, if penniless, who adored her, and she had no feelings for him. Meanwhile, her sister, little Flora, whom she loved, craved Os's affection more than life itself, but he never noticed because he only ever had eyes for Mary.

Even though Mary did not fancy Os, she couldn't help but like him, and she favoured him with a smile as she drew near, although his instant beaming grin in return made her regret it.

The gruff voice from inside the mill was a welcome distraction. 'Mary, my little angel! Where have you been?'

'Hello, Father,' she said happily.

'That's no way to greet your old man, is it?' he roared cheerily. He swept her up in his arms, a genial, powerful man with a bushy beard that all but concealed his face. Lifting her high above him, just as he had always done ever since she was a child, he smiled up at her contentedly. She could see his happiness, and she felt her own heart swell in response. When he threw her up and caught her, she put a hand on each of his cheeks and kissed him heartily. Only then did he enfold her in a great bear-hug, before setting her down on the ground and walking away, laughing.

'He is always happy,' she murmured to herself.

'Why shouldn't he be?' Os replied. 'He has a good mill, money to keep his children and wife, low rents, two daughters a man could be proud of. What more could he want?'

She had noticed the tone of his voice when he mentioned the daughters, and daren't look at him. A woman always knew when a man eyed her a certain way, as though he was peering beneath the clothes rather than at them, and although she liked Os as a friend, that was different from wanting him as a husband. Kindly he might be, but that was no substitute for . . . What? Excitement? Riches? What did she actually want? She had no idea.

'He is a good man,' she said a little distantly, deliberately ignoring his compliment.

'But fearful of the Lord.'

She cast a look at him. Os was gazing absently after her father. 'What's that supposed to mean?'

'Sir Ralph was here a little while ago,' Os replied. Suddenly he reddened and shot her a look. 'I'm sorry, I wasn't meaning to insult your father.'

'No, I am sure you weren't. But what about Sir Ralph?'

'He came here on his horse, puffed up like a cockerel, and walked straight into your home without a by your leave. Left your dad out here with his horse like a common hostler.'

She smiled at his hot tone. He sounded like a child who had been caught thieving apples and had been thrashed for the theft, who was later trying to explain that *he* was the victim of a crime, not the perpetrator. 'He has been good to us.'

'He is always after more from all his peasants.'

'So is every lord, but at least he has helped us. Did you know he introduced my father to my mother? If he hadn't worked to see them married, I might not be here. He doesn't treat us so badly.'

'You don't think so?' he snapped. 'Your father was offended today, and so was your mother. She was upset by his visit. It's not surprising. When he rode off, your father was glad to see the back of him.'

'Of course. No man likes to be watched over by his master,' she said.

It was true. There could never be peace while a man knew that his every movement could be monitored by his lord. Any activity which generated money could – and would – be taxed or all the profits taken without compensation. Some serfs, even here in Gidleigh, had so little for themselves after they had paid their taxes, spent their labour maintaining their lord's lands, seen to his cattle, helped repair his hedges, ploughed and tilled and sown his fields, that they were constantly close to starvation. Mary was just glad that her father seemed to have a little of Sir Ralph's respect.

That brought her full circle, to considering a husband. Any man she married must also be respected by Sir Ralph. She couldn't afford to pay the *merchet* fine for a man outside Sir Ralph's lands, because she knew he set that very high. He didn't want to lose good breeding stock, as she had heard him say with a chuckle.

'It's not so tough when you're a freeman,' Os said with a slight cough.

She was about to open her mouth to speak again, but shut it quickly. Anything she said would be misconstrued by Os, she knew that from long experience. While she wondered what to say to him to make her lack of interest plain, she caught sight of her brother, and this drove all thoughts of Os and marriage from her mind.

Ben saw how her expression changed, but it only served to make him smile. He sauntered over to her and Osbert. 'Well, sister. How do I find you?'

'I saw you today, baiting Sampson. He was bleeding when I got to him. Bleeding badly!' she said, her voice clipped and haughty.

'So what? He deserves it. They say he's got a demon in him. You've heard the priest talking.'

She had: Mark had spoken about a man in the Bible who had been possessed by demons, and Jesus had made them leave him. It had made many in the congregation think of Sampson because there had to be a reason why he was so slow-witted. His wide-spread eyes and round face marked him out, and surely he would only look that way if God had meant him to. 'That's not for you to decide, is it? A *little* boy with so few brains is hardly the best judge.'

'I've got good enough brains to see a fool. If he wanted, he could defend himself. He doesn't bother, and that's his lookout.'

'What's all this? What's he done this time?'

Mary was glad of Osbert's intervention and looked up at him gratefully. When she turned back to Ben, he had set his jaw.

'It's none of your business. I'm talking to my sister.'

'He was bullying Sampson again,' she said.

'You should pick on someone your own size,' Osbert said with a hint of contempt in his voice.

It was enough to goad Ben. He thrust his head forward, mockingly rolling his eyes. 'Yeah? Why, do you think you could do better, eh? You! A pathetic worker for my father! You try to harm me, and I'll see to it that you never work here again. How would you like that, big fellow? Never have a chance of staring at my sister's bubbies again. Never have a chance of fondling them, either.'

Os growled incoherently, and he stepped a pace toward Ben, but before he could get close, Ben had whipped out a slender eating knife from his belt and held it close to him, ready to strike, his left hand ahead, palm outstretched. 'Don't try it, Ossie! My father taught me plenty about fighting when I was a lad. You try something now, I'll kill you. All because you can't keep your eyes off my sister.'

'That's a lie!'

'Is it? Maybe it is! Sorry, sis. Perhaps I should leave you and him to talk. He'd like that.'

'Just leave Sampson alone in future,' Mary said.

'Why? What would you do if I didn't?' Ben asked. He gave a laugh, thrust his knife back in its sheath, and walked away, still sniggering.

Osbert cleared his throat. 'I'm sorry about that.'

'It's all right.'

'I . . .' he had blushed to the roots of his hair, and he looked down at his feet. 'It's not true, what he said. I don't always . . .'

'I know. I never believe anything he says,' Mary lied. She knew Os often glanced at her breasts when he thought no one would notice.

She stayed standing there a moment, watching after her brother. It was so difficult. Since that fateful day, Ben had been horrible to her, and she couldn't bear to be alone with him. There was something evil about him. She couldn't tell what he might do, not any more. He was capable of hurting Sampson just to get back at her. She had no one in whom she felt she could confide. Not Father, because he would beat Ben like a dog; not Mother, because she wouldn't be able to do anything; not Flora because it would only scare her. No. The only person she could talk to was Os – but if she did, it would be impossible for him to control his anger. She couldn't tell him unless he gave his oath to keep her secret.

'It's weird to me that he could have been born to the same parents as you,' Os said.

'Yes.'

Her quiet demeanour made him cast a look at her. She could almost feel his eyes studying her, but she didn't feel it was lascivious, only eager and loving. His obvious adoration was comforting. She felt as though while he was alive, no harm could come to her.

'Os, I have to tell someone, but I can't if anything would ever be said again. Can you swear to me, I mean it, swear on your mother's soul, that you won't tell anyone about this while I live? You can't tell anyone at all. Never.'

'Of course I won't.'

She took a deep breath. 'Ben hates me now, because he tried to lie with me. He wanted to make love with me, and I wouldn't let him.'

'I'll beat his brains to a pulp! I'll cut off his tarse and balls and—'

'Os, you swore to me! You mustn't tell anyone! Ever!'

'I won't. Not unless there's a good reason.'

'There can *never* be a good enough reason. You swore.'

* * *

Lives were short in the early 1320s, Surval was later to reflect. The Great Famine had wiped out whole families since it began in 1315, and some said that a tenth of the population of Oxford had died in 1316 alone. Many felt that they would soon follow their fathers, mothers, brothers and sisters to their graves, and they were shameless in their pursuit of pleasure, for what merit was there in caution? Better to live life while it was there, and make sure that a priest took your confession before you died, to guarantee your journey to Heaven.

In the cold winter of 1321, and on into February, the work was constant for all the people about Wonson. Rain it might, but hedges must still be cut back and laid; ditches must be cleared of leaves and twigs so that the water could drain away; roads must be repaired and fields ploughed ready for the grain. Even Surval must labour to keep his bridge functioning.

At the chapel, he knew Mark concentrated on his works: the round of services for the patrons of the chapel itself, and the construction of his wall, mortifying his flesh by unremitting mental and physical effort. Surval was sure that at the end of each day, the young monk was glad to find the peace of his bedroll, thanking God that he had not succumbed to temptation – except he had not yet been truly tempted, and when he was, Surval saw him fail.

It was in the late spring of 1322 that Surval noticed Mark's mood subtly altering. Suddenly he was less keen on walling, and he spent more time away from the chapel, walking about the lands of the demesne. For weeks he continued in this way, and then Surval saw him with Mary the miller's daughter.

That summer was sultry and golden; easeful. Many would later say it was the first real summer of the century, and youths and maids of all classes frolicked together in fields, in barns, in haylofts and in private chambers. Surval stumbled over them wherever he went. The passing away of Sir Richard in June was sad, but came as no surprise. He had been unwell for years, and his gradual death was explained by many as caused by his broken heart after learning that his lands were to be forfeit to Sir Ralph. News of his mortality was bruited abroad, but affected even his own peasants only slightly. Their time was taken up by the ceaseless round of work, repairing or building new homes for man and beast, and seeking members of the opposite sex.

In the glorious weather, long balmy evenings ran on from hot work in the fields, and couples went to drink in taverns and alehouses after slaving all day.

In retrospect, Surval was pleased that Mary's last year had been so happy.

In the bright hall of his new castle, in the early spring of 1323, Sir Ralph de Wonson sat still a short while after his Reeve had spoken, and his face blanched as he took in the news. 'But it's monstrous! he thundered. 'It can't be true. Have you been there yourself? Have you seen the body?'

His son Esmon sniffed and looked bored, but Lady Annicia put a hand out on her husband's wrist to calm him. She knew how his rage could explode.

Sir Ralph shook her hand off and glared at the Reeve. 'Well?'

'My Lord, there is no doubt. I haven't been there myself yet, but I trust Elias. He's no fool.'

'CHRIST'S PENANCE! If I find this is true, I'll take the man's *ballocks* with my own knife and feed them to him!' Sir Ralph bellowed and slammed a clenched fist into his left hand.

Then a thought struck him. His brother! The bastard had once killed a woman after getting her pregnant. That was why he had come back here to Gidleigh like a whipped hound, tail between his legs! Could he have taken Mary and realised that he couldn't stay here if his second offence became known?

'Christ Jesus!' he swore. He felt numbed, broken.

Lady Annicia pursed her lips, for she was always distressed to hear the Good Lord's name spoken blasphemously, but she curbed her tongue. It was only fair that her husband should be disturbed after hearing such terrible news, and in his present mood he was likely to strike her if she remonstrated with him.

'What did Elias actually see?' he asked, leaning forward in his new chair.

Piers Wike the Reeve was a slight man in his early forties, with narrow features and dark eyes. He had a strong cast in his left eye which lent him a somewhat piratical air that was entirely at odds with his nature. Shorter than the knight, he stood only some five and a quarter feet in his bare feet, but that might have been due in part to the bowed back, a defect granted to him at birth by a drunken midwife, so his mother said. 'My Lord, Elias said he heard a shout in the late forenoon, while he was out at Deave Lane ploughing. Said he was turning, heading away from the moors, when he heard it.'

'Heard what? Get on with it, fool! God's precious wounds, you would take an hour to describe a nail!'

'Elias said he heard voices, a man and Mary both shouting, and then she gave a scream, and there was a slap. There was silence for a while, and then someone ran off, up towards Throwleigh. He thought someone had been arguing, didn't think more of it than that. Didn't realise there could be anything wrong, what with no more shouting or nothing, so he didn't make a move. Then, later, when he left with the ox team to settle them for the night, he found her lying in the roadway, poor chit.'

'You mean to tell us that someone has killed one of our serfs?' Esmon drawled. 'Actually damaged our property? What a scandal!'

The knight stared at him and took a deep breath, his face growing purple. His mood was plain enough, even to an exhausted Reeve, and although Piers was tired out, he was no fool. He quickly continued, 'As I said, it was Mary, the older daughter of Huward the miller. She was beside the roadway, as though she had crawled there to lie with her back to the wall. Her skirts were up, Sir Ralph, and there was blood all about her thighs.'

'She'd been raped?' the knight rasped. He strode over to Piers and stood with his head lowered, staring at the man. His voice dropped menacingly. 'Is that what you're saying? She was raped by some bastard while that cretin wandered about with his oxen for company, dreaming about cider?'

Esmon was gazing at Piers shrewdly. 'You say that the old peasant heard voices shouting and so on. Who was the man?'

Piers glanced at his father, but Sir Ralph was clenching and unclenching his fists like a man with an anguished soul. 'I spoke to Sampson,' Piers said. 'He saw the priest from the chapel going up there.'

Sir Ralph felt a momentary relief. At least it wasn't Surval! But then his anger took over. He remembered seeing Mary at the priest's door two years ago, and he recalled pulling the little monk to him and threatening him, should Mark ever go near Mary again. He hadn't listened, though, had he? The little turd had gone ahead, and now he'd raped and killed her.

Esmon murmured, 'Christ's cods! A damned clerk raped and killed her!'

Piers found himself meeting Esmon's gaze. The lad looked amused! It was awful, and Piers had to bite back a comment. He met Sir Ralph's gaze, and his voice was hard when he replied, 'No, Sir Ralph. Least, if she was raped, it wasn't the first time. That young maid was with child.'

Chapter Four

Mark would have been grateful for any company, even if it meant his arrest and later death, he was so worn out from flight and mental torment after seeing her lying dead.

It was almost an instinctive thing at first, heading for the water, but as soon as he was in it, he knew he had to go where pursuit wouldn't think of looking. That meant following the stream to its source, he reckoned, heading northwards. Surely the Hue and Cry would think he was going to head straight for the coast, maybe following the river south to the Teign and thence to the sea. No. He'd not make his capture easy.

He was soaked. Shortly after slipping into the sluggish brown water of the brook, he tripped and fell headlong, slamming down onto the flat surface with a force that knocked the air from his lungs. His head struck a rock, and instantly he was overwhelmed. It was as though his senses were destroyed in an instant. His eyes could discern nothing, his ears were full of a rushing noise, and his mouth was filled with water. There was no up or down, no north or south, only this perpetual immersion: nothing had happened before, and there was no future, only an all-enveloping *now* of noise. Although a part of his mind knew he must surely die if he remained here, that this would be his grave, it was comforting, somehow. He was tired, bone tired, and just the chance of closing his eyes and shutting out the horror of the world was so attractive, that he allowed himself to be dragged along for a short while.

But then the world impinged upon him once more. He was rolled over, and air struck his face, bright sunlight burst upon his closed eyes. Coughing and choking, he realised that the air was so much warmer than the water, it was like a waft of dragon's breath.

The water pushed him gently into a shallow, and he felt his head bump another rock, but softly, as though the river itself was trying to stir him without alarming him, conscious of his suffering.

His suffering! What could water – yea, or earth or fire! – know of suffering? Mark felt as though he had been born to suffer, that his existence was marked by the endurance of pain and fear, overwhelming sorrow and misery.

Mark lifted himself from the river, shivering uncontrollably, and stumbled up to the bank, but he couldn't carry on. He threw himself to his hands and knees, retching, and while there, all he could see in his mind's eye was her: Mary.

It was the sight of her body that had made him bolt. He had hit her, yes, but not hard. Not hard enough to kill. Not hard enough to make her miscarry! He had slapped at her, the blow glancing off her shoulder and then, as she stared at him with her love turning to loathing, he had felt his life shatter like a window struck by a stone. He was supposed to be celibate, yet he had lain with this maid; he was supposed to be kindly, yet he had struck at her in rage. And then, when he went back later, he saw that he was dead, and he was sure that it was he who had killed her. Overwhelmed with horror, he fled the sight and that cursed vill.

He knew what he had done, knew that he was wrong to have lain with her, not once, but at every opportunity during the last summer and autumn, no matter how many times he had prayed to God. It was no use. Every time she had come to him again, drawn to him by some power that neither could understand, he had allowed himself to submit to his natural instincts. They had once tried to pray together, when he had insisted, hoping that if he were to ask help from God while she was there at his side, perhaps God could give him a sign, or merely eradicate every vestige of whoring from Mark's soul, but even that had failed. It was as though He had turned his back on Mark.

The young priest wiped his mouth on his sleeve, went to a tree-stump and slumped against it. Until today his whole life had been marked out: he would go on his journey, and when he returned, he would go to the university. From there, he would take up a senior position with Bishop Walter at Exeter, or perhaps, if the good Bishop was still Treasurer, then maybe Mark might be able to find a position with him in the King's Exchequer in London. His future had seemed bright and ripe for promotion; now all was lost, and all because he couldn't keep his tarse in his hose.

It felt as though the entire world had rejected him. Until today his life had been untroubled except by loneliness, but now his future had been snatched from him. His past friends would be his companions no longer; the teachers and choir at Exeter Cathedral would not stop to talk as had been their wont. All the delights he had anticipated, all the pleasures, all the duties, had been cruelly snatched away. His life was ruined purely because of one error – the girl, and a thoughtless fist.

He could see the pain in her eyes as soon as he struck her. She had fallen and he had hesitated, sickened, before bolting. Later, when he came to his senses and returned, there she was, lying on the ground, her legs parted and blood, blood *everywhere*! He'd nearly thrown up on the spot, revolted by the sight of his lover, exposed like a slab of pork on the butcher's table.

Standing there, his mind seemed to work with an immediate clarity. Everyone would think he had intentionally killed her. He hadn't, he'd only lashed out at her, but that wouldn't be enough for the locals here, Christ's blood, no! They would appeal him. He was an outsider who had got one of their women pregnant and wanted to avoid the shame and expense of an illegitimate child.

If he was found, if he was caught, he could claim Benefit of Clergy, demand to be tried in the ecclesiastical court, but he knew he'd be dead long before he could get there. No one in the village would try to protect him. He knew how the place worked: it was Sir Ralph's manor against the world. They looked upon a man who came from South Tawton as a foreigner, and that was a town only some four miles away. If the Hue was raised against him and he were captured, his life would be worth nothing. What was the value of a foreigner's life compared to the hurt and sorrow felt by a father for his murdered daughter? *Nothing!* They would castrate him and hang him from the nearest tree, rather than wait for the

Law to take its measured time to consider his case and release him into the Bishop's hands for trial.

The Bishop's court. He had been there several times listening to cases; once he had helped make a note of the transcripts of a case. Sitting there before the Bishop's steward and the clerics who would try the matter, he had felt as though their importance and glory was reflected upon him, just as light from a candle could illuminate the faces of three or four, although it was intended to assist only one man to read.

Once or twice, while the judges were deliberating, he had studied the man who stood so patiently before them. Pale, thin, worn down with work, he had been accused of stealing a sheep from the Cathedral. If he was found guilty, he would be hanged immediately. In his eyes, Mark saw resignation. No shame, no guilt, just a weary acceptance. He didn't expect sympathy. That was some seven years ago, 1316, and famine was killing people up and down the country: men, women and children lay starving, weakened by malnutrition, their souls weighed down with the grim weather. Oh, what weather! Mark could recall it only with horror. It rained all through the winter, and then on into the summer in those famine years. Harvests failed. Animals collapsed and died. It was as though God Himself had decided to punish the world. First the loss of the Crusader kingdoms, then the announcement of the crimes of the Templars, and now famine, pestilence – and the war in Scotland. No one would consider a man who stole to fill his belly to be deserving of kindness. If he were treated leniently, others would try the same. So he had been hanged.

Never, during that trial, had it occurred to Mark that he might one day stand there himself, pleading his own case. At least he wouldn't be hanged by the Bishop. Priests could anticipate a less rough form of justice. The penance might be severe, but it would not entail death.

That was the spur that had set his legs running originally. He couldn't simply wait there to be taken and executed without trying to save himself. He had pelted up Deave Lane, hardly knowing where he was going, through Throwleigh and out towards the mill east of the vill. There was a stream there that flowed from the moors. The Baron would seek him with dogs, he knew. He must escape by evading their noses.

The stream was cold enough to take the breath away, but Mark didn't care. He splashed on through the water, desperate to put as many miles between him and pursuit as possible. The way was hard, with trees and bushes snagging at his clothes. He had to duck beneath straggling branches, soaking his tunic with water so cold he felt his flesh creep. His chest was constricted, his breath ragged with exertion, and his toes and shins were bruised and barked from falls against rocks and tree trunks. A blackthorn branch was before him now, a sharp spike almost piercing his eye, and his breath sobbed in his throat as he took hold of it, moving it away from his face. His hands were already scratched from a thousand wild roses and brambles, and as he moved on, a spine slid into his palm. In his pain, he let the branch go, and it scraped along his tonsure, two splinters breaking off in his scalp. He wailed with the pain, but he had to continue, driving himself onwards, sploshing through shallows, wading noisily through the deeper waters, until at last he reached a tributary.

It was much smaller, approaching from the north, but it held the merit that the Baron and his posse would surely assume he would continue on the broader reaches of the river if they thought of coming this way. And no matter where this led, he must be out of the jurisdiction of Sir Ralph's court soon.

He took the turn, but first he spread water over some dry rocks further up, to make it look as though he had continued within the main stream and hadn't turned away. A little farther still, he grabbed a pair of stout tree limbs near the banks, hoping that a hound would notice it, and the hunters would carry on without turning off.

The tributary was much smaller, and he had to walk carefully to prevent his steps moving outside the water, where they could be seen – or smelled. Saplings and smaller trees fringed the water, and he kept well within their protective screen, peering nervously between the branches while not touching them. After a half mile or more climbing a shallow valley, at the bottom of which lay his stream, he saw some rude dwellings through the trees. A small barton. There was the odour of cattle, and the wind brought the distinct, almost human, stench of pigs' dung. One house stood higher than the others, but there were four or five stretched below it, all pointing to the top of the hill.

He was exhausted and starved. If only he had made time for a meal before leaving, but he hadn't. The thought of warmth and food was poignant in his present state, but he dared not ask for help. He wouldn't cut a very respectable figure in his present sorry state.

Just as he was thinking this, he saw a door open in the nearest house. A short man walked out, stopped, sniffed, and then ambled around the side of his house, a wooden pail in his hand, a dog scurrying at his heels. Before long Mark saw them wandering up a lane, into a pasture, and over to a cow.

Afterwards he would remember it with shame, but at that moment all he could think of was his belly. When he saw the man crouch at the side of the cow, Mark clambered out of the stream and tried to hurry to the house inconspicuously, although after spending so many hours in the cold waters of the streams, he was incapable of speed.

The opening was a rough affair with a long strip of leather supporting a wooden door. Splinters attacked his hand as he touched it, but he pushed it nonetheless. If he was asked, he would beg food, declaring himself a mendicant and relying on the peasants' respect for the tonsure, but when he opened the door, his breath caught in his throat at the smell of fresh bread. There was no time to consider. He snatched the loaf where it lay cooling, turned, and was gone, ripping shreds from the loaf as he went and stuffing them into his mouth.

Sir Ralph soon had his horse saddled and ready. Piers had arrived at the castle on his own sturdy little pony, but had left as soon as Sir Ralph bellowed for his mount. They were to meet with the posse out at the bottom of Deave Lane, where the girl's body still lay under the protection of the first man Piers had found.

The knight spurred his mount furiously and clattered out through the gateway, turning north up the road towards Throwleigh. His route led him under the great trees, whose boughs gleamed under fluffy, emerald mantles of moss. At several places, the muddy track was so full of puddles that the knight's horse threw up immense sheets of water on either side, but he didn't notice. He was thinking only of the dead girl.

That she should be dead was unthinkable! He couldn't believe it, wouldn't believe that he'd never again see her smiling face, hear her cheerful voice, thrill to the sound of her laughter. The light was verdant beneath the trees, the sun slanting through thin, new leaves, but he saw nothing of it. If he had, he would have thought it obscene that such freshness, such explosive fruitfulness, should be here still, when that beautiful, perfect child was destroyed.

The journey passed by in a whirl. He cantered up the hill towards Deave Lane and reined in at the sight of the men milling. There were a few on horseback, but most were afoot, all the villeins from the fields and houses nearby, from twelve years up to forty-odd, strong, hearty men, all wearing their horns and staffs, a couple with their billhooks in their belts, but most only armed with their knives. All about them were the hounds, great monsters with drooling jowls and powerful shoulders.

Stopping, Sir Ralph stared about him with his mouth agape. 'So few men? Piers! *Piers!* Jesus Christ above! Where in God's name have you got to?'

The Reeve had been talking to a pair of hunting men, but hearing the hoarse bellow, he immediately made his way to his Lord. There was no telling with Sir Ralph. Sometimes he could be sensible, but more often than not he was overbearing, taking no account of how others felt. Not that it was surprising. Sir Ralph's family was an old one. It was said that many years ago a clerk for the King had demanded to know by what right he held his lordship and the rights to his own court, and Sir Ralph had smiled, then fetched down a rusting sword from his wall. He threw it at the now anxious clerk.

'*There's* my right. That's the sword my father wore; it's the sword he used to kill the man who owned this land before him.'

'You're threatening me!'

'No. It was a fair fight in the tournament,' Sir Ralph had said softly, taking back the sword, but then he had suddenly swung it. It whistled as it sliced through the air, narrowly missing the clerk's head. 'But I won't give away my inheritance just because a pissy priest who took to the Law decides he must see papers. Tell the King I claim the right by ancient privilege.'

Ancient privilege, Piers thought to himself. That was all this family ever thought of. They certainly had little enough feeling for their servants. Looking about him here, at the men standing so quietly, he could see too many whose faces were gaunt. Scurvy again. The poor harvest last year, the depredations of the King's Purveyors, grabbing everything they could for his armies as they marched to Scotland, all the good food gone when the peasants here were already hungry.

'My Lord?' he said respectfully.

'Where have you been? I've been calling for you.'

'My Lord, I had sent those men to see if the priest was in his chapel.'

'Well?' Sir Ralph demanded, leaning forward. 'Did they find the foul scroyl?'

'No – there's no sign of him.'

'He's fled!'

'All the other men of the vill are accounted for, but he is gone, and I know some have said that he was sleeping with her. You know how rumours always start, but now . . . well, it looks very possible that it could have been Mark who killed her.'

'Right, then, organise the men to chase the mad bastard down! I want him – alive or dead makes no difference to me!' Sir Ralph bellowed at the top of his voice.

'If we can, Sir Knight,' Piers said, glancing about him with a feeling of helplessness.

'Is this all the men you could find? We need at least twenty men on horseback for the posse, and you have found only seven!'

'There aren't the men, my Lord. Who has horses in the manor? Too few. And not many can ride. We have all the men over twelve years here, but these seven are the only men with horses. Even my own son is here,' he added pointedly. Esmon, Sir Ralph's son, had not turned out for the posse, Piers saw, nor the castle's men-at-arms. The lad was no doubt sitting in his great hall, dreaming of owning it when his father died.

Sir Ralph gave the Reeve a long, cold stare. 'God's blessed will! If we don't catch this murderer, Piers, I'll have you flogged until I have the hide off your back, d'you hear me? Now get on your pony and let's be off!'

The dogs were ready, and as soon as they had sorted out who was to go where, the hounds were released and the small party set off.

Piers had already instructed the men in what they were to do. He and Sir Ralph would hasten along Deave Lane and use the hounds to see whether they could catch the priest. Meanwhile, the bulk of the men would follow, separating at the different paths. Messengers had been sent to neighbouring vills and Hundreds already, so that the population would rise and attack Mark if he appeared. Finally, a small group was to make its way to the priest's home and chapel and wait there, in case he returned to collect belongings while the posse was abroad.

Their way led them up along the old Deave Lane to where the poor girl's body had been found. Sir Ralph slowed as they reached her. She lay with her legs parted, a red mess between them. One eye was closed as though she was winking, but there was too much blood for her to live. Sir Ralph felt a dreadful hatred stir in his breast. He wanted to find her killer and skin him alive, cut out his beating heart, make him suffer all the agonies a man could, for this defilement.

It was not only he who felt this rage against the murderer. He could feel it among the men about him. There was a stillness, a silence, that spoke of their horror at the sight of that pretty young girl, her body violated – *desecrated* – by this foul attack.

'You! Put a shirt or something over her face!' Sir Ralph said.

At Mary's side stood a guard gripping a pole with a bill hammered onto the end as a makeshift weapon. This man nodded emphatically, then glanced about him. There was nothing near with which to obey, and at last he sighed to himself, set his polearm leaning against the hedge, and pulled off his own thin jack. He draped it over the girl's face, but as he turned away, picking up his weapon, the butt caught the material and snagged. His jack came away, and suddenly Mary's head lay oddly.

'Her neck's been broken, Sir Ralph,' Piers said, peering at her.

'The shit broke her neck,' Sir Ralph whispered. 'It takes effort to do that. He must have meant to kill her – this was no accident!'

'Many a priest has been accused of killing off his woman when she grew pregnant,' Piers said sorrowfully as the embarrassed guard set her head more naturally and draped the jack once more over her.

Sir Ralph swallowed his sadness and raked his spurs along his horse's flanks. The mount burst into action, throwing a large pool of black water up into the air. On they went, into Throwleigh and then north and east, the dogs eagerly following a scent, tails waving like so many saplings in the wind, occasionally baying as the excitement got to them.

'Huward's not with us?' Sir Ralph shouted.

'No, sir. I think Huward would tear him limb from limb, if he was to catch him,' Piers responded. All too true. If Huward caught Mark, the lad wouldn't last two minutes. At least this way, with a posse, Mark could be captured and taken back to Sir Ralph's goal.

'Bad. You should have brought him along.'

Piers opened his mouth, but then snapped it shut. In that moment, he realised that Sir Ralph intended executing the priest as soon as they caught him. He felt the urge to protest, but there was no point. Sir Ralph was within his rights to slaughter a fleeing murderer. An outlaw could be beheaded on sight, and there was no more obvious felon than a man who murdered a pregnant woman and then fled with her blood on his hands. Except that Mark was a priest.

'Where can he be heading?' Sir Ralph cried with frustration as the dogs took them eastwards, towards Frog Mill. 'This goes nowhere.'

Piers himself had little enough idea of the direction of the roads from here. In his youth he had once travelled to Oakhampton, but apart from that one journey, he had never been further than Chagford and the local market there. He'd never had the need of a longer trip.

Today the hounds led them down the track away from Throwleigh, but suddenly they bounded off north, through a large pasture shared by the vill, until they came to the Blackaton Brook. There they milled uncertainly.

'Devious scroyle!' the knight muttered as they waited for the hounds to pick up the scent. 'He's done this a'purpose. Running into the water to hide his trail.'

'What shall we do, sir?' Piers asked. If he had the choice, he'd head downstream a way, with some dogs on each side of the water. He doubted that the priest would have gone north and west, back towards the moors themselves. That was too dangerous. Only men who had grown up here knew the safe routes through the shifting mires, and the priest would surely be too fearful to attempt such a path. No, he must surely have followed this water until it met the Teign, and maybe hurried on the banks of that river towards the sea. Or until he met with more outlaws, he told himself gloomily.

Sir Ralph agreed with him. 'We'll go down the stream here. He's only a damned priest, not an experienced felon. He isn't used to hard walking. Chances are we'll find him down here, lying on the bank dozing. Come!'

Piers nodded and they went down to the stream, wading slowly through it where they must, at those places where the vegetation on either bank was impenetrable, at other times riding at the water's edge and watching the dogs all the while. Sir Ralph egged them on as keenly as any huntsman after a hart, hoping to catch sight of the murderer. He wanted the man who had killed the young maid.

Piers felt more ambivalent. He had liked Mary – who hadn't? She was a bright little thing, with a saucy manner when she flirted, but generally a kindly soul if she wasn't annoyed; if her temper was fired, she could be as ferocious as any alewife. Yet mostly she was a good, comely member of the vill, and Piers would have liked to see her murderer caught. His only concern was, if the knight should catch her killer, he might well run him through for what he had done to Mary, one of his own peasants. Piers didn't want that. He was content to see the killer pay for his crime, but it was wrong to execute a priest. They had protection from God, and Piers wasn't sure he could stand aside quietly and see Mark struck down.

For him it was a relief when, after hunting the priest for many hours, Sir Ralph finally called a halt to their search. Men had already gone to the other Hundreds to warn them that there was a renegade priest on the loose who had murdered his lover and his child. All should be aware, and all should have arranged for their own posses to search for Mark.

It struck Piers as odd, though, how badly Sir Ralph had taken the priest's escape. Once he realised that he couldn't catch Mark, he slumped in his saddle like a man who had lost everything. If he hadn't been a knight, Piers might have thought he was weeping. And all, Piers thought cynically, because a priest had robbed him of his property. For now, though, as the sky darkened, there was no more they could do.

For now they must wait and see what news was brought to them.

That night Sampson huddled, arms wrapped about himself, staring into the fire smouldering and hissing on the floor before him. Every so often a log cracked and spat out a small flame, throwing sparks far. One landed on him. Sampson didn't care. He flicked it away, his eyes bleared with tears as he thought of the girl: the lovely girl, her with the smiling face; her who radiated kindness when she spoke to him.

He hadn't thought to see her. No. When he heard the steps he wanted to hide, but there was the sound of a man ploughing, the noise of chopping in a field, and they scared him. They might attack him. Men did. He didn't know what to do. No, so he turned and limped unsteadily on his bad leg, until he was hidden around a bend. Out of sight. Safer.

There were thick roots in the hedge here. Clumsily, he pulled himself up until he could force his way through the hedge and topple onto the thick grasses of the pasture beyond. He rolled over and stared up at the grey clouds. He was safe. His head resting on the clean, cold grass, he panted.

Steps approached. Loud. A man's. He turned over, keeping flat to the soil, as though by making it impossible to see the traveller, he would render himself invisible.

More steps. Lighter, softer. Must be a girl's. Not like the heavy tread of the other.

'Mark! I've been to find you.'

'My dear.'

'That's a cool welcome for a lover.'

He didn't want to hear. Sampson knew them. Both of them. A hollowness came to his throat. He felt tears filling his eyes, couldn't do anything. He couldn't run. They'd hear.

'I am a priest, Mary. What do you expect from me?'

'A little affection, Mark. Am I so repellent now? You didn't think so before.'

'That was before I realised what we had done.'

'Your voice – you sound so cold!'

'How else can I be? Do you realise what could happen to me?'

'Would you like me to pretend nothing's wrong, then? Pretend *this* isn't real?'

'Listen, I have heard that there are potions, drugs, which can help us. Just take a drink, and all the problems go away . . .'

'I'll have nothing to do with such a thing!' she burst out. 'What – you, a priest, want me to take something to murder our child?'

'No! Not murder – simply make it never live. It's not a real person until it's born,' Mark mumbled. He sounded like he knew he was lying.

Sampson understood all right. He had seen them, hadn't he? Oh, yes. Almost a year ago, he'd seen them. They'd come out from Mark's dwelling, laughing. And then she had said something and darted away even as his hand grabbed for her. He missed her, but caught her wimple, and it came away. When she turned, her long dark hair was glinting and gleaming in the sun, streaming away like a dark smoke over her shoulder. She was running now, towards the trees that bounded the path to the river, and Mark suddenly bellowed in raw pleasure, ducked his head and pelted after her.

Sampson was worried. Thought Mark might hurt her. He chewed his lip to see the priest running like a greyhound after a hare. Mary was giggling, darting left then right, as if careless of capture. She wasn't evading Mark's outstretched arms, but stringing out the inevitable.

Then Mark's fingers snared her blouse and the material came away. Mary's chest was exposed, her bare breasts bouncing, and Mark gaped, a trail of linen in his hand, crimson with embarrassment and Sampson felt the flood of relief. She was safe. The priest wouldn't hurt her.

Mary had halted, and her hands rose as though to cover her breasts, but then her chin lifted and her hands fell away. She held her hands out, smiling. When Mark shamefacedly tried to pass her the material, she took him by the wrist and drew him towards her. Mark resisted, shaking his head, but she persisted and led him to the trees. There she leaned him back against an oak and softly put her hands on his shoulders, leaning forward to give him the kiss of peace.

At least, that was what Sampson had heard it called, the kiss of one mouth upon another. It was how monks and priests welcomed each other. Something here was different, though, and Sampson felt unsettled to see how there seemed little enough peace for them. He could feel his own blood coursing faster as, while he watched, their kissing grew more impassioned. There was a fumbling of hands, a lifting of habit and skirt, slow, sensuous stroking, followed by a more hurried and urgent fondling, before both fell to the ground and Sampson saw her spread her thighs wide, saw Mark fall between them, his bare buttocks lifting and falling.

Their voices broke in upon his thoughts.

She said, 'I don't care what 'tis called, I won't do it. It's against the law.'

'So was what we did.'

'That's different. It's natural.'

'It's wrong,' Mark said miserably. 'Think of me! It could ruin me. I might be left here for ever to rot if the Bishop heard.'

'Don't tell, then, if you hate it here so much. Go! Leave me and our babe, if we mean so little to you. I wouldn't want to be the cause of your shame, Father!'

'You know that's not what I meant.'

'Do I? How do I know that?'

His tone was pleading. 'Mary, you know I can't wed you. What do you want me to say, that I'll leave Holy Orders and run away with you? I have taken the vows, Mary, I can't. If I tried to run away, they'd seek me out, no matter where I went.'

'So deny us,' she snapped.

'Don't be so cruel to me!'

'You wanted me when your blood was up, when you were lonely and needed company.'

'I know. My lo— Mary, I tried so hard to ignore you, so I could escape this torment, but it didn't work. I was so despairing, and you were so beautiful . . . I couldn't help but want you.'

'And now you can't face the consequence.'

'It was impossible to reject you. When your blouse came away in my hand and I could see you . . . My God! A man would have had to have been made of stone to resist you.'

'That was the first time. What of the others?'

'Christ's bones, but I was so tempted,' Mark said, and there was a catch in his voice as though he was staring at Mary's body and remembering.

Sampson's brain whirled. After seeing them rutting by the river he'd known he could never have her. No, this priest had won her. But perhaps she could love him now. If her priest didn't want her,

Sampson could win her himself. She had been so kind. Surely she loved him? He would speak to her, soon as he could. Maybe tomorrow or the day after.

He heard a slap, then a great gasp. 'What have I done?' from Mark, and then nothing. Sampson lay still, and for a great while there was no sound, but then there was a retching, a loud hawking and a spit, and then there were the footsteps running away, as though all the devil's hounds were already chasing after Mark's soul.

A scant mile from Sampson, a second man lay huddled and weeping. Osbert was curled like an infant on his rough straw palliasse, while tears flooded his cheeks and he sobbed silently. There was nothing left for him. His life was ended. His Mary was gone.

Mary, his love; his life. The priest was said to have killed her after he got her with child. That was why Mary never wanted Os, even though he adored her, because she was sleeping with that skinny cleric. How could she fancy him, when he was so scrawny! Yet she did.

The only satisfaction was, it was not her brother who had killed her. When Os heard she was dead, that had been the first thing to cross his mind, that her brother had again tried to take her, and this time he had forced her to submit, or rather, had killed her when she refused. If that had been the case, Os would have killed him.

But it was the priest. Little Mark from the chapel. *He* had ended her life.

She had made Os swear not to tell anyone about Ben, and he wouldn't. It couldn't help her, so he'd keep it secret, as he had promised. Letting the secret out could only besmirch Mary's memory.

Chapter Five

Lady Annicia watched as her husband stalked out of the solar and into his hall. At this time of night, the hall was no place for a woman and he knew that she wouldn't follow him there.

She hadn't seen him like this before – reserved, distrait, all the while denying that there was anything wrong, and both of them knowing it was a lie. The escape of that priest had moved him oddly. Even though the girl had died, he would not usually have reacted so strongly. Mary was only a peasant.

Sir Ralph was badly affected: she could see it in his eyes, in his fidgeting, in the drumming of his fingers. It was ridiculous to try to deny it, his pain and anguish were so plain.

Perhaps he . . . . No, she wouldn't think of such a thing. Surely it was purely the anger that Mark had escaped which tormented him so, not rage at losing a lover.

She had never liked that little chapel-priest. The fellow was gormless-looking. Always stared at people with his mouth open, just like that poor mindless devil Sampson. The latter did the same whenever he came to the castle's door, skulking like a rat, shunning the people who milled about, avoiding Sir Ralph like the devil, snatching at food from the alms-dish and then hurrying back up to the little shack on the hill above the castle where he lived. Nasty little cretinous boy that he was. Sampson gave Annicia a real feeling of sickness, as though merely having him in the same shire was enough to transfer his stupidity to her or her offspring.

There was a sudden burst of laughter from some of the men-at-arms out in the hall, and she heard the low rumble of her husband, deadened by the heavy tapestries that hung over the door. Such a racket was common now, since Esmon's friends had come back with him.

It was impossible to like the men. It wasn't only the flagrant manner of that man Brian of Doncaster, it was the way that they all shouted and sang, scuffling when they were drunk, jeering and abusive when they were sober. None of them seemed to care whether Lady Annicia was there or not; none of them understood the principles of chivalrous behaviour, they merely acted as they wanted. In older days, men in a hall would have shown respect to the master of the hall, and to his lady, too, but not now. Now they took money, and didn't think that counted as the sale of a man's honour and independence. There was no integrity with such people. They had not even bothered to ride out with Sir Ralph today to try to find that foul little priest.

No loyalty. That was the thing. She'd prefer one old-fashioned retainer for every ten of this breed – a man who would support and protect his master because he was one of the household, nothing to do with money. That was how things used to be.

She poured herself a small cup of wine and set it beside her favourite chair in front of the fire before walking up the stairs to her chamber. Here there was a garderobe set into the wall, a small chamber that projected outside, with a seat set into it. Below sat a box filled with wood ash which was regularly emptied and used as fertiliser. She settled, frowning.

The world was going mad. Girls like the miller's daughter Mary enticing men like the priest. It was a great shame. Annicia could remember the girl. Tall and willowy, with lustrous eyes and a gentle smile constantly playing about her lips. Beautiful. No wonder that she might have tempted a priest from his oath of celibacy.

Oh dear. That nasty, disloyal thought was there again: what if she hadn't only tempted the priest? What if she had tempted her master, too?

It was a relief to see that the weather had eased a little, Sir Baldwin de Furnshill thought, as he mounted his horse. Once in the saddle, he felt at his side for his short riding sword. It sat so comfortably against his thigh that he often forgot he was wearing it, but in these troubled times it was a foolhardy man who undertook any journey without carrying a weapon of some sort.

In his new crimson tunic, a present from his wife, who deemed, probably correctly, that his old one was too threadbare to reflect his authority as a Keeper of the King's Peace, Baldwin felt slightly ill at ease. The rich embroidery at sleeve, neck and hem was too gaudy for a man who was used to the rigours of military life, and his green hose made his legs itch. Still, he would sooner cut off his own arm than hurt Jeanne's feelings, so he could only hope that the clothes would grow more comfortable with the wearing.

The ride to Crediton was not arduous. From his home near Cadbury the road wandered gently about the hill to the western-most edge of his demesne, and then climbed for a short distance before dropping towards Crediton, where he had his court. However, he was concerned these days that he might be attacked on the way. There were too many men-at-arms wandering the land without money, especially since the Scottish war last year. Before his marriage, he would have brought his steward, Edgar, with him on a journey like this, but not now. Baldwin preferred to know that a trained, professional and trusted warrior remained in the house while he was out.

It was ironic that he should have been created Keeper of the King's Peace, with wide-ranging powers in this, his area. He often thought he should have refused the honour when it was first suggested to him by his friend Simon Puttock, the Bailiff of Lydford. With a wry grin, Baldwin could recall his shock, bordering on horror, when he realised that his friend, who was then a very recent acquaintance, had proposed him to fill the post. At the time Baldwin was effectively a newcomer to the district. Beforehand he had been a loyal member of the Poor Fellow Soldiers of Christ and the Temple of Solomon, a Knight Templar, until the arrest of the Order on 13 October 1307.

For a long while after that date he had not believed that his friends and comrades would be sent to the stakes. All through the hideous testing of the men, while they were tortured, many to death, threatened, and some summarily executed, Baldwin had believed that the Pope must rescue them. The Pope had to recognise their innocence and proclaim that their arrest was all a hideous mistake. When it didn't happen, he wondered whether there was some vestige of truth in the allegations, and it was only when his Grand Master, Jacques de Molay, denounced his executioners and declared his innocence and the innocence of the Order, that Baldwin realised the truth: the whole matter had been staged in order that the French King and the Pope could grasp the wealth of the Knights Templar for their own advantage. The most noble Order of Knights had been destroyed, the most devout Christians murdered, in order that two implacably avaricious men should satisfy their lust for wealth.

It was that, so Simon had once said, which had forged Baldwin's suitability for the task of weighing men's innocence or guilt. Baldwin had seen how Justice could fail. He had lost faith in the Pope and secular rulers, for if the greatest Christian King and the Pope himself could be corrupt, how could a man trust those who worked beneath them?

The injustice and horror of it all had left Baldwin a cynical and caustic man in the years immediately following the destruction of his Order, but that aspect of his character had mellowed; indeed, these days it was all but gone. He still bore the same wrinkles and marks of pain which had grown to decorate his features during that lengthy period of rough living when his life was in perpetual danger, but now they simply looked like the honourable marks of a man who was older than middle age. Since he had been fortunate enough to find and marry Lady Jeanne de Liddinstone, his figure had filled out, and the expression in his eyes had lost some of the introspection of 1315. Today he was as likely to smile and laugh as to snarl.

Not that Sir Baldwin himself would admit that he had changed. If asked, he would have declared that he was the same man who had set sail in 1290 to join the defenders of Acre against the hordes of pagan Saracens. Yet he secretly knew it wasn't the case. He felt the same, held some of the same opinions and beliefs, but in the same way that his body would occasionally let him down with sharp aches and pains or grumbling muscles when he had taken too much exercise, his attitude to life had changed. He was cooler, calmer, and more fiercely protective of this land of his.

It was probably the effect of the parlous state of the realm itself, the mutterings of dissatisfaction with the King, the open contempt for Edward's two most trusted advisers, the Despensers, and of course the terrible disaster of the campaign against the Scots. There were certainly enough matters to cause an informed, intelligent man to pause and consider. Men muttered that it would be better to have open war and destroy the Despensers. That avaricious and murderous family ignored the law and robbed and imprisoned people without trial, purely to ransom them for whatever the Despensers wanted.

One man had even suggested, in Baldwin's hearing, that an assassin should be hired to kill the Despensers. There Baldwin drew the line. When he had lived in Acre, and afterwards on Cyprus, he had heard of the dreaded *Hashishim* of the Old Man of the Mountain. He was a terrifying mercenary who would point his drugged adherents at any man if he was paid enough, and his crazed killers invariably succeeded in their murders. To Baldwin, a Templar, the idea of a clandestine murderer of that sort was uniquely repellent. A man should stand and fight in the open, calling on his enemy to defend himself. How different from the single madman hiding beneath a bed or behind a tapestry, stabbing or poisoning. That was the act of a coward, an act which must lead to terror among all right-thinking men.

Following the roadway as it curved around the last hill, Crediton was at last laid before him. Over the last few years the Canons of the great church had built many new houses for themselves, their servants and novices, and now the view that met Baldwin's eye was one of bustle and confusion all the way out to the water meadow at the easternmost point of the town, especially near the church itself. There people milled about some more construction work. Craftsmen bawled orders to apprentices, smiths hammered, hawkers and tranters wandered shouting their wares. Over it all was the warm, light haze of the smoke from the fires.

He had little enthusiasm for business today, and he idled up the road. The shops and houses on either side gleamed, damp from the night's rain, while the ground beneath him was foul, spatted with excrement from the herd of cattle which he could still see being taken through the town and out to the pastures near the river.

When he arrived at the church's buildings, he made for the timber-framed hall in which he held his court. It was owned by the church, and there were stables behind where visitors could leave their mounts. Baldwin swung himself from his saddle and bellowed for the groom. The lad should look after horses for a few copper coins, but he was routinely late to observe a new client.

'Jack? *Jack!* Get out here now, you lazy son of a—'

The youth appeared in the alley that led behind the town's hall, rubbing the sleep from his eyes. 'Oh, Sir Baldwin, I didn't hear you. I was . . . er, filling the . . .'

'Do not lie to me, Jack. I can recognise a lie two miles distant.'

'I wouldn't think of lying to you, Sir Baldwin,' Jack said in a hurt tone.

'You should leave cheap wine alone, boy. Save your money until you can afford a decent drink. Maybe then you would not fall asleep.'

'Sir Baldwin, I haven't been drinking. Not much, anyway.'

'I can smell it from seven paces, Jack,' Baldwin said grumpily and passed him the reins.

'You are my favourite customer, sir. Out of all them who come here, it's you I serve first and keenest.'

'That says little for your treatment of other clients, since you are always asleep whenever I arrive! Now give my horse a good rubdown and rest. He has come far enough to warrant at least as much rest as you seem to think you deserve yourself.'

'Sir Knight, that's not fair.'

'I often think I should take my custom to the inn's ostlers. At least the men there seem interested to have my business,' Baldwin grumbled.

'Don't do that, please, Sir Baldwin!' Jack's face had paled, and he hung his head, looking up at Baldwin with sorrowful eyes. 'You know my wife and—'

'And three children would suffer,' Baldwin said testily. 'Yes, I know. You tell me every time I come here. But I *will* go to them if you do not stay awake and listen for my arrival.'

'Yes, Sir Baldwin.'

'So – see to my mount!'

The youth nodded, ducked his head submissively, and led the horse away towards his stable.

Baldwin watched him go with a glower fixed to his face. The trouble was, he knew that the lad was desperate for the money. If Baldwin stopped bringing his horse here, Jack probably wouldn't have enough income to keep his wife and children. That wasn't something Baldwin wanted on his conscience. He had seen enough suffering in the last few years.

It wasn't the fault of the groom that he was so sharp-tempered today. No, it was all to do with Roger Scut.

This morning's work was not difficult, but it involved much reading and agreeing of documents with one of Bishop Walter's clerks. There was to be a court of Gaol Delivery in Exeter in a matter of days, and Baldwin must go through all his cases in which a man had been sent to Exeter Gaol from his court to make sure that none had been forgotten and that the relevant material was all there. Then, when each case came before the men nominated to try it, at least Baldwin himself should escape a fine. He would hope so, for he was to be one of the Gaol Delivery Justices, and setting a fine upon himself would be embarrassing.

Never Baldwin's favourite task, today he looked forward to reading through the records with less than his usual good-humoured tolerance. All because of Roger Scut, who was in the hall as Baldwin entered.

The odious little man! Chubby and ingratiating, almost half a head shorter than Baldwin, Scut's hands fluttered as he spoke, as though emphasising his every point. What Baldwin found most annoying was Scut's habit, or perhaps it was a deliberate affectation, of tilting back his head and squinting along the length of his nose, as though it gave gravitas to his pronouncements. Not that his nose itself was particularly deserving of such attention, to Baldwin's mind. It was a short, bloated appendage with red and purple blood vessels spread liberally over it. A cider drinker's nose if Baldwin had ever seen one, which probably explained why the clerk's voice was so nasal as well. But his habits and his nose were not his only unattractive features. He possessed many others. His eyes, for example.

His eyes were like a ferret's, always looking about for something, as though he believed that there was a secret to be teased out of the woodwork if he could only but find it. That was another thing that Baldwin disliked about Scut. The way he would not meet Baldwin's eyes when they spoke. The knight had no doubt that the clerk was honest enough. Yet a man who would not or could not speak to you and meet your eyes was all too commonly concealing something. Baldwin did not trust Roger Scut, the oleaginous little shit.

Not for the first time, Baldwin reminded himself that a 'scut' was a common word for an arse on a rabbit or a woman. An old woman, he reckoned, glancing at Scut without amusement.

'Good Sir Knight! Godspeed, my dear Sir Baldwin. It is a pleasure to see you again. Do I find you well?'

'Well enough,' Baldwin said shortly.

Roger Scut was already sitting at the great table in the hall, a pile of papers rolled neatly at his side on the floor, most held in strong, waxed leather tubes. Sheets of parchment were spread before him, held at each corner by large stones wrapped in leather to prevent marking the records. Most people Baldwin knew would not bother with such fripperies. Provided that the stones were clean and not too rough, they would do no damage – but this was just another of Scut's little affectations. He hated dirt.

Roger Scut picked up a reed and studied the end. Taking up a small knife, he sharpened it and cut the end freshly. There were a number of reeds on the table, and an inkhorn was carefully propped against Roger's purse.

Baldwin shouted for a pie and a jug of wine, before sitting with a grunt and glancing at the papers before him. Records of crimes committed, money amerced, property confiscated, and then lists of witnesses who would have to be told to travel to Exeter. Baldwin found it hard to suppress a groan. The thought of spending hours alone with this clerk was deeply unpleasant.

'Please, Sir Knight, look at these first,' Scut said, pointing to the gaol delivery records.

Baldwin glanced at the figures and tried to fit an expression of interest on his face.

Chapter Six

While Sir Baldwin de Furnshill suffered the tortures of adding and subtracting the Latin figures, trying to reach agreement on the totals with Roger Scut, his friend Simon Puttock was returning to his own home after a lengthy meeting with his master, the Abbot of Tavistock.

Simon was a tall man, his dark hair sprinkled with silver now that he was nearing his middle thirties, but although his belly had grown in the last year, and he was the possessor of a second chin, he still rode across the moors often enough on Stannary business to keep his weight from exploding. His face was ruddy-complexioned from his hours abroad in all weathers, and the lines that marked his brow gave character to his features.

He looked relaxed enough today as he rode back from Tavistock to his home at Lydford, but that was only on the surface. As Bailiff, he was an official of Stannary Law, and all too often his expression must reflect the severity of the rough justice given at the Stannary Court. Outside the Court, he was contented enough, and judged by many to be a good companion, but when he was at his rest, his smile was often tempered with sadness in memory of his firstborn son, Peterkin, who had died some few years ago of a fever. The pain of losing him would never leave Simon, or so he felt. Death had marked both him and his wife; their grief was only moderated when their second son was born, named, like the first, Peterkin.

Now he had more to occupy his mind than memories of his dead child. Since the terrible events of the last year, life was becoming more complicated.

In 1318 Abbot Robert had paid three hundred pounds to buy the revenues from all the tin-mining in Dartmoor for three years.

It had proved a worthwhile investment, and in 1321 he leased the
revenues for one hundred pounds a year over ten years. It brought
in a good sum annually, and his most important official was
Simon, his Bailiff, the man charged with maintaining law and
order on the moors. It was Simon who must negotiate with miners
and landowners, who had to defuse arguments almost before they
started, who had to soothe the ruffled feathers of knights and
barons all around the King's forest of Dartmoor when the tinners
took it into their heads to divert streams or declare that another
prime piece of pasture was perfect for mining. There were
always rows between the miners and the other inhabitants of the
Stannaries or their near neighbours. When those disputes came to
blows, it was Simon who must perform his inquest and record the
details so that the matter could be raised at the next Stannary
Court and suitable fines or punishments imposed.

It was wearing on a man, but Simon had coped well so far.
Nowadays, though, he was losing his temper more and more often.
He wasn't naturally irascible, but he had problems enough to
distract him, and they made his brow darken now as he lurched on
homeward.

The problems had begun with his daughter, Edith, about a year
ago. Recently he had felt close to a form of peace with her, but
things had flared up again. He knew why, but knowing the root
cause of a problem was not the same as possessing a cure.

It started during the last summer. She had bitterly resented his
interference in her choice of a suitor, and she had become a
source of disharmony in his household. Meg, his wife, and even
his servant Hugh began to take her part in discussions, leaving
Simon feeling like an outcast in his own home. Later in the year,
she had appeared to submit to his authority, when her favourite
died, and for some time thereafter she had been friendly, as she
used to be, but now her attitude had suffered another reversal and
she was once more froward and uncooperative.

If it were only her, he wouldn't mind, but a sullenness had
infected his wife and other members of his household. Young
Peterkin sat and watched Simon and Meg whenever they were in

a room together, with an oddly adult expression on his young face, as though he was gauging their mood and assessing how he might make best advantage of their mutual antipathy.

Simon sighed deeply. He knew it wasn't Meg's fault – it was the way that her dreams had been so rudely shattered.

The whole trouble was, Simon was being promoted. Abbot Robert was so pleased with his work that he had arranged to send Simon to the coast because at the same time as leasing the mining revenues, the Abbot had acquired the position of Keeper of the Port of Dartmouth as well. Naturally he had no intention of removing himself to a place so far from his comfortable quarters at his Abbey in Tavistock, but it was plain that he needed a representative there whom he could trust, and since the death of the previous Lieutenant, he had decided that Simon should go.

Margaret was delighted that he had won so much favour with the good Abbot, as she often said. 'If you are happy in your work, my husband, I am happy.'

'But you'd be happier not to move to Dartmouth,' he had said last week when she protested her delight once too often.

She had bent her head slightly. 'I love our home here.'

'It took you a while to get used to Lydford, didn't it?'

'I adored our farm in Sandford.'

He knew that. They had married there, and set up their family in Sandford. That house was where their daughter had been born, and their memories of the place were all happy. The summers seemed longer and hotter, the winters more mild, and life itself had been simpler. 'You were unhappy to move here to Lydford.'

'Yes, Husband, but that was mainly because we lived in the castle itself, and that is a terrible place,' she said with a delicate shiver. 'The walls seem to echo with screams. I have been very happy here.'

That was obvious. Her manner had become calm again since they moved here, to the little house near the castle at Lydford. 'Perhaps you will find it as easy to like Dartmouth,' he said hopefully.

'Perhaps,' she said dully.

'I believe it is a pleasant enough town.'

'Filled with sailors? A nice place for Edith to mature,' she countered.

'We should be able to afford a good house. I believe people say that it is healthful to live next to the sea. It may be good for Peterkin.'

'Yes, Husband. Unless pirates raid the town and fire the house about our ears,' she retorted, and that was where they had left the matter.

Simon could have refused the post. He was almost a free yeoman, scarcely a serf owned by his master, but even an entirely free man who had taken his Lord's livery and salt must obey his Lord's whim. If Abbot Robert decided that Simon would be best used down at Dartmouth, to Dartmouth he must go, no matter what his wife thought, if Simon wished to remain in his service. There would have to be an overwhelming need and urgency for Simon to even postpone taking up his new responsibilities.

Meg could stay here at Lydford, but neither of them would enjoy so long a separation. Others left their wives at home when they went to their work: Hugh himself had to leave his wife and son miles away up at Iddesleigh while he worked for Simon, just as any other servant would. A household, whether it was a man's, woman's or child's, would only expect men to remain to serve their masters. Women were called in for specialist tasks, for wet or dry nursing, for brewing, or for jobs where their skills were valued, such as milking, but generally a servant was a man, and he left his wife while he served his master. Women tended to be too much of a distraction and cause of dispute in a household. For that reason some poor fellows didn't see their wives for months at a time. Simon could never leave his Meg that long.

He couldn't refuse the post, but he knew that his wife dreaded the idea of moving so far from their home. Especially with the dangers of pirates, as she said. There were always French ships prepared to test the defences of little ports like Dartmouth.

There was no way out of it. He had already received the seal from Abbot Robert, and now he must set about packing up all their belongings on carts ready to be transported to Dartmouth.

Not that he was looking forward to informing Meg that the date for their departure was agreed.

It was almost time for their midday meal when Baldwin heard hooves ringing loudly on the cobbles outside. There was shouting, a horn was blown, and he could hear servants chattering while a horse stood blowing, clattering its shoes. Scut looked up at the door with a face filled with annoyance, which was itself enough to lighten Baldwin's mood.

The noise was enough to persuade him that something urgent had brought the rider, although he would have been willing to break the meeting on hearing news of a wren dying, Roger Scut bored and irritated him so much. He stood quickly as the door opened to admit a servant and a mud-bespattered messenger.

'Who are you and what do you want here?' Baldwin demanded.

'Sir, I am Joel, from North Tawton Hundred. Two days ago we had a messenger from South Tawton, from Sir Ralph of Wonson. He said that the cleric of Gidleigh Chapel has murdered a girl and run away.'

'A priest? Christ's pain!' Roger Scut said, and crossed himself.

'I'm sorry, Brother. He got her pregnant, I heard. Punched her or something. Probably trying to kill the baby.'

Baldwin nodded, but he could feel the revulsion in his belly. Hurting anyone unnecessarily was repellent to him, but to harm a child while still in the womb was surely the worst crime. His voice was harsh as he said, 'It is not unknown for even a priest to do such a thing.'

'Surely it is very rare,' Roger Scut protested.

Baldwin ignored him. 'What makes you think he might have come this way?'

'There was a theft of bread from a farm,' Joel said, then explained how he had heard that the day before, there had been another theft of food and some ale reported from a farm near Spreyton. 'I may be wrong, but he could be coming this way, Keeper.'

'Then we must search for him!' Baldwin said decisively, smacking a hand against his sword hilt.

'Sir Baldwin,' Roger Scut said smoothly, his hand encompassing the piles of documents still lying on the table. 'We must complete this work before you ride away.'

'I am Keeper. I have a duty to find this man.'

'No, he is a cleric and therefore not your responsibility. Perhaps this fellow could ride to the Dean of the church here and advise him that our Brother has gone abroad. We shall have to learn why, of course.'

Baldwin barely acknowledged him. Seeing a watchman in the doorway, he said, 'Godwen, I shall be with you as soon as my horse is saddled. Raise the Hue with your horn and call for all the men with horses.'

'Sir Baldwin.' Roger Scut leaned his head back and peered at Baldwin down his podgy nose as though it was a cocked and ready crossbow. His voice was so oily, Baldwin could have used it to soften twenty-year-old leather. 'We have much still to do. Surely a man of your importance need not ride about for no reason? Especially when we have so much ground still to cover in here.'

'No reason?' Baldwin gave him a look up and down, and made no effort to conceal his annoyance. 'Brother, I am responsible for the King's Peace. Having a man wandering the land stealing from every house he comes upon is not conducive to maintaining the Peace. Apart from his offences, this priest may be caught and disturbed while in someone's property, and could be attacked – either he would add another murder to his crimes, or he might even die himself. I will not have that! Godwen, do as I said. Brother, I suggest you go through the cases in my absence, and we shall discuss them later.'

He spun on his heel and swept out from the room, a little ashamed at his sense of victory over the fool of a clerk, but mostly pleased to have escaped sitting in Roger Scut's company any longer. Except, as soon as he realised the source of his pleasure, he felt himself contemptible: he was no more than a hypocrite who was willing to use his official position and arguments of protecting others to evade an afternoon spent in the company of a man like Scut.

Mark shivered and wrapped his arms about his body once more as he stumbled and slipped onwards, hardly aware of his cracked flesh, the purple colour of his fingers and toes, the shivers which made his whole body convulse like a man in his death throes. His only aim was to escape South Tawton and get to Exeter, his sole guide was the sun, but fear made him avoid roads and lanes in case he was spotted. Instead he crossed fields, concealed himself in woods, made use of narrow runs created by deer and foxes, and tried to keep out of sight of farmers and other peasants.

As he trod along yet another tortuous path at the side of a stream, he turned and stared back, still fearing pursuit; however, there was no sound but the clattering of water over stones and occasional birdsong.

It was awful. He had stolen food and drink, he had worn his feet to a blistered mess, and he had no idea what would become of him. The more he considered it, the more the hollow fear grew in his belly at the thought of telling Bishop Walter about his crimes. Tears of self-pity sprang into his eyes again, and he snivelled miserably. His life was devastated, and why? Because the Bishop had chosen to send him to Gidleigh, that's why! It was damned unfair that he should lose his good name and honour this way. If he hadn't been dropped in that midden of a vill, with no other monks for company, he'd never have even noticed Mary. And now look at him.

The trees were thick down here, growing close together, and as he thrust himself forward, Mark could feel the brambles catching at his habit, pulling it apart thread by thread. He had a thick stick in his hand which he had fashioned from a young sapling, and he used it to prod aside the heavier clumps and smash down the thinner, but even so his progress was slow.

God's dear bones, but how could this have happened? All because he discovered lust after so many years. It was mad. Poor Mary! If it had been possible, Mark would have been happy to live with her, but that was impossible for a priest who intended advancement. Only a feeble-minded, semi-literate cleric of the type who would have been content to live in Throwleigh could have done that. And God preserve any priest who was found by Bishop Walter enjoying the comfort of a woman. He would soon be exiled to a much worse place – although how anywhere could be worse than Gidleigh was more than Mark could imagine.

Grimly, he recognised that Bishop Walter would no doubt find it easy. It would be either a miserable monastery on a bleak, windswept moor, or a church on an isolated island where he would be forced to live a hermit-like existence.

Well, he wouldn't accept it. He had never committed any form of crime until he'd been forced to. He hadn't meant to hurt poor Mary. He'd only slapped her – a little hard, yes, but not enough to hurt. Not enough to kill. Certainly not to kill, he repeated, as though his denial could reverse the events of two days ago. It was only the frustration, that was all. It had made him lash out. But he wouldn't hurt her on purpose! Not her!

'I didn't mean to, God,' he whispered, but God brought no comfort. How could He? Mark knew that behind him, somewhere, his own father was now chasing after him, bent on his capture and death. God could bring no solace that might ease that horror.

Piers the Reeve watched the Coroner leave, then hitched up his hose and belt with a grunt, making his way back along the lane to where the body still lay, her head slack and loose where her neck had been broken.

'Come on, then. Better get her up to the chapel,' he sighed.

There were three others from the vill still there. Huward, the miller, her father, was keeping the tears at bay, while trying to comfort his wife, Gilda. Sir Ralph had already ridden off, slashing with his whip at any folk who stood in his way, but Piers could rely on Osbert and Elias.

That poor fool Sampson had told his story haltingly. He'd seen Mark and Mary, heard Mark apparently thump her, gag, and run.

That was clear enough, then. They were justified in going after the bastard. Sampson hadn't heard the neck break, but the feeble-minded dolt had probably run off after hearing the punch.

'Let's lift her, then,' he said. He was glad he'd gone to the chapel before coming to this inquest. It had given him a chance to calm himself before the horror of the inquest, not that it had been his reason for going there. He'd gone to tell the men who were waiting there in case Mark should return, that they could forget their vigil. The priest had obviously made it clean away and they were needed for the jury at the inquest.

It was strange there without the young priest. The lean-to shack where Mark had lived was warm with the fire that the guards had set blazing in the hearth, but there was no comfort in the place. It was a bachelor's house, merely a chamber in which an exhausted man could rest from his toil. Piers thought it felt too much like his own home: bleak without a woman's touch to enliven it. Since his own wife had died, he was more aware of that lack than before. While Agnes lived, he assumed that the comfort he enjoyed was no more than that which all men had as their due, but then she died. A disease attacked her, and in the space of a few days, she was gone. Since then, he had come to realise that his contentment with her company was in reality due to her. A vast emptiness had opened in his life once she was buried. The sparkle had gone, and he thought, looking around Mark's little cell, that there was much the same atmosphere of loss here.

In the chapel he kneeled and gave a quick prayer for Mary, but also for his dead Agnes. Not a day passed that he didn't think of her, and he found the cool silence in the chapel conducive to reflection, giving him time to gather his thoughts before he came here to Mary's body.

She had been rolled onto a blanket, naked, while the Coroner studied her, prodding and prying with the subtlety and sympathy of a butcher with a hog's carcass before the vill's jury. All he cared about was the fines he could impose. Piers had observed a dignified silence while the money was totted up, convinced that the cash would mostly end up in the Coroner's pocket. You couldn't trust officials who collected taxes. Too often, most of the money they took would stick to them.

'You couldn't tell him much, could you?' he said conversationally to Elias.

The peasant was older than Piers by some four years or so; Piers remembered him being almost married when he himself was still being sent out to hurl stones at the birds pecking at the grain as it was sowed.

'What more do you expect me to tell him?' Elias snapped. He had not aged well. His wife had also died years before, but Elias had never learned to cope with his loss. It had been worse for Elias than for Piers, partly because his wife had died during the birth of his son, who also perished, and then his first and only child died during the famine seven or eight years ago, raped, and suffering a slow death. At least Piers still had his own son and daughter. The lad lived with him, while his daughter had married and moved away to Oakhampton. Still, Piers saw her every so often, and her children, when he went up to the market in South Zeal, the new town roughly halfway between them.

Up till his wife's death, Elias had been a cheery companion, always one of the first with a song or a story in the ale-house, but since his daughter's death in the famine, he had grown withdrawn and surly. His greying hair was unkempt at all times, his heavy, round head tended to hang like a whipped cur's, and his craggy features remained fixed in a scowl from dawn to dusk, his brown eyes all but hidden beneath his grim brows. He wore a thick grey beard that almost concealed his mouth and his solid jawline, but any strength it gave to his appearance was marred by the particles of bread and mashed pea that adhered to it.

If anything, his demeanour today was blacker than usual, a fact which gave Piers pause for thought. 'Nothing. I was just interested.'

Elias said nothing, but Piers saw him shoot a look towards Huward. The miller had left his wife to her grief, and was marching towards the men carrying his daughter's body.

'We can take her to the chapel,' Piers said comfortingly, but inwardly he wondered how he would cope were this his own daughter.

'Be damned to that! You think I want her body set down in there, in the place where *he* raped her?' Huward rasped.

The miller didn't speak directly to Piers. He couldn't. This was the saddest day of his life. Until he had been called to see Mary's body, he had known only happiness. His wife was a source of delight, his daughters were both adored by him, and he had a son to take on the mill after his own death. This sudden collapse from joy to despair had left him with a more acute pain at his loss that he would have thought it possible for one man to bear.

Since confirming that the body was his daughter's, he'd been filled with misery for the death of his little Mary – his little angel, as he always called her. He had the two girls, Mary and Flora, and Mary was always the calmer, quieter of the two. Flora, his flower, was sweet-natured, but more turbulent to live with. When she had a mood, all in the house knew it. Many was the time he had been forced to roar at her to be silent when she was teasing Mary or Ben, their brother.

Walking here, he had known that the inquest would be grievous. It was the hardest thing, burying your children. He remembered his mother saying that once, when his brother Tom died. She'd said that it was the toughest thing she'd ever had to do, putting him in his grave. Well, perhaps it was, but for Huward, the hardest part was the inquest. Seeing her poor, bloodied body being stripped and exposed for all to see. Every man in the vill standing there, eyeing her – oh, not with any lust, no, but that wasn't the point. They could all see her, his little Mary, naked, like a whore.

That bastard priest would regret his brief fling and murder, Huward swore to himself. The devil-spawn had destroyed more than Huward's little girl, he had killed off Huward's grandchild and taken away the peace of Huward's home. He felt as though with that one blow, the killer had slaughtered his entire family.

'You think I'd let you take her there?' he said brokenly. His hand reached out to stroke her cheek. 'Cold. She's so cold!'

Piers put a hand to Huward's shoulder. 'Come, let's go to the tavern and find you a good draught of cider.'

'I don't need cider. All I want is revenge.' He thrust forward and took his daughter up in his arms, forcing the men who held the blanket to relinquish their burden. Huward softly turned her face to him, then tucked it into his shoulder, his arms about her back and behind her legs. Then he turned away, and set off in the direction of Gidleigh and the church there.

Chapter Seven

When Baldwin ran to the stable and bellowed for Jack, he was aware of a strange feeling that things weren't right.

Partly it must be the fact that Edgar was missing. Every other time he had been forced to raise the Hue and Cry, Edgar had been at his side. When Baldwin rode in search of a felon or some other assumed miscreant, Edgar was a permanent guard, always nearby. But today Edgar was at the manor protecting Jeanne, Baldwin's wife.

Edgar had been his servant for more years than he cared to remember now, originally his sergeant in the Knights Templar. Every knight went into battle with a trusted man-at-arms to back up the knight's charge, to protect his flank and to fight at his side, loyal unto death. After the Templars had been destroyed, Edgar had refused to leave Baldwin's side.

However, his would not be the only missing face, Baldwin knew. The compact, wiry hunter, John Black, who had joined Baldwin on some of his early chases, was dead; he had fallen from his pony into a river during the floods of the winter of 1321. Tanner, too, who had been so successful as the Constable of the Hundred, a large, stolid man with a face and head that might have been carved from granite, had suddenly been stricken with a malady last summer, and had succumbed in three days.

Life was nothing if not fleeting. Baldwin couldn't help but notice that the years appeared to flash past with increasing speed, and the thought was sad. He had only just found a woman with whom he felt he could spend the remainder of his life, and he regretted the years before he had met her. They felt wasted. Although he was no modern chivalrous knight, a lust-filled, salacious fool like those who thought that the only battle worth fighting was that for a woman's virginity, he sometimes found himself thinking that if only he had met Jeanne earlier, he would have gained more enjoyment from his life.

He was getting old. He detested the idea that he might soon leave Jeanne, a feeling made still more poignant by the fact of his daughter, little Richalda. Almost one year old, she was utterly dependent upon Jeanne and him, and he felt that responsibility keenly. Perhaps for the first time in his life, he truly had a reason to live, or so he felt. He had loved Jeanne since he first met her in Tavistock nearly four years ago, and he knew that she loved him in return, but all the time he was aware that she was a strong personality in her own right. If he were to die, his widow would mourn him, mourn him deeply, but she would not expire for despair. Nor would he want her to.

Still, with the wind in his face and a powerful mount beneath him, it was impossible to feel gloomy. Men died on days like this, and if he were to die today, he would do so with a smile on his face, glad that he had spent his life honourably.

Unlike this priest, he thought, and the smile was wiped from his face in a moment. It was hard to understand how a man who had professed himself determined to live by God's own rules could slip so dramatically into such a mire of dishonour and shame.

Baldwin had never met the cleric from Gidleigh, but he had heard that the fellow was a youngster. If that was true, Baldwin could begin to comprehend the story: a lonely young man placed in a drear and miserable location near the moors. Long winter nights in which to brood; chill, wet weather to make him wonder at God's reasons for creating such a land; monosyllabic neighbours whose dialect would be largely incomprehensible and who would either distrust a foreigner or be so respectful to a priest that they would find it hard to open their mouths in his presence. And in the middle of all this misery, a sudden ray of light: a young woman, her lips promising soft kisses, her breasts begging to be caressed, her body suggesting fire and warmth and rest.

Baldwin had been a celibate warrior monk for most of his adult life, and he was all too aware of the temptations of the flesh. But he had not succumbed – apart from a few occasions before he had taken his vows – and there was no reason why this fellow should have done so either.

What was he doing heading this way? There were only two explanations Baldwin could envisage. Either he was expecting to escape: flee the shire by running east or flee the country by jumping on a ship; or he wanted to get to the Bishop's palace and put his side of the story in the Bishop's court. If he could make it that far, he would escape the secular authorities.

He would not be the first priest to do so, Baldwin knew. Stories abounded of priests who tried to avoid the shaming experience of being captured and gaoled, called liars when they claimed Benefit of Clergy, until they were taken to the Lord's court and could prove that they could recite the *Pater Noster*. That was usually good enough. It was rare for a lord to dismiss his claim after that, and for good reason. Woe betide the knight or banneret who dared flout the authority of Mother Church. She protected Her own. The Pope was the unchallenged ruler of the spiritual world, the successor to St Paul, more powerful than any monarch. A king could have you executed; the Pope could condemn you to hellfire for all eternity.

Charitably, Baldwin wondered if that was the cleric's aim, to get to Exeter, so that he could fall on his knees before his Bishop and apologise, confessing his guilt so that he could perform a penance that would save his soul. It was quite possible.

The alternative was that the fellow was making his way east or to Topsham to catch a ship. That was perfectly likely too, but Baldwin was not persuaded. If he wanted to avoid capture entirely, the easiest route away from danger would be away from the Bishop's authority. A man determined to survive outside the law could live rough for weeks on end in the woods and moors heading westwards, and there were plenty of ports that way, too. Why run the risk of a brother cleric recognising him by running straight towards the Cathedral where he had once lived, when he could head in the opposite direction?

No, Baldwin was comfortable with the inference that this cleric was trying to get back to the Bishop. And Baldwin was determined to prevent him succeeding. The murderer of a young woman and a child deserved a little discomfort by being held in the local gaol for a short while, so far as Baldwin was concerned.

When he had mounted his horse and trotted out to the roadway, there was already a crowd of armed men and boys waiting, most of them mounted on large horses better suited to ploughing or carting than galloping, who had arrived in response to the horn-blast and shouting of the man from North Tawton.

Baldwin had to stop himself glancing about for his old Constable, Tanner. Tanner would have made all these men sort themselves into some sort of order, arranging them by location, to prevent any fears of fighting among them. However, in Tanner's place there were now two Constables, Godwen and Thomas, both of whom were studiously ignoring each other although they sat a scant four yards apart. Seeing them, Baldwin groaned to himself.

This chase might well become more arduous than he had expected.

Piers walked behind Huward and his burden, his heart leaden as he saw how the miller stumbled and tripped in his misery.

At any other time it would have been a pleasant walk. For once there were no clouds, the wind had stilled, and the low sun was casting a bright light all about. Shadows stretched out against the dark soil, and trees looked stark without their leaves.

The lane was sunken between walls on either side, and Piers could see the great hills of Dartmoor to the west. At this time of day, the sunlight caught their southern flanks and lighted the heather with a golden hue. First thing in the morning, when the weather was clear, the sun had an oddly pink colour to it. It had always made Piers look. Somehow he never thought it looked natural.

Nothing was natural today, he reckoned as he set his jaw and glowered at the ground before him. The mud was almost ankle-deep again here, and he could feel it soaking into his boots and squelching between his chilled toes. He would have to clean the leather carefully later, when he had a chance, or he'd have to replace the boots before long, and that was an expense he could live without if possible.

Mary looked like a sleeping child again. Her eyes were closed, and her face rested on Huward's shoulder just as though she had dropped off in her father's arms. Just as Piers's own daughter used to. He sighed; when they got to the church, he would give thanks to God for the fact that his own daughter was fine, happily married, a mother herself. He could not imagine how he would have behaved if she had been slaughtered in this way.

It was plain lucky that the miller had a wife to look after as well as everything else. If not, Piers was sure that Huward would have run after the pissy priest, no matter what his master said. That would have caused many more problems, and Piers didn't want problems. His post was an annual elected one, and he saw no reason to make trouble. This death was bad enough. Fines for breaking the King's Peace, a fine for the weapon that was used, more costs would undoubtedly mount, and all when the vill had to cope with the death of a popular girl.

They had reached the top of Gidleigh now, and the road curved towards the castle and church. There Piers caught sight of Elias once more. The old peasant had a nervous expression on his face, and Piers could see him glancing from side to side as though anticipating an attack from some quarter. Then his eye lighted on Osbert, and his attention focused.

Piers saw his expression, and when he looked at Osbert, he could see why Elias was staring so hard. Poor Osbert looked devastated. He looked desperate to conceal his tears and misery as though such sentiments were unmanly, sniffing and wiping at his eyes with a hand that was quick and cursory, as though he was pretending that there were no tears there, that he was too strong to weep for a girl, as though he was simply scratching at an irritation. It was unnecessary. Everyone in the vill knew that he had adored Mary. Most men had, especially those who were marriageable.

Osbert must have dreamed of owning her, Piers thought, and they would have made a pleasing couple, her so slim and attractive, him bold and strong and tall. Yes, they'd have made a handsome pair.

The sadness assailed him again and Piers's mind turned to other things. He would have to stop with Elias and take a moment to speak to him, but the little band swept on, and it would have seemed disrespectful to the memory of Mary if he had tried to collar the older peasant.

He would have to talk to him later, Piers thought to himself as he followed the weeping Huward into the church itself. At the door he turned back, but instead of staring at Elias, his gaze went to Osbert. Osbert met his look for a moment, but then the young man turned and walked slowly back towards the mill.

It was much later that Ben walked into the house and spat at the floor when he realised there was no meal waiting. His parents were too taken up with grief to worry about mundane things like food. He wasn't, though. He was starving. Hadn't eaten since late morning.

He'd been supposed to go out and help Osbert with the hedging on Huward's fields after the inquest, but he couldn't be bothered. It wasn't as though his father would punish him, not if he kept his head low, and he didn't want to stand in a cold field, feet freezing to the soil, helping Osbert to cut part-way through branches until they could be bent back, fixing them in place by hooking them under stakes. They didn't have to be enormously strongly held, because it was the ditch and high turf wall that held the animals in their pasture, but it was good to tidy up the hedges at the top, if only because it was a useful source of firewood.

No, hacking at a blackthorn hedge was not Ben's idea of fun. Instead he'd gone to an ale-house on the Chagford road and drunk himself into a merry state as soon as the inquest was over. Not that the mood was going to last if he didn't quickly find something to eat.

'Come back, then, have you?'

'Osbert! What are *you* doing, sneaking in like that? You should—'

'You should hold your tongue, you should. I've been working while you've been out drinking again, haven't you? While your sister was being taken to church, too – dead.'

'Leave it, Osbert. I used up my grief when I heard she was dead.'

'You managed to make it last a whole day?'

'Very funny. I suppose you'll keep it going for a good long while, won't you? You'll make up for any lack on my part.'

'What's that supposed to mean?'

'You couldn't keep your eyes off her, could you? Always fancied her arse. Did you ever get a chance to feel her up?'

'No, Ben, I didn't. I wouldn't have if I'd been given the chance, either. Because it's not right that a man should do that to a woman outside of marriage.'

'Oh, it's all right, Os. If you want a woman,' Ben continued, eyes open wide in innocence, 'why don't you go to see Anna at Jordan's ale-house? I could give you a recommendation there. She's very good. The way she wriggles her backside is—'

'Be silent, you dunghill worm. You can treat me with contempt if you like, but on this day, when your sister's being taken to her grave, the least you can do is go there to witness it. Why do you stand here chewing at my ears when you should be with your mother?'

'Oh, by Christ's passion! Give me strength to cope with a big man's big heart. What good will it do Mary for me to be there? I grieved enough for her the day she died. There are other folk in church who'll say prayers for her. Who knows, maybe even I shall sometime soon.'

'You loved her before. Why do you hate her so much now?'

'I didn't love her. I never loved her. It's different for you, you wanted her body: that lovely scut and her breasts like two great bladders waiting to be squeezed. And she'd have liked it too. It's a shame you missed your chance. Losing her to a cleric! God's blood, I wouldn't have thought he had the life in his bone to satisfy her.'

Osbert had kept his patience, but he could feel it draining. 'I respected your sister, that's all,' he said quietly. 'And you should revere her now all you have is a memory.'

'Ah, yes, a memory. Sad, you don't even have that, do you? But I forgot! You did see her, didn't you? I was there. I saw you follow her down to the stream when she went to bathe last summer. I was intrigued to see why you were walking so quietly down that path.'

'I wasn't walking quietly!' Osbert spat. 'You make this up. You imagine the worst you could do yourself, then think others might copy you.'

Ben continued as though Osbert hadn't spoken. 'I went after you, and I tiptoed, just like you did. You turned into the wood, and when you came to the river, where she was lying naked in the water, I saw you. I saw you fiddling with your tarse . . .'

'I didn't, you liar!'

'All over the sight of my naked sister. Naughty, naughty Os.'

Unable to control his anger, Osbert leaped to catch Ben, but the smaller man slipped aside. Osbert felt a tingling in his arm as his momentum carried him onwards. When he stopped, he turned to catch at Ben again, but then he saw Ben had come around behind him, and now he stood with a dagger held ready, his head low in a fighting stance, eyes wary, alert to any movement.

'Try that again, and you'll get worse, Os,' he said, pointing at a long cut on Osbert's arm that dripped blood. 'And you shouldn't fear, anyway. I won't say anything. I know you adored my sister, you even went to watch her in the river naked, and I saw what effect that had on you, but I won't tell anyone. Why should I? I never liked her anyway. Bitch. It's better that she's gone. Especially since she seems to have been playing the whore herself. Think about it. You're better off without her!'

'She told me, you know!' Osbert spat. 'I know all about you.'

'What?' Ben demanded, waving his knife nearer Osbert, sweeping it back and forth.

'You accuse me of lust, but it was you who tried to take her,' Osbert spat.

The knife darted forward and Osbert had to slip to one side to avoid it.

'You're lying! She swore she wouldn't . . . I didn't touch her!'

Osbert laughed mirthlessly. 'She swore she wouldn't talk? She did. I know what you tried, *boy*!'

'I didn't try anything.'

'Perhaps it wasn't the monk killed her, eh? Maybe he just found her and thought . . .' Osbert's mouth fell open at the thought. 'Did *you* kill her?'

'Me? Why should I do a thing like that, eh?'

'To silence her! To stop her telling people how you tried to make her sleep with you!'

'No, and you're mad to think it.'

'You haven't liked her since then, have you?'

'It was the priest killed her. You're just mad with jealousy of *him*. That's why you're making up this tale. You're mad!'

Ben chuckled low in his throat. It sounded almost like a snarl. Then he cautiously stepped backwards, and sidled out through the door.

Osbert's anger had left him now, and in its place was an emptiness. He should have defended her. He should have fought Ben for that foul assertion. As if any man could think that beautiful Mary was in any way a whore. If he heard Ben insulting her memory again, he'd kill him. Yes, and take the consequences.

Osbert remembered what he had said and shivered. The thought that Ben might go about spreading that story to others was fearful. He couldn't deny it was true. That time, when he'd first seen her nude, it had snared his heart. She was so perfect, so beautiful. Small, but large-hipped and large-breasted, perfect.

If people realised just how badly Os had desired her, they might think he could have killed her after raping her. Ben would enjoy telling tales, spreading rumours. There was no point in it; it couldn't do anything to benefit Ben, or anyone else, but it would cause pain and shame. Ben was right about one thing: Os didn't want others to hear that tale. They would think that he wasn't enough of a man to take Mary. That was shameful. Nearly as shameful as their thinking that he had taken her against her will.

There could only be one purpose for Ben to spread the story, and that was to cause hurt. That was one thing at which the miller's son excelled.

Ben was bitter, but at least he had punctured the thick ox's self-satisfaction. How did he hear about that . . . Mary must have told him about it. No one else knew. Only him and her – yet Os knew. Mary must have said something, the cow!

There was nothing shameful about it. He was a young man, and she was a woman. He only wanted her to lie with him, so he could know what it was like. He did love her, after all, and all his friends had tupped girls in the vill. He had thought she would be willing, that she'd look on it as a great compliment. It wasn't as if it was rare for a brother and sister. He'd have agreed if *she* had asked *him*.

If only she had agreed, he wouldn't have hated her so much then. But she not only rejected him, she laughed at him. Made him feel stupid, small – nothing. She laughed at him, as though he had no manhood for her to consider, and that made him angry. He had caught her, made her hiss with pain as he pushed her to her knees, and then he hit her, to teach her to laugh at him. That was why he had grown to hate her, to loathe the sight of her. If he could, he would have killed her. Except there was always that little place in his heart which watched her with the jealous eye of a lover. A lover whose adoration could never be consummated. That was why he refused to honour her in death, even though part of him felt desolate that she was gone.

Flora was no better. He had never tried to sleep with her, but she was fearful of him – probably because Mary had warned her. If she had told Os, who else might she not have told? Shit! The bitch should have kept her mouth shut! There was no telling what trouble she could have brought to Ben.

Os had wanted her. He had watched her with his great bovine eyes whenever she passed nearby, almost drooling with delight. When she spoke to him kindly, he all but fell over at her feet like a puppy. Pathetic arse. He should have taken her. That's what a real man would have done.

Suddenly Ben had a vision of another man, the sort who would have taken her without compunction: Esmon, Sir Ralph's son.

'Esmon,' he muttered thoughtfully. 'You were up there the day she was killed, weren't you?'

He hadn't been with Elias quite all the time out in the field. Elias had gone to empty his bladder twice, and once Ben had gone himself, and that was the time when he had seen his sister alone there by the gate. Only a short time later, he had seen Esmon riding nearby as well. Everyone was off hunting down the wayward cleric, and yet if Ben was to mention that sighting, many in the vill would immediately think that the Lord of the Manor's own son should be questioned.

Ben gave a shrug. He didn't miss his sister – not really. She hadn't cared about him, so he wasn't going to waste his feelings on her. She was nothing to him. She had rejected him, while opening her legs for that damned priest. Fine. And the priest killed her.

It was interesting to think of Esmon being there, though . . .

Chapter Eight

As twilight came, Baldwin had reached the road that led north to
Eggesford, but after a few moments' thought, he took the road
that led almost due east in preference. Ahead of him, a lowering
hulk in the far distance, was the great mound of Cosdon, the first
of the huge hills of Dartmoor. To continue further was pointless.
He had tested his initial conviction that Mark was running straight
to the Bishop and found it persuasive. There was no need to carry
on west. The priest must already have passed by here.

'You want to go on, Sir Baldwin?'

The speaker was Godwen, one of Crediton's two Constables.
He was a small-boned and sharp-featured man with black hair
and bright blue eyes in a narrow but attractive face. Women
loved him, although many were jealous of his high cheekbones
and slender nose. His eyes in particular were startling. They
were the colour of cornflowers on a summer's day, and when he
turned them full onto a target, especially with his attention
concentrated so that he scarcely blinked, Baldwin thought that
they would be quite as hypnotic as a cat's. Together with his
gentle manner, soulful expression and tenor voice, let alone his
quick and assured movements, he must have his choice of women
in the town, especially with the expensive clothes he always
sported.

'I'm happy to carry on if you want, Sir Baldwin.'

This bass rumble came from the second Constable, Thomas, a
larger, slower man, with a heavy, square head and a jaw that could
have broken moorstone. His eyes were narrow slits that glittered
darkly as he spoke, especially when he caught sight of Godwen.
There was a perpetual antipathy between the two. Even in clothing
they could not have been more different: Thomas wore cast-offs

from his father that were so well darned that there was little of the
original colour or thread of the original.

Baldwin sighed to himself. 'We shall turn back now. All the
other men have had time to search out the smaller bartons. If we
head back along the road down here,' he pointed, 'to Coleford, we
should begin to meet up with some of them. Then we can make
our way back to Crediton if there is no news.'

'Very good, Sir Baldwin,' Godwen said, ducking his head
obsequiously, but then throwing an amused glance at Thomas.

It was that which irritated Baldwin. Godwen and Thomas had
always been on edge in each other's company. Once he had heard
it was because of some slight or insult that went back several
generations. He knew that their fathers hadn't exchanged a word
intentionally in twenty-odd years, and these two now continued
the feud. In another country, he reflected as he kicked his mount
onwards, they would have come to blows, or more likely, one
would already be dead. In most of the lands which Baldwin had
visited, enmity was not allowed to rest, and insults weren't
permitted to go without punishment. Luckily English peasants
were a little better behaved.

'We shall return this way. With luck, we should be back at
Crediton before dark,' he added. He had asked the groom to see
that a messenger was sent to his home to warn Jeanne that he
would be staying overnight in Crediton. 'I hope that fool Jack has
not fallen asleep again and forgotten.'

Godwen gave him a smile. 'You trusted *him* with something?'

'I needed a message taken home to my wife.'

'Jack is a cretin – he's always forgetting things,' Godwen said
dispassionately.

'He's a good man!' Thomas asserted harshly. 'Even the best
may grow drowsy with all the work he does.'

Baldwin glanced at him. 'What do you mean? He is a groom,
is he not? What is so tiring about looking after a few horses?'

'He's a groom during the day, yes, but he still keeps his three
cows, and has to look to them as well, and after all that is done, he
helps in Paul's inn. Poor bastard, it's no wonder he gets tired.'

'I did not know he had so many jobs,' Baldwin mused. 'Why does he do all that?'

'Needs must. He has a family to support.'

'True,' Baldwin said.

'And he's been fleeced by his landlord. His rents have been put up. Every time he's close to having enough to keep his wife and children in food and ale, his landlord takes more.'

'He's just lazy,' Godwen said, languidly dismissive. 'His family always was.'

Baldwin made a guess. 'He is related to you, is he not, Thomas?'

'Brother-in-law to my sister,' the man grunted with a sidelong look at Godwen.

They rode in silence for a good mile or so, through one small barton and out the other side towards Coleford. There they met the first of Baldwin's posse, two men whom he had sent to question the master of the seyney-house at the riverside. This was a resting place for monks who had become exhausted from their onerous duties. Baldwin sometimes wondered how tiring rising in the middle of the night and kneeling throughout long services actually was, but all monasteries had these small retreats so that brother monks could have their blood let, and then recover with less stress, better food and more sleep. No doubt if he had taken on the robes of a monk and was still serving an abbey or priory, he would occasionally feel the need of good food and more sleep, he admitted to himself.

He noticed that Thomas glared at the place. 'What is the matter, Thomas? You look as though you feel that place is the haunt of demons!'

Thomas said nothing, merely pulled his horse's head around and trotted away.

'It's the Brothers, Sir Baldwin,' Godwen said with a chuckle at his side. 'He never liked them, not since they started making Jack's life harder. You see, the landlord who keeps Jack on his toes, he's a Brother too.'

'What is his name?'

'He's a tight-arse, so it's appropriate, really. He's called Roger Scut.'

He wanted to stay. Huward's little angel had meant so much to him, he really wanted to remain there by her body all through the long night's vigil, but he had others to think of. His wife would remain here in the church, as would little Flora and some of the other women from the vill, but he was finding the atmosphere stifling. The smell of the incense was getting into his throat and irritating his eyes. He could have coped with it, but there was nothing to be done here, while he had something he desperately needed to do, ideally alone.

If he could have, he would have gone after that priest. He would have torn the devil limb from limb, pulled out his entrails and scattered them, ripped open his breast and fed his beating heart to the crows! That puppy would have suffered so much, he'd have begged for death. Perhaps he would still have an opportunity to kill him, too. If he was caught, there was a good chance that he'd be returned to the place where he committed his crimes. A double murder, mother and child! Hideous.

The priest at Gidleigh hadn't wanted to let them in at first. He'd said that he couldn't deal with the bodies of people from the next parish, especially women who died in childbirth. And the baby itself was not baptised, so it couldn't be allowed in the church. Huward had squared up to the skinny little streak of piss, and the other men of the vill were with him, muttering and cursing the priest so volubly that he retreated nervously, fingering his rosary. It was lucky Piers was there. Before Huward could set his daughter's body down, Piers appeared at his side, speaking soothingly, but quickly. He pointed out that the priest was standing in the way of a young girl's soul if he refused to bury her. In the end the priest agreed, but more because of the grim-faced men who watched him while Huward shoved him from his path and carried his daughter to the communal hearse, than because of the force of Piers's arguments.

'She lies here until she is buried by you, here in your graveyard, Priest,' Huward said calmly. He was proud of that. He wasn't angry, didn't shout or scream, just stated what would happen. His daughter had made her last journey. And his grandchild.

He walked from the place and took a deep breath. Although he wanted to sob, he couldn't. Maybe later. For now, it was hard to believe that his daughter had in truth been ripped from him. She was gone, for ever. He would only see her again on the day that all the dead were called to God. Perhaps even the priest who had killed her would be there . . . No. God couldn't allow that. He wouldn't make Mary have to see her murderer in Heaven, even if he swore his repentance.

Huward walked slowly from the church. There hung about him, ever so faint in the still air, the subtle odour of her. That buttery, sweet smell that he recognised so well. He had noticed it when she was suckling, and it had never left her. Not even now, in death. He sniffed at the shoulder of his jacket, then knelt, falling forward on one hand, the other covering his eyes while racking sobs convulsed his whole body, and yet still the tears wouldn't fall. It was as though her death had removed some part of him, so that while he could feel his despair, he couldn't fully appreciate the grief that she deserved. His angel, his little darling, was gone.

He remembered her life in a strange sequence. It was like a series of flashes, pulses of life bursting into his memory: the babe suckling; older, smiling and laughing as she gulped down meat already chewed and softened by her mother; a toddler who had taken a tumble, her knees all bloody, bravely trying to stop her sobbing; a child with her first illness, spewing and wailing with the pain and indignity of throwing up; a young woman proud of the new ribbon in her hair; a girl holding up her first blackened attempt at baking bread with the smile on her face that said she knew her father, if no one else in the world, would love it. She knew that if she were to hand him a crisp of charcoal, he would declare it delicious and swallow it, if it meant she would be pleased.

The scenes passed through his mind in an apparently endless procession. Mary helping at harvest, brushing the hair from her brow with a smile as she took a jug of cider from him; sitting and staring at her father as he told her ever more unlikely stories; that curious, still, serious expression she occasionally wore; the beaming smile; the bellow of laughter; the soft, gentle kindness of the perfect nurse.

Gone. All gone. His life was shredded in the face of his unbearable loss.

Wiping at his face, he stood, and now he set off with a fresh vigour and determination. He went north, down into the valley and through the ford at the bottom, then up to the chapel. He tested the door. It was unlocked.

Inside, he felt the anger rise until it seemed about to strangle him. It was like a thick fist in his throat that was slowly clenching, and as it did so, it cut off the air from his lungs. He was exhausted. All he wanted to do was return to his home. When he turned to shut the door, he almost did so. The urge to leave this place came upon him, and he nearly opened it again and fled.

It was the memory that stopped him – of that feeble, pimply youth the monk who had served the people here, and later served *her*, Huward's daughter. And murdered her. That thought brought to his mind's eye a recollection of Mary as he would always remember her, held up in his arms, smiling down at him; happy to see him, full of love. As he always had been whenever he saw her.

It was enough to stiffen his resolve. Although the altar stood at the far end of the room like a physical reproof and warning, he slammed the door and stared about him. There was little enough in here that looked as though it would serve his purpose, and he pursed his lips. Undaunted, he went to the chest at the back of the church and tested it. The lid was unlocked. When he threw it open, he saw that it was full of priestly garb. Even to touch Mark's clothing made him feel sick, as though it was defiled and could pollute him; it was foul, just like the soul of the evil priest who had worn it. Rich cloth, designed to enhance the aura of he who wore it, with silken threads and expensive velvets, had served only to conceal his true nature. They were a sham, false stuff that Mark could don or doff as it suited him, so that when he wanted a counterfeit integrity or honour, he could throw it on with these vestments.

Huward pulled the stuff free, making a pile near him. Then he looked about and found a small cupboard. In it was a book, and he pulled at the leaves of parchment, tugging them free and throwing them onto the clothes before shoving the whole lot into the middle of the room.

There must be more things to burn, and he went across to the priest's little home next door, finding just what he needed: the store of faggots and logs. Carrying them through to the church, he dropped the faggots on top of the small mound, and then he began the arduous task of striking sparks from his flint and his knife. Shreds of lint began to smoke, tiny wisps rising in the still evening air, and soon he had a small flame. Carefully he tended it, adding small pieces of material and parchment, before throwing the first of the faggots on. In Mark's house he had found a little oil lamp too, and this he hurled at the fire together with the earthenware jug that held spare oil. There was a *whoosh!* and it all began to shimmer with the flames. Then there was a roaring noise, and Huward could feel his brows begin to contract in the enormous heat.

Only when he had seen to it that all Mark's possessions, all his clothing, his bed, his stool, everything, all the little he owned, had been thrown onto the pyre, did he open the door and leave.

He looked back once, when he reached the ford. Even then the sight of the forked, reptilian tongues of fire licking upwards from windows and the door gave him no satisfaction. It was a job that had needed to be done, he considered. That was all. Just something that had to be done. He was getting rid of the evil that had lived there in the chapel.

Turning away, he set off homewards. It was going to be a cold, quiet night tonight, with his wife and daughter sitting vigil over Mary's body.

* * *

The Reeve had seen him go, and wondered whether he should follow his neighbour, but the sight of Huward's face was enough to put him off. It was undoubtedly the face of a man who sought, and needed, solitude. Companionship would not be welcome.

Instead Piers glanced at Elias. The ploughman was standing at the back of the room, frowning at everyone from beneath his brows as usual, but Piers was sure that his appearance was even more grim than normal. Elias's expression was that of a man who has newly discovered misgivings about all his neighbours.

Glancing at him again, Piers saw that Elias's eyes were now upon *him*, and the hostile expression remained.

With a grunt, Piers rose and crossed the floor to Elias's side. 'Come on, what's the matter?'

'Who's asking – my friend of many years or the Lord of the Manor's Reeve?'

'What difference does that make?' Piers asked with frank surprise.

Elias opened his mouth and investigated a loose tooth. He had lost two teeth over the last winter, and was worried that he would soon lose more. It was sometimes the way, he knew. When food was short, people lost their teeth. Soon he'd have to suck all his meals. Everything would have to be liquid. Nothing to chew. He spoke slowly. 'When you're my friend, you listen to me as a friend would. When you're Sir Ralph's Reeve, you listen to me like a tax-collector – *that's* the difference.'

'I always treat you the same, Elias.'

'That answers that, then.'

'What?' Piers demanded as Elias made to walk away.

'I need someone I can trust. I can't trust you if you'll run to Sir Ralph.'

'I swear I won't,' Piers said, more quietly now. He placed his hand on his breast and gazed at Elias meaningfully. 'What is this about? Is it Mary?'

' 'Course it is.'

'Well? What of her?'

Elias looked away. 'There was others down the lane that day. Osbert was working on the hedge. I saw that hermit, old Surval, too. And a rider.'

Piers felt his heart pounding with more gusto. 'What of it? Surely the priest must have done it. Why else would he have run off like that?'

'Why do you think? What if he thought the knight on whose land he lives was responsible for killing poor Mary?'

'The knight on . . .' Swallowing anxiously, Piers glanced about them to see if anyone else had heard Elias's words. 'You saw *him* there?'

'Sir Ralph. I saw him ride away, a broad smile on his face – the bastard.'

'When was this? Are you sure it was after she was killed?'

'I heard something. I didn't realise until later, but I'm certain of it. I heard her cry out. Then I was turning away, heading back along the next furrow, and it was when I got back that I saw him mounting his horse. He was on that big bugger. His head suddenly appeared above the hedge line.'

'He could have been riding along and—'

'Don't give me that!' Elias said scathingly. 'Think I'm as thick as Sampson? If he'd been on his horse all the way along there, I'd have seen his head moving along, wouldn't I? No, I saw him spring up into the saddle, and he saw me – and smiled. Like he was out for a happy little ride and fancied a—'

It was Piers's turn to silence Elias. He shot the peasant a look, held up a hand in admonition. 'I don't want you to say that, not in my hearing, and not in anyone else's. It's a villainous tale, Elias, and it'd get you into trouble.'

'That's why he bolted,' Elias said, a cynical grin twisting his face. 'The priest wasn't stupid. He came along a little after, when I was back near the hedge again.'

'You saw him?'

'No. But he's the only man who's run off, isn't he?'

'You're certain you heard someone running off?'

'I told you I did.'

'But you didn't mention our master at the time,' Piers said sharply.

'I missed that out,' Elias agreed. 'I like life. It was that priest who ran off.'

'Why'd he do that if you're right and Sir Ralph killed her?' Piers said more quietly.

Elias shrugged. 'He was a priest, and he got her with child. We've all heard of clerks who keep their women but try to kill them when they realise it could hurt them in future. He probably thought we'd all be after his blood. Anyway, he hit her – I'm sure of that. Maybe he was scared then – you know, shocked. Maybe he just saw her lying there and thought he'd actually killed her! He might've seen her and bolted.'

'He should have waited.'

'What – and let the Hue and Cry behead him in their rage?' Elias's smile seemed to hitch up the whole of his beard. 'You know more about the law than I do, Piers, but I say this: if I was a poor priest like him, I'd not think twice. I'd bolt and make for the woods. Or I'd go to my Bishop. I wouldn't bugger about here hoping for justice. Not when someone like Huward was hankering for my neck, and not when the man who owns the court was Sir Ralph; the man who'd actually killed the poor girl.'

Chapter Nine

Baldwin was already up before the landlord, and with the early dawn, he was in the inn's hall with his sword and dagger, practising thrusts and parries, blocking imaginary blows at his head, at his belly, at his thighs and flanks, each time manoeuvring to keep his feet glued flat on the ground as he blocked, maintaining his position as he swung away. That was strength in a battle: remember, feet firm to give a base from which to strike. The man who moves his feet while striking is the man who will suffer defeat, because he is unbalanced.

When he could feel the sweat running freely, he began his exercises, swinging his weapons from side to side, holding them out at arm's length and moving them in small circles, or up and down, until the pain in the junction of his shoulder and neck grew too extreme for him to continue. Only then did he set his weapons aside and take a deep breath, gradually relaxing all the tension. He drew himself a bowl of wine from the inn's bar and, adding water from the pot beside the fire, he sipped the warm drink.

'Most impressive, Sir Baldwin.'

The knight groaned inwardly. He had hoped to avoid the clerk today. 'Brother Roger. How pleasing it is to see you.'

Roger Scut was sitting at a bench near the door. 'I hadn't expected to find you with your sword drawn at this time of day, Sir Baldwin,' he said teasingly. 'I needs must be careful not to upset so warlike a knight.'

Baldwin used his tunic to wipe away the sweat. 'You should always seek to avoid upsetting a knight. Some do not possess such remarkable calmness of spirit as me.'

'Haha! I am sure you are quite right in that, Sir Baldwin!' Roger Scut laughed. He was aiming along his nose again, and

that, together with his irritating voice, was already getting to
Baldwin.

'You look damp,' he remarked through gritted teeth.

'The weather is inclement,' Roger replied. 'The rain is sheeting
down, and the wind tries to blow it through you.'

'Typical!' Baldwin said, thinking of his long journey homewards. He grimaced, then continued towelling himself dry.

'I assume you, um, failed to find the man yesterday?'

'We did not capture him, no. But I have men sweeping all
around the town today,' Baldwin said shortly.

'The Dean has asked that you present the priest to him when
you do catch him.'

'You may tell the good Dean that I shall consider his request.'

'It was not a request, I fear.'

Baldwin heard the slight intonation. He met Roger Scut's bland
expression with a keen look. 'I fear it was exactly that, Roger.
Dean Peter asked if I would present him with his murderous
priest. I shall consider his request when I catch the fellow. First,
of course, I have to catch the felon. Once I have done so, I shall
think about whether I should release him to Peter or take him
back to Gidleigh.'

'He is a priest, you know.'

'No, I do not. He is rumoured to have been living there as a
priest, it is true – but that means naught. What if this was a felon
who waylaid your priest on the way to his church? He might have
slaughtered your cleric and buried the body, then thought to himself
what fun he could have with a small congregation like Gidleigh's.'

'My God! You don't mean that?' Roger Scut said, blanching.
He nervously felt for his rosary. 'But how could a man hope to get
away with such an imposture?'

'Easily. I have known some outrageously bold felons in my
time. Why,' Baldwin said with a sudden sharpness, 'how do I
know that *you* are who you say you are? You could be another
false man.'

'I?' Roger Scut spluttered, his face suddenly reddening like an
apprentice caught with his buttocks bared with his master's

daughter. 'But I have been here for years, I am known to—'

'It was merely an example. I shall decide when I see the boy,' Baldwin lied mildly; his mind was already made up. The lad's crime was awful, and to Baldwin's mind it was neither fair nor just that he should be allowed to escape to the Bishop's court without having to face those whom he had wronged.

Gradually Roger Scut's complexion returned to normal. 'I am glad to hear it. So tell me,' he said, his head tilting back again until he was drawing a sight on Baldwin once more, 'why do you practise with your sword this morning? It is hardly the time of year to expect a war, is it?'

'There is no time of year when one should not expect a war. Especially now, with the King's army shattered again.'

'Oh, that!' Roger's face fell. 'We live in terrible times, Sir Baldwin. I sometimes wonder when we shall know peace again.'

'So do I,' Baldwin said with feeling. The Scottish had drawn the King northwards during the previous year at the completion of the latest truce, by swarming over the border and ravaging the lands of the north-west. King Edward II had gone with a massive, well-provisioned body of men. Yet the stories which were filtering back to the south were all of subterfuges and disasters.

The Scots had withdrawn before the might of the English host, refusing them battle, but also destroying all the food stores and animals in their path, with the result that the English were soon decimated by starvation and disease. The King had to pull back, but his orderly retreat was harried by Scottish forces, and one made its way even so far as the middle of Yorkshire. It was only with difficulty that King Edward II himself escaped capture in a skirmish near to Byland and Rievaulx. The whole of Yorkshire was struck with terror as their King fled and the upstart rebels from Scotland devastated their lands.

It was a disaster for everyone in the realm, with repercussions even down here in Devon. Simon, Baldwin's friend, had helped a King's Arrayer the previous year, organising men to be used in the King's host, and some of these fellows had limped back, but all too few. The rest, they said, had been captured and slaughtered by the mad Scots, or they had died of pestilence or starvation. Many died because, after suffering the worst pangs of hunger, when they came across food, they gorged themselves and their poor bodies couldn't cope. They died in terrible pain as their stomachs burst within them.

The cost was vast, too. Huge stocks of grain, meat and fish, all salted, had been taken to feed the men fighting for the King, but this was the food that the towns had expected for their own winter supplies, and without them, many households had gone hungry over the winter. Crediton itself was better stocked than many other towns, but Baldwin had several cases of families who must beg for food from Church stores.

'We can only hope and pray that the Scottish rebels will accept their fate,' Roger Scut said piously.

'Yes,' Baldwin agreed, although privately he wondered whether they ever would. It was all very well having the Pope's approval for the King's claim to the Scottish crown, but if all the people continued to refuse, point blank, and wouldn't offer battle either, but instead ran away into the bleak, miserable far north of their lands, it was hard to see what the King could do about it.

He was considering this miserable fact and wondering what miracle of strategy could be used to defeat the Scottish, when there was a sudden shouting and laughter from the road. Baldwin paid it little heed at first, thinking it was only some folk playing the fool, but then the noise drew nearer and he realised that the source of the row was already in the cross passage. He stood, putting a hand near his sword, but did not draw it. In a few minutes a group of cheerful men entered.

Godwen was first to walk in. 'Sir Baldwin, I think we have your man!'

'*That* is him?' Baldwin asked with ill-concealed disbelief.

Sir Ralph eyed the sky as he climbed up the three steps of moorstone and mounted his horse. It had been blowing like a horn since before dawn, and the rain had come across like a grey mist, obscuring everything behind it. Now at least there was a brief period of calm and dryness, but the grey clouds above left him feeling dubious as to how long it would last. The wind had not abated.

He shivered. It felt as if there was an ague in his guts. Since the death of Mary, he'd been feeling like this. It was hard to swallow food or drink, and he must force himself. It was no comfort to observe that the energy which had at last failed him would appear to have been transferred entirely to his son.

While a groom led him a short distance away, Esmon leaped lightly into his own saddle and nonchalantly pulled on his gloves.

Esmon was quite a chip off the old block, Sir Ralph had to admit, but he wasn't sure that it was pleasing. Certainly he had the fair-haired good looks and the appearance of hardness, but his mouth was all too often a thin line, displaying his petulance. Although his eyes were a clear, bright green like emeralds, they did not reflect mere jealousy but comprehensive and consuming avarice. He didn't care what his neighbour possessed: what he wanted, he would take. In many ways, he would be the ideal knight, Sir Ralph thought. He was not prepared to allow any rudeness or cheek to his honour, he wouldn't take any foolishness that might reflect upon him, and he had just enough sense to know when to hold his tongue when the odds were heavily laden against him.

That was the trouble with fellows today. Sir Ralph knew so many of them, men of strength and apparent intelligence, who would yet charge a thick line of Genoese crossbows and spears alone just because of an imagined slight. That was madness, in Sir Ralph's opinion. To join in a charge was a glorious experience, but as a military force he felt that it was overrated. He wasn't alone, either. Others too had witnessed the disaster of Bannockburn, when the mounted chivalry of the realm was shattered on the pikes and spears of the Scots like waves on the seashore. There was nothing that a knight could do to break into a solid, packed phalanx of men with good, long polearms. That was the job of footsoldiers.

It wasn't only Bannockburn, either. He had heard of the field of Courtrai, where the mad peasants had destroyed the French cavalry, and Morgarten, where the mountain men had wrought destruction on more noblemen. Both were examples of that most appalling of things, a slaughter of the knightly class by the lowest forms of life: serfs. In the Christian world, there were only three orders: the holy men, whose task it was to protect the souls of the living and the dead; the warriors, whose job it was to keep society in check; and then far down the list, the peasants and freemen. The knights' job was to control them and keep them in check. If serfs could fight knights and defeat them, the whole order of the world was topsy-turvy. It didn't bear considering.

However, the means by which they could win a battle was instructive. Clearly it wasn't because God was on their side – He would hardly support the peasant! – so it was the methods which they used. Even King Edward II was moving towards a mobile host of men-at-arms, who could ride to the point where they were needed, but who would then dismount and fight on foot, in among the archers and others. Dismounted knights, standing among the peasants! It was a horrible thought and yet it worked. The Scots had proved that. Rebels they might be, but they could fight – and win.

They were moving off eastwards, and Sir Ralph realised that they were soon to pass in front of Mary's home. His back stiffened at the thought. He could still remember his first sight of her body lying at the side of the path, under the wall. It was hideous. With the recollection he felt he must gag.

Almost as he had the thought, the little mill came into view. Os was just lifting a sack onto his back and carrying it to the door when he heard their hooves. Instantly upon seeing them, he dropped the sack and bent almost double in reverence. Huward was in the building, and hurried out. Seeing Sir Ralph, he ducked his head, without breaking contact with his eyes.

Sir Ralph saw his distrustful expression, but acknowledged him. 'Master Miller. A fine morning.'

'I hadn't noticed. Not with my daughter dead.'

'I offer you my sympathy,' Sir Ralph said.

Perhaps Huward heard the broken tone, the sincerity in his voice, because his reply lacked gruffness. 'I thank you. Godspeed, Sir Ralph.'

'Godspeed, Miller.'

Esmon sniffed loudly as they passed by Huward and muttered something under his breath.

'What?' his father demanded, more harshly than he had intended.

'Nothing.'

'You said something. What was it?'

'I just don't understand why you are so kindly disposed towards that family. They're peasants, and should be treated accordingly.'

'When you are older, Esmon, you will learn that things are never so simple, nor straightforward.'

'He's only a miller. What's so complicated? If he gives us trouble, we can throw him out of the vill and offer the mill to another. There are plenty of millers about the place. We should easily be able to find another – especially at the rent you demand!'

'It is my choice,' Sir Ralph said coldly. 'You may make your own decisions when you are Master of the Manor.'

'Don't worry, Father, I shall,' his son said.

His voice sounded carefree, but there was an undertone of contempt which was pitched at the perfect level to rankle. With his own little force of men under Brian of Doncaster, Esmon had grown more independent of late. He often sought to tease and annoy, but Sir Ralph was in no mood to rise to the bait today, not with memories of Mary so fresh in his mind.

They passed along the roadway, dropping down the hill to the bottom, then turning left towards Wonson.

'What have you heard?' Sir Ralph asked after a few minutes.

'The party is coming on Friday as usual. All merchants, no men-at-arms.'

Sir Ralph nodded. Each Saturday Chagford held a market, at which the miners from the moors would come to gain provisions, as would farmers and villeins from miles about. Many goods were always on sale, but the most keenly eyed items were the spices and mercery which had to come all the way, usually, from Exeter.

There were good profits to be made from meeting merchants on their way to Chagford for the market. A man could demand a toll for using a road, if he was bold enough. Or, if he had courage, he could take a portion of the goods for himself. And now that Sir Ralph had Gidleigh, he could state his price. He controlled the roads that led to Chagford Bridge, over which the merchants from the north would probably pass.

'Who is that?' Esmon called.

Sir Ralph scowled, annoyed that his thought processes had been interrupted. Then he saw at whom Esmon was pointing.

'Ha!' Esmon yelled, slashing at his horse's rump with a switch.

It was a woman. Sir Ralph shrugged. It was only natural that his son should seek to chase her. He was young, and many a buck saw fit to run down his doe. Already, hearing his exclamation, or perhaps his hooves, she had turned and caught sight of the two men. Seeing Esmon in pursuit, she dropped her basket and bolted. Only then did Sir Ralph see it was Flora, Mary's sister.

'Esmon! No!' Sir Ralph bellowed, but his son was already too far away to hear – or didn't care. With a sudden rush in his blood, Sir Ralph felt the choler taking over his humours.

'Come, Bayard!' He raked his spurs along his mount's flanks, crouching low as he felt his beast's muscles bunch and thrust, bunch and thrust. The mane was flicking across his face now, the mud spattering at either side, and he was pelting along at a full gallop; although the rage was there in his belly, he was aware of the thrill, the excitement. The thundering of hooves, the pull of the wind in his hair, the tug of his cloak, the slap, slap, slap of the heavy sword at his hip, all lent a curious exhilaration to the chase.

He could see his son almost upon the girl now. She was running, terrified, her face drawn into a mask of horror when she threw a look over her shoulder. Then Esmon was alongside her, and he lifted his arm with the switch to strike at her. Sir Ralph saw the short ash stick lift, and then he was pushing his mount between them. The switch came down, but it hit Sir Ralph's cheek. Enraged,

he grabbed his son's arm and pulled. He hadn't forgotten any of
the training he had been given by his Master of Defence, and he
made use of it now. Esmon's wrist was in his hand, and he hauled
it down and back, pulling on the reins at the same time. His horse
stopped almost instantly, while Esmon's carried on, and Sir Ralph
felt his son lift from the saddle. Esmon gave a short cry of shock,
and then he fell into the mud and filth of the lane while his father
gave a quiet smile.

'You may think you're better than me, boy, but you don't touch
that girl. Her sister is dead and you *will* show her respect.'

Esmon spat mud from his mouth and slowly stood, whirling his
arm about his shoulder, feeling the muscles with his other hand as
he did so. He gave a nod, satisfied that nothing was broken or
torn, and then looked up at his father.

'If you do that again, I shall kill you.'

'You may try, boy. In the meantime, you'll show that girl
respect.'

'I shall do as I wish, Father,' Esmon said quietly. 'And if I
desire to ravish her, I shall.'

Sir Ralph stared at him coldly. 'If you do so against my wishes,
you'll have to answer to me.'

'Yes,' Esmon said with a sweet smile. 'I will, won't I?'

Chapter Ten

It took little time for them to pack and prepare for the journey back to Gidleigh, especially since, to Baldwin's profound gratitude, Roger Scut disappeared shortly after Godwen and the others had brought in Mark. The clerk took one last appalled look at the priest and then scuttled away like a small beetle disturbed beneath a stone.

Thinking of Scut's expression made Baldwin stop and consider a few moments. Mark had been in a terrible state, soaked, frozen, his feet bleeding. His hands were scratched, his skin red, raw and in many places cracked and weeping, and he had fallen on his chin and scraped all the flesh from the point of his jaw. If there could have been any doubt about his guilt, it was removed at the sight of him snivelling and shuffling, his head hanging at a slight angle, as though he could already feel the hemp at his throat. It was somehow terrible to see a man whose whole life should have been one of moderate ease brought to such a pass. He stood downcast, flinching when Godwen or Thomas came too near.

He deserved little sympathy, though, if he were truly guilty of killing the girl, Baldwin told himself.

'What is your name?' he grated in a rumbling tone that conveyed his authority.

'I am a poor traveller, Sir Knight. Please, give me peace and a place to rest my—'

'I didn't ask what you were doing, I asked you your name.'

The Brother's glance shot up at Baldwin, and then slid away when he saw the grim determination on his face. 'I am named Edward of Axminster, Sir Knight.'

'Come, now. What name did you take when you took up the

cloth?' Baldwin asked silkily. 'What is your Christian, baptismal name?'

'I . . .'

'Then I shall tell you,' Baldwin said, sitting at a bench and fixing a blank stare on the unfortunate wretch. He often found that this persuaded criminals to confess and become more helpful, and so it proved today.

Mark was worn down with his grief and his shame. His legs were aching, and sores and blisters made his limbs feel as though they were gangrenous. He had managed to come so far, yet now he would be taken all that weary way back to Gidleigh once more. A sob broke from his breast, and he could feel the tears well and course down his cheeks. He felt as though his ruination was indeed inevitable. He was destroyed. His hands were bound so tightly that he could scarcely feel his fingers, and escape was impossible.

'Sir Knight, pity me!' he said hoarsely. 'I have done nothing wrong of my own volition, I am merely the dupe of fate. On the Bible, I swear, I have intended no harm to anyone.'

'And yet you bolt from your vill as though the legions of Hell were at your tail.'

'What would you have me do? Stand there and await the retribution of a father who is insane with rage to see his daughter murdered?'

Baldwin allowed no relaxation of his features. 'Why should her father think to accuse you, a priest?'

'I am ashamed to confess,' Mark said bleakly, and his head dropped as if he truly felt how unwholesome his behaviour must sound. 'I forgot my cloth and my honour with this woman, and I admit I was horrified to learn that she was with my child. If her father were to hear that, how else could he react, other than by trying to destroy me?'

In his years as Keeper of the Rolls of the King's Peace, Baldwin had heard many men's confessions, and he reckoned that Mark sounded genuine, but that made little difference to him and his duty. 'You shall still have to explain yourself in your vill, in your local court. Godwen, you will escort him there.

Take another man to help you guard him. He can't go like this, not with his feet in that condition. You shall have to demand a pony for him. Tell Jack I sent you, and ask for the healthiest mount he has for the lowest price. When he gives you a price, no matter how much it is, tell him you'll pay him five pennies less and he should be glad that I won't accuse him of trying to profit at the King's expense.'

Mark had listened dully, but on hearing Baldwin's calmly authoritative voice, he broke down again, and dropped to his knees. 'God's own body! Don't just take me there and leave me like garbage! They'll kill me!'

Baldwin eyed him without feeling. 'You must be returned to the vill where the Hue and Cry was raised against you. You know that. It will be for the vill's court to decide whether you are guilty or not.'

'But if you have me taken there, they will kill me without a hearing! You *can't* do that. I am a priest, I should be tried in the Bishop's court, not in that of a wayward and detestable knight like Sir Ralph! He will see me destroyed without trying to mete out justice.'

'You slander a knight? You, who have forgotten your vows to God? I have made oaths too, to keep the King's Peace and see justice done. I have my duty.'

'What of your duty to the law? You call yourself Keeper of the Rolls of the King's Peace, but if you leave me there, I shall die in hours. They will see to it.'

'Perhaps that is no more than you deserve,' Baldwin said bluntly.

'No man can tell that,' Mark protested. 'Please, Sir Knight, convey me to the Bishop's court, where I can be tried by men who would see me tested fairly – don't send me back to that terrible vill! It's too unjust! That I have sunk to lewdness and fornication, I admit freely but, Sir Baldwin, I am no murderer! Look at me! Could I be so cruel, so barbaric, as to willingly slay my own love and the child in her womb?'

* * *

As Brother Mark made his protestations, Saul the carter and his apprentice Alan were in the process of mending Saul's carts in his yard near the church at Oakhampton, prior to filling them with goods to take to the market at Chagford.

'Still don't see why we have to get ready so early,' Alan objected. 'The market's not until Saturday. Today's Thursday. It's not far.'

Saul grunted. A short man with grizzled hair and beard, his sharp, suspicious eyes gleamed brightly beneath his hood. He was carrying a heavy sack, and he threw it into the back of his cart and stretched. 'Because it means we have more time in the tavern the night before the market, that's why. And we avoid footpads, too.'

Alan, a weakly-looking lad in his late teens with a thin, wispy beard and sallow complexion, pulled a face. 'Footpads? What do you mean, footpads?'

'Nothing! It was a joke. What'd they do with us? Who's going to rob us, when we're travelling with so many others? I've made sure there are more than ten carters, and then there are the six others with their packhorses.'

'But you're worried about footpads?' Alan said anxiously.

'Come on, lad, I was only joking,' Saul said, but he didn't meet Alan's eye. Alan had been thinking again, always a mistake for an apprentice. He'd obviously been listening to the stories about the mad bastard at Gidleigh. Time was, that used to be a good clear road, that – when Sir Richard owned it. Now that cocky bugger up there had got so he wouldn't listen to anyone. Thought he was beyond the reach of the Justices. Maybe he was, too, Saul told himself glumly.

Indeed, Saul felt generally gloomy today. His sinuses were giving him a lot of pain, like sharp pins and needles stabbing at the back of his palate, and there was a tickling in his nostrils. He must be getting another cold. Wonderful! Six he had had last year – two in the middle of the summer, by God's wounds! His wife was growing peevish, complaining that he never did enough work, spent all his time at the tavern, and here he was with another flaming cold on the way. He needed a warm pot of spiced ale to drive it off, that's what he needed. Instead he was getting ready to join the convoy of carts on the way to Chagford and getting grief from his blasted apprentice as well. At least in Chagford he could go to a physician and maybe get bled.

'There's no reason to think he'd come to get us,' Alan muttered hopefully. 'Sir Ralph's sat there in his castle, and you've already said we're not going to go close. He can sit there waiting for us all week, if he wants, and miss us.'

'That's why we leave early. He's no idiot. He might have heard we're approaching, and then he'll demand money for passing his lands.'

'Demanding money doesn't mean we'll be at risk.'

Saul eyed him bleakly. Alan was a pleasant enough lad, usually cheerful and helpful, but there was no getting away from the fact that he was sometimes argumentative; he would take a stance and speak smilingly about it, apparently listening to other views but ignoring whatever was said. It was infuriating. Saul himself preferred to have a simple stand-up row about something.

Still, today Alan seemed less disputatious for the sake of it. He looked more like a boy who had been told to go and sit all day in the rain watching chickens on the off-chance that a fox might happen along. Sulky, that was the word.

'That's why we go early – so that even if he chooses to extort cash from us, we'll have gone already. What is it, lad?' Saul asked, leaning on the wheel of his cart and studying Alan carefully.

'It's just daft, going tomorrow,' Alan burst out. 'Why not go without me? You don't need me riding along.'

'Who'll drive the other cart, boy?'

'You could lead it,' Alan said.

'What is this? Are you 'prentice to me or not?'

'Anyway, he only takes money, doesn't he?'

'Yes, it's only money!' Saul spat. 'I suppose you have so much you'd be happy to give it all to him? Come on! What's all this about?'

'I don't like it, that's all.'

'Why? You don't mind going farther afield. We've been up to Hatherleigh, down to Tavistock – what's the matter with going to Chagford?'

'I went there once before.'

'Ah!' Saul thought he could understand. 'You never told me this. And he caught you?'

'No. I saw the ambush, and I bolted.'

'So what's your problem?'

'If they recognise me, they might demand the money I owed them from that last journey!'

Saul sighed. 'Al, if you escaped, they won't remember. They only pinch what they can from a few folks, that's all. I doubt whether they'll remember you, all right?'

'I still don't like it.'

'Well, get used to it, lad.'

'Master Carter. Are you going to Chagford?'

Saul groaned to himself and turning, found himself looking up into a familiar face. 'Well, well, if it isn't Wylkyn the miner.'

'No need to be like that.'

'You enjoying life up on the moors?'

Wylkyn smiled thinly. He wore good clothes, a heavy cloak of fine wool, a tunic of hardwearing fustian over a fine linen shirt, but all were worn and faded now. Once grand, now all was growing shabby. 'It's good enough.'

'Not as comfortable as your old life though, up at the castle, boiling herbs for Sir Richard, eh?'

'Perhaps. Is it true you're going to Chagford?'

'Yes. We'll be leaving early tomorrow.'

'I want to join you.'

'You? Why?'

'I have things to sell and provisions to buy. Where else should I go but the Stannary town to get them?'

Saul shrugged. 'You can come with us, if you have a mind. Why not? The more men the better.'

'Good, old friend. I'll be here tomorrow, then, with my ponies.'

'Aye.' Saul watched him walk away with an unsettled feeling in his gut. 'Why does he want to come with us?'

Alan shrugged. 'Why shouldn't he?'

'Are you as thick as a hog? Why do you think? We're all travelling together to be safe from the men at Gidleigh, but he should be safe enough. He was one of them, wasn't he?'

Roger Scut marched to the inn with Peter Clifford, the Dean of the Canonical Church, walking solemnly at his side. This early in the morning there were not yet many hawkers thronging the streets, but they must walk cautiously, avoiding the pots of night-soil being flung from upper windows and the excrement which lay in the kennel. While stepping around one, Roger felt his foot squelch and he smelled the odour of dog's mess almost simultaneously. It made him feel queasy – and still more irritable. It was not helped by the onset of rain. They were only fine drops tapping at his face right now, but yes, Roger was sure they would soon become thicker. The wind was getting up again, too. He was bound to get soaked on the way back after this meeting.

'I still think we should have brought some of our servants, Dean.'

'There is no need for force with a man like Sir Baldwin.'

'He is irrational, argumentative, and all too keen to resort to steel to impose his will.'

'Your words are intemperate,' Peter Clifford said, pausing and fixing Roger with a cold eye. 'What proof do you have that Sir Baldwin has ever drawn a sword to push through an unjust action?'

Roger Scut reddened. 'It is well known that knights are always prone to arrogance and haughty behaviour! You cannot think that this man is better than the others.'

'I state it firmly, Brother, and I suggest you moderate your own opinions of him. Sir Baldwin is fair, intelligent and just. It is a shame more knights are not struck from the same mould.'

'If you are wrong . . .'

'I said no,' Dean Peter said affably. A tall, grey-haired and wan-featured man in his later fifties, his back was bowed from sitting and reading by candlelight, and his thin, ascetic face gave him something of the look of an invalid, but his mind was perfectly clear and he was no man to be bent to another's will without reason. 'I know Sir Baldwin well. There is no need to try to scare him to a just solution. If there is merit in your proposition, he will see it, with or without guards.'

Roger Scut pursed his lips as they continued on their way. If anything were to go wrong, he would see to it that this refusal became widely known. The only way to deal with an arrogant bastard like this miscreant knight was with the threat of violence. Everyone knew that law officers were routinely corrupt, it was merely a matter of degree. Every so often Sheriffs would be cast out from their lucrative positions, Coroners would be told to go and Keepers would be changed. It was easy enough to see why. Each of them could influence decisions on a man's guilt or innocence. It was a matter of supreme importance to a noble that he should see any of his men released from custody with their innocence determined. All his retinue must be protected. Otherwise the actions of a small number of hotheads might reflect badly upon their masters. Better that they should be released and their crimes denied.

Not that it was only a case of saving face. Sometimes professional assassins must be reprieved from a court so that their lords might point them in the direction of another enemy whose passing would be little missed by the world.

'Men like this Keeper should be reminded occasionally that they do not control us in the Bishop's See,' he said, tilting his head back and staring down his nose at merchants and traders.

'Men like *this* Keeper need no reminding,' Dean Peter said with a chilliness in his manner.

'I am glad you believe so,' Roger Scut said equivocally.

They had reached the inn, and Roger Scut dived inside like a man gathering a last breath before jumping into a pool to grasp a shining bauble before it could be snapped up by a fish. Dean Peter sighed, tutted to himself, and then shrugged good-naturedly and followed. He was in time to see Roger Scut interpose himself between Sir Baldwin and the kneeling Mark, his arms held out dramatically as though he were pinned to a cross.

'Sir Baldwin, I insist that you release this prisoner into the custody of Dean Peter and myself.'

Baldwin gazed at Roger Scut with ill-concealed distaste. 'I fear I can do no such thing.'

'Dean Peter and I *demand* that you release him to us.'

Dean Peter met Baldwin's sharp glance with a mild smile, but said nothing.

Sir Baldwin turned his attention back to Roger Scut, but now his face, without changing expression, seemed to Roger to have taken on a deeply malevolent appearance, and the clerk took an involuntary step backwards, bumping into Mark.

'Roger, I shall do my duty as seems fit to me. I shall not be bent by you like a straw in the wind, but will obey the instructions of my Lord the King, and of the law.'

'Dean Peter, please persuade the Keeper that we should be permitted to take this fellow back to Exeter. I doubt very much that the Bishop will be content to hear that his will and authority has been flouted by a . . . a knight.'

Baldwin's features became glacial as Dean Peter cleared his throat. Roger Scut looked about to retreat still further, but then Baldwin was surprised to see the pompous little arse stiffen his shoulders, raising his head and returning Baldwin's look with determination.

'You don't scare me, Sir Knight. I am a man of God.'

'Roger, please,' Dean Peter remonstrated with a hint of annoyance. 'Sir Baldwin, my friend here has a point, if he perhaps lacks a little of the wit to explain it fully and politely.'

'He does!' Baldwin growled. 'I won't listen to his whining about this any further. Godwen, I told you to find a horse, I believe?'

As Godwen hurried from the room, Dean Peter took a deep breath. 'Sir Baldwin, you know that this man must surely be returned to the Bishop's court as soon as it is shown that he is a man of God? What use is served by taking him all the way back to

Dartmoor, deciding he is a priest, and then making the same journey back here again? It is foolish, surely.'

'You know that the law says I have to see him taken back,' Baldwin said. 'I can do nothing else.'

'If I am taken back they will kill me!' Mark said. 'Please, Dean, protect me! I cannot go back there. The father will kill me. Who would believe my story when they have my lover's body?'

'What is your story?' Baldwin pressed. He was standing now, and bellowed for the host to come and serve wine.

'I was there with her . . .' Mark shot a glance at the Dean. 'Father, please do not judge me. I have never done anything before which could cause me so much shame. Never before have I failed in my vows. It was that horrible place. All I ever wanted was to serve God in Exeter, maybe to travel, but I was sent to Gidleigh instead.'

'You were being tested,' Dean Peter agreed, adding pointedly, 'and you failed.'

Mark winced as though Dean Peter had slapped him. He held his hands to his face, and the Dean saw how dreadfully scratched and scraped they were. 'I know, I know it too well. I grew to desire the women, and even hearing their voices was enough to inflame my passions. I started building a wall just to occupy myself, exhausting myself to keep my thoughts pure, but it failed. I begged and pleaded with God to release me from my lusts, but He didn't answer me. And then I met *her*.'

'Who?' Dean Peter asked.

'Mary, daughter of the miller. She showed me kindness and calmed my fears, and when she also soothed my loneliness, I got her with child, God help me!'

'She is dead,' Baldwin stated flatly. 'And you bolted.'

'I spoke with her that day. She had told me a while before about our child, but I didn't believe her. It was impossible, I thought, but she swore that her monthly days had stopped. Then I saw that she was growing large, and I knew she had told me the truth. On the day she died, I spoke with her, and we parted in anger. Later, I walked back that way, and found her lying dead.

Dead! Someone had struck her down and killed her, and our child with her. I didn't know what to do!'

'You mean you didn't strike her?' Baldwin asked, thankfully accepting a cup of wine. 'You should have called the vill to arms, raised the Hue and Cry.' He sipped and grimaced. 'This tastes of the midden! Bring a cup of the other barrel.'

'I knew I should be accused and die.'

Dean Peter nodded. 'Because you might be thought guilty of murdering her to stop news of the child.'

'It is not unheard of,' Baldwin agreed, musing. 'Often a priest will try to punch his woman to kill the new life just growing. And sometimes the woman will die as well.' He frowned at Mark. 'Is that what you did?'

'I *swear* I am innocent of intending her death.'

'Did you hit her to make her miscarry?'

'Yes – *no*! I don't know! All I remember is, she struck me, and I struck her back, and then I left her.'

'You knocked her down? You struck her on the belly and she fell?' Baldwin said keenly.

Mark couldn't answer. He had fallen to his knees, hands back at his face as he knelt, weeping, shaking his head. 'I hit her, but not in the belly – and I didn't kill her. I couldn't! I *loved* her.'

'Many men who love have killed their wives,' Baldwin observed unsympathetically. 'Did you see her fall after you struck her?'

'No, no, she just turned away from me, and I was angry, bitter . . . I don't know . . . I just walked away to cool down, and think. I had to pray for help and forgiveness. But she didn't come past me and when I returned along that way to talk to her again, I found . . . I found . . .'

'Her lying dead,' Baldwin said flatly.

'Blood on her legs, and she was so still,' Mark said in a small voice, shivering at the memory.

'You spoke with her,' the Dean murmured. 'What of?'

Mark bowed his head. 'I desired her to take a potion I had acquired. It promised to end the pregnancy.'

'You said you spoke to her and left her angrily,' Baldwin said as the Dean's face set like granite on hearing Mark's crime. 'Was that because she refused to take the potion?'

'I loved her, I didn't want to hurt *her*, only the baby!'

'A potion like that will often kill the mother as well as the child,' Baldwin said coldly.

'If you take me back there, I shall be slaughtered! Please don't take me back!'

'You should have thought of that before you tried to make your woman miscarry!'

'Come, Sir Baldwin,' Dean Peter said after a moment. 'Won't you please let us take him to Exeter? Look at him! He is in danger, he says. I would be reluctant to see him strung up by angry villagers. No matter how foul, nor what, his crimes. Surely he may be quite right to fear for his life?'

'No. You know I cannot set him free.'

'Then I shall ride with him to this outlandish place,' Roger Scut said. He gave Baldwin a look which expressed only distaste. 'If the good knight won't protect this poor priest, I shall do it myself and see that no harm comes to him. I will shield him with my own body.'

Baldwin eyed him wonderingly. 'Why? What do you seek?' he wondered aloud.

'I seek nothing for myself, only to serve the best interests of this unfortunate.'

'I thank you, friend,' Mark said. He was weeping, and he humbly held his hands up towards Roger Scut in gratitude.

Baldwin grunted. He had intended to be home last night. Into his mind flashed a picture of his wife sitting at his great fire, the light gleaming in her red-gold hair, shining on her tip-tilted nose, sparkling in her green eyes. It was a most appealing scene, the more so because in it there was no place for Roger Scut.

'Won't *anyone* believe me?' Mark wailed. 'I didn't mean to kill her. I loved her. I couldn't have done that to her!'

'Done what?' Baldwin demanded harshly, brought back from his mild daydream with a jolt.

'Killed her . . . killed our baby!' Mark cried despairingly. He bent forward and burst into sobs of despair, exhaustion and self-loathing.

Baldwin watched him cynically. He had witnessed all too many felons who wept and moaned when their guilt was established. Often they would then declare their misery over a momentary lapse, a flaring of anger that resulted in a death. It was usually shame and sorrow for being discovered, in his experience.

And yet there was something about this lad. Mark was like a youngster caught filching a penny for food because he was starving. He watched the fellow, in two minds, then looked at Dean Peter. The older man appeared as doubtful as Baldwin himself.

'Oh, in God's own name,' he exclaimed, 'damn it all! Peter, could you send a messenger to ride straight to Simon Puttock? Ask him if he could come and help me with this matter. He works for the Abbot of Tavistock, after all. It's more his duty than mine to save this wretch from the people of his vill.'

'You mean, you will hand this fellow over to Simon?' Peter Clifford asked hopefully.

'I mean I shall go with this fellow and protect him.'

'I am so glad. I thank you,' the Dean smiled. And then, 'When all is done, you must come and speak to me, though. I will need to arrange a penance for your swearing.'

Chapter Eleven

Huward stood, drained his cup, and walked to his door when he heard the footsteps in his yard. He stood silently in the doorway, his thumbs hitched in his belt, watching in silence as Piers approached the house.

'Morning, Huward.'

'Reeve.'

Piers was shattered. He'd hardly slept at all. His son had snored after a night of drinking at Mother Cann's ale-house, but that wasn't the reason why Piers had thrown his blankets away and dressed in the middle of the night, walking out and sitting on a log near his door, staring up at the clean, bright white stars in the moonless sky. No, it was the peasant's accusation.

Sir Ralph was a hard bastard. No one who knew him even remotely could doubt that, and Piers could easily imagine that he might have killed the girl. Yes, and raped her too. It was perfectly easy to believe, as it was that he might have ridden away with a smile on his face. Sir Ralph was a killer, when all was said and done. He was used to getting his own way. If a girl thwarted his desires, he was capable of hitting her hard and then breaking her neck.

The worst of it was, if Sir Ralph was guilty, there was nothing that Piers could do. He was the Reeve to Sir Ralph's court, and the one man who couldn't be tried in a court was the man who owned it. Piers knew that, and he knew that Sir Ralph would have to be tried in another court, a court that was higher than Sir Ralph's own. Perhaps the Sheriff's – except it was too late. Elias had kept his mouth shut, so the Coroner had taken his money and fled. Just as they always did. So the murder was recorded as having been committed by Mark. The fact that he had bolted was proof enough;

it made his guilt apparent and the jury had been happy to declare him responsible.

So an innocent, perhaps, would be forced to pay for the crime committed by Sir Ralph. Piers wasn't happy with that. It made his gorge rise to think that a rich, greedy brute like that knight could benefit by seeing another convicted.

The sky had been no assistance to Piers's grim assessment. He had stared up for inspiration, but all he got was a slight stiffness and a sore arse. It didn't stop him looking up again now, though. He peered at the clouded skies for an age, trying to think how to broach the subject with Huward. It wasn't easy to know how to begin, but when the wind began stirring about him and the first drops of rain pattered gently on his back and into the puddles in the roadway, he made an attempt. 'Huward, I've just come from the castle. Was called there to look at the chapel.'

Huward shrugged without interest.

'Someone set the place afire, you see,' Piers went on. 'It happened last night, after taking your girl to the church, we reckon. One of the servants at the castle thinks she heard something after dark, but she didn't bother to tell anyone at the time. Probably thought it was the wind in the trees. Couldn't see from there, of course. So by this morning, there's nothing left but the stones.'

Huward scratched at his ear and scowled at the ground, impervious to the rain that had begun to fall around them. 'Probably that monk left a fire untended when he ran, and it flared.'

'Yes. Maybe it did,' Piers said distantly. 'If it didn't, I'd have to think it was someone here in the vill who did it. That would be terrible.'

'Bad enough. What makes you think it was deliberate?'

'Nothing, Huward,' Piers sighed. There was little point telling him that Piers had gone to the chapel and prayed there before the inquest. There had been no fire then, he knew, nor had there been the collection of rubbish in the middle of the floor. It was all made clear from the ashes: someone had built a fire in the place and left it to rage. Not that Piers cared overmuch. 'How are you, man?'

'How do you think?' Huward snarled. 'I've lost my daughter. That doesn't make a man happy.'

Piers could see that. The miller's face was pale, apart from the dark shadows under his eyes, and the lines seemed to have deepened at his brow and at the side of his mouth. He had been a cheery, happy-go-lucky fellow until Mary's death: it was awful to see the change wrought by her passing.

'Old friend, it's hard to lose a child, but life continues.'

'Ah! Life continues. Life goes on. One girl dies, but what's that? All the others must live,' Huward grunted. 'It's not very convincing right now, you know, Piers? Not what I'd call comforting. I loved her. She was my own, precious little angel, she was. Everything I ever wanted to see in a child. And now she's snuffed out, her and her child within her.'

'I know. It must be terrible.'

'*You* know? You *can't* know!' Huward suddenly raged. He felt his frustration and hurt welling up. 'I want to punch someone, kill them, take away another life. I want that snotty little scrote here, in my hands, so that I can strangle him, see the life slowly fade from his eyes as he feels his own death approach, then I'd release him, let him breathe a little, until he realised how precious his life was to him, and only then would I start to squeeze, squeeze again, until he was on the brink, and then I'd let him recover again. I'd do that ten times, or twenty, or thirty if I could. Make him suffer. Make him feel his own horror. Make him hurt like I hurt, like my poor wife . . .'

'How is Gilda?'

Huward wasn't weeping. He couldn't. The tears wouldn't come today, for some reason. Last night he'd cried like a baby when he huddled himself alone in his bed, but now there was nothing, as though he'd emptied his well of grief.

'She's still at the church, but Gilda is destroyed. She hasn't spoken to me yet. Not since hearing that Mary's died. She walks in a daze,' he said. 'That's what I find really hard, you know? I can't even talk to her about it. I can't comfort my own wife.'

He looked at Piers. The Reeve could do or say nothing to ease his pain. Huward had known Piers most of his life, but the two men had never shared their innermost secrets, they had never been close companions like some, and now in the depths of his misery, Huward looked at Piers and saw a stranger. Piers must have felt it, because the miller saw him half lift a hand as though to pat Huward's shoulder in a show of affection, but then he allowed his hand to fall and thrust it behind his back like a thief hiding his gelt.

'So I am a leper now, am I?'

Piers didn't raise his voice. 'I want to give you my sympathy, Huward, but I can't change what's happened. All I can do is try to help you and your family.'

'We don't need help. I just want to be left in peace.'

'They may catch the monk.'

'And what then? Would you allow me to kill him as I want? No, I didn't think so. I'll have to watch him be pulled up in the court before our lord, and then he'll claim Benefit of Clergy. There's no justice for my girl, is there?' he added bitterly.

'What do you want me to say? There's nothing I can do about it.'

'No. So all we can do is get on with things. Mill the flour and fill the sacks. That's all we're good for, isn't it? Serfs to our lord.'

Piers nodded, but less sympathetically. Everyone hereabouts knew that the miller was treated with generosity when the rents were assessed. He shrugged his head lower, and water dropped from his hat and dribbled down his neck. This weather was only good for ducks and fish.

'Hoy! Ben! Where are you going?' Huward suddenly roared.

'To an ale-house, Father. Away from this gloom-ridden midden.'

'Get back in that house. We have work to do. You can't go running about the vill today.'

'I can do what I want,' Ben said over his shoulder as he marched up the road towards Gidleigh.

Huward started as though to spring forward to catch his boy, but he stopped and bent his head, bursting into dry, racking sobs.

He waved Piers's hand away, spinning on his heel and leaning his brow against the doorframe, trying to regain control of himself.

The pause was embarrassing, but terrible too. Piers felt as though he was the unwilling witness to a man's death. That was how it felt. Huward had always been a strong man, strong in the arm and in the head, and to see him in this state was scary, like seeing the collapse of an oak. No matter how hearty the soul, any man could be felled by losing a daughter, he reflected. Somehow it was worse than losing a son. At least a boy might have marked his attacker. A girl would be less likely, especially if she was punched suddenly. She could have been unconscious when her neck was broken.

Huward whispered, 'Look at us! What can I do? My wife's lost her mind, my son's a wastrel, and look at *me*! I can't even control my son! What will become of us all? We're ruined, and all because of an evil priest's lusts! Nothing else. Just to satisfy a beardless lad's greed.'

'Is it a great deal further?' Roger Scut asked plaintively.

It was foul weather, and sure enough, he was soaked through already. He almost regretted his spontaneous offer to escort Mark back to the wild lands west of Crediton. The rain here seemed to fly horizontally, especially now that they had climbed a hill and had nothing in front of them to shield them from the miserable weather.

'We have only travelled some eight or maybe nine miles, Brother,' Godwen responded cheerfully. 'Not even a third of the distance, I reckon.'

'God, please give me patience!'

There was a brief lull in the wind, and Roger Scut looked up. The terrible rain had stopped, and as he peered, he saw a sudden break in the clouds. A shaft of sunlight lanced down, and he could see the country ahead clearly. Already the horizon was taken up with the grim, blue-grey grandeur of the moors.

Perhaps if the weather was better, Roger might have felt happier. After all, this was the best outcome he could have hoped for. All he had originally intended was to thwart the knight's aim of taking the monk back to Gidleigh, it being a firm principle of Roger's that the secular authorities should always be forced to bow to the might and power of the Church. Under no circumstances would he ever agree to allow a knight to put a cleric in court, for that was an appalling concept, and yet if there was one monk whom he wouldn't mind seeing in irons, that fellow was Mark.

Now that Sir Baldwin had made clear his determination to drag Mark back to Gidleigh, there was perhaps a benefit. Mark would certainly not be permitted to remain there in charge of the chapel whatever happened, and if Roger was there, he might be able to acquire the living. The man already present was more likely to be granted the running of the place than any other. He could take it over, smarten things up, and when the affair had blown over, install another young cleric so that Roger could farm the profits. There would be justice in Mark's shame and fall, then. Just the thought made his mood lighten.

He shot a look at the forlorn figure on the pony at his side, his wrists bound together. Poor Mark! So innocent, so good, so *bright*! The apple of the Chapter's eye at Exeter, he was. Such a talented singer, an elegant and accomplished scribe, mathematically sound, and a good logician – and also, although with his calm manner, soft voice and gentle, doe eyes, he was almost as pretty as a maid, he was considered to be sticking to his vow of celibacy. No one had ever disputed his godliness. He behaved and looked like a saint of old, so it was said.

Saint my ballocks! Roger thought to himself scathingly. The wastrel was no better than he should be. No better than any number of other young fools who thought that they deserved a better, easier life by mere virtue of their learning. *Learning!* It hadn't done much for young Mark now, had it? Roger tilted his head back the better to view Mark, but there was nothing to see except ordinary self-pity. That was it. The great fool was miserable because he'd been found out.

Roger wouldn't waste any sympathy on *him*. Nor would he try to save the bastard – he could ensure that Mark was ruined utterly.

That thought served to ease his mood as he jolted along on the broad back of his pony.

'Roger?'

'You should not be talking, Mark,' Roger Scut said, peering down his nose at the roadway. 'Rather, I feel you should be considering your sins – and how you are to explain yourself to Sir Ralph.'

'Oh, my God! I can't bear this!'

'What?' Roger said keenly. 'The weight of your guilt?'

'No! It's the thought that my own father could seek my ruin.'

'What are you talking about?'

'My father was a knight who passed through Axminster. He met my mother, and to his credit, he paid her handsomely when he realised that his dalliance had left her with child – me. Later the Bishop's man came to the town and heard of me. My Latin was good, so he took me with him to the Cathedral, and there I have stayed.'

Roger Scut made a small, irritable gesture with his hand. 'I don't care . . . so this knight, you say, who was he?'

'My mother told me he was Sir Ralph of Wonson. That was why I wanted to come here and see him. I thought he could help me, with patronage and support. Every bit of help is useful. You know that.'

'Oh, yes. Yes, of course.'

Roger Scut listened as Mark spoke further, but the boy's babbling intruded but little into his thoughts. He was not here to help Mark. No, Roger would be the next Parson of Gidleigh. Not that he would stay. He thought again of his plan to install a youngster – maybe Luke? – in the chapel for a small salary, and add the revenues from this place to his other profits. Before long, if he was careful, he would have more money than a Bishop!

However, it was most unlikely that Sir Ralph would pass the chapel on to anyone else, if he knew that Mark was his own son. 'Even though Sir Ralph knows you're his son, he's hunting you down?' he enquired casually.

'It's because he *doesn't* know I'm his son. Why should he?' Mark wailed. 'I never told him, because there never seemed to be the right moment.'

'Oh, I see.'

And he did. He could see how to win the chapel. All he had to do was make sure that Sir Ralph never learned of his son's parentage. Simple.

It was late in the morning when Flora reached the lane that led to her home. She was still shivering, but it wasn't the rain and getting soaked, it was the shock of being chased. The vision of that great horse bearing down on her, Esmon screaming with glee, knowing that she couldn't outrun his beast, kept returning to her. She couldn't get the picture out of her mind, nor that of Esmon reaching up with his switch held high, ready to swipe it down at her. The very thought made her shudder again; it was awful, terrifying. At that moment she had been convinced she was about to die, raped like her sister, forced to couple with the filthy, sweating Esmon.

The similarity between this and her sister's death made her feel as though her very marrow had turned to ice. She had told herself to run, and keep running until her heart gave out and her soul was freed, but she couldn't. Like a young rabbit caught by an adder's gaze, all she could do was stare in terror.

Then, with a suddenness that had made her feel faint with relief, Esmon's father appeared and forced himself between them, saving her. He glanced down at her, and she saw compassion in his eyes, she was sure. That made her feel a slight easing of her fear, but then she caught sight of Esmon's expression, and she knew that she was not safe. She could never be safe while he lived.

Now that she was almost home again, she glanced about her with her heart thundering in her breast. It was so close to the castle. At any moment Esmon might leap from the trees and assault her. She had never seen another man who looked so uncaring, so greedy. That was all she was to him, she was sure –

a slab of useful meat he could devour. And he could do so at any moment. She had no defence.

The wearisome vigil of the night before was wearing her down. Her knees ached, oh so badly, after praying all night for her sister's soul, and she felt dried out and scratchy. Her throat was rough with thirst, and her eyes felt as though someone had thrown fine dust in them. And all the while, she felt guilt at that feeling, that faint little feeling of relief at her sister's death.

She'd left her mother with Mary. Gilda couldn't do much more than sit on her haunches and rock, moaning gently as she surveyed the winding-sheeted body of her daughter. Even Sir Ralph had gone there and tried to speak to her earlier that day, before Flora left her, but Gilda had only stared at him with her broken eyes, then turned back to the corpse, crossing herself like a mad penitent. It had hurt Sir Ralph, Flora could see that, but for anyone to come close to madness was terrifying. Lunatics were usually ostracised, and best avoided by all sane and wholesome folk. Except when it was your own mother, of course.

The rain of the late morning had stopped, and although the sun was hidden behind clouds, the landscape glowed as though someone had washed every blade of grass, every leaf. Occasionally the sun would try to shove its way through and the rivers and streams glittered like silver, the trees shining as though their branches were scattered with fine diamonds, but then the cloud squeezed the sun away again and the land seemed almost to die without its warming light.

She wrapped her arms about her body in a bid to keep warm, but it was little help. More than the weather, she knew that it was the thought of that great horse bearing down on her that really chilled her to the core.

Esmon was a foul man. She was sure of it. In the vill there was talk that he'd grabbed young Avice Fletcher last month and raped her. Men said she was a flirt, that she'd lifted her skirts to show him her legs and she'd got what she deserved, but Avice had told Flora the truth of the matter. She'd been minding the flock out near Throwleigh when she heard a horse approaching at speed. It was coming along the lane at a gallop, from the sounds of it, and she'd climbed up into the hedge to see who it was. Esmon saw her at the same time.

He had often made eyes at the girls in the vill. With his handsome looks and aura of danger, many of the local beauties had been happy to flirt with him, hoping he'd take them. Some of the girls dreamed of being married to a man like him, being taken up to the great castle and allowed to live in luxury: fresh rushes on the floor each month, two, maybe even three dresses, a thick cloak for winter – and enough food and strong wine to fill even the hungriest belly. That was what most craved now, a surfeit of food, after these last seven lean and hungry years.

Esmon fancied several of the girls. Flora knew that he regularly tupped Margery, and he'd had Johanna as well. There were others, she was sure, but that was no surprise. He put his faith in his strength, and that was all the girls had to care about. If their menfolk dared to stand before Esmon and denounce him, he could beat them for insolence, and his father might well arrest them and hold them until his court next met, at which time Sir Ralph could order them to be hanged for petty treason, or merely order that their rent should be increased to a level where their lives were at risk. He owned the land, and he owned *them*.

But if those girls were willing enough companions, Avice wasn't. She was already sworn to marry Pike the shepherd's son, and wanted nothing of Esmon's rough handling, so she ducked down and pelted away across the field, trying to find sanctuary.

Esmon had hallooed like a hunter seeing a stag. He'd leaped the hedge, his mount digging great divots in the grass where his forefeet fell, and set off after her at a canter. She had almost reached the safety of a small copse, when she felt him grab her under her arm, his hand curling about her breast, scooping her up while she kicked and struggled. He laughed, lifted one leg over his horse's head, and dropped with her to the ground. There he pushed her backwards, forcing her onto her back, and all but ripped her clothing from her before covering her. She screamed and wept, but for all the compassion her cries aroused in him, she might as well have remained silent. He knew full well that there was no one who could hear her so far from the vill.

Flora had been walking from the mill towards Avice's home when she saw the girl. Avice was clasping the remains of her clothing to her breast, limping painfully, an eye blackened and swelling, and dried blood marking her thighs. She couldn't talk, only sobbed piteously, her hair bedraggled and scattered with twigs and leaves. Her lips were red and sore-looking from being crushed by his teeth as he tried to force her to kiss him, and her face was ravaged with shame and pain.

The memory of that sight would live with Flora for ever. Esmon and his father could take any woman who attracted them, and if a father or brother objected, and Esmon's blood was up, he might set about them with his sword. He was perfectly capable of it. It was strange that his father today had protected her. Flora had heard that other girls had been taken by him in just so rough a manner. Perhaps – she shuddered with revulsion – perhaps Sir Ralph wanted to save her for himself.

The idea that her father might realise what had happened and try to defend her honour by attacking the vile son of their lord was appalling, because it could only end in Huward being slaughtered.

'Oh God, thank you for saving me,' she whispered, the tears beginning to fall again.

'Come, maid! Try to dry your eyes. Your sister's gone to a good place where she'll live like a queen.'

She jumped almost out of her skin, but then she saw Piers smiling at her with that twisted grin of his, and she felt her heart recover a little – only a little, though. After being chased by Esmon that morning, she was wary of any man. Even one so friendly and decent as Piers.

'Would you like me to dance and caper, Reeve?' she asked directly. 'When my sister lies dead in the church?'

'My love, I wouldn't ask that. It's hard, when you lose a companion, I know. But there is still life in your breast.'

His words made her fear that he implied more than a casual interest in her feelings, but when she shot him a look, his eyes were kindly.

'I can hardly forget my grief.'

'Of course not, maid, and nor should you. Your sister was a generous soul. But you can delight in having known a life as easily as you can grieve for losing one. Look on her as having lived as long as she should, not as having died early. She had her time. You should celebrate her, not grieve for losing her.'

'How can you know!'

'Because I have lost, too. My wife. I do know what it's like to lose.'

'Mary was slaughtered like a pig!'

He gave her a sharp look. 'We'll catch the man who did it, Flora. He'll pay.'

'Him? A priest? How can you make him pay for taking her life?'

'There must be some way.'

'If he is punished, what will that mean to us? There are still other men who will prey on the women of our vill.'

'Who?' Piers said, his face hardening. 'You tell me who would dare, and I'll . . .'

'What? You'd go and murder your own master, would you? And his son?'

Piers's face fell. He avoided her eyes. 'Has one of them threatened you?'

'Esmon tried to catch me this morning. His father stopped him, but that doesn't make me feel any more safe. What if his father isn't nearby next time? How could I protect myself, any more than another woman?'

Piers sighed. The second indication that Sir Ralph's family might have been responsible. Sir Ralph was the man seen, though, he told himself. 'Don't worry, maid. The law protects you. You shouldn't fear rape or harm.'

'You say that, when I have just lost my sister? And who would bother to appeal a rape?' Flora scoffed. 'We would have to accuse him in court, show our wounds, show our clothing all bloodied and marked. If you were a woman, would you submit to that? Then, if the man defends himself by saying that he thought the woman was asking for it, she can herself be accused of lying, and be convicted. What is the use?'

'I still say that your sister didn't show any signs that she was unhappy. She must have been pregnant some little while, and she never showed anger or fear before, did she?' Piers said reasonably. He wasn't here to try to upset her further but to calm her. 'You're right: sometimes a man will get away with rape, but I don't think that Brother Mark was that sort of man. He wasn't bold enough – brash enough – to try to. I think he loved your sister.'

'He got her pregnant, though. The priest is saying he doesn't want to bury my sister in the graveyard or give her a service in the church, because she bears a child out of wedlock, when it was another priest got her into that state!'

Piers groaned. 'I'll go and see that fool. He's got his head up his arse most of the time. I'll see if I can extricate it.'

Flora wasn't listening. Her grief was overwhelming her, the misery materialising like waves breaking on a shore. There were moments of calm, when she all but forgot her loss, but then the next wave appeared, battering at her defences. The immensity of her misery was being forced upon her, and she felt as though she was drowning in it. 'Oh, what are we to do?' she groaned. 'Must I live with constant fear from now on? At any time Esmon could come and force me to lie with him, and I could do nothing.'

'First, maid, I'll walk you home to the mill. Then I'll go to see the priest and make sure he understands that your sister is to be buried there, whether he likes it or not. And then . . .' his eyes hardened, and there was a glint in them that spoke ill for any man who tried to prevent him '. . . and then I'll see what may be done about the master's pup.'

Chapter Twelve

Brian of Doncaster cuffed the boy about the head and made him squeal, then took up his cup and walked to the yard with it.

In the bright sun, the little court was baking. The heat seemed to reflect from limewashed buildings and the walls, adding to the heat, while the absolute lack of a breeze meant men sweltered in their thick woollen clothing. Brian himself found it all but unbearable. He was not used to such warmth, although that was no excuse for his men to be lolling on benches with emptied pots of ale before them.

Ach, there was time to get them up and working later. For now, maybe it was best to leave them to sweat and sleep off their drinking. Brian seated himself at a table near the hall, keeping an eye on the gate as well as his men. There was no sense in relaxing his guard. That was the way to receive a blade in the back. All these men were his, but only for as long as they reckoned his coin was forthcoming. As soon as his cash ran out, they'd be on to the next leader, leaving him, more than likely, lifeless.

Who cared? Brian didn't. Death didn't scare him – but lack of fear didn't mean he would hasten its arrival, so when he sat in a room, he kept his back to the walls and his head facing the doorway.

This was a weird set-up, this castle. A bunch of old fools, one youngster with fire in his belly, and a gorgeous Lady. None of the servants were a threat to Brian. All of them were older men, as weak in the arm as they were in the head, and they could be flattened by Brian's band of eighteen. Sir Ralph had been a cold, calculating devil, but now he'd gone soft. Hardly seemed able to concentrate for two breaths consecutively, since that miller's girl had been killed.

Esmon was different. He wanted things. Life, money, women. There was a fellow who'd go far, if he had a mind. He was as ruthless as Brian had been in his youth. Anything he wanted, he took, and that was all there was to it. He could make a good leader. Some of Brian's men already seemed to look on him like their own leader.

When Brian first met Esmon, he saw an easy time for a few months, nothing more. That was two years ago now, when Esmon was only fifteen. They had both been serving Hugh Despenser the Younger in Wales, just before the Despenser wars broke out and forced the Despensers, father and son, into exile. Brian had willingly taken Esmon's invitation to come down here with his men. After the fighting, there was nothing to hold them in Wales, and with the Despensers gone, there were no more opportunities to reward themselves. Better to leave and find a new master. Perhaps Esmon's own father would prove to be a warrior in need of a force, Brian had reasoned.

So it had proved. Sir Ralph had tasks for capable men-at-arms, and Brian and his fellows had earned their board and lodging. Now it seemed that some of his men would be content to remain here, taking orders from Sir Ralph and his son.

It was a state of affairs that Brian didn't much like. If his men started to look to some other man as their master, it left little space for him. Now Esmon was talking about ambushing a group of travellers nearby, with the promise of good rewards for all. Brian wasn't very pleased about it, although his men were delighted at the thought of money. They were content under the castle's roof – some had even muttered that they were better off here, living well, under the direction of Esmon than they had been before. Brian himself should seek opportunities for making money, if he wanted to keep his men with him.

There was something odd about this proposed raid, Brian thought. It was almost as though Esmon was searching for revenge against someone. There was news of someone dying out on the moors. Perhaps it was something to do with that – although Brian couldn't see how one man's death should affect the date of a raid on merchants and tranters. Esmon had obviously been waiting to have something confirmed.

Not that it was anything to concern Brian. He had pressing matters of his own to consider, like how to keep his men loyal. After all, a mercenary leader without men is only a mercenary. If Esmon was taking Brian's men from him, the least Brian could do was try to turn the situation to his profit. The question was, how to make cash from the position he was in.

As he had the thought, his attention was caught by the sight of a skulking figure at the gate. It was the dim one from the vill: Sampson, scavenging again in the alms dishes, taking anything edible for himself.

Pathetic! The cur was no better than a rat, sidling along walls as he went about collecting whatever he could. That was a sign of the feeble control of this place, the fact that he had been allowed to live. In most castles Brian had known, men like him would have drowned or fallen off a cliff by now. Not here. None of the peasants had the guts to kill someone. Only he and his men could do that sort of business. And Esmon.

It would, he mused, be very easy to take this place over. After all, there was no one to stop him. And the Lady Annicia, as he reminded himself, was still a marvellously attractive woman. She herself would be quite a prize.

Flora was nearly home, but she stopped when Piers left her, standing at the top of the track that gave onto her home. She was feeling odd, unsettled. It was Mary's death, she told herself – that and Esmon's attack. Nothing else. But she knew she was lying to herself. There could be few more revolting things than people who deceived themselves to make themselves feel better, she told herself sternly. She knew perfectly well what was behind it.

Yes, of course she felt deep sadness about Mary, but she was also glad, she couldn't deny that, because with the loss of her sister, she now had no competition. Mary's death had removed the most effective barrier to her own happiness.

Osbert had always had eyes only for Mary, and Flora had been made to feel like a silly younger sister. He humoured her, but he adored Mary. Maybe if Mary had even bothered to notice him, Flora could have got over her feelings of jealousy, but Mary had been embarrassed about Os's slavish devotion to her, and she'd scarcely bothered to hide it. That only made poor Os more devoted, but it also left Flora feeling bitterly furious. Like a vixen who sought to protect her cubs, she wanted to cradle Os and preserve him against her sister's uncaring disregard.

Down at the mill, she could hear chopping, and she knew Os would be there, swinging his axe at the logs ready for stacking. Some time perhaps, she would stand like this, listening to him logging, and he would be her husband, she his wife, and they would have children about them, all boys. It was a wonderful picture and Flora stood drinking in the scene as she saw it in her mind, feeling the wash of love cresting through her breast and belly. She adored Os; and she wanted him.

Mary was dead, but her death had given Flora new life. All she need do was look after Os and make him realise that his true, perfect lover was here still.

When the summons came late that afternoon, Simon Puttock was glad of the distraction.

'What is it?' he snapped when the messenger arrived at his door, directed there from the castle. Simon had been involved all morning in a dispute between two miners who were contesting a plot of land which both claimed to own. Simon could make no sense of the case: one had registered it, but then he rented out a part of it to a neighbour. Now the neighbour claimed that he had found tin on it, but the owner said that he had been digging in a plot that wasn't rented, so he himself owned the tin. It was not the sort of case which Simon cared to wrestle with now. He had dealt with it as fairly as he knew how, recorded the matter for the Stannary Court to deal with when it next met, and left them to find himself a little peace over a pot or two of wine.

Not that he was likely to find much with a wife who walked about the house like a pale and melancholic shadow and a daughter who had taken to accusing her father of trying to ruin her happiness because he was taking her away from the only man she would ever love and expecting her to live in a miserable hovel far from any marriageable men and how could he be so cruel to his own daughter and hadn't he married the woman *he* wanted when he had found her and . . .

If she hadn't fallen in love, to Simon's certain knowledge, three times in the previous ten months, he might have been more sympathetic. As it was, the thought of her endless complaints brought on a dull aching behind his eyes. All peace in his household had dissipated when he had been given his new job. It was all the more galling because until then it had been a contented, normally very happy home.

The messenger was a young lad of thirteen or so, with lank black hair and pale skin. Blue eyes gleamed as he glanced about him, but the rest of him looked simply soaked. Even as he stood before Simon in his hall, he was dripping onto the rushes. His cloak gave off a half dog, half woollen odour, and Simon could see that his hose and tunic were drenched. Fortunately he had kept warm with the ride, and appeared uncaring about it. He was much more interested in Simon's house than Simon himself, not that it was any surprise. His home was well appointed and well decorated. Margaret had only recently had the interior repainted, with pictures of St Rumon and St Boniface on opposite walls.

'Well?' Simon growled.

'A request from the Dean of Crediton Church, Bailiff.'

'Come on, then! Spit it out!'

The messenger took a pot from Hugh with a grateful grin. 'It's a thirsty ride in this weather,' he acknowledged as he lifted it to his lips.

'What was the message?' Simon ground out. 'Or should I find you a bed and leave you a week to recover before you pass it on?'

'A young woman has been murdered, her child too. The Dean ordered me here to pass on the message that Sir Baldwin of

Furnshill is on his way there with an accused man, a priest called Mark. Sir Baldwin fears the priest's life is in danger and begged that you might join him to ensure justice is seen to be done. The Dean felt sure the Stannary Bailiff would be interested.'

Simon gazed up the roadway. 'Where is this place?'

'Gidleigh.'

'Ah, I know of this case,' Simon said.

It was tempting to go. He had been told of the dead girl, for Gidleigh fell under his jurisdiction since there were miners trying to find tin near there, but this girl was a villein, nothing to do with the Stannary. If her killer was shown to be a miner, it would be a matter for Simon, but if the murderer was shown to be a priest, he would be tried in the Bishop's own court. Nothing to do with Simon.

There was another factor that weighed with him. If Baldwin asked for his help, it must surely be an interesting case. He never called for help unnecessarily.

However, Simon would need better reasons to leave his home just now. The Coroner had already been to view the corpse and record all the details about her wounds; she was probably already buried now, so there was little enough for Simon to do. Baldwin was capable of protecting himself, Simon could add little to his investigations, and so there was no point in making the journey. Especially when Simon had so many other problems to deal with at home. Disputes between miners and landowners were increasing, and he wanted to clear up as many as possible before he left to go to live in Dartmouth.

That was another thing, he thought. Would his wife want to go with him? She seemed so upset recently that it wouldn't surprise him if she decided to leave him to his own devices, perhaps stay here in Lydford with their children, and let Simon carry on. He couldn't live without her. The thought of taking on his responsibilities without Meg at his side was worse than daunting, it was fearful.

He put all thoughts of the dead girl at Gidleigh from his mind. There was nothing over which he need trouble himself going on down there. It was just a simple murder, caused by a lovers' row, no doubt. No more than that. Nothing for him to deal with.

Within a matter of hours he would be forced to reconsider that.

The next day it was after noon when Surval made his way home. He could feel his thighs and calves straining as he started his descent from the moors with his catch secure in a cloth pouch bound to his back, using his staff to make sure that he didn't slip.

It was not normal for a hermit to walk about so far from his cell, but Surval had heard two days ago that a man had died out on the moors, a terrible, lonely death, drowning in the midst of a mire. The thought of dying out there, so far from anyone, and no one to hear your shrieks for help, both appalled and attracted Surval. If he were to fall into a mire, it would be a natural thing, an accidental death. God Himself couldn't blame him.

Not that it would be right to seek death in that way. No, his death must be unintentional, unplanned, not suicide. Self-murder would be just one more sin to add to his existing crimes. Although he craved the long peace of the grave, that must come about in God's own time, not his own.

Still, it was always possible to die by accident out on the moors, so when Surval heard of a death out in the wilds, he would always go to pray for the dead man. This time, the victim had walked to an ale-house and, returning, had fallen into the great mire beneath Cosdon, called Raybarrow Pool. Surval had gone to pray there yesterday, and had found another miner, Wylkyn, already present.

'They all heard him. Screaming like a rabbit in a snare, he was, apparently. Screaming fit to tear the heart of a demon,' Wylkyn said, unusually pale and nervy. 'I was in town myself. If only I'd left with him, he'd still be alive.'

'Or you'd be dead too,' Surval grunted. 'We all die.'

'Yes, but to die like that!'

'You knew him?'

'He was my brother.'

Surval said no more, but slowly spread himself on the ground, his arms outstretched, and began to implore God's help for the poor dead sinner's soul. He often did so. Miners had a harsh existence, and there was always someone dying who would crave the aid of Surval's prayers, especially now that there was no priest here. That fool, the priest at Gidleigh, wouldn't bother himself over the soul of a miner; probably wouldn't dare make the journey to open moorland in case he got his hose muddy, the useless bugger.

He had prayed for hours by the side of that sucking green swathe, thinking how easy it would have been for the man to stand and walk into it, feel the waters rising up his shins and thighs, the cold caress reaching his genitals and on upwards until the soft wash flowed up and over his head, drawing him downwards while the breath left his lungs and God at last allowed him to give up this endless toil. My God, it was attractive! But Surval knew he mustn't give in, and that was that. He must carry on.

The miners had been grateful as always, and today when he'd returned to pray again by that mire, some men were there with a present for him. Now, walking back to his home beside the bridge, he must go carefully with the weight upon his back.

Admittedly a hermit was supposed to eat frugally, and many eschewed flesh altogether, but at present he had a good-sized mallard weighing him down, shot by a miner's sling, and there was no problem with that so far as he was concerned. It was another form of alms.

He reached the clapper bridge over the Teign and began the climb up toward the great stone circle on Scorhill. An odd arrangement, he always thought. A sequence of massy moorstone lumps arranged in a broad circle. Pausing to look it over once again, for he often paused here feeling that it added something to his contemplations, he glanced back the way he had come.

It was a glorious winter's day. The sky, for the first time in weeks, was clear of clouds, and the sun shone palely on the moors. All was still. Even the wind had abated, as though the elements were ashamed of their behaviour the previous day, although the evidence of the rains was all about. From here, Surval could see it. Rivulets, pools, tiny streams and waterfalls glinted and shone in the bright sun. Most were sharp and blue, discrete little patches of sky fallen to earth; others were pure silver, as though the tin that lay beneath had suddenly sprung to the surface.

Surval took a deep breath and let it out slowly, watching it shiver, his own personal cloud. This view was always calming to him. In other parts of the moors there were fires and noise from the tinners who were digging, smelting and working the ores, here it was peaceful. Miners had worked this land years ago, but all the available metal had been dragged from the earth a long time since. Now this was only a trail for peat-cutters, farmers and suppliers who led their packhorses along these damp, tortuous paths.

He turned east and made his way back towards the bridge and his home. The way soon took him down among the trees, and the sunlight was sprinkled between the fresh leaves like a green mist. On a whim he took a northern path. It would take a little longer, but in this glorious weather, he didn't care.

It was Surval's favourite time of year usually, but now he was worried; had been ever since the death of the girl. Such a terrible crime – so stupid, so brutal. It was the act of a coward, a man who would punish those smaller, younger or weaker than himself just to satisfy his own lusts or his desire for power over anyone.

'Oh God, forgive me!' he shouted suddenly, throwing back his head in his despair and staring with agonised eyes at the sky. 'Please, God, as You love men and share their pains, take my life. Please! Don't make me suffer so much! I killed her, I admit it. I am the foul murderer of a young woman because I wanted her so badly, and . . . and . . .'

That was it. To murder a girl who was scarcely more than a child was unforgivable. God Himself couldn't forgive him. And while he lived, the constant reminder of his murder would be here, the smell and sight of it would assail his senses, driving him mad. He felt more than a little mad. Was it a surprise? And all the while the foul atmosphere grew about him. It mattered not a whit how many good deeds he essayed, for that crime was always going to be there in his mind. That knowledge, the knowledge of his guilt, would not be dispelled by the sun or the wind: it would take more than them.

As he walked down the hill, near to the castle at Gidleigh, he heard a rattling, then shouts and the noise of hooves clattering over cobbles, approaching.

With a cold dread in his belly, he realised what that noise heralded, and he stopped as the row approached him. Soon he could see Esmon at the head of a force of men, all mounted, some with bows and crossbows, all armed with swords and long knives, ready for a fight.

'Out of the path, fool!' Esmon roared, and hurtled past.

The men followed him, none giving Surval more than a glance, as though he was an irrelevance. Soon they had all passed and the sound of their hooves faded into the distance. If it were not for the thick gouts of mud and horse shit which had been flung against him, he might have doubted that they had ever been here.

Chapter Thirteen

'Come on, cretins!' Esmon was feeling the excitement thrilling in his veins as he led the party on. He caught a glimpse of a shapely pair of buttocks bent over in a field as he passed, and wondered whose they might be, but he had no time to stop now. Whoever she was, the slut would have to wait until later. He had business to attend to first, but when he was done, aye, he'd be coming back this way and would look out for her.

Putting all thoughts of women from his mind, he slapped his mount's backside with his switch, urging the great stallion onwards. The beast was as black as coal, with one white star on his forehead and a single white sock on his front offside, and in this light he gleamed like oiled leather. He was a weapon, a trained and powerful warhorse.

He shouldn't be needed today, Esmon told himself. That was what he'd told his father earlier when they had spoken about this attack.

Sir Ralph had been disturbed, almost confused, as though there was a blasted great weight on his mind. Old fool! He had been like that since the girl Mary had died and that shit-head priest had bolted. It was a bastard to have lost the priest – that must be what Sir Ralph must be thinking: that it was shameful to allow a killer to escape. Esmon couldn't care less. Life was too short for regrets – especially on a day like today.

He had sixteen men with him, fifteen men-at-arms under Brian of Doncaster, all of whom had remained with him after fighting for the King and the Despensers. Afterwards Esmon had regretted coming back down here to Devonshire. The battles, the charges, all those available women in the taverns, the hand-to-hand combat had made life worth living. It was what a man was created for.

Even this was exhilarating. The chance of a good ride, rich
wagons, gold. All the things that a soldier needed. Perhaps there
might be a woman, too. There often were with these little troupes
of merchants and farmers. At least there would be Wylkyn, as
he told himself. It was a shame that the attack on him the
day before yesterday had failed. The fool of a miner had run off
into the middle of Raybarrow Pool, the filthy mire near the
commons, and he'd drowned there. All Esmon had wanted to
know from him was, where was that whoreson brother of his:
Wylkyn – the man who knew all about Sir Richard Prouse's
murder. Esmon had to kill Wylkyn. He couldn't get away again.
He'd escaped Esmon before and run to the moors, but today
he'd have him. Esmon had heard that Wylkyn was here, with
this party, and Esmon was going to put an end to the matter once
and for all.

When they came to the hill that led from Throwleigh to the
open moors, Esmon slowed to a trot. Foolish to make too much
noise, he thought. It would only alarm and forewarn the folk
whom he wanted to meet.

There was a slight sense of superstition, a faint feeling that he
had been here before, but that of course was different. That was
the day that Mary had died.

He hadn't ever intended her any harm. To him, killing a girl
who was so attractive was an appalling waste of beauty. Far better
to learn what it was that she craved, and then provide it in return
for her body. There was never any need to worry, because the only
thing he would never promise was his hand in marriage. That
would have been stupid. Poor Mary. She was so pretty, so lively
and God, she was sexy!

But he hadn't gone past her that day intending to hurt her. That
day he'd been riding up here to go and waylay Wylkyn again. He
had been told that the miner was going back up to his mine again
after spending a little time in South Zeal, and Esmon had ridden
up along the roadway that straggled along the side of Cosdon
Beacon, up to the open moors, but he found the wrong man. It
was Wylkyn's brother, not Wylkyn. The fool had refused to give

them information, or to plead for his life, and instead he ran away, straight into the great bog. A foul, repellent death.

It hadn't put him in a good mood when he rode back along the roadway. If he had been in a better mood, perhaps he would have been more polite to the girl.

At the top of the hill, the track became less muddy, more a grassed path. Here there were many cart-tracks and hoofprints marring the turf. Pools of water lay all about on either side. Esmon held up a hand to halt the men and listened carefully. Vaguely in the distance he could hear the squeaking and rattling of many carts, and he grinned at Brian and his men. Brian gave him a short nod. It seemed he was out of sorts this morning, but Esmon didn't care. The rest of his men were fine. For the most part, they were busy patting their mounts, watching the sky, checking swords and knives, easing the blades in their sheaths, one testing his knife on the ball of his thumb, dragging the corners of his mouth down and nodding to himself.

Esmon led them into the shadow of a thick stand of trees and waited.

It was his father who'd always led these raids previously. Esmon was the eager lieutenant, the boy, but never again. He'd as much experience as his old man – more, probably. There was no need for elderly fools to lead men – no need and no place. It was work for a younger man, a man with fire in his bowels and courage. A man like Esmon.

Sir Ralph had lost his sense of priorities. Wylkyn had to die, and Sir Ralph should have been here to make sure of it, but instead he was at home mourning that girl. There were plenty more. Perhaps, Esmon wondered idly, he should tell his father to go and see young Margery . . . But no! Sir Ralph was probably too frail now.

Esmon conveniently forgot that his father had yanked him from his horse only the day before, all but dislocating his shoulder and dropping him in the mud, because right now, with the feel of the wind in his face, the noise of his horse's hooves, the sense of power conveyed by leading a warrior band, he felt invincible. His father was too old for this kind of excitement. He had remained sitting in his hall, chin cupped in his palm, and waved his free hand dismissively as soon as the boy arrived to say that the convoy was leaving South Zeal along the Throwleigh Road. Pathetic old woman. Sir Ralph was losing his edge.

It was as he was thinking this that Esmon realised they were passing the place where he had chased Flora. The memory of his shame at being dragged from his horse returned to him, but so did the rage; it was a wild anger, all the worse for the fact that he couldn't satisfy his desire for revenge. Petty treason against his father was unthinkable. All this was because of the girl, Flora. The old man was trying to protect her, and Esmon wondered why. Sir Ralph had known of enough other girls his son had taken: half the villeins' daughters were fair game to him.

The noise was closer and Esmon found his thoughts leaping forward to the coming action. He could hear the distinctive squeak of one cart which was plainly in need of maintenance. Almost there, Esmon gloated. So close. And then he saw a horse appear, walking stolidly, dragging a well-laden cart behind it.

Esmon pulled his sword free and crouched expectantly in his saddle. This was the critical moment. Before him, the land rose gently to a flat plateau, which was concealed from here by the trees, but Esmon could visualise it with ease; he'd lived here much of his life, and he knew every field.

On the right flank of the travellers the land rose towards the moors; although it wasn't steep, it was scattered with moorstone so that a cart would find the way hard. To their left was a long stone wall that effectively cut them off, their only means of escape was forward, through Esmon's men, or back. That was hard to achieve for a man on a cart. Turning it took time, and before they could manage, Esmon's men would have cut off their retreat. That gave Esmon and his men free rein. When they charged out from their concealment, if they were swift, they could cut off any escape. Some might evade them and try to bolt up the hill towards the moors, but even if they managed to do so, it shouldn't be too hard to catch them. There wasn't much chance of a heavy cart outrunning a horseman, but it would be irritating to have to waste time herding them together again. He didn't need that sort of grief, so he waited, the blood humming in his brain, the soft, seductive tingle of sudden action thrilling every nerve and fibre in his body. War: it was what he had been trained for from birth.

The first carter sat hunched on the boards, his head jolting with the cart's motion. Gradually more carts and men came into view, trailing behind the first, spread over the grass so as not to follow the tracks of previous wheels and break the surface too badly. That could mean a cart getting mired, perhaps damaging a wheel or axle.

They were so close Esmon could all but feel the breath of the leading horse. Nearly time, nearly ... When the first two carters had passed, that would be the perfect time to spring the trap, he thought – and then he saw the carter snort, hawk, throw back his head to spit, and suddenly catch sight of the men watching him from the still darkness of the trees. The carter choked, the phlegm catching in his throat, and Esmon knew that he had only a moment to retain the benefit of surprise. '*Now!*' he roared, and spurred his charger on, waving his sword about his head.

The horse exploded into life. Esmon felt the cantle of his saddle pound into the small of his back and then he was flying forward at a tremendous pace, and he was shrieking, and his men were howling and bellowing, while the carters grabbed reins, trying to move from their path and escape. One was stuck when his horse reared and the traces snapped, another tried to turn his mount up the hill, but that was a vain hope. The heather and furze there were thick enough to clog the wheels of a cart.

Further back were the packhorses. These were Esmon's target. His plan had been simple: his men would ride out a little further up the hill than their quarry, and then they would drop down on the carters' flank. Total surprise should work in their favour, for they had never attacked this far from Gidleigh. Usually they sprang their assaults nearer to Gidleigh or Chagford, and that was why so many merchants had changed their route to the market. An attack so far from help was a terrifying experience for travellers.

Towards the rear of the line he found what he sought. He wheeled and glanced back. As he had ordered, his men were strung out behind him, and when he pointed, they all rode down, using their momentum to panic the men and their animals still more.

It worked. The packhorses whinnied and tried to bolt. Their owners were stuck for a choice: protect their property by drawing a knife and see their packhorses disappear into the distance, or fight to control their mounts and hope to see to their attackers later. In the event, some saw fit to draw steel, and their horses were herded away by the three men Esmon had ordered to catch them. The others were soon forced back, swords from the back of a horse being more effective weapons than knives in the hands of merchants and tranters. The carts were forced to halt.

Only one man stood his ground against the raiders. He was walking beside a pair of heavily laden ponies, their broad backs weighted down with leather satchels bound securely to strong cross frames. As soon as the men burst from their cover, Esmon saw him pull his ponies swiftly down towards the stone wall. There he tried to scramble up and over, but the wall was mossy and slick with rainwater, and he couldn't manage it while holding onto his ponies' reins. In the end, he slithered to the ground and drew a long-bladed knife.

He was a sturdy fellow, was Wylkyn, thick-shouldered and with the wild hair of a moorman. His eyes flitted over the men of the ambush and at last rested on Esmon as though recognising he was the leader. 'So, felon! You're still in charge of this rabble, are you?'

'Hold your tongue, Wylkyn!' Esmon shouted. 'Get back up here and sheath that knife, little man or, by Christ, I'll take your hand off. Bring your ponies.'

'You have the look of a knight, but the behaviour of an outlaw. I'll not bring my ponies to a robber! You want them, you'll have to take them from me. But it's not them you're after, is it? It's me, you shite!'

The man glanced over his shoulder at the wall as though guessing whether he could leap it in a bound, but then he stepped in front of his ponies, set his shoulders and gripped his knife more firmly. '*No*. You want me, you'll have to take me.'

'You miserable bastard son of a poxed whore!' Esmon screamed. His blood was still up, his anger easily ignited after the recollection of his father's treatment of him, and he was in front of his men, too. He had to show them that he wasn't fearful of a peasant, no matter how grim his features with those narrowed eyes and thin line of a mouth, all but hidden behind the pepper and salt beard.

He spurred his horse and aimed at the man, intending to run him down, but the fellow darted aside at the last minute. Esmon wheeled his horse and Wylkyn sprang out of the way again, but Esmon laughed and rode on past him, scaring his ponies. They whinnied and bolted, running up the hill. Esmon saw Brian leaving the main body of travellers and haring after them, whooping with excitement.

Esmon shot a look up the hill to make sure that they were caught, and then smiled coldly at the miner. 'So much for your defiance, peasant!'

'At least I behave like a man of honour, better that and penniless than a mere thief who sports the outer livery of a man of chivalry while his soul is blacker than night in a mine!' Wylkyn spat. 'You are dishonoured and a coward! I name you felon and outlaw! Come, fight me fairly, if you dare. You've already killed my brother.'

'It should have been *you*!'

'I know. You thought it *was* me, didn't you? Just because I was in town.'

'And now he's gone to Hell in your place, Wylkyn.'

'He won't be there when you arrive, *murderer*! He'll be in Heaven,' Wylkyn cried hoarsely.

Esmon looked at the sun. There was no time to prolong this. Luckily Wylkyn was inexperienced as a fighter, for all his bluster. Dispassionately Esmon watched to make sure that the travellers were being led away, and once they and his men were out of sight, he ran his horse once more at the man. This time, although the miner slipped to one side, Esmon didn't give him the opportunity of escape. He swept his sword around in a great arc and Wylkyn coughed and stared down as though in disbelief at his knife. It lay on the ground a short distance from his arm, still gripped in his hand, the fingers twitching, while the blood pumped brightly from his wrist where it had been severed.

He looked up at Esmon with cold contempt. 'You fucking coward!'

That was enough. The bloodlust washed over him. 'Die, you prickle!' Esmon shrieked and urged his horse forward. He swung again, and his blade sank deeply into Wylkyn's shoulder. He grunted, a deep, pained noise that snorted in his nose like a final snore, and Esmon had to kick at his horse and use the leverage of his mount's movement to free his blade.

Later, when he was riding back to the castle at the head of the travellers, he felt a crust on his upper lip. Scraping at it with a tooth, he realised it was Wylkyn's blood, and he smiled. It felt good to have killed again – and now, once he had dumped this lot at the castle, he could go and find the owner of those buttocks. He could do with a tumble on a woman now.

It was the next day, late in the forenoon, that Simon received his second messenger. He had suffered an interminably lengthy explanation of a dispute between two angry miners, neither of whom had bothered to mark their claims with the customary turves piled at the edges. They had simply started digging, and soon thereafter fighting. He fined them both when he grew bored with their whining and arguing.

As he reached his home, desperate for a bowl of thick stew to warm him after the draughts and cold of the castle, Simon saw his wife appear in the doorway. Tall, slim and elegant, with her long blonde hair coiled under her wimple, he adored her even after many years of marriage. When she smiled, he was unaware of the passage of time; it was as though he was seeing her, once more, as she had been when he first met her. As she drew nearer him, all he was aware of was the calmness which she radiated, and his first impression was that he could rest here.

She said, 'A boy has just arrived. There's a problem over at Gidleigh.'

Simon scowled and swore. 'God's belly! What do they want of me? I've already said that I won't go there. Where's the messenger?'

'In the buttery. I sent him there to refresh himself. I wasn't sure if you wanted him to take back a message.'

'The only message I'm likely to send is one that tells them to stop wasting my time,' Simon said bitterly. 'I'll speak to him later.'

'Good, Husband.'

There was a jarring tone in her voice that rankled, but Simon swallowed his irritation and tried to sound conciliatory. 'I am sorry to have spoken so grimly, my love, but I have had a sorely trying morning.'

'I understand. Your work is important.'

'Meg, please! It's not as important to me as you are.'

She turned to face him. 'It hardly feels like it, Husband.'

'Why do you say that?'

She wouldn't meet his eyes. 'Simon, our daughter is very unhappy to be going away.'

'I know, but what would you have me do – leave her here on her own? You know we can't do that.'

'I could stay here with her . . . Simon, don't pull away like that! Please, we have to talk about this. I know you have no choice about the work . . .'

'Do you? It sounds as though you blame me for accepting what was never mine to choose,' he said bitterly.

'No man is free of a master,' she agreed sadly. 'But we should still take account of Edith's position. She is in love, she thinks.'

'Thinks!' Simon expostulated. 'And how often have we heard *that* in the last few years?'

'No matter. She is firm in her belief and . . .'

Simon gazed at her. There was a hesitancy about her that made him listen intently. 'And?'

'And she says she has given her word to marry him.'

'Christ's blood!' Simon roared. 'I'll teach her to—'

'Simon, please!' Margaret said, putting a hand on his arm. 'Be still for once and listen.'

'I always listen,' he glowered. 'I am more patient than many.'

'Then listen now, and stop shouting. She hasn't given her pledge in terms of present intent.'

He felt his heart's pounding slow a little at that. If she had given her words in present terms, she was legally married, and there was nothing Simon or even the Church could do about it. Well, not if she'd done it in front of witnesses, anyway. But if she'd sworn to marry in the future, that was different. It was a far less binding covenant. 'Then what?'

'She won't marry, she says, without your approval.'

'Who is this wastrel cutpurse who would filch my daughter, then?' Simon asked uncharitably. He was already unhappy about his move to Dartmouth, and the effect it was having on his wife and his daughter. The thought that young Edith could have gone ahead and offered herself in marriage without speaking to him first rankled.

'He is a good boy, Simon. A freeman.'

'What sort of a freeman?' Simon asked suspiciously.

'Apprentice to a merchant,' she said, but quietly, as though slightly reluctant to admit it.

'Merchant?' he repeated blankly. 'But there's only one merchant here. I . . . Oh, Christ's cods, not *him*!'

'Now don't be like that, Husband,' she entreated. 'He is a perfectly well-meaning lad, and I don't think he—'

'He's as gormless as a newborn mastiff,' he said bluntly. 'Dim and vapid. All he ever thinks about is the tightness of his hose! Spends as much time staring at his own ankles as at hers, I expect. Damned pansy! All these modern trends for fashion and high-living, furs and silks and other fripperies! Christ's blood, what can she see in him?'

Margaret took a deep breath. 'Simon, if you speak to Edith like that, she will run away with him tonight. She loves him and wants to be with him, but she won't dishonour you by disobeying you unless you force her to.'

'Me? I wouldn't force her to disobey me!'

'If you rant at her like that, you'll make her run away with him,' she said with calm, knowing serenity. She had moved to a turf bench, and was sitting on the grass with her hands crossed in her lap.

'What do you recommend?'

She patted the grass at her side and remained silent until he accepted her invitation and sat. 'Try to imagine how she feels. She thinks she is in love – in the same way that I was with you when we met.'

'That's completely different,' he said hotly.

'Perhaps. And perhaps she doesn't feel so.'

'And what then?'

'Then you can suggest that she may continue to see her swain, but that you would wish her to join us when we go to Dartmouth,' she said emotionlessly.

He put his hand on her thigh. 'I know you don't want to go, but I have to.'

'I know that. We have to serve. I just don't want to lose our daughter when we go.'

'Would she be satisfied with being able to see him?'

'If you tell her that you will allow him to visit us in our new home so that they can woo in comfort, she might.'

'I shall consider it,' he promised.

It was difficult, he told himself as he entered his hall. No sooner had a child been born than she was ready to leave home and begin to raise her own children. 'She's too damned young!' he murmured.

'Sir?'

Looking up, Simon noticed at last that there was a tired-looking young man standing near the fire. 'Who are you?'

'Sir, I'm Osbert. I've been sent from Gidleigh by Reeve Piers to speak to the Bailiff.'

'Osbert, eh?' Simon said musingly. 'And you are here to tell me about this dead girl, are you? I've already told Sir Baldwin and the Dean of Crediton that I can't come right now. Tell your Reeve that he's already had the Coroner and that there's nothing I can do to help now. I don't understand why he wants me there anyway. It's not my place to deal with a murder when it's nothing to do with the Stannary.'

'It's not Mary, sir. It's the murdered tinner.'

Simon blinked. 'What?'

'A man has been found dead, sir, and someone has suggested that he might be a tin miner. He was on his way to the market at Chagford, but never arrived. We thought you should know.'

'Bugger!' Simon spat, then roared, 'Hugh!' making the messenger quail. 'Pack clothes and tell the grooms to saddle our horses. We're going to Gidleigh.'

Chapter Fourteen

It was just typical, so far as Piers was concerned. He crouched down at the body's side again, trying to ignore the stench, but it was impossible. It was pervasive, this odour of blood and decay. Cloying, it stuck in his nostrils and made him want to gag.

'Who could have done this?' he choked.

'You serious?'

'Elias, what do you want me to say? I didn't expect this.'

'Huh! I don't know anything, and I'm not going to know anything. Don't want to. What, start talking and end up like that?'

Piers winced as he glanced again at the corpse. Somehow the fear and bitterness of Flora came back to him. At the time he had said he would see what could be done about Esmon, but his words had been intended to calm her rather than indicating that he had a means of punishing their master's son. Short of committing murder, he couldn't see how to effect that.

'There must be something,' he muttered under his breath.

'What?'

'Nothing.'

Unless Esmon was found guilty of committing a crime which could be taken to a higher court, there was nothing anyone could do to bring justice to him. He would continue doing whatever he wanted. In theory, killing a miner, one of the King's own villeins, would be enough to guarantee that he would be punished, but Piers knew that was a forlorn hope. The King's officers could demand that Esmon be called to court, but they were all his peers. Who ever heard of a knight's son being convicted and executed?

Someone had to prove it was Esmon who did this, yet Elias wouldn't even admit to seeing Sir Ralph at the road when Mary was murdered, let alone allege that Esmon might have been here.

No one would risk death in the hope of inflicting justice on Esmon.

Piers stood, averting his eyes. The dead man had been butchered as though in a rage, with slashes and cuts all over his body. His hand lay nearby. 'We can't let this carry on.'

'I suppose you think we can stop it?'

'Someone has to.'

Elias sneered, then turned away. 'Good – well, you be a hero, Piers. Tell you what, if I find you afterwards, I'll report it to the Hundred Bailiff personally.'

'Wait a bit, Elias,' Piers called, and there was enough irritation in his voice to make Elias reluctantly stop and walk back, staring down at the hacked body.

'Poor bastard.'

'Yes,' Piers snapped. 'I know. That's why I want to see to it that he's the last. Is this how you found him?'

'Yeah. Think so.'

'Did you find him yourself?'

Elias didn't speak, merely nodded his head once. Piers was sure he was lying, but when Elias wanted to be stubborn, he could give lessons to a mule.

'Have you sent for the Coroner?'

Piers shrugged. 'For what good it will do. I sent Osbert to tell the Hundred Bailiff, then to go to Lydford. The Stannary will be interested if this man genuinely is a miner.'

'He is. Don't you remember him? His name's Wylkyn. He was servant to Sir Richard before he died.'

Piers stared. 'Wylkyn?'

The name was familiar, and so too was this man's face now he had a name. Piers had always been Sir Ralph's serf, and hadn't mixed with the men of Sir Richard Prouse's demesne, but Piers had seen Sir Richard's steward on occasion at markets and fairs, buying exotic spices and herbs for his master's potions.

'I recall his face,' Piers said slowly.

'Wylkyn was a good enough man. As soon as Sir Ralph took over the castle, he ran for the moors and joined his brother. Called himself a miner. He's been quite lucky, so I've heard.'

'His luck hasn't held for him today. What was he doing up here?'

'What do you mean?'

Piers threw him a look. 'Don't be stupid! Why would he come by this route, rather than cutting across the moors? It's far out of his way.'

'I expect he had his reasons.'

Piers glanced about them, at the tracks of many carts. 'He wasn't alone, either.'

'The castle's full, I expect.'

'Did you see them?'

There was no need to say who. Both knew that he meant Sir Ralph and his son. Elias slowly shook his head. 'No, but who else would rob and kill like this?'

'Someone has to stop them.'

Elias curled his lip. 'Aye, well, you keep saying that, Master Reeve. Fine, when you've got an idea how to, let me know. I'll be interested. But don't forget, these men are friends of the Despensers. If you want to go against the King's friends, you try it, but don't expect anyone here to help you, because they won't.'

When he reached the castle, Baldwin thought how pleasing it looked, representing security, warmth and food, and he urged his small party on, calling to the gatekeeper as he approached the outer stockade. Surprisingly, he found that the gate was closed and barred. This was a quiet enough part of the realm, and he would have expected the gates to remain open all through the day, only being closed at night, like the gates of a larger castle or even a town. Everyone tended to welcome travellers, for they brought news, and in a small castle like this, one without a huge amount of money and miles from busier roads, there was little likelihood that the place could be threatened by a gang of outlaws.

After he had bellowed and demanded to speak to the lord, there was a rattling and squeaking as a bar was slid back from the gate, and then Baldwin was confronted by three men, two of whom

were clearly guards and who gripped long polearms in their
callused hands, while the other held his arms crossed.

'Who are you?'

'Are you steward to Sir Ralph?' Baldwin asked.

'You could call me that. I am Brian – Brian of Doncaster. I
serve Esmon, Sir Ralph's son, with my men.'

Baldwin heard the note of pride in his voice. This man was no
servant, bound to his master by ties of loyalty and honour, but a
paid employee with his own small host of men. Baldwin was
immediately struck by the thought that the master of this castle
might be well advised to protect himself from this Brian and his
gang. It was not a pleasant thought, that a man should be forced to
guard himself against his own hired men. It was, in its way, still
more dreadful than the idea of assassins and the Old Man of the
Mountain.

Brian had been eyeing Baldwin with interest, but now one of
his men nudged him and pointed at Mark, and suddenly Brian's
face lit up like a torch thrust in a fire. 'God's flaming cods!' he
burst out, and then sent the guard in through the gates.

While he waited, trying to control his annoyance at being
kept out here, Baldwin glanced through the gate at the castle's
tower. It was only a small keep with a ground floor and one
upper chamber which lay enclosed within a stockade, which was
strengthened in two places by some more solid moorstone
walling. Baldwin was reminded of the little enclosure at Lydford.
That too had stabling on the left of the entrance to the stockade,
a series of outbuildings ringing an oval space in which men
could practise with their weapons, groom horses or watch dogs
fighting for their recreation.

This place looked prosperous enough. There were a number of
carts, he saw, some loaded with goods, and the stables were filled
to overflowing with packhorses. They had passed some pastures
on the way here, in which still more ponies and sumpter horses
had idled, and Baldwin reckoned that the place had more than its
fair share of horseflesh for a castle of this size.

'Godspeed, my Lord. How may we help you?'

The man who spoke was older, perhaps not far short of Baldwin's own age, and had the carriage and indefinable authority of someone who knew his own value. Baldwin was sure that he had seen him before, and there was a faint frown of recognition in the other's face, too, as though he could almost recall Baldwin's name, but not quite. On Baldwin's part, he would not have remembered Sir Ralph's name had he not heard Mark mention the name.

At his side was a younger man, plainly his son, from the similar colouring and looks, and especially the dimple in the chin. Esmon, Baldwin said to himself. The boy looked much more dangerous, standing with a certain haughtiness that bordered on rudeness. His manner was very different from that of his father, who looked as though he carried the world's troubles on his shoulders.

'I am Sir Baldwin de Furnshill, Keeper of the King's Peace, and I am bringing a man here for justice,' he said formally. 'I had thought that this castle was the property of Sir Richard Prouse?'

Hearing his first words, the younger man had gasped with delight. 'You have him? We can—'

'Quiet, Esmon! I am Sir Ralph de Wonson, Sir Baldwin. You are very welcome. I remember you from the last shire court. You were trying some matters there, I recall.'

'I was there as a Justice of Gaol Delivery,' Baldwin agreed. 'Tell me, where is Sir Richard? Did not Sir Richard Prouse own this manor?'

'Alas! He died. He lost his wealth to a banker, and when the banker died, his debt was taken over by my Lord Despenser. When Sir Richard died, Lord Despenser gave this land to me.'

'I see,' Baldwin said suavely. He had no intention of disputing the man's right to the castle if the Despensers were minded to give it to him. The most powerful family in the realm could do such things and no man could prevent them. 'This man, the alleged priest Mark – I believe you wanted him captured?'

'We are very grateful to you,' Sir Ralph said. He motioned to the two guards, who set their weapons aside and strode over to where Mark sat quivering on his horse. Seeing them approach, he tried to withdraw, but Thomas, who held the reins, snarled at him to keep still.

'Sir Baldwin, don't just desert me here! I shall be murdered!'

Roger Scut interposed himself between Mark and the men. 'I cannot allow this monk to be imprisoned here! He is a man of God. Let us take him to the chapel and I shall guard him there, in the sanctuary of the church.'

'Oh, aye?' Esmon said innocently. 'That would be a good, safe place for him. You don't mind the cold and the wet, do you?'

'A man of God cares nothing for such things,' Roger said loftily. 'Only that his duty to God is performed rightly.'

Esmon grinned, but his father interrupted him. 'I have a gaol here, and he will be safe enough in there. Safer than his victim was on the road.'

'I will not have him left in the care of this knight,' Roger said stubbornly.

Baldwin gave him a sour look but again it was Sir Ralph who spoke.

'Master, I shall speak for his safety while he is within my walls and until he comes before the court.'

'That is good,' Baldwin said, ignoring the priest. 'You may take him. Except . . .'

'Sir Knight?' Sir Ralph enquired.

'I shall be here to help you to hear his case,' Baldwin said.

'There is no need. This is a matter for the vill. He was caught red-handed.'

Baldwin glanced at the lad shaking in his saddle. One of the guards drew his knife and roughly cut the thongs that bound Mark's wrists to his saddle, and the two pulled him ungently from his pony. He stared appealingly at Baldwin, and a small worm of uncertainty began to wriggle in the knight's belly. The young priest looked so lonely, so devastated, and there was something about the knight and his son that he didn't like. Revenge was a natural emotion, and these two might be willing to ensure that Mark died just to satisfy their own anger.

'Perhaps we could discuss it over a cup of wine? It is a thirsty ride from Crediton, and we have been riding for three days.'

'Three? It should not have taken you so long,' said Sir Ralph.

All their eyes were on the shuffling figure being taken in through the doors. Baldwin had expected that the two would move aside and let him pass in as well, but they stood their ground. It was discourteous, and Baldwin felt insulted. 'It would not have taken so long, but the rivers were too turbulent for us to cross and we had to turn back to an inn. Will you not spare some wine for us?'

'I fear that my home is filled, Sir Baldwin. We have no space even for a serf, let alone a great Keeper. Would it be possible for you to visit and stay at the local inn? It is only a short ride from here.'

'Do you mean that you have not even some space in your hayloft?' Baldwin asked politely, indicating Thomas and Godwen, Roger and himself. 'We require very little.'

'We could scarcely allow you to suffer in a hayloft, my Lord,' Esmon said. 'And I fear we have many guests just now. Finding space for one alone would be hard. But there is a man to lead you to the inn, if you want. Hi, Piers! Come here!'

There was a small group of men-at-arms in a corner near the tower, and they watched as Brian gripped Mark's shoulder, and walked him towards the stables. Meanwhile Baldwin was sure he could hear sobbing coming from a room in the gatehouse nearby, but then it suddenly stopped. In the silence, it was almost as though there had been a death. It was a grim reflection, as he told himself, and his anxiety grew at the thought of leaving Mark here.

Baldwin turned his attention back to Sir Ralph, who was gazing after the prisoner with real hatred on his face. 'I suppose you have too few cups to offer us wine, then.'

'I am sure we could find you a cup,' Sir Ralph said.

'No. I am sure I don't wish to be the cause of trouble.' Baldwin pulled his horse's head around, ready to ride to the inn. 'Sir Ralph, I hold you personally responsible for the well-being of that priest. Please remind your gaoler that a man who is held in prison is still entitled to be treated as a human. Killing him, or being responsible for his death is a felony.'

'You threaten me, Keeper? Perhaps you should know that I answer only to my master, and he, Sir Baldwin, is Lord Despenser.'

Baldwin turned in his saddle and offered the furious Sir Ralph a mild, apologetic smile. 'Ah, I am sorry, friend. I knew that already. Perhaps you had not considered, though, that Mark's master is the Bishop of Exeter, Bishop Walter? I am sure we do not wish to see a dispute between the King's Treasurer and his favourite adviser, do we?'

Sir Ralph gave a tight nod of agreement, but Baldwin wasn't content. He wished his friend Simon Puttock was here. There was something about the knight that worried him. Sir Ralph looked like a man who was beyond fear of the law, and that was not the sort of man into whose custody Baldwin was happy to leave even the murderer of a woman and child.

His tone hardened. 'And in the meantime, if any harm comes to that fellow, I shall personally appeal you in court.'

Piers was not best pleased at having to lead this grim-looking band anywhere, but when his lord and master ordered him, he had little choice.

'You are the Reeve?' Baldwin asked him as they wandered the lanes towards the inn at Wonson.

'Yes, sir. I have been Reeve here for almost a year. Never thought I'd have to cope with a murder, though.'

'There are not many in this quiet area, then?'

'Until Mary's death, the last one was poor Elias's own daughter. She was raped and killed not far from her home. Poor lass. That was during the famine. Terrible times.'

'He was the man who found the body, wasn't he? I shall want to speak to Elias,' Baldwin said.

'Of course. Now? He's there, at Sir Ralph's warren.'

Baldwin followed his gaze and saw a grim-faced peasant at a stone-built warren. Rabbits were not very successful at making their warrens here in the forbidding area of Dartmoor. Often lords would create warrens for them for their meat and fur. Elias was at one now, and as Baldwin watched, a rabbit sprang from a hole into a purse-net. It was bundled up in a ball as the net slipped tight, and Elias darted to it quickly. He carefully retrieved the rabbit and held it by the hind legs while he reset the net ready for the next, and then squatted on his haunches, stroking the little creature and calming it. Then, in a smooth movement, he pulled the head with a swift jerk, and gently set the dead body with others. Another net was filled, and he darted to that one.

'Not now,' Baldwin said, thinking of his sore buttocks. 'It can wait until morning. He looks efficient.'

'Very. He's the best ferret-man in the vill, is Elias the ploughman.'

'What of others?'

Piers described all the peasants and their duties while Baldwin listened carefully. Finally Piers mentioned Sampson.

'Who is he?'

'His name is a joke, I'm afraid. Ironic or something. He's a half-wit. Sometimes happens that you get one even in a good, healthy vill like ours,' Piers said defensively. 'He lives on his own. He's built himself a little shelter on the hill south and west of the castle.'

'Interesting. I shall look forward to meeting him. And now, master Piers. Where were you on the day this girl was killed?'

Huward was resting his legs and back at the ale-house when the little cavalcade arrived, and he shifted back in his seat when he realised what sort of men they were. Baldwin was clearly a knight, and he strode to a table and sat at it with the calm self-assurance of those who are used to command. At his side Huward saw the cleric, and the sight of another churchman made his mood darken and his belly churn like a butter barrel.

It was not only the fact of Roger Scut being there. There was something about the sight of the rich and powerful that made him want to puke. He drained his drinking horn and would have hurried from the place, but then he saw that two guards stood near the door like statues, one, to his eye, looking like a youthful rake, while the other looked as grim and forbidding as the Gather-Reeve when his piles were playing him up.

The sight of them made him walk to the buttery and demand another jug of ale. He carried it back to his table, his ears straining to catch any words he might, but all he caught was the name 'Sir Baldwin'. The fact that the fellow was a knight was little comfort. All knew what knights were capable of. With one daughter hideously killed, he was suspicious of any strangers in his vill, any man who might take it into his mind to attack Flora. She was his only daughter now, and he would die rather than see any harm come to her. He was so proud of his daughters that it hurt, it actually hurt. Even now, just the thought of his little Flora suffering pain made him draw in his breath. There was a sharp sensation in his breast, and the hairs prickled on his scalp. It was as though a ghost had blown a breath from the grave all down his spine, and he shuddered.

It was that which kept him in the ale-house, the idea that the slim, good-looking guard at the door might think of attacking Flora. Perhaps he was being unreasonable, but he didn't care. The man looked the sort of arrogant brute who'd not think twice about taking a girl just because he took a fancy to her, or because the ale had been flowing too well that night.

His friend looked even worse. The way the man scowled silently about the room made Huward certain that he was dangerous, a wild animal. If he decided to grab at Flora, he'd treat her no better than a dog.

Huward suddenly wondered whether there were any more of these men. They looked so dreadful, he wanted to know where his wife and daughter were. Gilda should be at the mill, and Flora should be back at home . . . but she might be out still; she could even be talking to another man-at-arms, not realising what sort of a desperate bastard he was! In fact, even now she might be opening her mouth in shock as he shoved her to the ground and . . .

In another moment he would have stood and run from the room, knocking Thomas and Godwen aside, but then he saw that Baldwin was peering at him while Piers spoke.

It was odd, but in that moment, somehow Huward felt that his life was changing. He couldn't guess how, but the man's face told him that no matter what else happened, he had a friend. The stranger knight stood and walked over to him, leaving Piers and Roger Scut at the other table. As Baldwin motioned to the alewife to fetch more ale for Huward, the miller saw that the priest was leaving the room, his nose in the air, and the absence made him feel a little better.

'Friend, I am called Sir Baldwin de Furnshill, and I would be grateful if I could speak to you for a moment.'

'Why, sir?' Huward grunted.

The knight was a curious-looking fellow. He was well-dressed, and appeared quite wealthy, but there was a kind of shabbiness about him, as though he had been given riches, but money couldn't change him. His face spoke of great sadness and loss, and sympathy for Huward, but Huward could only dimly appreciate that. For the moment, all he could see was Sir Baldwin's social position – one which was so far above his own that he must shout to be heard. Yet when his eyes rose and met Baldwin's own, he saw that there was something else, too. A strong desire for justice burned in them.

'I want to make sure that your daughter's killer is found and pays for this murder,' Baldwin said.

Chapter Fifteen

Sampson waited while they all stood talking. Talking, talking, talking! And here was poor Sampson, his tummy rumbling, hungry as a hound, and the alms dish out by the gate where he couldn't get to it without walking past the great men on their horses.

Ah! At last! They're going. As the grim little party turned away and rode towards the inn, Sampson sighed with relief. His tum needed filling. That was what. He'd get there, to the dish, now. That'd be good. Find some meat, some bread.

It was good the new lord gave away food. The Church ordered one tenth. Sampson was grateful for anything. He hurried to the bowl, took up the nearest hunk of brown bread soaked in thick, greasy, cold gravy, and rammed it into his mouth, turning and sinking to the ground, his back resting against the wall.

Then the crust was kicked from his hand, and Sampson squeaked in fear, raising his hands to protect his face as he recognised Esmon.

'So, boy, you thought you'd take food?'

Sampson cringed in fear, and Esmon curled his lip in disdain. This poor cretin was little more than a dog. No brain at all – and yet he might be useful.

The sight of a Keeper of the King's Peace at his gate had seriously alarmed him. At first, he had thought that he was to be accused of the robbery; luckily Sir Ralph hadn't been dumb enough to let the Keeper into the castle, because he might have heard one of the carters complaining of the robbery if he had; however, Sir Baldwin would certainly be told of the body. Esmon was suddenly convinced that it would be foolish to let him find Wylkyn's corpse. A man couldn't be accused of murder when there was no body. If only he'd removed it as soon as he'd killed

Wylkyn, but the red mist of rage had smothered him, and being rational and sensible was impossible. At least no one had seen Wylkyn die. It was only now that he realised how stupid he had been. Not that he regretted his actions. No. Wylkyn had to be killed. It was his potions that killed Sir Richard, and a murderer deserved his punishment.

Sampson was wailing now, reaching for the bowl as though expecting to see it kicked away and all its contents spilled into the dirt. ' 'Tis for me! 'Tis why it's put out!'

'It's not for lazy and stupid people. I think I'd better stop it getting put out. You don't need our food, you need work, that's all.'

'Can't! No one hires me. No money!'

'Everyone needs work, boy. I tell you what – I'll give you a job. Then you can earn your food, can't you?' Esmon said.

It didn't take long to explain. Esmon soon finished, and then the unhappy Sampson went scurrying off like a cur with his tail between his legs after a good whipping. The sight brought a smile to Esmon's face, and he resisted the temptation of hurling a stone after the fool.

With a little luck, Sampson would take away the evidence, and then Esmon would feel more secure. And if Sampson failed – why, he would be bound to leave marks that would lead to his own arrest! Esmon wandered off grinning with self-satisfaction at the thought.

They had missed their road, and Simon was still swearing as they headed westwards out of the Stannary town of Chagford; they had gone at least two leagues out of their way.

'Don't see why we need to go to Gidleigh anyway,' said his servant Hugh.

Simon bit back the curse that sprang to his lips. 'Because I am Stannary Bailiff, and I am responsible if a miner's robbed or attacked, Hugh. It's that easy.'

Hugh was annoyed at being called away from the house at Lydford. He had been hoping to take a weekend off to go and visit his wife, but Simon had demanded that he should come to Gidleigh too, and he was determined that his master should know how dissatisfied he was.

Simon had been like a wolf with a sore tooth ever since he'd been promoted to the job in Dartmouth, but that wasn't Hugh's fault. All Hugh craved was a stable life, no more wandering about the place, like he'd had to do when he was a shepherd. It was a source of pride to him that he'd managed to catch Simon's eye and get work with him, early on as a general servant but gradually becoming a close friend as well. He knew Simon laughed about him, but he also knew that Simon looked on him as an ally and associate. It was that which tore at him: his divided loyalty.

Hugh had a wife now, Constance, who lived north, towards Iddesleigh. Constance was calm, quiet, and a little reserved because her child, whom she had named Hugh, was not Hugh's son, but that didn't affect Hugh's love for the boy and his adoration of Constance. To him, she was the ideal woman. As gentle and kind as Holy Mother Mary herself, but bright and bubbling with laughter. She had a reputation for midwifery in the vill already because she had been trained as a nurse, and all in the area had grown to love and respect her. Hugh travelled to see her when he got the chance, whenever Simon gave him an afternoon of freedom, and to his credit, Simon sent him as often as he might up to Hatherleigh. Their master, the Abbot Robert, owned the fair there, so there were always opportunities to make use of a messenger.

It wouldn't be so easy to invent reasons to travel there once Simon was moved to Dartmouth, though, Hugh thought. That was far from anywhere, that was. Miserable journey every time he wanted to see Constance, and it'd be longer between each trip. He'd be lucky to see young Hugh at all.

Thoughts like these kept circulating in his mind, causing depression. And Hugh was not alone. He was all too aware that his friend and ally in Simon's household, young Edith, was as set against the move as he was himself. It was her opinion that Simon should give up the post, that he should become something else –

maybe a farmer. There were worse jobs, she had said to Hugh.

Worse maybe, but few that offered such opportunities for suffering the most bitter extremes of weather, to Hugh's way of thinking. He'd lived that life, he'd been out in all weathers, he'd led the plough teams of oxen up and down the fields, covering miles each day, he'd got soaked and frozen, he'd got cut and stabbed by bushes while hedging, and he'd seen friends die: one man kicked in the head while wrestling a young calf to the ground, another squeezed against a wall by a dull-witted ox until his entire chest cracked with a rippling noise like tearing cloth. It wasn't the sort of life Hugh was keen to return to, not while there was a warm indoor room with a roaring fire, and plenty of ale and wine to be drunk. But it would be hard, very hard, to go so far away. At least being a merchant was safer, he thought, but he wasn't convinced that Simon would be able to 'merchant' for a living.

'It's not as though you have to worry about the job much longer,' Hugh grunted.

'While it's my job, I'll do it as best I can,' the Bailiff said sternly.

Osbert rode a short distance behind them. 'It's not far now, Sir Bailiff.'

'It would have been a damned sight quicker if you'd not got us lost!' Simon snapped.

Osbert ducked his head as though Simon had aimed a physical missile at him. He had tried to warn the Bailiff against using that route, but Simon had insisted upon it. The path had become a quagmire, and there was the risk that a new mire had opened up there. If that was so, they could have ridden to their deaths. As it was, they were forced to turn back and take the longer way east to Chagford because they had already passed so far from the other track that would have taken them to Scorhill and thence to Gidleigh. However, Osbert wasn't going to mention that at this particular moment.

The Bailiff had looked grim all the way, riding stiffly as though he was expecting a barbed comment at any moment from his

servant, who in turn had looked like he'd just bitten into a crab-
apple. Osbert had taken the safest approach, leaving them to their
bickering, like a long-wedded husband and wife, but it was
difficult and made for a tense journey. At least the rain had held
off, he thought wearily.

'What do you know of the dead man?' Simon suddenly shot out.

Osbert gulped. 'Wylkyn? He was steward to Sir Richard.
Looked after his master with potions and powders to cure his
aches and pains. He left when Sir Richard died. Went to live with
his brother the miner.'

'What's his brother's name?'

'John of Chagford.'

'I know him,' said Simon, who had an encyclopedic knowledge
of miners on the moors. 'Why would Wylkyn have gone up there
after a relaxing life in a warm castle?'

'Like I said, he went as soon as Sir Richard died,' Osbert said
evasively.

'Not when Sir Ralph took over?' Simon asked.

'It was the same thing. Sir Ralph was here with his son when
Sir Richard died.'

They were at the bottom of the hill, close by Chagford Bridge,
when he saw the old hermit, and Osbert groaned, hurriedly making
the sign of the cross.

'Masters, Godspeed!' Surval called.

Osbert kept his eyes averted, but Surval seemed to take an
especial pleasure in speaking directly to him. 'Come, Os, why the
long face? Surely you're not fearful that men such as this great
Bailiff might accuse you of anything?'

Although he tried to ignore Surval, Osbert felt his face colouring, and it was a relief to hear the Bailiff speak and take Surval's
attention from him.

'You call me Bailiff? How do you know my position?'

'There are no secrets here, my Lord. Surval the hermit knows
people to speak to, and when a friend like Os is sent away to act
the messenger, calling on an important Bailiff to come and inspect
a corpse which might be that of a dead miner, it's easy to guess

who might be with him when he returns. I don't think,' he added, gazing at Hugh from beneath his lowered brows, 'that this man would be a Bailiff, somehow.'

Simon chuckled at that, especially when he saw Hugh's glowering mien. 'Come, then, master. Have a coin for your words, and may my thanks speed you.'

Surval caught the coin with a swift hand, and then glanced back at Simon as though daring him to mention it. Simon smiled, slightly bemused at the sight. A hermit with such quick reflexes was rare. Most were worn down with their way of life, if they were genuine, because a poor diet and harsh living conditions meant that they were always near to starvation while their concentration on prayer and God's will meant that all too often they could forget to throw on a robe.

'Hermit, you have a good position here,' he said.

'Thank you, Master. I keep it as clean as I can. There's no point in squalor for squalor's sake.'

Simon shot a look at him. It seemed that the hermit was unaware of the irony of his words. Simon had meant the location of his place right beside the bridge, where he was sure to win plenty of alms from travellers, for it was the only bridge for miles over the river and almost all must cross at this point, but looking at the hermit's face, or what was visible above the bushy mass of his beard, Simon was sure that Surval was proud of the hovel in which he lived.

It was constructed of stone. That much was obvious, because where the limewashed daub had flaked and fallen away, the rocks were plainly visible. The fact that it was thatched was easy enough to guess at, because where the thick green felt of the mossy covering had broken apart, and where the ivy hadn't yet colonised, Simon was almost sure he could see signs of rotting straw. It facilitated egress for smoke from his fire, but Simon was convinced that this filthy place must be chill and unwelcoming at the best of times. At least it was in keeping with the woods all about here, green and grey like the trees, and so ramshackle and dilapidated, it could be missed by a traveller in a hurry.

All created the impression of a genuine holy man who lived without consideration for his own wants; indeed, a man who was far removed from earthly desires and troubles. Like other hermits, he would labour to God's praise, mending the bridge when it failed, working with the rocks and stones to repair all damage. It was his life's work, keeping the bridge operating, because all men must use bridges; preserving a bridge was good for all in the vill. Especially here, where it was the main route from the north to reach the important little town of Chagford with its busy market.

There were many hermits infesting the country, Simon reminded himself as they rode up the steep hill towards Murchington and Gidleigh beyond. Some, of course, were charlatans, masquerading as religious men in a bid to conceal their felonious pasts.

'Osbert, you were quiet enough in his presence. Why?'

'I don't trust him. When Sir Richard was alive, he didn't either. Said Surval was a mad escaped felon who shouldn't be here, and that one day soon he'd evict him, but then he died.'

Simon considered this for a while, and then decided that he would have to ask about this man and see what sort of hermit he was: genuine or fake.

Baldwin was impressed by Huward. There was a kindness in his face, which was clouded by the knowledge of the terrible fate of his daughter, but it was still there. He looked like a clear-thinking man, an honourable, upright sort who would work diligently for his master without complaint, although his present state of distress was obvious; all the time, while Baldwin spoke to him, he was fiddling with his drinking horn, a cheap pot of badly glazed earthenware, chipping with his thumbnail at a piece of encrusted dirt on the rim.

'I am sorry about your daughter,' Baldwin said.

'I just want justice – but I won't get it, will I? He'll get sent to some court for priests and that's going to be that. They never pay like we do, do they? If they're churchmen, they're safe.'

He spat the last words, avoiding Baldwin's eye, and the knight considered before continuing.

'The Coroner held his inquest?'

'Yes. Her neck was broken. Coroner reckoned the weapon might have been a stick and charged us a shilling for it. Wanted to take all the priest's stuff, too.'

Baldwin knew that the Coroner would have taken an estimate of the priest's worldly value so that the amount the King could expect would be known. An outlaw lost all his possessions – they were forfeit to the Crown – so one of the Coroner's more important jobs was to assess the value of an outlaw's worth so that it could be recouped from the vill in which he had lived.

'Neck broken,' he mused. It didn't tie up with what Mark had said about striking Mary and nothing else, but many a murderer was a committed liar. 'What did the Coroner learn about the death of your daughter?'

Huward drank deeply, then put his hands over his face a moment. When he pulled them down again, Baldwin saw that his eyes were glistening with unshed tears. 'Elias heard it, most of it. Heard my little Mary, he did, heard a woman's voice, then a slap, but thinking it was just a lovers' tiff, he turned his plough and went back the other way. When he returned, there was nothing more to hear. Later, when he was done, he walked down the lane and found her body.'

'He could see them from the field?' Baldwin asked. 'Through the hedge, you mean?'

'No, the lane's very low there, and the hedges are overgrown. It was just voices.'

Baldwin narrowed his eyes. 'But if a man is ploughing, it must be difficult to hear voices, surely? The noise of the blade cutting through soil, the hooves of the oxen, the calls and whistling of the boy leading them – how could he have heard so clearly?'

'You'd have to ask him. I don't know.'

'I shall want to see this field. Who was leading the ox team?'

'My lad, Ben. He often works with old Elias.'

'Did anyone else see or hear anything?'

'That fool Sampson said he heard them talk about killing her baby, then he heard a punch when Mark got angry, then a sound of vomiting, and then he ran away. He reckons Mark made for the chapel, but he must have been wrong.'

'Why?'

'Because that was the wrong way. Unless he went there to fetch food and clothes, then bolted.'

'I must speak to this Sampson,' Baldwin muttered. 'So it comes to this: your daughter's and the priest's voices were heard, but no one actually saw him hit her, let alone break her neck?'

'They didn't need to, did they? She was dead.'

Baldwin was about to speak, when there came a great clamour from the doorway. He spun around in time to see Godwen staggering backwards, a hand clutching his belly, and Thomas staring at him, then gazing at the man in the doorway with admiration bordering on adoration.

The sight made Baldwin sigh. 'Simon, I *asked* them to keep people out. There was no need for that.'

Roger Scut waited with his toes tapping on the ground while the ostler fetched and saddled a pony for him. He already had some directions, but he made sure with the ostler just to be safe and then set off for the chapel.

It was a fine afternoon, albeit chilly, and he pulled his cloak about his breast to shield himself from the worst of the breeze, not that it stopped the whole of the icy blast. Some seemed to dive down to his breast like a fish. That was what it felt like, a dead fish slipping down between his tunic and his throat, cold as death itself. The reflection made him shiver.

The land was pretty, if you liked the wild. It certainly wasn't cultivated like the fields and gardens about Exeter, but then he had always been told that Exeter was the edge of the civilised world. Other monks spoke with horror in their voices of the desolate lands further west. They implied that the sole place of any interest was Tavistock Abbey, and beyond that institution there was nothing of any merit whatever. The people were rough, untutored, and good only for manual labour.

In his humble opinion, the folk around here looked the same.

They would be easy enough to lead. No doubt a priest like himself with a good understanding of people would be able to give them some direction. He would get them to do his bidding, and quickly find another priest to take over the duties here, and then he would live on the money which was sure to come in. A portion would go to his parson, but the rest he could pocket. That was the way for a man to make some money. Get someone else to do the work, while you yourself rested.

The roads were confusing, but before too long Roger had to ford a stream, then climb a hill before wandering along on the flat. When the roadway began to drop, he turned left, then forked right through trees.

Yes, it was good land, if uncultivated. The trees grew tall and strong, the soil looked dark but fruitful to his untrained eye, and he was sure that with some effort on the part of the locals, this place could be turned into a small Garden of Eden. All it took was a little labour, and there must be enough hairy-arsed workers down here. He would have to speak to the local lord and point out that he was failing in his duties to his local priest by not allowing the villeins enough time to work on the chapel's lands.

He had almost reached the little brook when he recalled that the ostler had said, grinning, that he should have reached the chapel before he got thus far. There was nothing to see here, though. All he could discern was the faintly sweet odour of burning, as though someone had been coppicing recently and had burned some spare twigs to warm himself.

Looking back to his left, to the north, he pursed his lips. Either that boy at the ale-house was a fool, or . . .

As he caught sight of the ruins, his mouth fell open with stunned despair. 'My God!'

'A sad sight, eh, Priest?'

Roger Scut saw a tall figure at the door whom he recognised from the castle. 'Master Esmon?'

'Yes. Look at this! The bastards could have left it, couldn't they?' he said, kicking a blackened door-timber from his path and standing at the open entrance, hands on his hips as he glared inside. 'What a shit-hole!'

'Who was responsible?' Roger Scut said, hurriedly dropping from his mount and going to the door. The sight that met his eyes made him groan aloud. His dreams had shattered like glass. All his hopes of creating a small area of lucrative peace here in this pretty valley had been broken and now seemed to lie at his feet in the mess of soot and ruined wood.

'Some hot-head from the vill. If I find out who it was, he'll regret his actions!' Esmon said with a quietness that was more menacing than a bellow.

'Perhaps it can be salvaged?'

'Look at the place!'

Roger felt his shoulders droop. 'I was hoping . . . Ah, well. God's wonders can be curious on first sight.'

'You were wanting this place for yourself?' Esmon shot out suddenly. 'I see. And now you have nothing.'

'Nonsense! I came here to prevent that lad from being murdered illegally,' Roger said, but as he spoke, his eyes went again to the ruin of the church's interior.

'Perhaps we could see a new chapel built. A place suitable for a man of your calibre, Priest.'

Roger Scut faced him. There was a light in Esmon's eye that Roger wasn't sure he liked. 'What does that mean?'

'You have travelled far, Priest. Come with me to the castle and share a quart of wine. Perhaps we have some interests in common!'

Smiling, Esmon returned to his mount. This, he reflected, was indeed good fortune. The priest was with the Keeper's party. Provided Esmon could remain on friendly terms with him, Roger Scut could become a most useful informant.

Looking at him, seeing the despair on his face, Esmon was sure that Scut had wanted to acquire this chapel for himself.

'And then we can discuss rebuilding the chapel,' he said as he swung his leg over the saddle.

Chapter Sixteen

'How was I to know?' Simon grumbled. 'I try to walk into an ale-house, and some scrawny churl tells me to go and service my mother: what would you expect me to do? I only tapped him, anyway.'

Baldwin had finished with Huward and sent him on his way with Piers, and now he and Simon sat at a bench near the buttery. Godwen and Thomas sat at opposite ends of another bench, Godwen glaring at Simon, Thomas smiling openly for the first time in Baldwin's memory, a fact which did not ease Baldwin's mood.

'I've apologised already,' Simon added pointedly.

'God's cods – just look at them! They hate each other, and there is nothing I can do about it. Undercurrents, Simon. There are undercurrents in Crediton, but nothing to compare with this place: the knight and his son; the girl's father . . .' He shook his head, unsettled.

Simon was eyeing Godwen. 'What's their problem?'

'A family argument which goes back deep into the mists of antiquity. Perhaps Godwen's grandfather's father once took an apple from Thomas's grandfather's father's orchard. Who can tell what motivates such disputes?'

'Come, then, tell me what you know of this murder.'

'The girl had her neck broken and . . .'

'No, the Coroner's already seen to *her*. I want to know about the miner.'

Baldwin blinked. 'I know nothing of this. I am here to protect the priest. Did you not receive my message?'

'Yes, but I couldn't drop everything for that. It was only when I heard that a miner had been attacked that I realised I must come.'

'What miner?'

'A fellow called Wylkyn,' Simon said and told Baldwin what he had heard from Osbert. He glanced at the unshuttered window and pulled a face. 'I should go now and see the body, but I've been on horseback all day, and I won't be climbing back into the saddle again unless I have no choice.'

'I do not suggest that you do,' Baldwin chuckled.

'So you are here to learn what you can about this girl? Why?' Simon asked. 'The Coroner must have seen to her already.'

'He has, but I am reluctant to see justice imposed without thought on the priest. He is an unlikely murderer.'

'Many are,' Simon objected.

'Very true! And yet I find it hard to imagine this man in particular murdering a girl. It is not his nature, I believe.'

'So you will be tied up with that, rather than aiding me with my dead miner?'

'It is curious that there should be two such deaths so close together,' Baldwin mused. 'Perhaps they are connected in some manner?'

'Perhaps. And perhaps they aren't.' Simon laughed. 'Hugh! What do you reckon?'

'Me? There's not much I wouldn't put past a priest.'

'There you are, Baldwin. The man gets married, and that's now his opinion on priests!' His expression became quizzical. 'Are you serious? You really think that the lad might be innocent of the murder?'

'I have no idea,' Baldwin admitted, 'but I do not like the look of Sir Ralph or his son.'

There was no denying it. About the castle there had hung a foul atmosphere. The man-at-arms had carried it about him like a banner, and then the way that Baldwin and the others were treated was alarming in its own right. Being sent to find an inn without even the offer of a cup of wine like a beggar . . .

'Ach! That is for tomorrow. Come! Tell me about Meg and the children.'

* * *

It was just as dark was settling over the land that horses arrived at the inn's yard. Soon there was shouting, then a scurrying of feet, and marching boots approached through the screens.

'I'm glad to find you awake still. I had thought you might be abed,' Sir Ralph said, glancing about him with the distaste plain on his face as he entered with Esmon. Brian and another man lounged by the door, watching the people in the room with attentive insolence. The landlord was clearing away dishes and platters. 'You have eaten?'

'Oh, but yes, I thank you,' Baldwin said with effusive sarcasm. 'The host here is most welcoming and attentive.'

Esmon glanced about the room. His eyes settled on Roger Scut sitting in a corner, a short way from this knight. Good. Roger had eaten with him at the castle, and afterwards Esmon and he had both agreed that it was probably better that their discussion should not become common knowledge until they were ready for it.

Sir Ralph waved at the innkeeper, who scuttled over anxiously to take his order for wine, then hurried away like a harvest mouse on an urgent mission for a farm cat, desperate to give no possible reason for complaint.

'I hadn't realised my own board was so meagre,' Sir Ralph said, pointedly staring at the plates before Roger Scut. 'You appeared to eat your fill in my hall.'

'I merely desired a light meal to settle my stomach,' Scut protested. 'Your food was excellent, my Lord.'

'You have already eaten?' Baldwin exclaimed. To his mind, gluttony was one of the worst of the sins.

'Perhaps my food was not to his taste. I believe it could be thought too rich,' Sir Ralph said. Looking up, he saw that Baldwin was considering him as he sat a short distance from the table. Sir Baldwin, he saw, glanced at the gap between Sir Ralph's lap and the table. Distance was important. Any knight who was in a situation in which there could be danger always left a short space between himself and the table, if only to make sure of room to draw a sword.

Sir Baldwin was obviously a fighter. He knew the signs that

showed another man was on his mettle; and was also proud. Sir Ralph was sure of that. His words that afternoon had confirmed that fact. No mere rural man-at-arms with a long lineage and limited funds, Sir Baldwin saw himself as an important magnate. It was good that he knew Sir Ralph was allied with the Despensers. It didn't mean Sir Ralph was entirely above the law, but it showed that in this vill he could rule with impunity. He chose to do so with an iron will, and the innkeeper's speed was proof of that. Seeing the man respond like this to his Lord would demonstrate to Baldwin the sort of power Sir Ralph possessed here.

He could have sighed. None of it mattered now. Not since Mary's death. Mary! Even the thought of her was enough to bring a sob to his breast. No, he mustn't submit to his misery. He must set aside all thoughts of grief and get on with his job here, talking to this dunderhead knight who had such a high opinion of himself.

There were rumours about Sir Baldwin. Sir Ralph had heard of him before. Tales of his intelligence abounded, most of them implying that Sir Baldwin was a cross between a saint and an alchemist who possessed the power to divine a man's soul. It was enough to make Sir Ralph nervous. He had no wish to lose his son.

Esmon was a fool! Why get that cretin Sampson involved? His son had been absorbed on their ride here, tied up with his thoughts. It took some prodding for Sir Ralph to get him to admit what he had done, as though he had no respect for his father, and when Sir Ralph had heard his story, that he had told Sampson to move the body, the knight had almost knocked him from his horse for his stupidity. What good moving Wylkyn would do was beyond Sir Ralph: the body might as well have lain there. Moving it now would only attract still more interest. At least Wylkyn was dead now, that was the main thing; he had been punished for his crime.

Sir Ralph felt heavy and tired, as though he had run a long race only to lose. Esmon had done the right thing in killing Wylkyn. They had agreed on that an age ago. But this action was different. It would have been better to use one of his own men. Esmon explained that this way, if someone was suspected, the finger would likely point to Sampson. He would be certain to make a mistake, and then people would assume he was the killer, not Esmon. At least Esmon was certain that no one had seen him kill Wylkyn, and without a body, he should remain safe.

It was worrying, though, that his son only admitted what he had done when pressed. Sir Ralph was suddenly struck with the thought that Esmon didn't trust him any more. It was no surprise; since Mary's death, he felt as though he was walking in a continuing dream. Still, he must impose his will on Esmon, he thought. If only he could simply leave and go to his bed, he thought distractedly. He was so tired.

The innkeeper was back. Sir Ralph stopped the man before he could pour wine into a cup, peered into it himself, winced, and then shrugged. It was hardly worth worrying about a little dirt in the cup, when he was exposing himself to the filth in this tavern. It was well known that bad air could kill a man, and this place must have some of the worst in the vill.

Concentrate! He sipped at his wine, watching Sir Baldwin coolly, feeling a little like a dog preparing to enter the ring to fight another. There was some shrewdness there in Sir Baldwin's eyes, and he certainly held himself like a knight who practised with his weapons. His belly was quite flat, he bore no second chin, and his hands moved with that calm precision that only efficient martial artists displayed. Yes, Sir Baldwin would be an efficient killer, Sir Ralph reckoned. A worthy foe. Esmon could sense it too; Sir Ralph could feel his tension where he stood behind Sir Ralph watching and listening.

The others were nothing. There was the grim-faced man whom Baldwin introduced as the Bailiff of Lydford, a Stannary official, and next to him a servant, while there were two scruffy peasants with weapons as well; watchmen, no doubt, sent to watch over the priest. Mark would hardly need more to guard him. The feeble-minded cretin was practically in his grave already. Before long he would be, if Sir Ralph had his way.

Sir Baldwin had not commented, and now Sir Ralph spoke again.

'I desired to apologise to you for my hurry when you arrived at my door, Sir Baldwin. I should have come here with you to make sure that you found the place. I hope you do not mind that I could not drop everything at the moment you turned up?'

'Not at all.'

'I trust you found your way here without mishap?'

'Yes, I thank you. It is an easy road, and Simon and I have travelled this way often enough before.'

'Good. Then I hope you will be able to find your way home again before long.'

'Not very soon, though,' Simon interrupted. His face was partly shadowed, giving him an evil, demonic look. 'We have these deaths to hear about first.'

'Deaths?' Sir Ralph enquired impassively.

It was the other knight who answered. 'You have had the Coroner here about the girl, I understand?'

'He held his inquest and had his records written down, but there was little need. Mark had bolted, so he was obviously the culprit. We had raised the Hue and Cry, so that was really that.'

'The day that the girl died – who was the First Finder?'

'An older peasant called Elias.'

'But she had been dead some time when he found her?'

'I believe so.'

'Was there anyone else up that road on that day?' Simon asked.

'I wouldn't know,' Sir Ralph said stiffly. 'You should ask Elias and see what he thinks.'

'We will,' Simon promised him.

'You have not heard that anyone else travelled that road who saw her – either when she was alive, or when she had died?' Baldwin pressed.

'If someone had, wouldn't they have reported the find as First Finder?'

Baldwin smiled without speaking, but Simon leaned on an elbow and picked at a tooth. 'Did someone else?'

'Sampson came up later and reported that she was dead, but he probably couldn't understand that someone had already found her. He's the local fool, I'm afraid. His brains were missing from birth, and he's a figure of ridicule now. He lives out near the moors, if you want to speak to him. Many folks here will be able to show you where, if you wish.'

'But you don't think we'd achieve much by talking to him,' Simon stated.

'If there was anything to be learned, I am sure that the Coroner would have learned it.'

'Where were you on the day that the girl died?' Baldwin asked.

'Me? I was out hunting, and later, at home again, I heard about this girl's murder. I instantly called up a small posse and rode off after that damned priest.'

'Where did you go hunting?'

'Around the vill. I didn't go over the Chase of Dartmoor, if that's what you mean,' Sir Ralph added drily. 'I wouldn't trespass on the King's lands like that. His venison is safe here.'

'You believe so? Where was your son on the day this girl died?'

Sir Ralph stiffened a fraction. This was the question he had feared. 'Esmon was with me. I rode back with him from the hunt. He didn't rush away to commit murder, I assure you!'

Simon glanced at Esmon. 'You confirm that?'

'We were together, yes.'

'What about the day that the miner got himself killed? Where were you then?'

Sir Ralph interrupted. 'Is this an inquest? I only ask, because I find your questions are growing impertinent, Bailiff.'

Baldwin shot a look at Simon, then continued for him, 'But you will understand, Sir Ralph, that we have a duty to look into this man's death. Do you know anything about it?'

Sir Ralph looked from Simon to Baldwin. 'No.'

Simon looked at Esmon, who shrugged.

'Well? A man died, did he? What of it? I saw many men die during the wars.'

'Were you on the moors when he died?'

'It is true enough that my son spoke with some merchants who were disrespectful and refused to pay his legitimate tolls. That is all, though. I am sure no man was killed,' Sir Ralph said.

'The body of a man called Wylkyn lies up on the moors,' Simon grated. 'That is why I was called here.'

'Does it affect us?' Sir Ralph asked, feigning disinterest.

'I don't know,' Simon said suavely. 'Perhaps if you let your son answer, I'll find out!'

'Wylkyn used to be steward to the castle, to Sir Richard Prouse,' Baldwin said.

'He wasn't when I took over the castle.'

'No, he left as soon as Sir Richard died, I was told,' Simon said. Sir Ralph shrugged.

'It seems odd that he should bolt from the place as you take the castle, and then appear dead on the moors.'

'Ah, well. People are superstitious on the moors. Perhaps there was an argument, and a passerby thought that murder had been done? I am sure you will find that there's no body up there,' Sir Ralph chuckled.

He glanced at Sir Baldwin, and the two men locked eyes for some moments. It didn't matter. Sir Ralph knew he was speaking the truth.

Shivering, his teeth chattering, Mark spent a terrible evening in the cell. It was a dank, foul-smelling hole deep underneath a stable, with rock-lined walls that dripped steadily with water and with liquid excrement and urine from the horses above. Whether it was intended that the gutter should run into this little sewer, he couldn't tell, nor did he care. He daren't lie in the half-inch or so of moisture, so he must stand. That was all he knew.

The cold was deadly. He slapped his hands against his shoulders, trying to invigorate them, but it did no good. It was as though they were already turned to ice. Hitting them hurt his palms; it was like thumping slabs of wood.

There was no light. That was shut out by the solid trap door above his head. When he had been dropped in here, he had caught a fleeting glimpse of his cell: small, square and foul. Less than six feet wide and broad, and maybe seven deep. He huddled in a corner, listening to laughter and shouting above his head, and suddenly tears sprang forth. All he wanted was human contact, the companionship that a man needed, but he could hope for nothing. He wanted to pray as well, but couldn't. The words wouldn't come; the idea of offering a prayer to God from this hole was somehow disrespectful.

When he heard vague splashing at the far end of the cell he told himself that it was the dripping of water from above, perhaps a horse had defecated, and not the pattering of tiny paws. It was all too easy to imagine ranks of rats watching him, waiting for him to lie down and sleep so that they could attack him. If he could have found a stone or pebble, he would have hurled it, but there was nothing that he could feel with his feet in the filth, not that his feet would necessarily have detected anything, so cold were they.

A shudder ran through his frame and he had to control an urge to sob. He felt desolate, lonely and forlorn, and fear was making his bowels loosen. Terrible to think that he could beshit himself through terror. That was not something he'd have thought of when he was sent here, that he'd be in such fear of his life that he could soil himself.

He had hoped that the friendly cleric, Roger Scut, who had vowed to protect Mark from all enemies and persuaded that Keeper, Sir Baldwin, to come back with them, might have kept up a conversation with him on the ride back here, but of course it wasn't fair to expect that. Roger was supposed to be preventing a miscarriage of justice, making sure that Mark was saved from the rigours of the local court and instead was appealed before the Bishop's own, thus he had maintained a dignified silence.

God, but it was so cold. All the long hours of his escape, he had never once had the chance to warm himself, and since capture, he had been able to spend only a few moments in front of the fire in the inn at Crediton before they whisked him away on the long ride back here. Even when they had been forced to resort to an ale-house because the river was in spate after the rains, they had seated Mark near the door, far from the fireside. He was a suspected felon: he didn't deserve comforts.

There was a rattling and when he looked up, a few stray pieces of damp stuff fell from the trap door and into his face. Coughing with revulsion, spitting bits of straw, he looked up in time to see that a ladder was being lowered and his heart suddenly felt as though it might burst with joy. Someone was going to let him out of here! Someone had taken pity on him! He was about to be saved and given food, drink, a place near a fire! Oh, my God! Flames, heat, warmth! He couldn't stop the loud sobs that racked his breast, and he grabbed at the ladder, clambering up it as quickly as his frozen fingers and toes would permit.

At the top, he was already babbling his thanks when he was blinded by the light from a torch. Covering his face, he squinted about him. 'My Lord, I am so thankful . . . That place . . . Might I beg a little warmed wine? My mouth . . . I am so famished . . .'

Without warning, a fist slammed into his kidneys, and he gasped as he went down, his head striking the cobbles with a hammer blow. A boot kicked at his back, then his neck, and he curled into a ball while feet pounded into his already frail body.

'Think you're going to escape, priest? No one wants that!'

He recognised that laughing voice: Esmon, the son of Sir Ralph. There was yet another kick at his arse, catching his cods and making him whimper.

'You thought you were going to get away, didn't you, priest? Thought you'd get to Exeter. Perhaps you thought you'd be safe if you brought your friends here, that you'd be allowed to get to the Bishop's palace if they spoke for you in court? Well, we aren't having that, little priest. You aren't going anywhere. You will die right here, whether today or tomorrow, I don't care, but you're dying here.'

Only one glimpse did he catch of the men. There, at the front of them, watching while Esmon beat him, Mark saw Sir Ralph, his face twisted with hatred.

'Father,' Mark said, but no one listened, and no one cared as he screamed, cradling his head in his arms as the boots and fists hammered into his soft and unprotected body.

Least of all Sir Ralph.

Chapter Seventeen

Baldwin and Simon were up early the next morning, demanding that Piers come and take them to Wylkyn's body. To Hugh's disgust, he was ordered to leave his warm bench and follow his master as soon as Piers arrived, while Baldwin's two watchmen were permitted to remain in the tavern's cosy hall. They asked Piers to join them while they completed their breakfast, and he sat a short way from the table. Roger Scut was with them, eating quietly and watching them all suspiciously. He was still bitter that the chapel had been fired.

'You want some meat or bread?' Baldwin enquired.

'No, thank you, Sir Baldwin,' Piers said. 'I've eaten already.'

'Some of us eat even when we've already taken our meals,' Simon observed, glancing sidelong at Roger Scut.

'I have not!' Roger said, flushing angrily. 'I have only just woken!'

'You had a meal here with us last night when you had dined earlier with Sir Ralph, didn't you?' Simon accused.

Roger Scut chose the safest approach of saying nothing.

Baldwin studied him thoughtfully. 'Tell me, Scut – what was it like there in the castle?'

'A sumptuous meal,' Roger Scut said, 'served by attentive and thoughtful servants. Any who were slapdash risked a thrashing, so all were careful. I didn't like the Grace being said after eating, though. I prefer to hear it said beforehand.'

'I don't care when he says Grace, and I don't care how attractive the food was, how careful the servants, nor how elegant the surroundings,' Baldwin said irritably. 'I meant, did you see any signs which showed why we weren't allowed into the castle?'

'Nothing. The place was neat and tidy, and his carts were all moved out of the way.'

'So! You're the Reeve?' Simon asked. 'Do you know why my friend was rudely refused permission to enter the castle?'

Piers shrugged good-naturedly. 'Oh, Master, the ways of great knights are beyond me. I'm only a simple peasant.'

'Really?' Baldwin asked, one eyebrow lifted slightly.

Piers was glad to escape further questioning until they were all mounted on their ponies and ambling northwards to where Wylkyn had been found. Roger Scut remained at the inn with the two Constables, apparently sulking at the untoward allegation that he ate too much.

'You raised the Hue and Cry when this new body was found?' Baldwin asked.

'Yes, sir. We advertised the murder as soon as we could, but there's been no news yet.' Piers sighed glumly. 'We'll be fined again when this comes to the courts.'

'You still have some days,' Baldwin said reassuringly as Piers led them out on the road towards the moors. Once the Hue and Cry was raised, the vill had forty days to find the culprit before they were liable to a fine.

'Yes, sir, but I fear we won't find those responsible.'

'Did you know the dead man?'

'Vaguely. I am Reeve to Sir Ralph's Manor of Wonson, and Wylkyn was steward of Gidleigh to Sir Richard Prouse. I saw him sometimes.'

'The First Finder is honourable?' Simon enquired.

'Elias is an honest man, not a thief,' Piers stated. He recalled the expression on the old ploughman's face as they spoke about the body and about Sir Ralph. The only illegal behaviour he could be guilty of was assaulting a knight, he thought.

'Elias again? How honest is he?' Baldwin smiled. 'Honest enough to refuse money to find a body?'

'I don't know what you mean.'

'He also found the girl Mary's body, did he not?'

'I think so, yes,' Piers said loftily.

'We know what I mean, then. All First Finders have to pay a fine, do they not? And they must provide two sureties who will also lose their money if the First Finder does not appear in the court. But a man can only be fined once to make sure he goes to court. A First Finder who discovers one body may often miraculously find other dead bodies in his vill. What would be the point of someone else finding a fresh corpse if the First Finder of another would be happy to state that he found it? I wonder how much Elias was paid to find this tin miner.'

'I am sure that Elias wouldn't . . . um . . .'

Baldwin chuckled softly. 'There is no need for it to go any further. However, I shall want to speak to Elias and ask him who suggested that he should walk that way when he found the body.'

'Elias will tell you exactly the same as I have,' Piers said. He felt a little mournful. It would have been good to be able to unburden himself about Sir Ralph, about Elias seeing him just before finding Mary. Piers was also convinced that Elias knew something about this latest body as well. He had been very shifty when talking about Wylkyn. It wouldn't surprise Piers to learn that Elias had not been the First Finder.

'Remind us about this body,' Simon said.

'It's a miner called Wylkyn. I heard his brother died the other day, as well. Fell in a bog. He was travelling down here – probably on his way to Chagford for the market.'

Simon snorted and gazed about them. 'To buy, then.'

'Why do you say that?' Baldwin asked.

'He wouldn't come here laden with goods to be sold. Too much risk of being robbed. He probably had only a few pennies on him to buy some flour and a capon.'

'He wasn't alone, Master,' Piers said. 'He was one of a band.'

'What happened to them?' Baldwin asked. 'Surely the other travellers would protect him – or was it the travellers who killed him?'

Piers was torn. He would have liked to tell the truth, that Sir Ralph and his son regularly beat and robbed travellers, but that might put his own neck at risk. He would be so glad to see Esmon arrested and sent to Exeter Gaol for the next court . . . but he knew that was unlikely. Judges didn't gaol knights or the sons of knights. 'I don't know. I daresay they were so fearful that they ran straight to Chagford,' he said lamely.

'Really? Leaving one of their number dead? But when they arrive, they must surely tell the Port Reeve and call the Hue and Cry?' Baldwin said.

Simon nodded slowly, studying the Reeve. 'I think we should send a messenger to Chagford and ask for the men who reported the murder.'

Piers led the two men at a swift pace much to Hugh's annoyance, for he loathed being on horseback, down one hill and up another. It was at the top of this, a scant mile away, that Piers waved to a lad standing near a blazing fire. As the men approached, Piers could see that the boy was terrified. His hands were shaking and his face was deathly white.

'What is it, Henry?' Piers asked gruffly.

'Father, thank the Good Lord! Christ Jesus, but I was scared!'

'This is your son?' Simon asked with some surprise. The lad looked too sturdy in build for Piers, with a strong, slightly round face fringed with a thick, tousled mop of reddish-brown hair. The pallor of his face lent fire to his remarkably bright green eyes.

'Yes, Bailiff. This is my son Henry,' Piers said, ruffling his hair affectionately.

'You look as though you have had a great scare,' Baldwin said gently. 'What is the matter?'

'Sir,' Henry said, glancing at his father and seeing the nod of approval before continuing, 'it was the wind which unsettled me, and then, when it got dark, I couldn't sleep because of the dogs.'

Simon nodded understandingly. 'Wild dogs and wolves are a nuisance all over the west of Devonshire, just as they are in other parts of the country. Did any get close?'

'I don't know. I don't think so.'

Baldwin gave him an encouraging smile. 'You lit a fire, that was a good idea. It would have scared away any animals.'

'Most, yes,' Henry said, and wrapped his arms about his chest as though protecting himself from the very memory of the previous night. 'Not all. One group came close, very close. I thought I might be attacked and eaten, because they weren't worried about the fire at all.'

Hugh was all sympathy for the lad. He'd spent enough time alone on hills to know how, every so often, a particular noise could frighten you – the way the wind caught in the branches of a tree from one direction, maybe the way that a branch creaked against another. Sometimes it could be just the sound of a bird stirring in the branches, or the awareness of something that couldn't even be heard, like the grey, silent drift of an owl shearing through the air without the faintest rustle to mark his passing. That could be truly terrifying, Hugh remembered – until you realised it wasn't a ghost but a damn great bird which might soon carry off a newborn lamb.

Still, Hugh reckoned it odd that dogs would approach a living man when he was near to fire. Flames scared off most animals, in his experience.

'But you stayed close and protected the body?' Baldwin pressed him.

'Oh, yes! I wouldn't sleep, sir,' the lad said with some asperity, as though his integrity shouldn't be in doubt.

'Good. Then where is this body?' Baldwin asked.

'Over there, sir,' Henry said, pointing.

He was indicating a shallow dip before a wall that surrounded a pasture. Baldwin walked to it, peering all about him. 'Where?'

Piers shot him a look, then stared hard at his son a moment, before joining Sir Baldwin. 'He was there, Sir Knight,' he breathed. 'Some bastard's made off with his body, damn his rotten soul to hell.'

'Yes,' Baldwin said musingly. 'So, boy, it seems you weren't that close after all.'

Simon nodded. 'Aye – and it would seem that Sir Ralph was quite right, too, when he said we wouldn't find a body.'

* * *

Surval watched the flames of his fire for a long time that morning, on his knees in the dirt like a man praying, exhausted from his exertions the night before.

He had been out most of the previous night, up near the road where Wylkyn the miner had been found dead, because he wanted to go and pray over the poor soul. Wylkyn was a pleasant enough fellow, the sort of man with whom Surval would have enjoyed sharing a pot of ale in the past, especially after receiving that bird. It had been delicious.

Instead he had seen Sampson.

Usually Sampson was content to sit with Surval while the hermit cooked something for him or prayed for him. At such times Sampson would stop squirming and a light like a heavenly pleasure would seem to illuminate his features. Surval always thought that seeing Sampson sitting before his altar, the light from a candle shining on his simple wooden cross, made Sampson look like an angel. He was handsome at those times.

He hadn't wanted to talk last night, though, and there was no ease in his face. Instead he had stammered and whined, pulling at Surval's arm until the hermit had gone with him and helped him. Surval hadn't wanted to help when he realised what Sampson intended, but Sampson explained that Esmon had told him to, and then Surval agreed.

This morning, he wondered why Esmon had been so keen to have that body hidden. He could have got his own men to move the corpse if he was truly that concerned about it, but instead he had told Sampson to go up to the moors and conceal Wylkyn. Not that hiding the body was difficult. Surval knew of several ideal hiding-places, and the one he had picked was perfect, especially with a few stones piled over it to protect the body from wild animals. Henry was fast asleep before they got there, so he was no obstruction. Dunderhead! He would pay for his failure. The Coroner would demand a princely sum for failing to protect the body from theft.

Gradually the noise of hooves broke into his thoughts. He rose and strode to the door. There, at the bridge, were a number of carters, their faces pale, their manner urgent and fretful, starting at every noise. Surval stood at his door, grasping his staff and leaning upon it like the old man he felt himself to be as he recognised their fear. These were the men captured and ransomed by Esmon. 'Is there no end to their damned rapacity?' he muttered to himself.

'Old man! This is the right road to Chagford, isn't it?' The speaker was Alan, and Surval took in his thin, wispy beard and pale skin. Weakly-looking fool, he thought.

Alan sported a blued and half-closed eye, and he spoke with a slight slurring, because his jaw was bruised after being punched, but overall he felt happy enough. His worst fear, of being recognised as having escaped Sir Ralph's men before, had not materialised, and he was still alive. That was better than the alternative, he reckoned.

'Yes. You must follow the road up the hill there. Are you well, boy?'

'I'm fine. Yeah, fine. Are there any footpads between here and the town?'

'Hoy, Alan!' another man shouted out. 'We've told you there's nothing else. For God's sake don't keep whining.'

'Oh, shut up, Saul!'

'What is he complaining about?' Surval demanded grimly.

'We've been ambushed, our goods ransacked, a companion taken from us, and there's nothing we can do! Why – should we expect another attack?' Alan asked.

'Shut up, boy! Don't talk about what you can't change!' The second man was a thickset fellow with the ruddy, well-lined features of one who spent much of his life in the open air. He had a bushy beard and black, suspicious eyes, which were made malevolent by their red rims, which Surval at first thought were due to lack of sleep or torture, but then he saw the man wipe his nose on his sleeve and heard him snort loudly. It was only a cold.

'Wylkyn has gone – disappeared, for God's sake! Do you feel nothing for him?' Alan burst out.

'No. Little enough. Can I bring him back? No. Can I give him back his goods? No. So what's the point of complaining? We can't do anything about it, so that's that. Meantime, I've got a wife and children to feed. It's buggers like you make that hard. Oh!' He wiped at his nose again, muttering, 'This damned cold. Flies in summer, colds in winter. You can't do anything about either, damn them! Why did God send such pests to plague us?'

'It was murder. *Murder!* They must have killed him! And now we've been held in his castle while his men go through all our goods! Does everyone passing through here get taken and held, their goods snatched from them?'

The older carter shrugged. 'Yes. It happens. And we didn't see anyone killed, did we? Maybe he ran off and we'll find him waiting at Chagford. More to the point, if we don't get on, we'll miss the market altogether, and then we'll lose the rest of our goods. My cheeses won't last in the wet for long. So stop your bloody dawdling, boy, and get on!'

'Hermit, what would you do?' the boy Alan appealed. 'You're a man of God! In His name, what would you do?'

Surval could say nothing. The lad stared at Surval as though hoping for some sort of answer, an explanation for what had happened to him, a suggestion as to a course of action that might return that which had been stolen from him, but Surval remained silent. He bowed his head in shame, knowing that if he was a real holy man he'd be able to make this man feel better. But he had nothing to give. God knew, he'd tried often enough to help people, but how much use was he? It was bad enough trying to deal with his own shame and guilt.

The lad spat at the ground, disgusted by his rough treatment at the hands of Sir Ralph and Esmon's men and equally disgusted by the hermit's inability to offer even verbal support. He snapped his reins.

'Godspeed, hermit. Buy a capon!' the older man called. He flicked a penny at Surval, who automatically caught it and bobbed his head in thanks, then watched as the group ground past him, the axles squeaking and grumbling, the iron tires cracking over small stones and making pebbles fly.

Surval watched them go with a feeling of emptiness in his belly. He knew better than Alan or Saul what had happened to Wylkyn.

'Poor Wylkyn!' he murmured, shaking his head. It seemed obvious that Esmon and his men must have killed him, and yet there was little he dared do about it.

With that thought, he re-entered his chamber and prostrated himself before his cross, praying for the man's soul, while all the time at the forefront of his mind was the picture of Wylkyn's body lying in the shallow grave while he and Sampson set the stones all about it.

He could have gone to the Port Reeve at Chagford and told him all, but here he was, lying before his altar, begging God to forgive him. It made him feel his cowardice. If he had courage, he would go, and damn the consequences. Esmon and Sir Ralph were ruthless, they would trample any man who stood in their path. They should be restrained. Yet there were loyalties too strong to be broken, and Surval couldn't throw the two to the dogs, even if they were guilty of killing Wylkyn.

'Forgive me, Wylkyn!' he implored.

They spent as much time as possible searching along the line of the road, then up and into the moors, before Baldwin took a look at the wall and peered over it. 'Could they have taken him over here?' he wondered aloud.

'Baldwin, look at the sun!' Simon said. 'We have to get back for the court.'

Regretfully, Baldwin agreed. He went to his horse, but could not help staring over the wall again.

Simon noticed the direction of his gaze. 'The boy Henry was asleep there. If someone took the body of Wylkyn away, they'd hardly drag it right over the lad's head, would they? They must have carried it over that wall, I suppose, but where in all this shire did they hide the damn thing? Perhaps we could use dogs to find it.'

'That's possible,' Baldwin agreed, and allowed himself to be led back to the castle. Once there, he found that many of the peasants still hadn't arrived. On a whim, he turned to Piers. 'How far is it to this boy Sampson's home?'

'Not far.'

'Simon, would you mind sending Hugh to our inn and telling Thomas and Godwen to come here? I have a feeling we might need them. In the meantime, we could ride on to meet this Sampson and see if we can find out anything more about poor Mary.'

With that agreed, Piers took them down past the castle's entrance, then right, heading westwards, along an old track. After a half mile or so, he climbed from his pony and led the way in among the trees. 'There it is.'

It was a rough dwelling of the sort that charcoal-burners might construct: rough timbers with the spaces filled by mud, and a roof of thick thatch stapled in place by hazel spars.

'Sampson? You there?' Piers called.

A vacant, fearful young man appeared, crouching to duck under the lintel. He had a nervous smile that twitched at his lips and made him look as though he was more stupid than Baldwin thought he probably was. In his experience, the men described as 'fools' could remember things as accurately as the brightest men. Not that it said much for the intelligence of the brighter men whom Baldwin had known.

He smiled to put Sampson at his ease, climbing from his horse. Sampson seemed to have a lame foot. It was something which often went with foolishness, Baldwin knew.

'Master Sampson. I hear you were in the road when the poor child Mary was killed. Is that right?'

Sampson nodded slowly. He had told the Coroner already. He didn't like that man. He was suspicious. This one was kinder. Had a nice face. Sampson quite liked his face.

'Could you tell me what you saw?'

'I didn't see. I was lying down so they wouldn't see me,' Sampson explained.

'I quite understand,' Baldwin said. 'What did you hear, then?'

'They argued. He wanted her to take something. Something to stop her baby. No, she wouldn't, no. Not that. Killing her baby. No. So he grew angry. Hit her. Heard that. He smacked her. And then he says, "What have I done?" and he cries, and he's sick, and he runs off.'

Simon looked up sharply. 'He was sick? And what of her?'

'She was quiet.'

'She must have miscarried,' Simon said to Baldwin.

'If so, she was unconscious, or she would have been crying out, calling for help,' Baldwin mused. He looked at Sampson. 'Was she still, as though she was asleep?'

Sampson frowned with the effort of recollection. 'No, master. She was sniffin'. Sad. Very sad. Didn't say anything, but wept.'

'It does not sound as though she was in mortal pain or aware that her child was to miscarry,' Baldwin murmured. 'Sampson, did you hear a loud cracking sound?'

'Cracking?' Sampson queried, mouth hanging slackly.

'Someone broke her neck,' Baldwin explained. Something made him frown. A fact which niggled, but he could not put his finger on it.

Sampson sniffed, and his eyes filled with tears. 'I didn't know that. No. Didn't know that then. Only heard later.'

'Did anyone else walk by on the road?' Simon pressed.

Sampson averted his head slightly. Didn't like the Bailiff. He was loud; scary. Sampson didn't want to be scared. Didn't want to say Sir Ralph came by. Sir Ralph was scary too. Sir Ralph was on a horse, though, Sampson remembered slyly. 'No one *walked* by.'

'What, then?' Simon demanded. 'Did she sit, did she walk away, did she hit herself?'

Sampson shrugged. 'I came home,' he said simply.

'Can you remember seeing anyone else there who might have had something to do with her death?'

Sampson remembered what Surval had said only the night before. 'No. No one.'

'See, Sir Baldwin? Easy. And now,' Piers added, looking up at the sky, 'we should get back to the castle. The court must be about to start.'

Chapter Eighteen

Baldwin glanced about him when he walked into Sir Ralph's hall that afternoon with a feeling that this would not be a straight-forward meeting.

He had told Godwen and Thomas to wait outside. There was no point in additional witnesses, and from the look of the men traipsing in from the fields, there would be enough and to spare.

'But do not drink too much, and for God's own sake, try to resolve your problems,' he said crossly.

'Nothing to sort,' Thomas grumbled.

'I fear that any conversation I attempt is a little too far over his head,' Godwen said with a chuckle.

'Try to behave like sensible adults, not warring children,' Baldwin snarled as he left them.

It was not only the two men, it was his frustration. Piers's son Henry had obviously slept all night, and his fear and anxiety had stemmed more from nervousness at what his father would say when he realised Wylkyn's body was missing, than from terror of wild dogs overnight.

For all Baldwin's diligent searching, all he had learned was that Henry had slept in the shelter of the wall, away from the body, to be out of the wind. After he fell asleep, someone had come and taken Wylkyn away. Obviously that man would avoid Henry, so he dragged or carried the body away, and yet Baldwin had found no sign. It was infuriating.

Now he stood in the hall with Simon; Hugh stood behind them wearing a fixed scowl that seemed to demonstrate that he would have preferred by far to be out in the buttery with Godwen and Thomas, their ongoing feud notwithstanding, than in here with a reeking population of villagers.

Baldwin ignored him, concentrating on the men in the hall. Huward was there, he saw, at one corner of the room, while Sir Ralph had taken his seat in a carved chair like a throne on his dais, a table before him. He sat impassive as the men filtered into the room. Baldwin could see that Sir Ralph had brought in all the men of over twelve years to act as jury, and Piers was there among them all. Esmon loitered against a wall.

'A good-sized hall,' Simon muttered.

'Good if you want to entertain the King and his Host,' was Baldwin's murmured opinion. 'It is larger than a small castle like Gidleigh warrants, I should say.'

'It was built smaller originally.'

Baldwin nodded. He too had seen the tell-tale marks on the walls where the place had been extended and limewash painted over the new plaster. 'No doubt before long Sir Ralph will attach it to his keep and construct a real moorstone wall about the place.'

'Provided he can solicit the necessary permits to castellate.'

'I doubt,' Baldwin said, 'that he would find that to be a difficulty if he remains on close and amicable terms with Hugh Despenser the Younger.'

'True enough.'

'So what do you think?'

Simon snorted. 'That young fool dozed and the murderer returned to hide the body.'

'But *where*?'

They had searched carefully in and around the place but found nothing. Blood was spread thickly where the body had lain, but there was no sign to show how or to where Wylkyn had been removed. It was maddening, but it pointed to a serious urge to conceal the murder. Fine. So Baldwin and Simon must seek more diligently, then.

Baldwin glanced about him. The hall was certainly generously proportioned, and the roof timbers seemed as high overhead as a cathedral's, although he knew that was an illusion created by the warm fug. The room was filled with the odour of dirty, soggy men and their dogs. Smoke from the fire rose to the rafters. All the tables had been stored away around the walls, their trestle-stands collapsed and set in front of the tables to stop them toppling. Thus the floor was clear, apart from Sir Ralph's great throne and his wife's alongside.

On the walls of what Baldwin took to be the older part of the room were faded paintings of saints. Left was the great window which lighted the room. It was open, unglazed, and with square sectioned wooden bars rising to cover the space. At the back of Sir Ralph's dais hung a pair of matching tapestries which Baldwin assumed gave out to the solar block of the hall. That was where Sir Ralph would retire when his work was done, with a strong door to lock out intruders. The tapestries could be moved aside to allow escape from Sir Ralph's retainers and servants when all went to sleep. As he gazed at the heavy hangings, both depicting a hunt for a white hart, Baldwin noticed that one of them trembled. A moment later, he saw a dainty white hand slip out and pull the material away, and there stood a woman whom Baldwin could only think of as beautiful.

She was in her mid-thirties, a slender woman clad in a long, pale-blue tunic, her hair carefully bound up beneath a wimple, and her wealth and position made clear by her posture and carriage. She had an oval face, slightly slanting almond eyes, and a fine, long neck. As she walked, her head did not turn to inspect the servants and men waiting for the court, but instead appeared to stare over their heads.

'Is she all right?' Simon whispered from the corner of his mouth.

'If I didn't know better, I'd say she was very tired,' Baldwin returned. There was a snigger from behind him, and he cocked an eyebrow over his shoulder at Hugh.

'She's about as tired as a ploughman who's finished the strong ale at breakfast.'

'That is a villainous thing to say,' Simon said, scandalised. 'Remember, you are in her hall with her husband about to open his court.'

'I hate to admit it, Simon, but I think Hugh is right this time,' Baldwin murmured.

It was not only her own appearance, but the expression on Sir Ralph's face when he saw her that persuaded Baldwin. The knight stood as his wife came close, but even so, neither attempted to take the other's hand as she took her seat next to him, in a chair which a servant hurriedly pushed forward for her. Once sitting, she remained still, calmly staring ahead as though she was entirely alone. It was as if she was blind and deaf, unaware of others in the hall with her.

'She looks unhappy about something,' Simon said, studying her with his arms folded over his breast, occasionally throwing a suspicious glance at Sir Ralph.

Baldwin had no doubts about Simon's ability to read a man's character quickly, and the same skill often worked with women. Now, watching the Lady closely, Baldwin was sure there was misery in her features. Even from this distance her eyes looked as though they were red from weeping. It was all too common for a knight like Sir Ralph to beat his wife, but somehow Baldwin doubted that Sir Ralph was forged from that mould. He was no gentle lord to his servants, and his behaviour towards Baldwin and Roger Scut had been cavalier yesterday, but there was an apparent tenderness in his treatment of her even now. His annoyance was based on the fact that she was so obviously drunk in public, but even so Baldwin was sure that he caught sight of several sidelong glances from Sir Ralph, as though he feared that her spirit might fail her, and that insight intrigued Baldwin. What could he fear in this, his own hall?

Then Baldwin caught a glimpse of Sir Ralph's face and saw, not the simple arrogance of a man at his wife's drunkenness, but the face of someone whose soul was already tormented in Hell. His eyes were too wide, grown immense, like a hunted stag's when the raches catch him at bay, and the gaze Sir Ralph cast at his wife was not accusing, Baldwin saw. Rather, it was apologetic, penitential almost, like a man who had been forced to confess to a serious failing. It reminded Baldwin of Simon's expression when his drunken snores had kept his wife awake all night – but more serious.

Baldwin was about to nudge Simon and see whether his friend had noticed, when Sir Ralph's expression hardened and the misery disappeared, and he was once more the lord of his own court.

There was a vague shuffling as men moved aside, and Baldwin turned to find that Roger Scut had entered, a servant following with arms full of parchments rolled inside leather tubes. Roger walked to the side of the hall and waited pompously while a table was set before him. He eyed his stool doubtfully before sitting and motioning for his bag and parchments to be delivered. Immediately he set about sharpening his reeds and cleaning a large parchment, held down as usual with his leather-covered stones.

'What's that polished-arse doing clerking for the knight?' Simon asked coarsely.

'He likes money. Perhaps he has been offered cash for helping,' Baldwin said lightly, but he was concerned. There was something wrong here. Uncharitable thoughts about Roger Scut began to develop in his mind.

'I don't like this, Baldwin.'

Baldwin nodded in agreement. Then he shot a look at Hugh. 'Fetch Godwen and Thomas, Hugh. Bring them in here.'

To his credit, Hugh did not hesitate. He instantly slipped out, pushing and shoving his way through the crowd, but before he could reach the door, there was a dull rumbling noise from the people, and Baldwin turned to see Mark.

He had managed, just, to stay awake all night. With the pain from the beating, the cold, the threat of rodents attacking him, and the fear that in such temperatures were he to fall asleep he might never reawake, Mark had passed a miserable night.

It was not only that his present predicament was so grim, but also that he was sure he would be unable to show that he should be sent to the Bishop's court. And that would mean that this was his last night, in all probability. Through the long hours of darkness, he had stood shivering, or pacing frantically, trying to imagine a means of escape, a brilliant plan that would allow him to spring free from this hellish place, and find himself back in the Cathedral, but he could think of nothing but his bruised kidneys, his black eyes, his torn muscles. His mind went blank when he tried to envisage his own future. When he thought of anything, it was his darling Mary, dead . . . and then he wanted to weep, but couldn't. It was as though that part of his life was only a dream. All that truly existed was this misery, this dreadful underground tomb. Even when he tried to call to mind Mary's face when they had been happy, it was impossible, as though all memory of their bliss had been eradicated.

When they threw open the trap door, he was blinded. After the dark, it was like staring from a long tunnel into a brilliant white light, and it lanced into his eyes like pure heat, as though it was burning not only his eyes but his brain as well.

There was a harsh scraping noise, and then he was relieved to hear Roger Scut's voice calling to him gently. Slowly, my God, how slowly, he managed to clamber up the ladder, his eyes all but closed against the sun's rays. At the top he had to close his eyes again. When at last he felt he could open them again, he found himself being watched by Roger Scut, Brian of Doncaster and two burly watchmen.

'My God, Mark, you *have* suffered. I did all I could to get him to release you from that sewer, but Sir Ralph wouldn't listen to me. I am terribly sorry.'

'My friend, my Brother, I am grateful. God gave me some solace,' Mark said. His voice was hoarse. 'Do you have any water? My throat, I am so . . .'

Hands took him by the elbows as he swayed with weakness, and the men half-carried, half-led him to a barrel in a corner. There he was seated, and he had to bend over, retching, with giddiness and hunger. A cup of almost pure water was pressed into his hand, and he drank it quickly. His belly tried to vomit it back as soon as he had swallowed, some spurting up into his sinus, and it was only with exaggerated gulping that he kept it down, holding out the cup for another.

'Are you ill?' Roger Scut asked. He was crouching at Mark's feet, and looking up at him solicitously.

'Yes. I feel so bad, so *foul* and tainted. The shame! And I don't know what to do! All I want is to be safe in the Cathedral, but look at this,' he motioned to his ruined tunic and robes. 'This is all I am now, a churl with only a common fame! Who would believe in my innocence? Even *I* thought I must have killed her when I saw her body lying there!'

'My Brother, don't speak like that,' Roger Scut urged him. 'Pray to God and trust in Him, and you will be saved. Don't let that knight browbeat you, but stand your ground, tell the truth and damn him if he dares try to hold you.'

'I must tell him that he is my father, too,' Mark said, glancing about him to check that Brian and the guards couldn't overhear. 'That should save me.'

'Mark,' Roger Scut bent lower, 'you are about to enter his court, with his wife there, and his son. If you say you're his son, they'll think you invented it to curry favour and he'll probably be harder on you than he otherwise would! I'd not mention that you're his son until later, when you've proved your innocence.'

Mark stared at him. 'How much longer must I keep this secret?'

'As long as you need to. You are innocent, Mark. And you can claim Benefit of Clergy. Prove that you are a cleric and you will be all right.'

'How do I do that?'

'He will ask you to recite something – the *Pater Noster*, I expect. It's what all clerics remember.'

'Yes, yes. Of course.' Mark closed his eyes and spoke the words again, his tongue using the Latin easily. After so many repetitions, he could say them with ease.

'That is good,' Roger Scut said, although his face looked no easier. 'Now, simply remember, don't allow Sir Ralph to push you into accepting his court or his justice. You have your own court under Bishop Walter. This is a farce here, nothing more than that.'

'Yes, yes, I thank you, my friend.' There were tears in Mark's eyes at the thought of how kind this brother cleric had been to him. His generosity of spirit was stunning, spending time with a man of notoriety like Mark. 'I shall pray for you.'

Roger Scut withdrew, but not fast enough for Mark to avoid seeing the revulsion on his face.

'Holy Mother,' Mark whispered, 'take pity on a poor sinner. Ease my torment.'

Roger gave him a faint smile as though to encourage him, but then it fell from his face as he left the room with an over-burdened servant. Mark watched them cross the yard and enter the hall. He shuddered, as though someone had walked over his grave.

'Come on, you.' It was Brian and he pulled Mark to his feet and bound his wrists with strong thongs. 'Our master wants a chat with you, little priest.'

There was no cell in the land which was designed to be comfort-able, as Baldwin knew too well, but the sight of Mark blinking, stumbling, his head smeared with filth that yet did not obscure the swollen temple and split upper lip where he had been punched, made him feel a welling of sympathy and sorrow, and anger. But also that curious niggling sensation, as though something was jarring his soul.

The crowd didn't bay for blood like hounds. It was a more intimidating front that they presented to Mark. As he entered, all talking ceased, and men stood and glared at him. Not a soul there spoke, and Baldwin was sure that where Mark was, passing along a narrow way between the men, all he would have seen was utter contempt and loathing. It was that which probably made the fellow duck his head, evading eye-contact with any of the men amongst whom he had lived, if only for a short while.

'You are Mark, the priest of Gidleigh Chapel?' Sir Ralph rasped and then, when Mark dumbly nodded his head, he suddenly roared, 'You will answer!'

'I am Mark, the Parson of Gidleigh.'

'You know why you are here?'

'Yes.'

'You have been appealed by Huward, father of Mary, the girl you murdered with malice aforethought on—'

'No, I never murdered her, you have to—'

His quavering voice was silenced as Brian punched him in the lower back with full force. Mark flew forward, arms out to break his fall, and stayed there, retching, as the pain ebbed and flowed about his kidney. Rough hands were thrust under his armpits and he was lifted, still bent and weeping, until he could stand on his own feet again.

Seeing the boy slammed to the ground, Baldwin was about to go to him, but even as he took his first step forward, he felt Simon's warning hand on his shoulder, and then, while the guards ungently lifted Mark, he heard Simon's gruff murmur. 'I don't like it either, but there's nothing illegal about it. Interrupt the court and you'll probably make matters worse for him.'

It was difficult, but Baldwin gave a curt nod even as Sir Ralph thundered, 'Elias? Speak!'

While Mark tried to gather his breath, Elias told his story again. He wouldn't look at Mark, Baldwin noticed, but gave his evidence to the wall over Sir Ralph's head. Soon Huward was called to assert that Mary had not had a boyfriend that she had told him of. She had been too dutiful and obedient a daughter to seek out a callow youth. Mark must have raped her, then murdered her to silence her.

'Piers! What did the Coroner say?'

Piers sighed. 'That the girl was murdered. She'd been made pregnant and the child was dead. Mary's neck was broken and . . .'

Mark's mouth fell open. He couldn't have done that! When he struck her, that was shameful, but he hadn't hit hard enough to break her neck, he'd just thumped her from frustration, and that had been enough to make him retch with horror. It was a reaction to how low he had sunk, nothing more – he couldn't have killed her! Now, overwhelming his caution, his sense of complete innocence made him open his mouth. 'But I didn't touch her head or face! I couldn't have been her killer!'

This time the fist missed his kidney and crashed into the side of his chest. It felt like a leaden hammer, and he didn't truly feel it at first. It was as though he was outside his body, slightly breathless, but without fear. Except he couldn't speak. Then, when he gasped for breath, a raging, icy agony exploded along his left side. He must have broken or at least cracked a rib or two.

When the Jury had declared their suspicions, Sir Ralph spoke again. 'It seems to me that you are guilty as the Jury believes. They have presented the case against you, and I find it convincing. Have you anything to say before I declare your guilt?'

'I . . . I claim the Benefit of the Clergy. Benefit of Clergy! You can't keep me here. You have to give me up to the Cathedral.'

At this point, Simon saw Esmon shoot a glance at Roger Scut. There was something in that look, and Simon was certain that he saw Roger Scut give a slight nod. There was no need for them to speak: they had an agreement, Simon thought, and he wondered what that agreement might be. He was relieved to see that the two watchmen had returned with Hugh.

'So you, Mark, say that you are a clerk and you cannot and will not answer here. Well, if that's the case, we must deliver you to your lord's court, but before you are delivered, your character must be determined. So we shall have to find out the truth of the matter.'

'You cannot try me! I am one of the clergy! Please, Fa—' Before he could call on Sir Ralph as a parent, Brian's fist whirled into his belly, and he collapsed, choking.

'This is no inquest. We are merely determining your character, so that we can deliver you to the court of the Bishop, and we find that you are guilty. Your guilt was proven by your flight. Your goods and chattels are forfeit, clerk.'

'Release him to my custody,' Baldwin said heavily. 'I shall take him back with me and have him carried to Exeter.'

'I fear I can only release him to an ecclesiastical officer,' Sir Ralph said coolly. 'And only after proof of the lad's clerical status.'

'If you wait that long,' Baldwin said reasonably, 'he might die. Look at him now! He's been left to starve, hasn't he? Have you fed him?'

'His feeding isn't my responsibility,' Sir Ralph said with sudden sharpness. There was an edge to his voice that to Baldwin sounded more than a little like madness. 'I'm only holding him.'

'Neither food, nor water, I expect. He could die of the cold in this weather, too. Bishop Walter would be displeased if he heard that you had seen to it that one of his clerks was dead.'

'He'll be well looked after,' Sir Ralph shouted, and his arm snapped out, pointing northwards. 'Better than he looked after that child out there!'

'Come! Father, there's no need to upset yourself,' Esmon said silkily.

'No . . . No, of course not,' Sir Ralph said, and wiped a hand over his brow. 'Now, we must see that he is ordained by letters from the Bishop. Where are the letters?'

'In my chest at the church,' Mark gasped.

'That is good. Then I shall send men to fetch them. If they are in order, you may be released into the hands of any official whom the Bishop may send.'

Baldwin happened to glance at Piers at that moment, and saw him lift a hand as though to object, but then his brows pulled together and he stood studying Esmon with an expression of disbelief.

'I claim him,' Roger Scut said.

Baldwin shot him a look and saw him tilt his head back and peer along his nose at Mark, who remained on his knees, weeping silently. 'There, Mark. You are safe. You shall come back to Exeter with me and await the court there.'

'How do we know he's a priest?'

It was Esmon. Baldwin gazed at him, wondering what new peril threatened Mark, for peril there clearly was. Piers was chewing his lip now. He looked up and caught Baldwin's eye; Baldwin thought he was ashamed.

'He could have murdered a cleric and come here after stealing his letters.'

'My son, please be silent,' Sir Ralph said.

'What if he's no priest anyway?'

'I said, *be silent*! If he is a priest or not, we have to hold him safely. If he is determined to claim Benefit of Clergy, he can go to the Bishop's court, and there, if he's no priest, he will be punished for imitating a cleric. Our duty is to hold him and send him to the Bishop in one piece.'

Esmon shrugged with apparent good humour and returned to lean against the wall.

'That is better. Now, boy, we should test you, I suppose. What can we ask? I know: recite the *Placebo*.'

'The *Placebo*? But clerks usually recite the *Pater Noster*,' Mark said, his voice quavering.

'I don't care. Begin.'

Mark searched his memory for the words, but under the hard stares of the men all around, he found it playing him false. The form of the service was there, right at the forefront of his mind, but the words themselves would not come. He closed his eyes, opened his mouth, as though by the mere mechanical exercise he might be able to tempt the words from the dimness at the back of his mind, but they remained hidden.

'I . . . I can't remember it! I've never had to recite it here. There's been no corpses to bury – how would I know that off by heart? I can give you the *Pater* . . .'

'Clerk, you told me to ask for the *Placebo*, but as you see, he can't recite it. What do you say?' Sir Ralph asked, turning to Roger Scut.

Mark gazed at him thankfully. Roger had saved him once, Roger would save him again. They were both clerks. But Sir Ralph said that Roger had told him to ask for the . . . Suddenly Mark felt a fresh thrill of horror washing over him.

Roger Scut gave him a stare down the length of his nose, and declared, 'Any real clerk would know the *Placebo*.'

Mark cried, 'No! Roger, please! Father! Help me – save me!' but his words were drowned out by the roar of anger.

Chapter Nineteen

The room erupted. Suddenly the peasants were roused, thinking this was proof that Mark was not even a clerk, that he had been misleading them all the months when he had been at the altar.

'That bastard!'

'He's a liar!'

'Are our souls damned?' one man asked, looking fearful.

The fellow at his side had a more mundane interest. 'Where did all our gifts to the chapel go, then?'

As the men started to move towards Mark, Baldwin grabbed the arms of his Constables and shoved them forward so that they stood at Mark's side, Thomas with bared teeth like an enraged mastiff, Godwen languid, but none the less intimidating for that, like a snake lying bathing in the sun. Baldwin whipped his sword from its scabbard and roared for silence. One man pressed forward as though to reach Mark, but Baldwin's point pricked his arm, and he changed his mind, withdrawing with a scowl and a curse. Simon, he could feel, was beside him, Hugh too, with his long-bladed knife in his hand, and it would be a hard fight for any man who wanted to reach Mark. Yet unless Baldwin took control, it was possible that the men might try just that. They were furious, believing that they had legal sanction to attack this man who had professed to being a clerk.

He did not know, nor did he care, what motive Roger Scut had for implying that Mark was no cleric. All he knew was that unless he acted swiftly, Mark would be hanged out of hand like any other felon whose guilt had been established.

'*Silence!* I am Keeper of the King's Peace, and I will see justice done here!' he roared at the top of his voice, glaring balefully at Brian, who had his hand resting on his sword's hilt. Baldwin pointed at him. 'You! Help to keep order in your lord's court. You want to see a murder done in his own hall? All of you: LISTEN!' he bellowed, feeling his face redden with sudden anger. 'If this man is harmed I shall order the whole vill to be amerced to the *fullest* extent for petty treason against your lord, for mutiny and murder! You are all in *Frankpledge* – any man who tries to attack me or this man here will suffer the consequences in *my* court as Keeper of the King's Peace.'

There was a less enthusiastic shuffling now. Baldwin caught sight of a man who looked as though he might try to push his way forward, but saw another grab his hand. The threat against their *Frankpledge* was working.

It had all happened so swiftly, it seemed that most of the men were stunned, many of them shocked by the urge to commit sudden violence. Five men, Baldwin saw, were left with different emotions.

Sir Ralph and Roger Scut had not moved. Sir Ralph sat as before, but his face showed his rage. He had wanted Mark to be killed, Baldwin guessed. Roger Scut, who had appeared excited and hopeful as the crowd jumped to pull Mark outside, now looked merely bored, although Baldwin caught a glimpse of something when their eyes met – perhaps frustration that the near execution, caused by his own deliberate lack of enthusiasm in Mark's defence, had not succeeded. It was a consideration that made Baldwin want still more to have a chance to talk to him.

Esmon, still at the wall, had made no move to protect his parents, nor to go to the defence of Mark. He still leaned against the wall, a couple of men-at-arms at his side, conversing with one, and staring, Baldwin noticed, fixedly at him.

Piers was the only man from the vill who had sprung to Mark's aid, and he stood at Simon and Hugh's side, a sturdy club in his hand, glaring about him like a crazed warrior waiting for the first blow to be struck – eager, so it seemed, to retaliate.

'You thought you'd break our master's hall? What's got into you all? Are you gone mad? Calm down, the lot of you, before I use this to calm you meself!'

'You blame us? That priest there tells us that this turd is no man of God, and you blame us for our anger? What's the matter with you, Piers? Lost your cods? You'd be happy to see the killer of my daughter walk free just so that you can announce there's been no fighting in the court? Ballocks, I say!'

'Huward, restrain yourself. Would it serve Mary's memory for you to be hanged because of disrespect to your lord? You want to die like that?'

Baldwin was glad to see that Huward hung his head and turned away. He could have sprung forwards even so, but other men, probably those from his own *frankpledge*, were there to surround him, shielding Mark with their bodies, and Baldwin felt safe enough to gaze about him again, meeting the faces of all the men in the room and staring down those who looked most truculent.

'Sir Ralph, I demand that this court be closed now so that men might recover their senses. It is clear enough to me that the boy here is a priest and that he deserves the protection of the court and all your men.'

'I don't need you to tell me my responsibilities. The priest here only said that any cleric should know his *Placebo* – he didn't say this man wasn't a priest.'

Baldwin slowly surveyed the room. 'Sir Ralph, I demand that you release this fellow into my hands as Keeper of the King's Peace. It is clear to me that your villeins are convinced that he is not entitled to Benefit of Clergy and that his life is at risk.'

'He is under my protection,' Sir Ralph said testily. 'This is my court, and I will not relinquish him.'

'I demand—'

'You have no right to demand anything!' Sir Ralph suddenly spat. He leaned forward in his seat as though to launch himself at Baldwin, but his wife put a hand out and caught his wrist. The knight hesitated as she spoke.

'Sir Baldwin, I agree with you. Any harm that might come to him will be the responsibility of Gidleigh. His safety must be paramount.'

'You shall look after him, then, until Scut and I can get him back to the Bishop,' Baldwin said with a slight bow.

'Yes, I shall hold him.' Sir Ralph smiled humourlessly. 'I shall keep him safe in the comfort of my little gaol.'

'If he dies, I shall inform the good Bishop that you allowed his death through negligence,' Baldwin stated sharply. He had little choice, he knew. This was Sir Ralph's court.

The knight shrugged. 'You know as well as I that the death of a prisoner from cold or hunger is death by natural causes. I'm sure he'll enjoy my hospitality while we wait to receive the letters he says the good Bishop sent him and which are held in his chest. No doubt they will prove his innocence.'

'The chapel is burned! Any letters have been destroyed!' Esmon called. 'He can't recite his prayers and I say we should hang him. He killed the girl, let him pay.'

'I will reserve judgement until I see the letters,' Sir Ralph said. 'If they have burned, we must send to the Bishop for copies or confirmation that this man is a priest.' He spoke as though reluctantly, and Baldwin was struck with the feeling that Sir Ralph had aged in the last few minutes, like a man who has realised he has failed someone he loved. Baldwin could not help but glance at Annicia as Sir Ralph waved an arm, stood, and walked heavily from the room.

Lady Annicia was sitting as though she was entirely indifferent to the outcome of this discussion, but her face was blank only in appearance because she was controlling herself with difficulty. Utter dejection was revealed on her face. As Baldwin watched, fascinated, he saw her eyes glitter with hatred, and he saw that she was staring at Huward.

'What in God's name can you have against him?' he wondered, but then he gladly helped Mark to his feet and watched as he was taken away.

He himself was not convinced of Mark's innocence, but he was quite sure of one thing, that Mark was definitely a priest; and, he reminded himself as he looked towards the table again, that Roger Scut had betrayed him.

Walking from the room, he didn't notice that Lady Annicia motioned to a servant, pointed to Huward, and spoke softly.

Elias had intended to escape the place as soon as Sir Ralph declared that the court was to adjourn, but he wasn't fast enough to escape Simon. Before he could reach the roadway at the front of the castle, Hugh had caught up with him. 'My master wants to talk to you.'

'Who is your master? That knight?'

'No, he's the Bailiff from Lydford,' Hugh said.

Elias scowled. He had heard of Lydford – who hadn't? The Stannary court there reckoned itself competent not only to try a man's guilt and deliver him from gaol, often they would do so before the King's Justices had time to arrive. Their power was absolute, and they had little regard for serfs. Many miners had once themselves been serfs, but had escaped to the moors, where they lived the easy life of freemen, owing service to no one.

The Stannaries were fiercely protective of their people. Elias knew he must be careful responding to the Bailiff's questions. He waited, chewing his lip. It wasn't his fault he was the only man who admitted to finding the body of the girl. Nothing to do with him, whoever had killed her. Nothing at all. But he'd be the man who was fined first and hardest, just because he'd stumbled over her corpse.

'You're Elias? I am Bailiff Puttock of Lydford.'

Simon wasn't the sort of man to make Elias feel at his ease. He loomed over the peasant, while Hugh wandered idly around behind Elias, making him wonder whether he was about to be arrested. 'Yes, sir, but I've done nothing, I just found the bodies, that's all. I can't help that.'

The knight was at the Bailiff's side now, two evil-looking watchmen behind him. One glowered at him as though suspecting Elias of raping his wife. The other looked bored stiff. The two were so incongruous together that Elias found himself staring at them. Baldwin's voice made him jump. He had all but forgotten the Keeper.

'No, Elias,' said Baldwin gently, 'you are not held to be at fault. Nor shall you be if you tell us the truth. Now: the body you found up on the moors, the body of this miner – are you *sure* he was dead?'

Elias ducked his head, confused by the question. 'His neck was broken, and his hand had been hacked off, like someone had gone berserk . . . Have you seen a man survive something like that?'

'I think we may safely conclude that he was dead,' Baldwin grunted. 'Did you recognise him? Piers tells us it was probably a man called Wylkyn. Is that so?'

'Yes. I'd seen him often enough. Used to be a servant at the castle – back in the days of Sir Richard, that was.'

'Is that why you were asked to find him?' Baldwin asked suddenly, cutting into his speech.

'Asked to . . .?'

'Don't pretend to be stupid. Just tell me quickly: *who* told you where to find that body?'

Elias stared dumbly at the ground. 'I don't know what you mean.'

'Oh, I reckon you do,' Simon said. 'Come on – how much were you paid?'

'Nothing.'

Baldwin leaned down. 'Elias, we can ask you here, and you can answer, or we can have you taken to Sir Ralph's cell and leave you there until you choose to respond. Of course, if you refuse, we can have you taken to Exeter to answer to the Justices there in the county court. It is up to you.'

'Which will it be?' Simon rasped.

Elias was loath to answer. He didn't know what to do, where to look, so he kept his head down, staring at their feet while he tried to think of an answer that would be safe, that would allow him some room for escape. It was a huge relief when he recognised the voice of Piers the Reeve.

'Master, Sir Baldwin, I am glad you found our First Finder. Elias will help you.'

Elias shot him a look of hatred. He had spoken to Piers as a friend, as a neighbour and member of the same *Frankpledge*. Under the unwritten but perfectly comprehended rules of the vill, his words about Sir Ralph should have remained secret, but Piers's tone gave him little hope that the Reeve would either leave him in peace or support him.

His feelings were plain, and when Piers glanced at him, he all but winced to see Elias's face, but nothing would change his mind. Ever since he had walked with Flora towards the mill and learned that Esmon had tried to rape her, he had grown more determined to see Esmon pay for his crimes. 'Elias may not know that Wylkyn's body has disappeared, though.'

The old peasant stared at Piers dumbly. 'Wylkyn's gone?'

'Somebody scared the shit out of my son last night,' Piers nodded. 'Took the body – we don't know where. With all the rain, there's little chance of tracking it down now, either.'

'Elias,' Baldwin said, 'we don't care about your role in reporting the body. The only point that concerns us is finding the body again for the Coroner. You understand? Otherwise the entire vill will be fined for concealing a murdered man.'

'It was Osbert told me about him. Osbert was walking out that way and heard a fight or something, and when he carried on, he saw a body lying in the gulley near the wall there. So he came back here in a hurry and asked me to report it. See, they can't fine me again – but it wouldn't have been kind to Osbert to have that as well as poor Mary hanging over him.'

'Poor Mary?' Baldwin enquired. 'What was she to him?'

'Everyone knew Os adored her,' Elias said shortly. 'We hoped he'd pluck up courage and ask for her hand, but he never did. And she was a bit flighty. Didn't want one of the dull-wits from round here, she used to say.'

'Osbert?' Simon mused. 'Is that the lad who came to fetch me?'

Elias nodded.

'Could this Os have raped and killed her in frustration, if he was so keen to possess her?' Baldwin wondered.

'We all know who killed Mary,' Elias said gruffly. 'It was that priest, Mark.'

'You were there when the girl died, weren't you?' Simon asked.

'Yes. Ploughing.'

His voice was toneless. Baldwin spoke softly, soothingly. 'Friend, all we want is to find out who could have done these terrible things, that is all. Could you tell us anything you saw or heard that day?'

Elias told them again. He had repeated his tale so often in the last few days, it sprang to his mind as though he was watching the scene again even now.

'It was quite a clear day,' he began with a sigh. 'I'd got up to the edge of the field, and the first few times all I could hear was the chopping of wood from hedge-laying on the other side of the lane. That was Osbert.'

'I see. Right, continue!'

'One time, when I came up to the top of the field, I heard voices. I knew them both. I've heard the priest often enough, and I've known Mary all her life. Didn't think anything of it – why should I? The priest can talk to whoever he wants, can't he?'

'You're sure you didn't stop and listen a while?' Simon said suspiciously.

Elias gazed at him scornfully. 'You think they wouldn't notice a plough suddenly stopping? They wouldn't notice if Ben stopped urging the team on, if I stopped shouting, if the blade in the soil went quiet?'

'Who's this Ben?' Simon asked.

'Mary's brother.'

'So if he heard something odd, he'd have sung out by now,' Simon said.

Elias was doubtful. 'Perhaps. Ben never liked her much. Not recently, anyway.'

'His own sister?' Baldwin said.

'No,' Elias said, glancing at Piers for confirmation.

'It's true, Sir Baldwin,' he said reluctantly. 'There were rumours.'

'There are always rumours. What were they?'

'That Ben tried to molest his own sister.'

Baldwin felt as though he was closer to understanding the undercurrents of the vill. 'You mean he tried to sleep with Mary?'

'Yes. And she rejected him. It is only rumour,' he added miserably.

'Where did it originate, I wonder?'

'With the young lads of the vill, I think. For my part I find it hard to believe, because it is so unnatural for a brother to lie with his sister, yet . . .'

'Yet?'

'Mary was a very pretty child. All the men would watch her when she passed by. And during a long, cold winter, a boy could seek comfort and solace in the arms of his sister. Who knows? Perhaps one thing led to another. And then he bragged about it with his friends, perhaps. I have heard of such things before.'

'So have I,' said Baldwin. Unnatural though such behaviour was, it was not unknown.

He gave Elias a nod. 'Continue.'

'That was all. When I was done, I sent the boy to open the gate, and I went out after the team. He stayed there to shut the gate while I carried on back towards the barton . . .'

'Where would this be?' Baldwin asked smoothly.

'Down at the bottom of Deave Lane, by the ford at the brook.'

'Go on.'

'When we got along the road a ways, we saw her. Down on the ground by the hedge.'

'Which side of the lane?'

'On my right.'

'So the opposite side of the road from your ploughing?'

'Yes. She was there, and there was blood all about her . . . you know. Her legs were wide enough to see where it all came from.'

'You noticed her instantly, so I assume anyone else passing there must have seen her?'

'Oh, yes. No one could have missed that sight.'

'You saw no sign of the priest at this stage?'

'No, he'd been long gone, I'd reckon.'

Simon sniffed. 'You say there were rumours about this Ben. Did he leave the field at any time?'

Elias scuffed a boot in the dirt. 'Not that I remember.'

Baldwin eyed him. There was a strangeness about him, as though Elias thought this was hardly worth his consideration. Perhaps he was merely convinced of the priest's guilt, he thought.

'So you did . . . what?'

'I didn't want Ben to see his sister like that, so I sent the boy down to the barton to call for help, while I stood there with the oxen. They grazed on the stuff at the side of the road.'

'What of the man laying the hedge . . . Osbert, you said?' Baldwin asked, glancing at Piers.

'He was gone by then, but he'd not have done anything to hurt her.'

'Why?'

'Because he loved her, Sir Baldwin. Everyone knew that. He was after her like a tom cat after his queen.'

'Sometimes I have found that those who love the strongest are also those who are swiftest to kill in jealousy,' Baldwin commented. Something made him glance up at Piers. The Reeve was staring fixedly at Elias. The peasant was clearly feeling more comfortable, his head was up again, and he had stopped staring at Baldwin's boots.

'Tell me, what else did you see that day, Elias?' he asked suavely.

'Nothing.'

'There was something that made you very fearful for your own safety, wasn't there? Did you see the murderer – is that it?'

'I didn't see no murder,' Elias said doggedly, his head dropping again.

'But you saw something else, didn't you? Or was it some*one* else? Yes, that is it, is it not? You saw someone riding past, before you saw her body. Did that someone ask you to report the body so that they could make good their own escape?'

'No, nothing like that.'

'Then what? Come along, man – speak!' Baldwin burst out, and then he felt Simon's hand on his arm. The realisation hit him like a blow as he saw Elias's eyes flicker up at the castle walls behind them. *That* was why he thought Ben was irrelevant! There was genuine fear in his face, as though he was worried that Sir Ralph himself might have heard the demand and might seek to punish the man who spoke and gave away secrets to a foreign Keeper.

'Nothing,' Elias said, his head drooping once more.

'It was Esmon, was it?' Baldwin said.

'I didn't see *him*!' Elias stated.

There was no doubting the sincerity of his voice. 'Are you sure? Then it was Sir Ralph.'

Elias hunched his shoulders as though hiding his head. 'I didn't say that.'

'I am Keeper of the King's Peace. Do you deny you saw Sir Ralph?' Baldwin demanded. 'If I learn you have lied to me, Elias, I can have you gaoled in Exeter until you decide to answer. Do you want that?'

'I have to choose that or saying my master's a murderer, do I?'

'All you need do is speak the truth!'

'It was him,' Elias sighed. 'I saw Sir Ralph ride past, but not Esmon.'

Simon was watching a group leaving the castle's gate. Two men caught his eye. One was Osbert, the other a younger lad with dark eyes who glanced in Simon's direction and then looked away quickly, as though anxious not to attract attention to himself. 'Who's that with Osbert?'

'Ben, Mary's brother.'

'Hugh, fetch them here,' Simon said and, grunting rebelliously, Hugh made his way to them. Soon they were standing before Simon and Baldwin, Osbert plainly worried, while Ben made a show of being unconcerned, but they stood uncomfortably, some little distance apart, as though disliking the fact that they were together.

Simon considered them a long moment, but then he noticed a bush tied over the doorway of a house further up the road, a little way from the castle, and he glanced at Baldwin. 'Let's get away from this castle. It's giving me the feeling we're constantly being watched.'

Chapter Twenty

It was only a cheap ale-house. The farmer's wife made a few pennies by selling ale to passers-by when she had a little too much brewed. It wasn't the best ale Simon had ever tried, but it certainly wasn't the worst either, and he sat on a table outside her doorway, Baldwin beside him with his arms crossed, while they questioned the men.

'Osbert. We've heard that you found Wylkyn's body. Why did you hide that fact?'

Os shot Elias a look, but the older peasant was staring at the bush over the door, and Os had to resort to cursing him inwardly. 'I . . . I knew Elias had already found one body. It made sense to ask him to look for Wylkyn as well.'

'To evade your fines,' Baldwin observed. 'Never mind that for now. When the Coroner arrives, perhaps we can give him the facts and save your money for you. In the meantime, what can you tell us about Wylkyn's body?'

'He'd been badly cut about. I heard his screams and went up there, but then I saw that it was quite a band of Esmon's men, and didn't get involved. I'd just have got killed. Later, when they'd gone off with the carts to get them to pay their tolls, I looked over the place and found Wylkyn.'

'Why would Esmon's men have gone there?'

Osbert shrugged. With Mary's death, life meant little to him any more, and if he could help put the noose about Esmon's neck, so much the better. Everyone feared him and his men-at-arms after their robberies and rapings. 'To rob them? They've often raided travellers, demanding tolls where none are due. That's what they did the other day; they killed Wylkyn, but took all the rest to the castle. I suppose they went through all the goods and stole what they wanted.'

Simon and Baldwin exchanged a look. This was a serious felony. Osbert's evidence, if corroborated, could lead to Esmon and his father being arrested. Not, Baldwin told himself, that it would mean they would be forced to suffer the full penalty of law, for they had friends in high places, but even so, it would lead to shame.

He nodded towards the road that led to the mill. 'What of the girl Mary? We hear you loved her.'

Os reddened. 'I did,' he said stoutly, as though daring anyone to comment.

There was no laughter, but for a small snigger from Ben. Baldwin immediately turned his attention to the lad. 'You were with Elias here when your sister was killed. Did you notice anything about her body?'

'Yes. She was dead,' Ben said sarcastically.

'How could you tell?' Baldwin didn't like this boy. Ben was glib and disrespectful, which was not the attitude of someone trying to help find the murderer of his beloved sister. He stood insolently, as though scarcely listening to Baldwin's questions, a small-framed lad clad in a good quality woollen tunic and soft linen hose.

Ben shrugged. 'Elias told me.'

'I tried to keep the sight from him,' Elias explained sombrely. 'I went to her and left Ben holding the oxen. When I saw what had happened, I sent him to fetch help and stayed with her body.'

'You did well,' Baldwin said and turned back to Ben. 'Do you think Mark could have killed your sister?'

'Him? I suppose so. She was all over him most of the time. Slobbering like a bitch on heat. Probably thought she could get him to throw in his place as a priest like old Surval the Hermit.'

'He did what?' Baldwin said.

Piers said, 'He used to be a priest, but got thrown out of his church because he did something. Don't know what, but he feels the guilt still.'

'We shall ask him. Osbert, you were out there that day when Mary was killed. Do you think it could have been Mark?'

'I was working at the hedge at the time. I didn't hear anything apart from the noise of the oxen and Ben calling to them. And I couldn't see anyone in the roadway. Only someone on horseback would have been visible to me.'

'You had left before Elias and Ben?'

'Yes. I had to go to the mill and help Huward.'

'You did not see the body when you went to the mill?' Baldwin said.

'I didn't go by the lane,' Os said. 'I went over the fields back to the vill, then took the lane from there down to the mill.'

'Did you see Sir Ralph or his son?'

'I saw Sir Ralph,' Osbert agreed, frowning with the effort of recollection. 'He was down at the bottom of the road on his horse when I saw him. That was where I reached the road myself.'

'What of Esmon?' Simon asked. 'Did anyone see him?'

'Yes,' Ben said. 'He was down near the castle when I got there. He had mud all over his legs, as if he'd been riding up on the moors.'

'Why would he have gone up there?' Simon wondered aloud. 'Was he hunting?'

'He had no dogs.' Ben shrugged.

Baldwin was watching him closely. 'Master Ben, you seem entirely unaffected by losing your sister.'

'I have another one!'

His glib reply made Simon want to hit him, and he was seeking for a sharp response when he saw Osbert's face. The strong peasant looked as though he could break into tears at any moment. Rather than upset Os further, Simon said, 'Where were you on the day that this Wylkyn died?'

'I was in a tavern. There were plenty of men there to vouch for me, too.'

'Is there anything else you want to tell us?' Baldwin said, looking from one to another of them, but all their long faces told him that there was nothing more to learn here. The only one who looked less than worried was Ben. He waved at the alewife to demand drink as Baldwin watched. His insouciance was insufferable, but there was nothing Baldwin could do about a man who was so uncaring about his own sister.

'We should go,' he muttered. 'We have to find the body of this Wylkyn and ensure that Mark is released into our custody.'

'I don't understand what you keep asking about Mary's death for anyway,' Ben said. He had a large pot of cider now, which he drank steadily, spilling some down his chin and throat. Gasping, he signed for another pot. 'The Coroner and everyone else are content that Mark was Mary's murderer. What do you expect to find?'

'Perhaps I don't believe that Mark killed her,' Baldwin said, rising. It was time to return to the castle. 'Reeve, I suggest you organise a hunt for this missing miner's body. We shall need to have something to show the Coroner, or you will be very heavily fined, won't you?'

Piers grunted noncommittally, and turned away with Elias along towards the barton and his home. Soon Simon and Baldwin were alone. It was as Baldwin beckoned the two Constables to bring his mount that he saw Huward. The miller was walking from the castle, his face white as a winding-sheet, and his eyes filled with a terrible horror that grabbed at Baldwin's breast and made him stand aside as Huward passed.

It was a momentary thing. Huward had been there, and now he was gone. A broken man, his life destroyed. It shocked Baldwin to see how Huward had changed since the night before. The miller had looked a large, hale fellow even after the horror of losing his daughter, but now he looked as though he was bent beneath a still more extreme misery. Baldwin wondered how he himself would have reacted if someone were to murder his own little daughter Richalda, if he was sure he knew who the killer was, and he had to witness the man's escape on the technical issue that the murderer had once trained as a priest. It would appal him. Perhaps this was only the natural expression of a man who had lost his daughter to a murderer who must escape the usual penalty for his crime.

The sight of Huward made Baldwin still more determined to see that the murderer should pay. If it was Mark, he would see the priest in the Bishop's court – but he found himself wondering anew whether Mark could have been the murderer. After seeing the lad's expression and alarm in the court, Baldwin found it hard to imagine a less likely murderer.

The priest had confessed to hitting her, Baldwin reminded himself. Mark had also admitted to an affair with the girl, to getting her with child, to arguing and even to striking her . . . but he strenuously denied murder.

To break someone's neck took considerable strength. Baldwin could remember seeing Elias in the field, his muscles bunching with the effort of ending a rabbit's life; to pull the bones apart in a woman's neck would take much more force. Mark was no peasant with corded muscles that could snap a human neck; he was a rather weakly-looking fellow. To strike a woman, yes, that was in his power, but breaking her neck was a different matter altogether.

'Simon, I don't think Mark would have had the strength to break her neck,' he said.

'I find it hard to believe,' Simon agreed.

Try as he might, Baldwin could not get the picture of Elias from his mind, gently smoothing the fur of a rabbit before tugging at the head. 'That boy Ben didn't leave Elias, according to the old peasant.'

'No. The two stayed together.'

Baldwin nodded. 'Perhaps both took a break. Ben didn't like his sister.'

'Baldwin, disliking her is different from actively helping to kill her.'

'Perhaps. Yet some boys can grow to hate their sisters. And we have heard that Ben might have been rejected by her. Shame alone could have made him want to kill her.'

'Perhaps. What should we do?'

'Simon, you go with Piers. Arrange for a messenger to Chagford to find Wylkyn's companions. I shall take a moment to speak to Huward again.'

* * *

The mill was dark and grim. Since Mary's death it had been silent but for the weeping of the women. The gears that operated the massive wheel had been still because Huward had closed off the leat that fed it. Somehow, in the absence of the grinding of the stones together, the void where before she had always known the clicking and graunching of the teeth of the mechanism, Flora felt as though the death of Mary had affected the machinery itself. It was just as if the whole building had died with her. No, it was worse than that: it was as if the family itself was gone, as though she'd lost her father and mother as well as her sister.

The burial over, Gilda had returned home and now sat in the darkest corner of the room near the grain store, like a woman whose life was ended. She scarcely responded when the family spoke to her, nor did she now, when Flora walked to her and rested a hand on her shoulder.

'Mother, you have to eat. Do you want some pottage?'

Gilda groaned and clutched at her clothes, pinching at her upper arms, shaking her head and uttering a long, low moan. Startled, Flora withdrew at first, but her shock soon turned to sympathy and compassion. This was her mother, the woman who had protected and nurtured her through her childhood. It can't have been easy. Even though Sir Ralph had always been kindly about their rent, nonetheless the famine had affected all in Devonshire, and Gilda had been forced to work hard for their money along with Huward. Flora went to her mother, throwing her arms about her and cradling her just as Gilda had cradled her when she was young.

He was a good man, Huward. Kind and loving, he had always insisted that he had no favourites, only four people to love equally, although Flora was certain in her own mind that Ben was less well-liked by their father. Huward had craved a son. All men did: a son was proof that their name would continue, that their family line was secure. A daughter, when all was said and done, was only a breeding dam, to be sold and served by the buck who attracted her father's attention, but a son – a son could carry on the business, take responsibility for a mother and father too old and infirm to shift for themselves, and increase the family's fortune, multiplying it for the future. Unfortunately Ben was in no sense an ideal heir.

Flora adored both her mother and her father, but her father was more warm and affectionate than her mother. With Gilda there was always a slight reserve, as though she couldn't entirely give herself to anyone, not even her own daughter. Even now, with Flora's arms about her, she averted her head, only slightly, but enough to remove her cheek from contact with Flora's, and the girl felt tears stinging her eyes at the sensation of her mother withdrawing from her touch.

It was hurtful, but if Gilda didn't want Flora to comfort her, Flora couldn't force herself upon her. She gently pulled away, saying, 'Mother, Mary wouldn't want you to starve yourself! You have to eat something.'

'Leave me! I don't want food, I want peace, only peace.'

'What do you mean?' Flora asked. Was her mother's mind becoming unhinged?

'Just go, Flora!'

'Not until I see you eating something. Will you take some bread?'

Gilda muttered angrily, but finally she agreed and picked at the coarse maslin that Flora placed before her. It was enough. Flora left her when she saw that Gilda had consumed a little, and walked outside.

She could weep. Her father wasn't here yet – he and Ben would be at the court, and God knew how long that might take. If the priest decided to argue the toss, he might delay all the men there a good few hours. Perhaps they had held their meeting, and had gone to an ale-house to recover their humour after hearing the judge declare the priest safe because of Benefit of Clergy. Flora was not sanguine about the likelihood of even Sir Ralph deciding to thwart the power and influence of the Bishop of Exeter. He was one of the most powerful men in the country.

Osbert was there as well. She felt so alone right now, with even her mother rejecting her, that the thought of Osbert's calming arms about her, just holding her, was so attractive, she couldn't restrain a small gasp of longing. Her heart was his. Perhaps . . . with Mary out of the way, she could win his heart. There was no one else for him. Oh, she wanted his arms around her so much, right this minute!

'Where is your father, girl?'

The strange voice made her heart leap. When she was able to recognise the man, Flora asked: 'Hermit, what do you want here?'

'Answer the question.'

'He's at the court, I think. All the men are.'

'That's good. Where is your mother?'

'Inside – why, do you need alms? Leave my mother alone, I beg! Since my sister's loss, she has been very sad. It is hard for a woman to lose her child.'

'It is as hard for a sister to suffer loss,' he observed gruffly, peering at her from under the old felt brim of his hat.

'Perhaps less hard,' Flora said uncertainly.

'You sound like someone who shoulders a little of the blame.'

'No! I had nothing to do with my beloved sister's death,' she burst out.

'I never thought you did, child. Yet you feel responsible.'

'A little. It's just that . . .'

'What?'

'I don't think I ever had quite so much of my mother's affection as Mary did. Maybe I'll never match up to her measure of me. I'll be a disappointment for ever.'

'If you are, it's not your fault; it's the fault of a foolish parent who didn't think of you as a person but as a "thing" to be possessed. You are as good as your sister, child,' he said with firm reassurance.

'You sound like my father,' she smiled.

'Maybe he is an intelligent man,' Surval said, peering over her shoulder into the mill. 'Is she there?'

'Yes, but please, won't this wait?'

'Because of the loss of your sister? No. And don't blame yourself for your mother's attitude towards you. She loves you greatly, but she is scared ... and her suffering goes back long before your birth, child.'

'You mean there was a problem with Mary?' Flora asked, frowning with incomprehension.

'Oh no. This goes back before *her* birth even,' Surval said, and ducked inside.

'Hello, Gilda,' he said as he caught sight of her.

'Surval. What do you want?'

'An opportunity to offer you my sympathy,' he said, resting on a stool. 'I have known you all your life, after all.'

'You have,' she said bitterly. 'So I suppose you're really here to see if I know why your relative is dead.'

'My relative?'

'You didn't know?'

'I guessed,' he said, and sighed heavily. 'So it was as I thought. I am glad I came here when your husband was out.'

'My *husband*!' she burst out, and covered her face with her hands as she began sobbing.

Surval watched her for a while, but her grief was too all-consuming for him to feel at ease. Powerful emotion was unsettling to him. Quietly he rose and walked from the place, heading back towards his home, wondering vaguely who actually *was* her husband.

Ben belched and swallowed hard. The cider he was drinking was rough and thick, and he could feel it fighting back in his stomach. He should have eaten something, but he wasn't hungry. Already his head was growing dull, but he didn't care. Not now. It was good to have evaded the eye of the Bailiff and the Keeper.

'You were quiet enough about seeing the others, weren't you?' he chuckled to Elias.

'I told all I had to.'

'But you forgot Sir Ralph and his son passing by.'

Elias was startled. He shot a look at Ben. 'I didn't see the boy.'

'I did when I was up having a leak. He was there, all right.'

'I only saw his father,' Elias said.

'What of it? It must have been that priest, anyway. The shit got between Mary's thighs and made her pregnant, then killed her. Why else would he have run off like that? He deserves to have his neck stretched!'

'But if Esmon was there as well,' Elias said, 'it could have been either one of them.'

Baldwin followed Huward but didn't try to catch up with him until they were out of sight and earshot of the castle. There was something about the place that was making him feel very wary. The little uproar in the court had been perfectly judged. If Baldwin had not reacted so swiftly and had not thrust the two watchmen into the midst of the crowd, Mark might already be hanging – and there would be nothing which Baldwin could have pointed at in order to appeal either Roger Scut or Sir Ralph. Neither had openly incited the peasants, the mob was merely incensed by the implication of their words.

'Master Miller. Please wait a moment!'

Huward's expression was that of a man who was about to be tortured to death and who was intimately acquainted with each device designed to inflict the maximum pain. 'What do you want?'

Baldwin had left the watchmen with Simon, and now he was glad. Huward stood strongly, a large man with thick fingers and a broad back. He stood slightly bowed, as though he was preparing to spring, and Baldwin kept his attention fixed firmly on his eyes, watching for any sign that he might attack. However, Huward looked more like a man at the very end of his tether than one who was about to explode into murderous violence at any moment. Except there was something else in his face, Baldwin thought: a terrible, rending sadness that was wrenching him apart, a horror more overwhelming than any Baldwin had seen in many long years. It made Huward seem as though he was on the brink of complete collapse, as though he was about to submit to a fit of sobbing.

'Huward, I know this must seem like a terrible time for me to ask you more questions, but I have to.'

'Why? What about?'

'Come, let us walk.' Baldwin had a shrewd suspicion that a man used to working hard, either with his hands or simply with his muscles and his own lifting power, was easier to question when moving, as though a part of their minds only functioned when their bodies were engaged upon some activity. Huward appeared to have sprung from that kind of mould. His tension visibly reduced, and he moved his arms as though every muscle within had been tensed for action.

'You haven't said what you want to talk about.'

'There are two matters, of course. You know that perfectly well. The death of your daughter, and the death of Wylkyn the miner.'

'We know who killed my daughter,' Huward said dully. 'The Coroner said it was the priest. The mad monk.'

'It is possible,' Baldwin conceded, 'but answer me some questions. Your daughter, she had many boyfriends?'

'None. It made us rib her about it. She was never keen on any of the boys here.'

'Perhaps because she was seeing the priest already,' Baldwin said. He was silent a few moments. 'She was a good and dutiful daughter?'

Huward cleared his throat. 'She was perfect. Beautiful as a young doe, obedient and loving. I couldn't . . .' He broke off, coughed, and wiped at his face with an angry hand. 'Whoever did that to her, if I could just get my hands on him for a few minutes . . .'

'You mustn't dwell on it. If it was that boy in court today, you cannot touch him. You know that.'

'I don't care what some Bishop in his great palace says. That shit killed my little angel. *My* angel,' he repeated firmly. '*My* Mary. What do words from some priest above him mean to me? If he was here now, I'd pull his head off with my bare hands.'

He was flexing his fingers as he spoke, and Baldwin could all too easily imagine them gripping Mark's head and pulling until his bones cracked and his flesh submitted. Hands used to hefting

great sacks of grain were more than capable of tearing a lad like
Mark limb from limb. It brought to his mind a picture of a woman
with her neck broken. A neck was a tough construction, with
strong sinews and muscles. Breaking one was not easy with bare
hands.

'What of the miner? Did you know him?' he asked.

'Yes. He was all right, Wylkyn. He made up potions and salves
and helped Sir Richard.'

'Why should someone kill him?'

Huward glanced at him. 'He was waylaid and robbed. It
happens.'

'By whom?'

Huward threw out his hands. 'By whom? What do you care?
My angel is dead. Isn't that enough? Christ's cods! What do you
want from me?'

Baldwin spoke soothingly. 'I understand. But the miner: did
you see anyone up there?'

Huward stopped in his tracks. He didn't face Baldwin as he
spoke, but stood with his head lowered like a peasant who has
been found stealing and knows he must expect the stocks. 'I saw
the son of Sir Ralph with his men.' He stared at Baldwin. 'There!
Are you satisfied? If you repeat that to anyone, I shall be killed
too, I expect. Let that be on your head, knight.'

'Why should he kill that man?'

'Because he thrives on violence. He loves battle, and adores
money. They think they're impregnable, those bastards! They kill
and rob, and because they have powerful friends they can get
away with it.'

'The body has been stolen. Do you know who could have done
that?'

'Only a fool. If any man thought to avoid the Coroner's fines,
he didn't think well enough. He should have realised that once
Piers heard of it, news would get out,' Huward said scathingly.

'Who, though?'

'I don't know, nor do I care. All I care about is my Mary, and
what I am to do now with my family. My children . . .' His wide

eyes stared unseeing up the lane towards his mill. 'My wife and children . . . Oh, God! What have I done to deserve this?'

'Huward, I want to ask you one more question. Think carefully. I do not wish to expose you to more suffering, but I have to know what you think of this. If the boy, Mark, did *not* kill Mary, it must have been someone else. I understand from Elias that Sir Ralph passed by that road that day. Could it have been . . .?'

There was no need to complete the question. Huward's face had crumpled like a rotten apple stamped into the ground. When he spoke his voice was a hoarse whisper. 'He saw Sir Ralph?'

'I am truly sorry,' Baldwin said genuinely. 'He was reluctant to confess, but yes. He saw Sir Ralph.'

Huward tottered as though about to fall. He stared up towards the heavens, and Baldwin could see the tears running in thick streams down his cheeks. 'My God, I wish You had killed me with my Mary. *My Mary!*' He choked, and then Baldwin saw he was chuckling to himself without humour. It was a repellent sight, and Baldwin was about to strike his face, to try to calm him, when the chuckle became a groan, and then a racking sob. 'Oh Mary, my little angel! What can I do now? How can I live with this? Sir Ralph raped and murdered you? That's the worst! Is there no end to my misery? Will no one just kill me and remove this horror?'

'Friend,' Baldwin said, glancing at the way ahead, 'let me walk with you to your door. You shouldn't walk alone today.'

'I can walk to my own mill without help,' Huward retorted.

'Who is this?' Baldwin said. A young, swaggering figure was strolling after them, whistling. Baldwin recognised the fellow as soon as he saw the jug dangling from his fingers. It was Ben, and he was plainly drunk.

'Who is that, you ask? That is my son, Ben,' Huward said thickly. He watched Ben's approach with an expression of wistfulness, but when Ben stumbled, swearing foolishly as he dropped his pot and spilled his drink, Huward saw that he was drunk. Instantly his features radiated loathing and rage. 'When his sister is dead, he goes and . . .'

'Father. Have you finished at the court?' Ben slurred.

'Don't call me Father! You are no son of mine!' Huward spat, spun on his heel, and strode back towards the castle.

Chapter Twenty-One

Simon watched as Baldwin strode off hurriedly in the wake of the miller, and when he saw Elias and Piers exchange a look, he shrugged. 'He knows where we are going. Let's be off.'

They were walking along the road towards the barton where Elias and Piers lived, when there came a clattering of hooves, and a figure on horseback bolted from the castle's gates. Piers and Elias immediately hurried out of the way, and Simon glanced at them suspiciously, thinking that they were about to make a run for it, but then he heard a shout, and felt someone slam into his flank. To his astonishment, he found himself flying through the air, only to land in a large muddy pool.

Struggling upright as the noise of hooves died away, he saw it was Hugh who had knocked him down. He opened his mouth to roar at his servant, when he saw the blood starting to spread thinly, like an oil slick on water, over Hugh's face from a deep gash at the back of his scalp. At the same time Hugh's eyelids fluttered, and then he gave a loud gasp before slowly letting his head fall.

Baldwin could have wept to see how hurt Huward was by his son's behaviour. He felt like punching Ben as Huward stumbled off, but Ben had no interest in Baldwin or his father. 'Old cretin!' he muttered, tilting his jug to see whether there was any cider remaining. Seeing there wasn't, he flung the jug from him and set off towards the mill with a disconsolate frown.

The sight was repellent. Baldwin was about to move away when he saw another man observing Ben. It was the old hermit, clothed still in his worn and shabby tatters, leaning on a long staff. Seeing that Baldwin had noticed him, Surval made his way slowly towards him.

'It is a fine afternoon, Sir Knight.'

'Yes.'

'You sound like a man who has unasked questions. Carry on! Ask me what you want.'

'I've heard you used to be a priest.'

'That I was. Ah, but you want to know more, don't you? Very well. I was a priest in London. I always had what I thought was a vocation, and I was delighted to be so honoured. But then I learned to love. It is a terrible thing, to love. I adored a woman. She was young, fresh, beautiful, and determined to see me succeed in my profession.'

'So you were another Burnell?' Baldwin asked unkindly. Robert Burnell, the Bishop of Bath and Wells and sometime Chancellor of England until his death in 1292, had been notorious for promoting and helping his many 'nephews'. Archbishop Peckham hinted that he had fathered five boys from one woman alone.

'I was not so prolific,' Surval smiled sadly. 'I had one child by her already, and then I committed the worst of sins. My woman was arguing about money she needed when she was pregnant with our second and I – well, I was drunk. I beat her up, and that was the end of her *and* the child.'

'What happened to the other child?'

'He is here. But no – I shall not say who he is. That would only leave him open to still worse opprobrium.'

Baldwin felt the man's pain, but he could give no comfort. This man was hideous by his own confession. 'I suppose you claimed Benefit of Clergy?'

'I am alive, aren't I?' Surval asked. 'Tell me, do you think that priest killed Mary?'

Baldwin sniffed. He didn't want to remain in this hermit's company longer than he must. 'Perhaps. I am not sure.'

'I am: he couldn't. When you hit a pregnant girl, you realise what a terrible sin you have committed. You might remain at her side to ease her agony or, if you're a coward, you might run away – but you wouldn't run away and then return to finish her off by breaking her neck.'

'How do you know that's what he did?'

'The vill's idiot, Sampson. He was in the next field and heard the argument, then Mark run away. A short time later, he also heard Sir Ralph on his horse, but remained hidden because he was so fearful of the man. Later, Mark returned, and that was when he saw her.'

'Sampson did not tell me that. You are saying Sir Ralph killed her?'

'My God, no!' Surval said with obvious shock. 'Sir Ralph would not have harmed a hair on her head.'

'Then who did?'

'I don't know. I didn't see anything myself.'

'What about the death of Wylkyn? Do you know what happened to him?'

Surval gave him a look from under thick, bushy eyebrows. 'You know he was keen on potions and herbs? And Sir Richard died quite suddenly after a short illness. He had been prone to all kinds of illnesses, the poor man, but that was the consequence of his willingly ignoring the Pope's words and taking up weapons to entertain people in the joust.'

'You do not approve of such things?'

'I told you about my sin. I could never think to hurt someone again, and since my woman's death, I have taken the Pope's instructions very seriously. I could never commit such a crime again. No. And others should obey the Pope, too. Sir Richard suffered greatly. If he was fortunate, it will mean that he will have swiftly risen to Heaven. Like a leper, his pain will allow him more quickly to reach God's side, while those who remained hale and hearty all through their lives, enjoying wealth and power, will suffer the torments of devils!'

Baldwin sought to distract him from a long-winded sermon. 'What sort of illnesses did he have?'

Surval scowled as though struggling with the attraction of a lecture he had practised, but then shrugged. 'He had inflamed joints, fevers, gout . . . many afflictions.'

'Inflamed joints and gout wouldn't kill a man.'

'No, but a fever can, and he endured many. It was a fever finally killed him.'

There was a certain tone in his voice that made Baldwin pause. He said, 'You think Wylkyn poisoned him?'

'Stranger things have happened. And that would explain why an honourable man like Sir Ralph might want to punish him, mightn't it?'

'By murdering him?' Baldwin growled.

'No, by executing a murderer like any other felon.'

Walking along the road, Huward suddenly came upon the castle, and instantly he stopped, staring at it, wide-eyed, his mind, at first, quite blank. Gradually, as he recalled that mad bitch's hate-filled words that she spat at him like venom, his mind began to work again.

He couldn't stand the sight of the castle; he had to move away, go somewhere else, but his heart was pounding with a sickly rhythm. There was nowhere for him to go: his home was his no more, it was lost to him. He knew of nowhere he might go and find peace. Stumbling slightly, he crossed the road, away from the castle, and took the track up towards the moors. The way was dark, deeply wooded with great beech and oak trees rising on both sides, and with the sun moving behind the hills ahead, the whole area was grim and gloomy. Soon Huward felt a little calmer. Away from other people, he could see things more clearly. Perhaps there was a way through this mess. Unbidden, a picture of Flora appeared in his mind, and he choked as he recalled her beauty, her smiling face and calmness. He felt sweet affection for her – and revulsion.

Suddenly he was through. The trees fell away on either side, and he was climbing a shallow hill with a thin scattering of rocks about a rushing stream. As he continued, the wind played at his hair, whipping at his tunic and gusting occasionally hard enough to make him lean into it. A fine spray of mizzle was in the air, and he could feel it flick against his cheeks like fine needles.

Over the brow of the hill were the dark shapes of the ring of stones. All the men of the vill knew these stones, the Scorhill circle, and he walked to it, sitting with his back to one of them, staring eastwards towards the vill where he had been born, where he had grown, where he had married, and where he had been so utterly betrayed.

He had never guessed: how could he have been so stupid! A week ago, perhaps he would have disbelieved her, maybe even dared to scoff at her, if he had been in a more optimistic frame of mind, but in his present mood he knew that she was telling him the truth. There was no point in her lying to him. She could have no motive to lie – but plenty to tell him the facts. Christ Jesus! The *poison* in her voice!

The recollection of Lady Annicia's little speech tore at him. It had felt as though his very soul was shredding under the torrent of words, as though her cold anger and loathing for him and his entire family were penetrating him even now, so far from the castle. Wrapping his arms about himself, he dully registered that he was not dressed for a night on the moors. He should return to the security at least of the trees, if not the safety of his mill, but he daren't do that. He didn't know what he might do if he went back there. No, better to sit here, maybe to die here. There was nothing for him to live for, not now. All he valued had been taken.

He heard the sound of splashing water, and then, as he squinted up the hill, he saw a figure, a man, dressed in filthy grey clothing, with a thick, bushy beard and dark, grim eyes: Surval.

The hermit slowly made his way to the miller and stood leaning on his staff, gazing down. 'I thought you'd be here.'

'You knew. All this time, you knew.'

'No. I only learned today; before, I only suspected.'

'I suppose I am too stupid to have realised.'

'You were always too kind for your own good. Others are more cynical.'

'And now little Mary is dead. Is that my fault too?'

'None of it is your fault, friend, you were just unfortunate.'

'It's a bit bloody easy for you to say that, isn't it!' Huward snapped. 'For me it seems very straightforward, now I can see the facts for myself.'

'Perhaps you are wrong to fear? They could all be your children.'

'Instead of *his*!' Huward spat bitterly. 'Yes, but my wife still cleaved to him, even when she was married to me. My whole marriage is a lie.'

'I had wondered. I had seen him with her many long years ago,' Surval said sadly.

'Why did she marry me, then?'

'Perhaps because she knew she could never marry him.'

'So instead of her being miserable alone, she has ruined all our lives. I shall have to leave. I don't know if either or neither of them are mine.'

'Or both.'

'You expect me to remain on the off-chance?' Huward sneered.

The hermit grunted, then slowly eased himself down to sit at Huward's side. 'It's always easier to see things after the event.'

'Oh, *good*! I suppose you mean I should be glad to have seen it at last. It's no comfort, hermit. No comfort at all.'

'No. God doesn't offer comfort, miller. Only hard effort and the will to resist temptation.' The very thought made him shiver.

Huward noticed. 'It's cold, but where else can I go, Surval – eh? Where can I call home? My family is no more, my life is ended. How can I find peace?'

Surval didn't look at the miller, but stared out over the trees towards the castle. 'A good question. I wish I knew the answer, old friend. All I can say is, that tonight you may come to my home and stay there with me. I have a duty to help poor travellers.'

'Yes. That's all I am now, isn't it? A poor traveller. An outlaw,' Huward said. 'And through no fault of mine! I have done nothing wrong.'

'Then *you*, my friend, are truly fortunate,' Surval said quietly.

Baldwin found Simon at the castle gate. Piers and Elias were helping to carry Hugh, and the knight stared down at the man's bloody face with astonishment and concern. He had only left them a few moments ago. 'What is this?' he asked. 'Has Hugh been attacked?'

'That cretinous son of a mutinous Breton pirate, Esmon, rode past and all but ran us down!' Simon hissed. 'If Hugh hadn't knocked me aside, I'd be here instead of him, but as it was, a hoof caught his head.'

'Where?'

Simon pointed out the shallow slash in Hugh's scalp where the horseshoe had sheared though his flesh and exposed the pink bones beneath. 'I want a quiet room with no draughts and a good fire,' he said curtly to a servant.

The servant, a fat but curiously cheerless-looking fellow, shrugged and glanced across the courtyard at Brian, who lounged against a wall. Simon grated, 'Fetch your master! I don't want to stand out here all bloody night.'

He saw the fat man peer again at the man-at-arms, saw that worthy curl his lip and give a short shake of his head, and then turn away as though uninterested. The servant pulled a face, and then drew away.

It was enough to fan the fire that was already glowing in Simon's breast. Hugh had been his only servant for many years. When he married Meg, it was Hugh who had helped organise the nuptials; when they moved to Sandford to their new farm, it was Hugh who made sure that their belongings arrived safely; when they travelled to Lydford, it was Hugh who made the castle as welcoming as he could. Hugh was an integral part of Simon's life, and Simon's family. Surly, he was, yes, grim-featured at the best of times, monosyllabic and dour, but he was Simon's friend, and he had saved Simon from attack before now, he had saved Simon's wife, and he had won this wound by saving Simon from death once again.

He reached out and grasped the fat servant's shoulder. At the same time he drew his sword. It all happened as though he was watching it through an all-enveloping red fog, a swirling mistiness that shimmered about him. '*Get your fucking master now, or I'll cut out your liver and feed it to the hogs, you beshitted worm,*' he ground out.

The servant gaped, his chins wobbling. As Simon loomed over him, he gave a squeak, turned, and bolted like a rabbit which has seen the hound. There was a shout from the castle walls and a rattle of metal, and he looked up to see that a guard was desperately trying to haul the string back on a crossbow. Brian had drawn his own sword and was approaching them, while behind him more men were coming from the hall's door, all wearing weapons. One held a short dagger by the point and was throwing it in the air and catching it meditatively while watching Simon.

Baldwin saw that the two watchmen were eyeing the guards with trepidation, but not fear, and he was pleased that they were not intimidated. 'Hold!' he shouted, his hand in the air. He too had seen the man trying to string his crossbow, but pulling back on the string with main force was all but impossible. He needed a crank or belt hook, and he seemed to have neither. Baldwin turned his attention back to the men-at-arms on the ground nearby.

They were a mixed bunch, probably aged from twenty to forty or fifty, and all looked like men who had profited from war while accepting the buffets that combat brought. There were many scarred faces and several missing fingers among them – and no cowards. All walked forward steadily until the little group was surrounded. Piers and Elias looked very unhappy at this turn of events, but Baldwin kept his eyes on the leading man.

'Where is Sir Ralph?' he called mildly.

'He's busy,' said Brian.

'So busy he wants to see two King's officials attacked in his own castle?' Baldwin chuckled. 'I think you will find that if either the good Stannary Bailiff or I myself are harmed, the men responsible will pay very dearly.'

The leader of the men snapped his fingers under Baldwin's nose. 'If we want, we can lose your bodies! There are places on the moors where a man can be lost for ever.'

Baldwin smiled broadly at the man. 'Is that what you did with the body of the miner?'

'I don't know what you're talking about.'

'I wonder who did move him, then.'

'Nothing to do with us,' the man said confidently.

There came a roar from the other side of the yard. 'What is this? Brian, what are you doing there?'

Baldwin held Brian's eye as he responded, and was sure that there was a certain annoyance in his face as he spoke.

'It's the Keeper, Sir Ralph. I knew you'd be busy, so I wouldn't let him interrupt you.'

'You didn't think you'd interrupt me?' Sir Ralph said with a calmness that heralded a storm. 'That was very kind of you, Brian.'

'You were with your priest.'

Baldwin pricked up his ears at that. Sir Ralph's 'priest' must be Roger Scut. What the man was doing here was a mystery to Baldwin, but whatever it was, it must be directly to Scut's benefit.

'All you men, withdraw. Now!' Sir Ralph bellowed.

The men drew away, for the most part reluctantly; the knife-thrower tossed his blade up one last time, and then suddenly caught it and sent it whirling into the door at the hall's entrance. It struck there, quivering, a few inches from the fat servant's head, and the man gazed at the knife with terror in his eyes.

The good Sir Ralph had best evict these warriors before they tried to take over the castle, Baldwin thought. There were plenty of others who had attempted to capture the castles which they were supposed to protect.

'Sir Baldwin, Bailiff Puttock, I offer my sincere apologies,' Sir Ralph said as the men dispersed. He walked to them from the door to the hall. 'I had no idea you were being molested until I heard the shouting.'

Over his shoulder, Baldwin saw Roger Scut peering through a doorway, but he turned his attention back to the knight as Simon explained angrily about the rider who had almost knocked him down.

'My son is very careless, I fear,' Sir Ralph said. His face was pale, and he kept drawing up the side of his mouth, like a man who had a hole in a tooth and was probing it with his tongue. Baldwin thought he must be more worked up about these men of his son's than he wanted to admit.

'What of my man here?' Simon ranted. 'Who is the best physician in this vill? I demand that he be called immediately. Do you hear me? If this man is harmed, I shall see you and all your household fined. Is that clear?'

His angry voice set a vein throbbing in Sir Ralph's temple. He peered at the furious Bailiff. 'Don't give orders me, Puttock! You may have power in your little castle of Lydford, but here, it is *my* word which counts. Yet I shall send my wife to help you. She is good with wounds. Take this fellow into the hall and she'll see him in there.'

Piers and Elias lifted Hugh gently, and he groaned, a sound that made Simon throw him a fretful look, and then they followed Sir Ralph into the hall. The knight roughly ordered some remaining men-at-arms from the room, and before long they had the place to themselves.

'Did he try to ride you down?' Baldwin asked Simon quietly.

'I don't know. He came on me from behind, so I couldn't see him or what he intended, but know this, Baldwin: if a rider approaches a man on foot from behind, if there is a collision, it is not the fault of the man who could not see or do anything to avoid him. It's always the rider's fault.'

'Yes. That bastard has some questions to answer,' Baldwin said. Not only about this latest incident, either. According to Huward, Esmon was the leader of the men who had robbed the carters on their way to Chagford, and according to Surval, he was motivated by the need to punish a murderer. Not that Baldwin could count on either making their accusations in court. Any denunciation against their own lord must result in their being punished severely, and without it, there was little likelihood that Baldwin could secure Sir Ralph's or Esmon's arrest for the murder of Wylkyn. Baldwin must find a means of ensuring that someone might appeal them, but also he must persuade a jury that they would not be in danger if they decided to uphold the conviction. He would have to call juries from the nearest four vills to secure a conviction here, he reckoned.

'This is a curious matter, Simon,' he murmured. 'Consider: the death of the girl, then the murder of the miner, and robbery of his companions, and now we have this careless attack on you. Why should someone want to harm you? Especially that fool Esmon. Most people seem to think that Mark is responsible for the girl's death; but some think it might have been Sir Ralph or Esmon, and many believe that Esmon could have killed the miner; now he tries to ride you down.'

'He won't do that again,' Simon swore softly. 'When I meet him next, I'll teach him to try to hurt a Bailiff of the Stannaries.'

'You must be cautious, Simon. He has many men-at-arms here,' Baldwin warned. 'If he feels strong enough to rob carters, he will feel strong enough to destroy you as well. Perhaps he fears you.'

'Fears me? Why should he?' Simon scoffed.

'You represent the Stannary. If he could say that you were killed in an accident, it is possible that the death of Wylkyn might go uninvestigated.'

Simon merely grunted, but Baldwin knew he was not foolish enough to risk escalating problems while they were all in Sir Ralph's castle.

'I never had time to send to Chagford!' Simon realised.

Lady Annica's soft, slightly slurred words silenced both. 'Come. Let me see this man's wound. What has happened to him?'

Baldwin and Simon exchanged a look. There was nothing to be done immediately. They went to speak with the Lady of the castle.

Chapter Twenty-Two

Alan, Saul's apprentice, tipped the bowl back and felt the cool draught wash down his throat, taking away the dust from the journey as it passed down his gullet. That was the trouble with riding in a line with other carters when the roads were drying. Wherever there was dust, everyone swallowed it. Refilling the bowl, he could sense the warmth spreading from his belly through his body. It was just as though someone had lighted a fire in his stomach.

'Careful, boy. You'll get drunk again!'

Alan gave a pale grin. His calmness had almost returned now that they were in the small town of Chagford. They had at least managed to sell most of their goods at the market, and Saul himself was delighted with the prices he had won for his cheeses: the men here paid good sums for produce because Chagford was so far from civilisation and the roads leading here were appalling. Most of the buyers were miners who had little money, but they were happy to pay for Alan's stock of iron blades for shovels, for his spikes, adzes and hammers.

'After the last couple of days, I wouldn't mind getting drunk.'

There were so many people in this inn it had taken an age to reach the large plank of wood which was the bar. All about them, men sipped their ales or ciders while keeping an eye on all these foreigners. Men who lived in market towns like Chagford might need the money that carters and buyers brought, but that didn't mean they had to like the folk that brought it, and several of the older men in this tavern looked as though they would be happier if all the market people would clear off. Traders were welcome in the market, but not here in the taverns, where all they did was block access to the bar.

It wasn't only the older locals who eyed Alan and his friends askance, either. There was a wealthy-looking fellow in one corner who appeared as unhappy about the noise and commotion as any. He sat on a low stool, his legs thrust out before him. Although he was clad in an expensive-looking tunic of some velvet of crimson, it had faded. His hosen were of a soft green material, but were heavily bespattered with mud of red, brown and black, and his boots were scuffed and stained. A thick grey riding cloak with a leather hood sat rolled into a bundle on the floor beside him, and his upper body was encased in a leathern jacket, cut long to fall to the knee.

His dark eyes looked unpleasant and cold; his was the sort of face which Alan thought would suit one of the men who had swept down the hill at him on the day that the raid had taken place. He had the same blank look of a man who was used to dealing in death. Alan shivered.

Saul drained his pot and belched, wiping a hand over his beard. 'There will always be footpads about, boy, and it's not worth worrying about them. Leave that to the Sheriff. You concentrate on what you're good at: helping me buy and sell for a profit.'

'So they can rob us again?'

'If you have a brain you won't come that way again,' Saul said thickly. The cold which had assailed him on the way here had developed, during their incarceration at Gidleigh Castle, into a real snorter, and he ran his nose over his sleeve again, leaving a glistening trail. His eyes lowered to the table and his voice dropped at the same time. 'I don't think you should go talking about it too much, though. They're powerful men, them who robbed us.'

'I see. Let the buggers get away with it, you mean?'

'Get involved in something like that, and you'll never get away from the town, boy. You'll have the Keeper of the Peace demanding you turn up in his court, the Sheriff too, and then you'll have to come back when the Justices return. Do you want all that?'

The idea of accusing men the like of Sir Ralph made Alan feel queasy.

'That's right, boy! Just leave things as they are.'

Alan nodded into his bowl. Sir Ralph was a knight, and knights could do much as they wanted, because the law hardly affected them. Esmon had been seen by many witnesses leading the attack on the carters, but that wouldn't have much impact. He was the son of a knight – what, would anyone expect a knight's lad to be held in gaol ready for the Justices? Of course not. Esmon would be out of court in minutes, his father's friends putting up money to meet the cost of his bond, and then he would make sure that the Justices would have no one to accuse him in their courts: he'd personally murder Alan, or maybe he'd simply pay one of his men to do it. Either way, he'd be safe and Alan would be dead, which was not a prospect that appealed much to Alan.

The tavern was raucous, and they had to raise their voices more than once as they talked over the robbery. It was a small place, built of solid moorstone, and stood a short distance from Chagford's marketplace, which was why at present it was filled with shouting, laughing and swearing miners. Two wenches were negotiating their services at one corner, Alan could tell, because the crush of drunken men was thickest there, and outside at the back there was a cock-fighting pit, with a regular turn-around of protagonists, so the noise swelled and broke from the cheering and cursing spectators there, making conversation still more difficult.

'This isn't our *Frankpledge*, after all,' Saul added persuasively. He had to shout to make himself heard.

'But it means letting a man's murderer go unpunished.'

'Oh, sod that! I never saw a man die. Maybe he escaped! If it makes us more secure, leave it alone, that's what I say.'

It was as he spoke those fateful words that Alan happened to glance across the room. The well-dressed man was staring at them both with a frown, as if displeased at something he had heard. Slowly, to Alan's concern, the man pulled his legs back and stood. He picked up his bundled cloak and walked over to Alan and Saul.

'I heard you talking about letting a murderer go. I don't think you should do that.'

'None of your business.'

'Isn't it?' The man pulled his jerkin back to show his sword and long-bladed knife as he took a stool and sat on it. 'I would have thought that a murder would always prove interesting to the King's Coroner. Now, suppose you two tell me about this murder of yours.'

Lady Annicia was gentle as she and a woman-servant washed Hugh's bloody face and scalp. With the help of Godwen, who held Hugh's head still, she shaved it before inspecting the gash.

Simon was easy about this, but Baldwin felt decidedly uncomfortable. It was one thing to see a dead body being prodded and poked, but to his mind it was quite another to see someone who was still alive being treated like this. Or maybe he didn't like to see a personal acquaintance lying there. Whatever the reason, Baldwin couldn't face remaining in that room. When Annicia stood and mumbled about fetching herbs, he was first to the door to open it for her.

They didn't speak. Baldwin took deep breaths of the clean, smoke-tinged air as he trailed after her. There was a faintly sour sweetness on the air, and he realised it was her winey breath. He hoped that she had found time to doze after the court session, because he didn't want Hugh to be harmed by being tended to by a drunken angel. As he considered this, she walked to the small room built on the side of the gatehouse, and opened the door.

When he peered in, he gave a low whistle. 'A marvellous stock.'

'Hmm?' she asked, glancing up. 'Oh, yes. It's Wylkyn's store. He used to make all sorts of things to ease Sir Richard's pain.'

She sounded as though her mind was elsewhere. Baldwin set his head to one side. 'My Lady, are you well?'

'Well? Yes – why?'

'My Lady, I merely noticed that you seem a little distracted, that is all. If it is something with which I can help, please feel free to ask.'

To his consternation, her eyes suddenly filled with tears. 'I am a foolish woman, Sir Knight. I was told a secret today, and just

because I was in a fey and foolish mood, I told another. I fear that
my husband will be very displeased with me when he hears. But
no, there is nothing you or anyone else can do to help me.'

She was still slurring her words slightly, but it was hard now to
see that she was drunk, apart from a certain deliberation in her
movements. Baldwin watched her carefully as she moved among
the potions, but she looked safe enough. Only very sad.

'Sir Richard died suddenly, I heard.'

'No. He was in his bed for a few days, but then he often was.
Poor man. I think he gave up in the end. He knew he couldn't keep
this place.'

'His back and face must have been constantly painful.' Baldwin
glanced at some drying leaves, and then he frowned.

'Not just them. He had an awful case of gout in his good leg,
which made it impossible for him to walk. That was why he took
to his bed in the first place.'

'Gout? That wouldn't kill him.'

'No.' She had found the jug she wanted. She shook some
powder into a cloth, then added some more from a second
earthenware pot. Transferring them to a mortar, she began
grinding and mixing the powders with the pestle. 'He died, I
believe, when he had a spasm, and that was that.'

'Oh? I had thought he died from a fever.'

She squinted at him. 'Not exactly. He had a bad case of gout, to
which he was prone, and took to his bed. Then a mild fever
attacked him and he was ill for some days.'

'What were the signs of his illness?'

'Blurred vision,' she said, 'I remember that. Then he grew
giddy and complained of his head aching, and slept a great deal,
but then he fell into delirium. In the end he had great convulsions,
and during the last one, he died. I don't know what could have
done this to him. If he had cut himself, I should have thought it
was one of those fevers, and I would have expected an inflamed
limb, but there was no sign like that. Perhaps we should have bled
him more. With such diseases, it is hard to know the best cure.
And he had suffered so much during his life, with all his twisted

and badly-set bones. Even eating was a torment, because of his mouth.'

Baldwin remembered Sir Richard's face. It had been all but sliced in two by a massive sword-blow. One eye was gone, and his jaw had been shattered on that side. His hideous injuries can have given poor Sir Richard no peace from the moment he received them.

Baldwin glanced at the leaves again. Gout could be helped, he knew, by the leaves of henbane, but life could be ended: henbane was a fierce poison.

When they returned, rather than staying in the gloomy hall, Baldwin walked to Thomas, who stood watching the yard outside.

'Are you all right?' he asked the Constable.

Thomas shrugged. 'I'm here, miles from my home, far from my wife, and stuck with *him*.'

Baldwin didn't need to glance in the direction of his jerked thumb: he knew Thomas was indicating Godwen.

'Come with me, then,' he said, and strode out into the yard.

'What do you want out here?' Thomas asked, trotting to keep up with Baldwin's long stride.

'Roger Scut. I want to know what he thinks there is in all this for him.'

'Him? He'll see money. That's the only reason he ever puts himself out for anything. Money or gold for himself.'

'How could he see money in this place?' Baldwin wondered.

Thomas glanced about him. 'He'll see some advantage, he always does. Same way as he always fleeces people – like poor Jack.'

Baldwin was listening with only half an ear to his mutterings, but the mention of the groom in Crediton made his ears prick up again. 'What is all that about Jack? You said that Roger Scut is his landlord and that Jack's rents are always going up, didn't you?'

'Yes. Jack is one of his serfs, but he used to be successful until Scut took over his demesne. Scut inherited the land and all the free or servile tenants on it.'

'Get to the point.'

'It's this. Until Scut arrived, Jack was doing well. He had bought land, animals, commuted his service by paying the Manor to get someone else in to do his work, and then increased his wealth and his animals by his efforts.'

'That is good.'

'Yes. Except Jack was a serf, so he couldn't own anything without his lord's agreement. Scut took the land back, then increased Jack's rents and let him rent the extra lands back for still more money. He also told Jack that he couldn't sell his produce anywhere except direct to the Canons at Crediton – and he had to agree to whatever price they offered. Now he can't afford to resow his fields with grain, and he has to scratch a living by grooming horses, helping out at the tavern and trying to manage with his three cows.'

'That is immoral. How can a lord take away lands that he never gave to his bondsmen in the first place?' Baldwin asked. It was all too common, he knew, but he hated it nonetheless. It was an abuse of the power a lord held over his serfs.

'There he is!'

Following Thomas's pointing finger, Baldwin saw Roger Scut walking from the small chapel beyond the castle's hall.

He looked pale, Baldwin thought, like a man who had swallowed a shellfish and realised that it did not agree with him. 'Scut, I want to speak to you,' he called out.

'Yes, Sir Baldwin? Oh, and your Constable. What do you want?' Roger Scut said, peering down his nose at them enquiringly.

'What are you up to here?' Baldwin asked. 'You came here with us to protect the lad, or so you said, and then in the court you betrayed him badly.'

'I surely said nothing that could have been construed as a betrayal? I listened hard to what he had to say, but when I commented on his abilities, that was *your* fault, Sir Baldwin.'

'*My* fault?' Baldwin grated.

'At the inn at Crediton, you suggested that Mark might not even have been a cleric, that he could have been an outlaw who had filched the papers of a clerk from one of his victims. Naturally, when he was asked to speak the words of a prayer, and could not, I began to wonder whether your initial scepticism might have been justified.'

'Do not try to blame me for your actions,' Baldwin said, incensed that this pompous little fellow was attempting to put the onus for Mark's position on Baldwin's shoulders. 'You should have merely claimed him for your lord's court. Instead you chose to throw him to the crowd like meat to a hunting pack.'

'I did no such thing. All I did was make a comment on his ability.'

'Which was the same thing. Scut, what do you seek here?'

Roger Scut's face altered subtly and Baldwin instantly knew that the man was about to lie. 'Why, Sir Baldwin, all I wish to do here is support a fellow cleric. If he is one, of course.'

'If he fails to convince, he will be executed here,' Baldwin stated.

'I sincerely hope not! Surely our Bishop will save him,' Roger Scut said, adding meditatively, 'But I shall have to remain here, no matter what. There are so many poor souls desperate for comfort, and I should wait here until another cleric is nominated to take his place.'

'In that chapel?' Baldwin said, recalling vaguely a small one-roomed building with a lean-to at the side from his last visit to the area. It did not strike him as being particularly attractive.

'Well, when the new one is built, yes. Until then I shall have to stay in here, I suppose.'

'What new one?' Baldwin demanded. 'What are you talking about?'

'The new chapel, of course. Didn't you know the old one was destroyed? Someone burned it to the ground.'

Baldwin shook his head. 'A terrible act.'

'Sacrilege, yes. The people here will have to pay dearly for their destruction,' Roger Scut said. 'But fortunately I have experience of making serfs work and be obedient. Perhaps this is my true vocation in life, to see to it that this place has a decent church.'

* * *

Annicia left Hugh feeling pleased that she had been able to alleviate a little of the man's pain. She hoped he would recover. Perhaps he wouldn't. It was always so difficult to predict whether a patient would or wouldn't survive.

Simon had watched her closely, but he was relieved to see that she was as capable and self-assured as any physician.

'You are well practised, Lady.'

She looked up at Simon, who had moved silently to stand beside her.

'Yes. This castle has always been well provided with people to be practised upon!'

Simon glanced at her enquiringly.

'Sir Richard, and since him ... well, there have been others. My son's men are often hurt in their training.'

He nodded. 'Is there anything else we should do for Hugh?'

'Your concern does you credit, Bailiff, but I think the main thing he needs right now is plenty of sleep and a good bleeding. I'll send a messenger to Chagford in the morning to fetch a phlebotomist. It is lucky you were so close to the castle when he was knocked down.'

'Perhaps if we'd been further away your son wouldn't have tried to do this,' Simon said ungraciously.

'Esmon?' she said, a hand going to her throat. 'Why should he do this?'

'I don't know, but my man there saved my life by throwing me from the path of Esmon's mount. If he hadn't, I'd be lying there instead of Hugh.'

She looked back at Hugh, then wished Simon a good night before leaving him, her mind whirling, and not only from the slight dizziness of a mild hangover.

Attacking the Bailiff was a ridiculous thing to do, Annicia thought distractedly. She would have hoped that Esmon would have shown more sense. His father was cleverer than to simply try to ride down a Stannary Bailiff. Sometimes subtlety was needed. Why couldn't her son behave more circumspectly, the fool! His father had always been more sensible, more pragmatic, she reflected. The memories brought a smile to her face.

Then her smile faded. Her husband was as much of a fool as her son now, she thought. Ever since he had acquired this castle by devious means, befriending the King's favourite and making himself politically useful, he seemed to have lost his integrity. She deplored his behaviour.

Sir Ralph had told her that morning of his affair with Huward's wife. Gilda had been his concubine since before his marriage to Annicia, whom he had wed for the reason that he craved her father's lands: in marrying her, he gained them as well. The union was rational and steady, if unfulfilling, but it was humiliating to think that he had gone to Gilda, a rough, untutored peasant with the coarse hands and skin of a villein, rather than to her own fragrant bed.

Annicia set her jaw. Yes. It was deeply shaming to think that her husband could have committed adultery with a woman like Gilda when Annicia herself was willing to submit to him. That was why she had spoken to Huward and told him about their spouses, told him the truth about his children. It was pure spite. Perhaps, she thought, Huward would go home and beat Gilda. She deserved it!

Her brow furrowed, she sat back, listening to the sounds of the castle closing for the night. Thinking of Sir Ralph's errant behaviour made her head ache, as well as the shouts, footsteps pattering across the yard, men roaring for ale and food, and laughter. There were few enough women in the place. Women were always thought of as a distraction, Annicia considered, just like Mary. She had *definitely* been a distraction!

Standing, Annicia went to the window that gave out on the court. The windows here had no glazing. Sir Richard had had no money to install glass, and in the time since they had taken possession of the castle, Sir Ralph had not had the opportunity to address such matters with all his other responsibilities. Not that it mattered in most of the rooms. They had strong shutters that either pulled inwards and lay flat against the wall, or dropped vertically in runners, held up overnight by a strong thong which hooked over a peg in the wall above.

Annicia had grown up with shutters. It was no hardship to live with them. It was better that a door should block the harshest breezes, and that shutters should exclude snow and rain. There was no need of glass.

Suddenly her eyes were drawn to the old castle keep on her right. The upper chamber was built into the hillside, and the upper door gave out onto the grassed sward beyond. No doubt in years past, there had been another wall planned which would have secured this area, making it impossible for an attacking force to reach the keep itself, but Sir Richard had never possessed the money for that either, so a thin palisade stood there to protect the whole of the court area. It was sufficient to keep the odd draw-latch or cut-throat away, but that was about it.

She thought about her son. Trying to kill the Bailiff in broad daylight was stupid. Executing Wylkyn was different, of course. That evil man had to die for what he had done.

She had felt nervous in Wylkyn's old room when Sir Baldwin started asking about Sir Richard's death and looked at the henbane. Although she was reasonably sure that she had concealed her alarm at his questions, she was convinced that he had guessed. He must have some leach-craft. Well, never mind. If he had, he would see the same as Annicia – that Wylkyn had killed his own master. He deserved to die for that. How any man could wish to kill a poor soul like Sir Richard was beyond her, but she had no doubt. That was why she had spoken to her husband and son, why she had told them what Wylkyn had done, and persuaded them that someone who could commit petty treason like that had to be slaughtered like a rabid dog, without compunction, before others got the same idea.

It had been her aim to have Wylkyn brought back to the castle, to be held there and killed before her eyes, but perhaps it was better this way. If Esmon was arrested, she would be able to state that they had wanted to arrest Sir Richard's murderer, but he refused to surrender. And then, with the Keeper in the vicinity, they grew alarmed.

There was some truth in it, after all. Esmon had had the body hidden rather than leaving it at the roadside. Hiding it satisfied Annicia – it meant that her son was safe from accusations of murder, for no man could be convicted when there was no body, and she knew Sir Richard's murderer had died unshriven and now lay concealed on unhallowed ground. A suitable end to him, so she felt.

'Damn him!' she hissed suddenly.

Chapter Twenty-Three

Mark couldn't help himself. As soon as they hurled him bodily down the ladder into the cavern, his chained hands catching on a rung and all but dislocating his shoulder, utter despair overtook him. The ladder was hauled out, the hatch slammed shut, sprinkling a thin smattering of filth over him and blocking out much of the sun. Only a couple of cracks in the boards of the trap door showed that it was not yet night-time.

This situation was impossible. He must die here. His belly rumbled its complaints at remaining empty for another night, but the despair he felt was nothing to do with mere hunger, it was the ruination of himself.

As the light overhead faded and disappeared, he remained squatting on the floor, his back to the wall, weeping uncontrollably. He felt much as a child who had suddenly discovered that there were hideous depths to human nature. He had come here seeking his father, and instead he had discovered love – and loss. Now, blamed for the death of his lover, his own father was determined to destroy him. There could be no more desolate person in the entire world.

The bolt moving above him made him give a small bleat of fear. They must be going to beat him again. Dully he watched as the ladder slowly descended, and then suddenly fell with a faint splash into the ordure of the floor, spattering him again. This time he was past caring. There was nothing that could make him smell or look worse, and he was not of a mind to worry even if there had been.

There was an odd silence. He had expected the same noise, the same torchlight as last night, but there was nothing. Only the ladder and blackness above.

It was a terrifying hole. Beyond it, he was sure, was a group of men who wanted to prove their courage by beating him. Men who only last week would have obeyed his commands because they came from God Himself through Mark.

He cringed back, an arm up to shield his head, peeping up through his fingers. Not a sound, not a flash of light, nothing broke the monotony of the silence. He could almost imagine that God had immolated all the persons in the castle, leaving only Mark to survive. But why should God do that?

Up above him he could hear the normal noises of a stable. The soft splat of fresh dung as a pony lifted its tail, the murmur of a horse, a hoof moving against cobbles. All sounded so peaceful, so comforting, that Mark was tempted to climb the ladder, but knew he'd be battered if he tried.

When the voice came, it was a relief purely because it put an end to the waiting. Now, he thought, he knew his fate. The men of the vill were determined that he was guilty and they were going to make him pay for killing Mary. If Huward was there, he'd want to see Mark screaming for forgiveness. He'd want to see Mark in intolerable pain.

He tried to hide himself in the corner of the cell, not that there was any point. If they lit a candle or a lamp, they'd see him soon enough. Any moment now, he thought, they'd launch themselves down the ladder. This silence was their way of increasing his tension, making his anxiety mount so that by the time they actually came for him, he'd be incapable of self-defence. Perhaps if he was more courageous, he could surprise them, scramble up the ladder and attack them. He might escape – but no. There was little hope of that. Still, he could make sure he was killed quickly, without torture. But he wasn't brave like that. The thought of throwing himself at men like Esmon and his father filled him with dread.

There was still no noise. Just the steady drip of water and the occasional clop of a hoof as a horse shifted. That was strange. If there were many men up there, the horses would have been upset, and he'd have expected a dog to bark and complain at being woken. Yet there was nothing. It was as though his gaolers had left after throwing open the door to his cell.

If this was intended to increase his fear and alarm, it was working! He felt as though he was about to void his empty bowels.

And then the irritable voice called down to him: 'If you want to hang, stay there. I'm for my bed. But if you want to escape, go to the side of the keep. There's a ladder there to the top of the wall, and you can escape easily. The key to your shackles is here.'

Mark listened to the footsteps receding, his mouth gaping. This must be a cynical ploy, another way to increase his terror – give him an apparent escape route and then capture him at the top of the ladder to this cell, or at the foot of the other – if there was one.

Yet the idea of escaping was so sweet, he could have wept.

A drip landed on his head, and he could smell the strong taint of horse's piss as more followed it, flowing down his back. This decided him. He strode to the ladder and climbed, feeling as though he was ascending to the waiting rope. As promised, the key to his chains lay on the cobbles.

As he turned the key in the locks and the chains fell away, he felt lighter, refreshed, like a man newly born.

'Simon, wake up, quickly! The damned priest's escaped!'

Simon slowly came to as a harsh braying sounded from outside. 'Sweet mother of God, what is that?' he grunted.

Baldwin gave an exasperated exclamation. Simon was always bad after an evening's drinking, and last night he had excelled himself. Baldwin had been more cautious, thinking that Sir Ralph might seek to remove the two thorns in his flesh at a stroke, but nothing happened. The food was plentiful if bland, which suited Baldwin's palate, and the ale and wine was of good quality. After the meal, Baldwin had watched as Roger Scut stood and pronounced Grace. He had worn a satisfied smile on his face, and Baldwin wondered what he had been discussing with his neighbour, Esmon. Something that would be of advantage to Roger Scut, and no help to Mark, Baldwin was sure. Lady Annicia had not been present. Perhaps she was nursing a headache after her drunkenness earlier in the day.

It had taken all his diplomatic skills to keep Simon from offering violence to Esmon. He had sat glowering all through the meal, but even in this mood he wasn't stupid enough to actually draw a knife against the son of a magnate in that magnate's own hall, in front of the whole of his household. Instead he had taken as much ale as he could and fell asleep snoring loudly on Baldwin's shoulder.

'In God's name, Simon, wake up, will you? That's the horn of the Reeve: the local Hue and Cry are trying to find Mark, and we must get to him first.'

'Let them. If he's bolted, that's as good as a confession.'

'If the locals get to him, they will tear him limb from limb. We have to find him, and bring him back here as quickly as we may, so that he can be safely installed in his cell.'

'They won't dare harm him,' Simon yawned. 'He still claims to be a blasted priest. Sir Ralph won't want to upset Bishop Walter.'

Baldwin threw Simon his tunic, and his usual calm was gone as he grated, 'Your mind is still sleeping, Bailiff. The chapel in which Mark lived has been razed to the ground. If Mark had any letters confirming his position, they were surely in the church or his home, and they are both no more.'

'That doesn't matter, does it?' Simon yawned again, closing his eyes and shoving the tunic from his blanket. 'The Bishop can always send a new letter.'

'Yes, he can, once he learns of Mark's position, but that could take weeks, and in the meantime the boy is likely to die of malnourishment, mistreatment or fever. There is nothing here to confirm his position in the Church. He has lost everything!'

At last his words sank into Simon's fuddled brain. He reopened his eyes and gazed about him blearily, then reluctantly sat up, scratching the bites at his armpits where fleas had attacked him. 'So he has nothing to verify his post?' Simon said, pulling his tunic over his head.

'No, Mark has nothing to prove his clerical status,' Baldwin said, watching as Simon pulled up his hose. 'And although that should not matter, we both know it will! The men of this vill are already so enraged about the murder that they'll seek to kill him as a confessed felon. His escape is all the proof they want, although Bishop Walter may choose to extort a high price for their behaviour later.'

'Even my Lord Bishop will be reluctant to impose too stiff a penalty on Sir Ralph. We have heard him say that this damned priest should be protected. He said so before witnesses.'

'True enough, not that it means a thing,' Baldwin observed. 'He made sure that he said the correct things in court, while still inciting his villeins to fury. But enough of him! We have to try to find this miserable priest before someone else does.'

'He must be mad,' Simon muttered as he tied his sword belt and shrugged on his coat. 'Running away in this weather.'

'What has happened to him here at Gidleigh would be enough to turn any monk mad,' Baldwin said sharply. 'But how much more mad would he have been to remain in that cell, knowing that all he was waiting for was death?'

'Perhaps,' Simon agreed, 'but running away simply means he'll find death that bit sooner. How did he get out, anyway? I thought the cell was locked, and I'd have expected him to be shackled.'

'We can find that out when we have caught him.'

'All right, all right. I can take a hint.'

He followed Baldwin out to the court, where Sir Ralph had already gathered a large posse. Near the door to the hall Simon saw Hugh glowering evilly at the throng, a heavy strip of grey cloth bound about his head. Hugh was sitting on a bench, a large staff nearby, and although he winced occasionally as the sun came out from behind clouds, or when a horse whinnied too loudly near him, he looked on the road to recovery. In fact, Simon thought he looked like a man who was waiting for the first funny comment before letting his fists fly, which was pleasing. It was good to see his servant returned to his usual state of truculence, even if he was still very drawn-looking; he appeared slightly yellow about the face, and had dark bruises beneath both eyes. At his side was

Thomas, whose grim expression seemed the perfect companion to Hugh's own.

Piers sat on a little pony, clutching at his reins like a man who feared falling, and Simon could see Hugh watching him with that mixture of sympathy and contempt that he always reserved for people, like himself, who were uncomfortable on horseback. In Hugh's opinion, he concealed his own fear admirably; in Simon's opinion, it was a touching piece of self-deception.

'Sir Baldwin, will you join our posse?' Sir Ralph shouted across the court.

The men in the area were silenced by his bellow. Simon felt as though all the eyes in that yard were suddenly upon him and Baldwin, and he was irritated that Sir Ralph should roar at them in this unseemly manner, in front of so many scruffy villagers.

Baldwin's response was mild. 'I fear we have other business to conduct. It would be wrong of us to join your host – we should only be in your way, not knowing the roads and byways about here where a man like the priest might run.'

'There's surely a duty on all men to join the Hue and Cry,' came Roger Scut's reedy voice.

Simon saw Baldwin's back stiffen. The monk stood with a smile on his face, head tilted back and a little to one side as though he was contemplating some new form of beetle before crushing it.

'You are quite right, of course,' Baldwin said suavely, and Simon could hear his anger in the precise, clipped tones. 'It is the duty of all those in the Hundred to join the Hue and Cry. I do not come from this Hundred. Further, I have the duty as Keeper of the King's Peace to perform my inquest and review all the facts of a matter. I shall do so. In the meantime, clerk, perhaps you should return to your *own* duties.'

'Of course you must do what you think is needed,' Sir Ralph said, and was about to ride off, when Simon called to him.

'Is your son with you, Sir Ralph?'

Sir Ralph glanced at him. 'Do you see him? Neither do I.'

'Yet it is the duty of all in the Hundred to pursue an escaped . . .'

Simon swallowed the word 'felon', quickly substituting, '. . . man like the priest.'

'If he *is* a priest.'

'That,' Baldwin shot out, 'is for the Bishop to confirm, is it not? You will not attempt to slaughter this man as though he were a common outlaw.'

'We shall see. Even a cleric who draws a weapon on the Hue and Cry to evade capture may be forced to submit.'

'He has no weapon,' Baldwin said more loudly. 'So I shall myself appeal any man who uses a weapon or excessive force to capture him. Any man.'

'Perhaps he has acquired a knife, Sir Baldwin,' Sir Ralph said angrily.

'Where is your son, Sir Ralph?' Simon asked doggedly.

'I don't know,' Sir Ralph admitted after a moment. 'He left the castle last night and has not returned yet.'

With that, he turned from them both, shouted a command, and the men pelted out through the open gates.

Esmon belched and rested his hand on the girl's flank. She squirmed a little at his touch, but then twisted under the blanket and offered her mouth to him. With a grunt, he rolled between her thighs and smiled down at her.

She was a saucy little strumpet, this Margery. Slim and attractive, she had the great advantage over other girls in the vill that her father was a carter and often away from his home. With him gone, Esmon could often hope for a warm welcome in this hovel with her.

He left her a few minutes later, standing in the doorway while he pulled on his shirt, then his padded leather jack and a cloak against the cold. While Margery mumbled her farewells, no doubt cradling the little gift of coins which he had left at the side of her bed, he stared out into the roadway over the small yard.

From here he could look all along the lane towards Gidleigh. It wasn't very far from here, but in this rolling country it was well concealed. Esmon took a deep breath of the air and sighed contentedly. This was good land, this. He loved it passionately. As he loved his freedom. The idea that he could be cooped up for some appearance in court was unappealing. That was why he'd let his annoyance take him over yesterday, trying to ride down the Bailiff. If he'd managed to kill him, he could have explained it as an accident, and disposed of the Stannary officer, the man most likely to want to avenge the death of a miner. A miner! Wylkyn was no more a miner than Esmon's mother; he'd just run off to the moors to hide from justice after he murdered his own master and Esmon had visited justice on him.

He knew the legal logic of his case, but that was no comfort. The law was unreasonable and foolish. Too often the wrong people were released while good men were convicted. It was all mad. Far better to remove an irritating officer and put it down to an accident. Shame the attempt failed.

That Bailiff and his friend the Keeper seemed convinced that the priest should be let go, and Esmon in all fairness saw little reason not to let him. Esmon had no interest in Mark. It was his father who wanted Mark to suffer for his crime, if he did indeed kill the wench. Probably he did. There was no other reason for him to have run away like that unless he was guilty.

Satisfied with his logic, Esmon wondered why his father should be so keen to punish the priest. Perhaps it was merely the instinct of a man who has lost his property to a thief. His father always valued his belongings, and Mary was one such: an item on his inventory.

His father had always coveted Gidleigh, largely because it had that castle, but Esmon was less interested. Times were changing. The whole realm was like a ripe plum, ready to be consumed by any man who was bold enough. That was proved by the Despensers. They had come from nowhere, and now they were the most powerful men in the country after the King himself. Perhaps not after him; maybe they were more powerful now. Everyone Esmon had heard talking about the King's court seemed to think that Edward II had abrogated responsibility for the realm and handed all authority to the Despensers, especially Hugh the Younger, Sir Ralph's friend.

This was a time for younger men, Esmon thought. No need for the life of subservience to his father; better that he should ride with his own company and make his fortune. There were opportunities for a man like him. The country was in the power of a strong family, so Esmon should himself join with them and make sure that as their power waxed, so did his own influence.

It was not far from here that he had been born, a quarter mile eastwards, down that hill on the right. That was the old manor in which he had been raised until Sir Richard Prouse had died and they had moved to take over the castle. It was while he lived in the manor that he had taken a shine to young Margery's body, and she had made herself available to him. A handsome wench, he reckoned, although not so attractive as that other daughter of Huward's. Flora was a very fine-looking filly.

On a whim, Esmon decided he would go and see her. It would warm his heart just to look at the girl. He shouted to Margery's brother to fetch his horse, and ambled around to wait.

Chapter Twenty-Four

Simon and Baldwin's horses were soon ready for them. While they waited, Baldwin strolled over to the gatekeeper and spoke to him. Simon meanwhile went to ask Hugh how he was.

'Feels like someone's been using my head for target practice. It's like it's more full of arrows than a quiver,' Hugh grunted.

'Be grateful to Lady Annicia for her careful nursing last night,' Simon returned.

'When she gave life to the man who did this? I suppose it's a family business, is it? He knocks men down, she mends them.'

'Just sit and enjoy the sun, Hugh. With luck we won't have to stay here for much longer, and soon we can get back on our horses and go home.'

'Aye – to Dartmouth,' Hugh muttered sombrely.

'It'll be Lydford for the nonce, anyway,' Simon said, a little sharply. His nerves were still raw when it came to discussing the move to his new post.

'Simon, please come with me!' Baldwin called.

He led the way around to the side of the castle, and there he explained all he had learned the night before.

'So this Wylkyn could have killed Sir Richard?' Simon breathed.

'Yes, and Esmon sought to make him pay for the slaughter of a knight.'

'He would have been better served to accuse the man in a court.'

'True enough, although I think he would say that you don't wait with a rabid dog, you kill it immediately. This was the same situation.'

'So what are you saying?'

Baldwin shrugged. 'If it's true that this Wylkyn killed Sir

Richard, he deserved death. Perhaps we should forget about it.'

'There's still the matter of Esmon charging tolls on the King's roads,' Simon reminded him.

'Yes. But no one has complained about that, so we can't do anything.'

'Careful where you put your feet, Baldwin!'

'Hmm?' Baldwin glanced down and saw that at his feet was a box filled with wood ash and human faeces. Above them was a garderobe, a little chamber set into the wall of the upper solar chamber and overhanging the box. 'Ah!'

'Yes. I suggest we move a little away,' Simon smiled. 'What were you staring at?'

There were several thatched buildings built into the wall and the castle's keep. The nearest was the stable block. Inside, the horses were ranged on both sides, and their urine was channelled from their stalls down into a gutter that ran down and out through the wall here, to a drain. Next to it was a good-sized manure heap where the horses' dung was deposited each day. This filled the angle of the wall between the stables and the keep. Baldwin was staring past the stables to the wall.

'It's not very interesting,' Simon said, casting a look at Baldwin to see for what his friend had brought him here.

'Don't you think so?' Baldwin said, pointing at a ladder, puzzled.

Simon cleared his throat. 'Very well, Baldwin. Why are we here?'

'The gatekeeper said that the gate was locked overnight, same as always. It was still locked this morning. There is a heavy sliding bar which locks the gates, and if that bar had been moved to open the gates, the gatekeeper would have heard it and woken. So we can assume that Mark didn't get out that way. Besides, if he had, the gate would have been unbarred this morning, unless the priest had a confederate who went and shut the gate after him. I suppose that's possible, since he was released from the cell. Still, I reckon he escaped from here. There is the ladder, and it would be an easy climb to the top of the wall.'

'And as easy a way to break a leg as I could imagine,' Simon said. He went to the ladder, tested a rung, and then climbed upwards. At the top he cautiously peered over. 'Ah! Perhaps not. The land is higher out here.'

'I thought so. The wall is partly built into the hillside so the ground is higher outside than in. That wall was not built for security, but to increase the space here in the yard,' Baldwin said. 'Is there any sign that he could have jumped down there?'

'I can see prints. He went up this hill, I think. Towards the moor.'

'I am glad. So, we can leave the posse to find Mark out that way, and meanwhile we must search for him nearer.'

'But where?' Simon demanded as Baldwin strode back towards their horses. 'I said, his steps were heading for the moors, almost due westward.'

'If that's where he is, we can assume that Sir Ralph will find him,' Baldwin mused. 'The posse rode in that direction, and they know all the places of concealment, I daresay. However, if I was Mark, and I was trying to escape, I would leave a trail that was obviously pointing in one direction, and would then hurry back in a different one.'

'You think a priest could reason that rationally?' Simon grinned.

Baldwin took his horse from Godwen and mounted swiftly. 'Yes. I think he'd think very clearly and rationally. If he could plan to get out of here, surely he'd plan a sensible escape.'

'What if he didn't plan it? He could have grabbed a chance and gone.'

'Or someone else planned it for him,' Baldwin wondered. He was silent for a few minutes, frowning with concentration. 'That raises several possibilities,' he admitted. 'But if I am wrong, we can be sure that Mark will be found – and killed. Let us hope I am right, for his sake.'

'And if you are right?'

'He didn't go west to the moors. But he wouldn't have gone north because he escaped that way last time, and he would expect to be caught there. I don't think he's the sort of man who would try that again.'

'So he's gone south or east?'

'East, if anywhere. There is a bridge down that way . . .'

'Ah yes, where the old hermit lives. I remember it,' Simon said, thinking of the old rangy figure of Surval.

'Precisely. If anyone would lend their aid to an outlaw, it would be a hermit,' Baldwin said, but then he shrugged. 'This is all guesswork. What I need are facts.'

Sampson heard the hooves approaching, and he dropped to his belly in the mud just inside the line of the trees, eyes darting hither and thither, petrified, as the horses came nearer and nearer, and then, blessed relief, passed by and thundered off into the distance. Scrambling up, he looked about him with the wide-open eyes of a startled creature, a faun expecting the hunt, before making his way back homewards.

Soon he reached a hill between the moors and the castle, its sides covered with oaks and beech, chestnut and elm, and in the thick leafy mould on the ground, his steps made little sound. As he entered the peace of the trees, he felt a little of his fear slipping away. It wasn't so bad. He'd been naughty, but he hadn't been found out, and now he had a friend.

It had been late last night that he'd heard the anguished sobbing, the stumbling gait, and he had pressed himself further back into his shelter, shivering with terror. This must be a demon, like the ones that he'd heard of in church, for no one else would be out at this time of night.

But as he listened to the sobs shuddering on the wind, he felt that this was nothing to be feared. A man, it was; a man in mortal pain. Someone who'd been hurt, needed help.

Sampson pulled his blanket over his shoulders and peeped out through his little entrance. The sobbing came from further up the hill. Sampson slid out from the entrance, then crept carefully up the hill on all fours.

It was the priest. Sampson recognised him immediately.

Mark sat with his head bowed, face in his hands, consumed by overwhelming grief.

He was a nice man – Sampson knew that. He liked the monk. Mary had liked him, too. He'd been kind to Sampson. No one else was, only Mary. She was good – but now Mary was gone. Sampson shivered at the memory of all that blood. He'd touched her face. Her eyes were open: they didn't move. He'd left her, crying. Went through the hedge again, into the field. There he'd seen the hermit.

The hermit was kind, and often gave him food. Yes, when the castle had little, the hermit shared with Sampson. Not that day – not when Mary died. Sharp eyes, he had then. Sharp and cruel. Sampson was scared by him. The hermit looked through him, saw the nastiness in his soul. It was scary.

This monk never looked through Sampson. Never looked at him like that. He was nice. He'd let Sampson sit at his fire. He'd been good – told those boys not to hurt Sampson. Now he himself needed help.

But maybe the priest had changed. He might hit him. He'd hit *her*. Sampson had spent his entire adult life running from people who threatened him. He waited now, watching Mark weep, watching him cradle a hand, sniffing with despair, eyeing a long gash in his wrist. Blood trickled slowly, and the sight made Mark wail and cover his face again.

He'd only got up here after failing to find his way in the dark. Desperate to put as many miles as possible between him and Sir Ralph, he had come to a road, and hoping to find his way to the moors, he'd rushed on down it, only to find himself at the door to the castle again. Stopping in horror, he turned and bolted, careless of his direction, only caring that he might get away from this hellish place. It was like a nightmare: at every corner he was convinced that he would find himself confronted by Gidleigh Castle once more.

He had flung himself into these woods hoping to find security. Not daring to stop for brambles or blackthorn, he ran on while the breath whistled in his lungs and the muscles in his thighs and calves started to tense. His legs were heavier than lead. The time he had spent in the cell with his arms bound had taken its toll, and he tripped and stumbled as he went, driven by his terror. Behind him was the horror of death, before him the uncertainty of fleeing to – to what? Some sort of safety? He had thought he could announce his relationship to Sir Ralph, but now he knew that had been a false hope. Everyone would think he was trying to curry favour with his chief accuser.

There could be no safety for him now. Not unless he could reach the Bishop's court, and to do that he would have to pass through Sir Ralph's men and all those other Hundreds on the way to Exeter. There was no security for him there. He could find a church and Abjure the Realm, it was true, but where could he go? It was impossible to think of life in one of the King's foreign possessions, even if he survived the journey. He'd heard of sailors who had offered passage to abjurers, but who then threw the felons overboard when the ship was in mid-channel.

He sank his face into his hands again, heedless of the warm blood trickling down his sleeve. When he heard the steps approaching, he froze. At first he wanted to climb to his feet and just bolt, but his legs wouldn't obey him. The breath sobbed in his breast again as he gave himself up to his doom. There was nothing to save him here, in the middle of nowhere. He stiffened, waiting for the sharp whistle of the blade which would cut off his head, but nothing happened.

'Are you tormenting me? Is that it?' he cried at last, and threw his hands down. To his astonishment, he found himself staring into the nervous, half-smiling face of Sampson.

'Master?' Sampson said slowly. 'Sad?'

Mark looked away. Sampson had always reminded him of the despair of this place. His disabilities were reminders to Mark of his own physical dislocation from the places that he loved and where his career should have been continuing on its calm, unhurried course, rather than in this midden. If only he had never been commanded to come here, he told himself again. But he had, and now look at him.

'Yes. Sad.'

'Food? Eating food? Water?'

Mark closed his eyes. The nausea which washed through his frame at the thought of food was curious, mingled as it was with the sharp urge to eat anything and everything as quickly as he could. He tried to shake his head, but somehow he failed. Instead, he allowed his head to drop onto his hands again. When he looked up again, Sampson was hurrying away, down the hill.

Sampson felt a thrilling in his blood at the thought that the priest had come to him. All his hatred for the priest, for what he'd done to Mary, was gone. Sampson didn't care. She was dead, and her image had almost faded from his memory, and it was nice to have a companion.

That night he had fetched everything he possessed to make Mark's life easier. He had gone to his little store and shaken the beetles and woodlice from his bread, he had beaten the maggots from his small piece of cheese, and carried them to Mark. He had watched with pleasure to see his meagre supplies eaten, at first with slow, meditative chewing, but then with a ravenous hunger that alarmed Sampson. When Mark was done, Sampson had led him to his own little shelter and settled him on his soft bed, made of mosses, herbs and grasses, before Sampson himself settled down and curled into a ball at his side on the hard-packed soil of his floor. He didn't mind; he didn't grudge the priest a little comfort.

Sampson had a friend again. Yet this morning he rose early to fetch water for his friend, and when he got back, the place was deserted.

The tears threatened, but he blinked them away. He shrugged and accepted it, just as he accepted life itself. Only . . . Mark had eaten all his food. He must find something to eat. The castle always put out food for him and other needy people, but he didn't want to go there. Not today. Men at the castle always had questions. Especially that son. 'Hide this'; 'Hide that'; and 'Where did you put it?' Sampson didn't want that.

A smile spread over his face. He would go to the hermit. Surval always shared his bounty with Sampson. A recollection of cold, sharp eyes staring at him made him hesitate, but then memories of little kindnesses from Surval came to him and made up his mind.

Hugh watched his master and Baldwin ride from the yard with Godwen in their train. The thought of riding again made him wince. Then, 'So what's the problem with you and Godwen?' he asked Thomas.

'Why does there have to be a problem?'

'Don't know, but there is. Just need to look at you once and you can see it.'

'Our families never got on. During the old wars, I'm told, my father's father's sires supported the King, but Godwen's supported the traitors.'

'You tell me this is all because of a war from before you were born?' Hugh said sceptically.

Thomas grunted, then sat at Hugh's side. 'Him and me used to want the same woman.'

'Oh. And he got her?'

Thomas scowled at Hugh. 'No, *I* did. He's been a bastard ever since.'

'Oh.' Hugh glanced at him doubtfully.

'Always niggling at me, digging. He thinks he's better than us, just because his family has more money. Well, I don't care! My family work hard and we earn our crusts. He just lives off his father's money.'

'What does his father do?'

'He's a tailor in Exeter. He's not free, he's a serf to the Dean of Crediton Church, but the Dean is a generous man with his serfs. Provided they pay a bit to commute their services, and cough up their rents each year, he's happy to let them make as much as they want.'

Hugh grunted. 'It all comes back to them in the end, doesn't it? When Godwen's old man dies, the Dean will want his death duties.'

'Perhaps,' Thomas said, brightening a little. 'I must tell Jack that.'

'Who's Jack?'

'My sister's husband – he's a groom now. Used to be a farmer. Every time Godwen sees him, he laughs at him . . .'

Hugh turned his head to peer at him, wincing slightly as more pain shot through his head. 'What? You forgotten what you were going to say or something?'

'No. It's that son of a donkey over there,' Thomas said, pointing.

Hugh could just make out the portly figure of Roger Scut walking quickly towards the stables. 'What about him?'

'He's the thieving goat who keeps putting up Jack's rents so that he can't survive on his money,' Thomas grated. 'I have a good mind to go in there and give him a pasting, just to give him a taste of his own medicine.'

'You do that and you'll be in the gaol before you can swing a second punch,' Hugh said, nodding towards a group of guards lounging at the stable entrance. Then he frowned. 'What's he up to?'

'Who?'

'That Roger Scut. What's he doing, sidling into the stables?'

Chapter Twenty-Five

Simon and Baldwin had ridden for the best part of an hour, sweeping around in a great arc with the castle at the centre, hoping to see some sort of sign that Mark had passed by, but after returning over their own tracks, Baldwin pulled a face and shook his head.

'There is no point in continuing this. Look, you can hardly see where our horses have gone in among all these fallen leaves. It would be unrealistic to hope that we could catch a glimpse of Mark's footsteps.'

'If he came this way,' Simon added sombrely.

'Yes. I have no firm conviction on that,' Baldwin admitted. 'But if I were him, I wouldn't go in another direction.'

'What of the hermit at the bridge?' Godwen asked.

'Aye,' Simon returned. 'What of him?'

'He's a holy man. Wouldn't he stop a felon from running away?'

Simon snorted. 'You think a hermit at a place like Chagford Bridge is going to be careful of the law?'

'If he's a holy man he would.'

'If he was a holy man, he'd be in a chamber in York or Winchester or Canterbury, or if he was even more holy, he'd be living in the middle of Dartmoor,' Simon scoffed.

'Come, Simon, it is possible,' Baldwin said. 'But Godwen, you must know that most hermits are people who have no knowledge of the religious life? There are many frauds and vagabonds who claim alms. I have even known of some outlaws who pretended to be religious and preyed on the weak and foolish who passed.'

'You mean he could be false?' Godwen said, shocked. 'That's disgusting! Taking money and charity from anyone who travels past here pretending to be able to pray for them ... It's outrageous!' He had a high respect for money and corresponding distaste for theft.

'Yes,' Simon grunted. 'And it's as natural as breath itself to many of these fellows. I had one bastard up near Oakhampton who preyed on the women passing back and forth for weeks. He told them that God had given him the ability to pardon all sins. All he had to do was get them to kneel before him and lean forward so that he could pray with them, but behind them. It took ages before any of the women complained.'

'No, well, you can't trust women, can you?' Godwen said bitterly. 'Even when they make promises, you can't be sure that they mean them.'

Baldwin eyed him for a moment. His own marriage was so happy that a man who could slander the female sex was strangely repellent.

Godwen caught the tail end of his look and felt himself colouring. It was irritating that he should still be so angry at losing her, but she was a beautiful girl when he had wooed her, and then that clumping, bone-headed cretin Thomas had got her instead. Until then, he and Thomas had been, if not close, then at least closer than their parents for many decades. Thomas's great-grandsire had fought for some queen who called herself Empress, while Godwen's had fought on the other side. That was enough, apparently, for their parents to quarrel, but Godwen and Thomas thought it was foolish to continue that strife. They had met, and they had been friendly enough. Until they both met Bea.

Bea was a breath of fresh air in the town. Only short, she had a thick body with strong hands and heavy breasts, but her nature shone through. No man who had ever had her large green eyes fixed upon him while she laughed, her cheeks dimpling, her mouth open to display her small, well-formed teeth, could have failed to have been smitten, and Godwen was completely under her spell still. He had married, and his Jen had given him several children, but still, when he dreamed of a woman coming to his bed, it was always Bea. Even now, miles from her, and some distance from

Thomas and the castle, Godwen could feel his jealous anger simmering. There was no cure for it.

They were passing along a winding road that followed a fast-flowing Dartmoor stream, and Godwen came to as they splashed through the uncommonly deep ford.

'Take care!' Baldwin called before he entered. 'The rains of the last few days have swollen it.'

He watched Godwen as the guard steered his unwilling mount into the water and through it. Luckily the ford was not broad, and the horse had little time to grow alarmed, but Baldwin reckoned that they would have to be careful before long. The streams and rivers about here were all swift-flowing and dangerous after rain, and God knew how much rain had fallen in the last few days.

Godwen was an odd character, in his opinion, and had the appearance of a man who had bottled up a grudge over the years, but Baldwin had other things to occupy his thoughts than the mood of a watchman.

'We have no evidence which would point to anyone, apart from witnesses who say Esmon is involved in robbing travellers. He may be involved in the death of the miner, whose body we cannot find,' he noted.

Simon nodded grimly. 'And that murderous little shit's made an attempt on me, don't forget. It was all I could do not to challenge him last night. Smirking up on the top table like that!'

'I was not going to forget him, old friend,' Baldwin said. 'No, but we shall have to be cautious with him. I do not want to have to fight him, especially with all those men-at-arms about his castle. The sooner we can get Hugh up and about, and back at the inn, the better I shall be pleased.'

'And I too,' Simon agreed, but absently. He was peering ahead. 'I think we're near now. I remember this hill, and then we go through a small hamlet, and the road drops again. At the bottom is the river.'

'Then let us discover what this good hermit has to tell us,' Baldwin said lightly, but when Simon shot him a look, he saw that Baldwin's face showed no humour, only cold determination.

* * *

Hugh gasped as his foot caught a loose stone in the yard and jarred his wound.

'Are you sure you should be doing this?' Thomas hissed.

'Oh, belt up!' Hugh responded. 'If a man can't walk about the yard to get some exercise, what can he do?'

They were at the door to the stable now, and Hugh peered inside.

To his right, on either side, heads facing the wall, were the rings for the horses. Most, of course, were out with the posse, and Simon and Baldwin had borrowed more, so the place was all but empty.

The trap door that led to the cell was wide open, and Roger Scut was crouched by it, a guttering candle in his hand, apparently staring down into the little room. As Hugh watched, he rose slightly and used the candle to gaze at the floor near the trap door.

'Dropped something, Brother?' Hugh said loudly.

There was a sputter, a low curse, and the candle dropped into the cell with a dull splash. Roger Scut stood and surveyed the two men in the doorway angrily. 'Why aren't you with the posse?'

'Look at my head!' Hugh said. 'What are you doing in here? You lost something?'

'No. Why should you think that?' Roger Scut said, his head tilting back.

Hugh had had enough. His head hurt, he didn't want to be here in this castle, he didn't want to move to Dartmouth, and he didn't like people who stared at him imperiously down their long noses. 'You got a problem? Blocked nose or something?'

'No.'

'Then why are you doing that?'

'It is nothing,' Roger said defensively, sniffing slightly, and then quickly looking up, as though he had always intended studying the rafters in this little stable.

This servant was an infuriating little serf. He would have to speak to the Bailiff and complain, when he had a chance – but then again, perhaps no. Roger Scut disliked the suspicion in his eyes, the way that his attention flew from Roger himself to the trap door and back. 'Do you want something from me?' he asked haughtily.

Hugh turned slowly and peered up at Thomas. 'What do you think, Tom?'

'I don't want anything from him.'

'No, I don't reckon many would.'

Roger Scut felt his face flush with anger at the man's insolence. 'I shall speak to your master as soon as he returns, and you will regret your rudeness!'

'Yes, you do that,' Hugh said. Then he did something which Roger Scut found more alarming than anything else.

He smiled.

Surval had finished his prayer when he heard the sound of horses. He got up, genuflected, and then unhurriedly made his way to his door, where he stood staring up the road. No traveller could miss him.

The trio was not an ordinary set of passers-by. The man at the front looked like a knight. He had the arrogance and confidence in his own power, and the man at his side was clearly also a man of authority. Both stopped and sat in their saddles, making no move towards their pockets, nor did they appear to be in a hurry to continue their journey. The last man was plainly a guard, but he merely surveyed the hermit's property with a suspicious glower.

Surval took his staff, a useful weapon in defence as he always said, and leaned on it like an old man. 'Lordings, Godspeed. I hope I see you well?'

'Hermit, we would like to speak to you.'

'What if I don't want to speak to *you*?'

'I think you'd prefer to talk to us here than make us have you arrested and held in a gaol for a night or two,' Simon said curtly.

'I am a hermit, Bailiff; you think to threaten me?' Surval said, but without rancour. He looked them both up and down and quickly formed his opinion of them. Both looked serious, which was good. When a lord decided to turn bad and started abusing his power and privilege, that was a situation that called for intelligence and caution, and these two looked like they might indeed be able to deal with a dangerous fool like Sir Ralph. Indeed, he hoped they could deal with his son as well, that murderous oaf Esmon.

In fact, looking up at them, he felt some amusement in this meeting. He had the distinct impression that they were not the sort to make empty threats, but nor did he think that they would abuse their own powers. Not that they'd need to, he reminded himself. If one was a Keeper and the other was a Stannary Bailiff, they had enough power to do what they wanted.

'Do you normally welcome people with threats of gaol?'

'Only when we are in a hurry,' Baldwin said.

'And why should a great lord like you be in such a hurry, Sir Keeper?'

He did not see fit to answer. Instead, he jerked his chin towards the hermit's breast. 'I see you lie to pray, as men used to of old.'

Surval glanced down at the dust covering his rags. 'I believe it helps a man's prayers to wing their way to God if we show our understanding of Christ's suffering. Yes, I prostrate myself in imitation of the cross. Perhaps if more men did so, the world would be a happier place.'

'Perhaps it would. You say you do not believe the accusation of murder against the monk.'

Surval closed his eyes and sighed. He had thought that the two must have come here for this, but he had hoped not. 'I do not believe accusations unless I have witnessed the attack. I didn't. I leave accusations of guilt or innocence to God Himself.'

Simon asked, 'Did you know Mark?'

'Of course. He and I used to pray together often,' the hermit said. He could see that Simon was surprised to hear that, and a wry smile twisted his beard. 'Ah, so you reckoned I was one of those lazy, runaway serfs who claim to be hermits to avoid hard work, did you? Not all are dishonest, Bailiff. I break my back here, maintaining that bridge. Do you know how old it is?'

'No.'

'Nor do I, but look at the span of it. Either side, the metal tires of carts passing by have cut into the stone. On the right there, near the pillar, you can see where the tracks have worn through the stone, and you can see the river beneath you. There were three other holes until recently. I have mended them all, and now there is only that remaining. I keep this bridge, Bailiff, and with every spare moment I tend to the poor folk about here, see to their spiritual needs and pray for their lost souls when they die, so don't think to accuse *me* of laziness!'

His voice had risen, and he had to calm himself. If only he didn't feel the need of his penance so strongly, he wouldn't react so angrily when people said to his face that they thought he was one of those men who took up a counterfeit religiousness in order to avoid working for a living. All he ever tried to do was ease the toils of ordinary people.

'Master, we meant no insult,' Baldwin said.

'No. You never do, you great lords and masters, do you? You look on all serfs as serfs, nothing else. You can insult people with impunity, without a care for their feelings, can't you? But some of us are as honourable as you. Some of us more so, perhaps.'

'Perhaps,' Baldwin allowed with a grin. 'Yet some, you will admit, leave something to be desired when it comes to their holiness! Do you find charity is freely given here?'

Surval looked up at him, and through his anger, he felt a grudging respect. This was the sort of man whom others would instinctively trust, he felt. The sort whom others would follow willingly. 'Not always without men being reminded,' he acknowledged. Then he raised his staff with a quizzical smile. 'But there are ways of reminding them.'

'And you receive plenty of pennies and halfpennies?'

'Aye, and often the odd old farthing, too. But rarely minted coins,' Surval said. 'They think that a simple hermit doesn't know what's been going on in the world outside his sphere and seek to offload their quarters and halves on me.'

Baldwin could smile at that. 'I am sure you quickly disabuse them of their foolishness!'

It was more than twenty years since farthings and halfpennies had been minted as coins. Before that, a trader who needed a halfpence would simply cut a penny in two, or four for farthings. There were still many such pieces about the place, but few traders wanted them any more.

The tale always made Surval feel bitter, but standing here in front of Baldwin, he could almost see the funny side of it. There was a lightness and cheerful calmness in Baldwin's eyes which was rare to find in a knight, and something else: a determination, as though he had decided to see the matter through. He would find Mary's murderer, no matter what.

'So you want to find the monk Mark.'

Simon was instantly alert. 'How did you know he was gone? We didn't say that. Who told you?'

'Come, Surval. What do you know of him?' Baldwin asked.

'I was woken by him this morning. He banged on the door and called for me.'

'Why did he come here?' Simon wondered.

'He wanted advice from someone who could help him. Poor devil! He had admitted his offences to that priest you brought with you, such as they were, but he realised he couldn't trust the man.'

'Why?' Simon said.

'Mark, the priest, is the son of Sir Ralph. He told me so this morning, and I believe him. Sir Ralph has many children! His mother was a widow of Axminster and Sir Ralph wooed her many years ago, before he met his Lady Annicia.'

'That cannot be true!' Baldwin exclaimed. 'I find it hard to believe that he would pursue his own son.'

'He would if he didn't know anything about it,' Surval said. 'Mark took your priest's advice and told Sir Ralph nothing. The man has no idea Mark is his son. The monk never screwed up enough courage to tell him in all the time he lived here.'

'Where did he go?' Simon demanded, glancing about them as

though expecting to see Mark's face peering at them from around a tree trunk.

'What with the murder of Wylkyn as well, I think he's run away as fast as he can.'

'That is another matter: Wylkyn. What can you tell us about the miner's murder?' Baldwin asked.

'Miner? Well, he wasn't that for long, was he? He was a servant to Sir Richard Prouse, the man who used to own the castle before Sir Ralph took it. I think Sir Ralph and his appalling son thought Wylkyn did something to kill Sir Richard. They sought to punish him.'

'I wondered about that,' Baldwin said. 'Wylkyn certainly had plenty of poisonous plants and powders in his room.'

'What,' Simon mused, 'if it was Esmon or Sir Ralph who murdered Sir Richard, and Wylkyn saw? That would explain why he bolted to the moors, and why he had to die.'

Baldwin said, 'True. Surval, did the Coroner view Sir Richard's body and hold an inquest?'

'Why should he? A sick man who was a mass of twisted muscles and bones died in his bed. There was nothing surprising about the end of his life, so no reason to call the Coroner.'

'True enough,' Baldwin agreed. 'So: Wylkyn. Do you have any idea where the body may lie? If you do, it would be better to tell us now. We could carry it back to the scene of the murder before the Coroner arrives, which would save another fine for removing it.'

Surval considered. 'I may be able to find it.'

'One other thing. You have met Mark and spoken to him. Yesterday you said you thought him innocent – do you still?' Baldwin asked.

Surval led Simon and Baldwin to the bridge and stood staring reflectively down at the water.

'I am all the more convinced Mark is innocent because of my family.'

'*Your* family?' Baldwin asked.

'I am brother to Sir Ralph. Although I am older, I early decided to take up the religious life, as I told you, Sir Baldwin. I enjoyed the desires of the flesh. And then my woman fell pregnant again and one night, when I was angry and drunk, I gave her a beating. It . . . it killed her and our child.'

Involuntarily, Simon took a step back.

'Yes, Bailiff. I am not a pleasant man. I did it. I killed my own woman. Not intentionally, but in drunken frustration and anger. And afterwards, I came here because it was close to my old home of Wonson.'

'Your Bishop allowed you?' Baldwin asked.

'Alas, he never realised. That all happened back in 1307. Walter Stapledon was being elected to the post, but Robert Winchelsea objected, and Bishop Walter wasn't consecrated until October 1308. In that time, I had run away. I wandered a great deal, and then came here. I've been here ever since. At least it has meant that I can protect the poor and infirm.'

Simon gave an exclamation of disgust. 'Even if that's true, so what? Why should that make you decide Mark is innocent?'

Hearing voices and the rattling of carts, Surval threw a glance over his shoulder, irritated to have his train of thought broken. He had much to think about, especially since hearing from Mark this morning.

'Because bad blood can run in a family. I believe it does in mine.'

'So it runs in Mark's blood too,' Simon observed.

'It's possible, but I think it more likely that my other nephew Esmon holds foul blood. I saw him riding along near that road on the day that Mary died.' He had seen Sir Ralph too, but no one could think his brother could be guilty of murdering poor Mary. Esmon, though, yes – he was capable. Especially if he didn't know the truth. Esmon could well have raped and killed her.

'If Mark is your nephew,' Baldwin said, 'then surely he would be capable of the same offence as you. You killed your woman while you wore the cloth; his woman has now died in the same way. Why do you think him innocent?'

'The two are not the same,' Surval said. 'I was drunk; he was sober. I punched my woman in the belly in rage; he merely slapped his in irritation. I sat and drank more, unable to see what I had done; he was overwhelmed with remorse and bolted from the scene, only returning later. And of course, his woman died from a broken neck. I cannot see him breaking a neck, can you?'

'But Esmon is more powerful,' Simon said. 'He could have snapped her neck with ease.'

Baldwin nodded absently. He was thinking of Ben, and wondering whether he had the strength in his arms to be able to break a neck. Would his sister's rejection of his advances give him the resolution to kill her in that way? It was possible.

Simon said, 'Again, do you know where the miner's body lies?'

Surval stood watching the doorway to his home. 'It must be well hidden,' he said.

Before Baldwin could respond, there was a gruff rumble from a man on horseback. Baldwin had not seen his approach behind two carts, and now the sound of his voice made the Keeper whirl round.

'Aha! Well hidden, is it? No doubt it was some Godless heathen did that. I expect it was some mad Keeper of the King's Peace, don't you, Master Bailiff?'

'Greetings, Coroner,' Baldwin said evenly. 'I had not looked to see you so soon.'

'No, I doubt whether you had,' Coroner Roger of Gidleigh said with loud delight. 'Still, I am sure you'll want to fill me in on the details of this matter, won't you? Um, shall we see the body straight away, or . . .' he glanced coldly at Surval '. . . leave it a short while to give people time to find it again?'

Chapter Twenty-Six

Sir Ralph swore and lashed with his whip at a bush to vent his frustration.

'So where has that miserable shit of a priest gone, then?'

Piers was at his side, holding his hands out in acknowledgement of his own bafflement. 'I don't know. I'd have thought he'd have come straight up here, but there's no sign of him.'

Sir Ralph cursed again, while the men about him waited. Dogs sat and scratched, one discovered a pile of something unpleasant, and rolled enthusiastically in it until Sir Ralph's whip caught his flank. 'He can't just have vanished.'

'Perhaps we were wrong and he went a different way?'

Sir Ralph pursed his lips. The bastard must have come this way. It was the only choice that made any sense, both because of the logic of the route away from the castle avoiding all those folks who could have apprehended him, and also because Mark knew that he should be safe on the moors if he only declared himself a miner. That would usually work, but today Sir Ralph had the right of Hue and Cry to catch his man, and so he would. And when he did, he would make sure that the young cur died for the murder of his Mary.

The land here should have yielded up a fugitive without difficulty. 'If he came here, we should have seen his prints in among all this black soil.'

'Yes. But there's no mark at all.'

Piers was speaking the simple truth. The land here was flat, with few rocks or bushes behind which a man might conceal himself. They had passed over the winding streams with their ancient clapper bridges, and on to the broad, flat plain. Here they ascended a long ridge of hills and now they could gaze out over some miles in all directions.

All the flat plains were soaked with water. Any man trying to escape over that would have been slowed, but also his prints would have been visible to the men whom Sir Ralph had brought with him. He had already led his men up and down this ridge; all were spread out and walking their mounts perpendicular to the direction of Mark's flight. Or the direction that his flight should have taken him, anyway.

He thrust his whip between his thigh and the saddle while he considered. This was ridiculous!

'Do you want us to carry on to Steeperton,' Piers asked respectfully, 'or shall we go back and see if the dogs can find a scent nearer the castle?'

'Don't try to tell me how to hunt a man, Reeve! I've done it often enough!' Sir Ralph saw Piers pull a face, and knew why. He'd been so certain that Mark must have come this way that he hadn't even bothered to take the dogs to the spot where Mark had escaped over the castle wall. Instead, he had led the posse up here, past the stone circle and onto the moors themselves.

Mark must be laughing. He had got out of the castle, and now he was concealed somewhere. Perhaps he was in a tree overlooking the castle even now, giggling to think how he had evaded the trap set for him by Sir Ralph.

It was infuriating to realise now that Mark must have guessed Sir Ralph would try to set a trap for him when he was released from his cell. Sir Ralph should have known his motive would be transparent.

'Come, we'll return and see if we can get his scent even now!' he shouted, and turned his horse back to the east.

At all costs, he must see that little pile of dung dead. He didn't care how, but Mark must die – and slowly, too.

That was the reason why Sir Ralph had gone and set him loose, after all.

Esmon sent the boy to take his horse back to the castle. There was no need for it today. The weather was fine, and the sun was out again, so he decided to walk the mile or so to Flora's house. After all, he didn't want to catch the girl and then be discovered by the miller who might notice Esmon's horse tethered at the place where he was enjoying Huward's younger daughter. A man the miller's size could inflict severe damage on a smaller man like Esmon, and he had no wish to suffer a beating at those giant hands.

Easier by far to take the girl away, scare her by threatening to have her father killed if she refused to submit, or if she told her father later what Esmon had done to her. Much easier for all concerned.

The lanes were still muddy from the rains, and the scent of warmed earth made him feel at home. It was a scent which had been with him all his life, but at the castle of Gidleigh, he missed it, because the natural odour was overwhelmed by the stench of unwashed men and the little midden behind. Here the soil's own rich tang was predominant, and in the warmth of the sun, with the dampness in the air, it felt as though he was walking through a fine mist of peat.

It was good that Wylkyn was dead. The man had deserved it, and it was always satisfying to visit punishment on the guilty, just as he must soon punish Mark the monk. And then he would sit down with Brian and plan what they were to do next. It was clear enough, from the exultation of the men after the raid during which Wylkyn had died, that they needed more excitement. The band was growing bored with sitting about; they craved war. Only in fighting did a man reach his true potential, only when shouting defiance with a sword in his hand did he achieve that peak. There was nothing else like it. Afterwards, sex with a willing wench was good, but even that wasn't as thrilling as the actual fight itself.

If he had been master of the castle, he might have decided to stay. It was a good place. Comfortable, spacious, and with the potential of ready money from raiding travellers, but while his father was the master, it was better that they should find somewhere else to go.

Especially now, since his attempt on the Bailiff. Esmon didn't want to be taken as a felon. He could count on the Despensers having him freed, but that wasn't the point. If he could have ridden Simon down, that might have given him a breathing space. Instead, by missing, he had further infuriated the Bailiff and given him a motive to find Esmon guilty. A Stannary Bailiff had many powers. If he wanted, he could feasibly arrest Esmon and have him installed in the Lydford Gaol. It didn't bear thinking of. He wished now that he hadn't let his impetuousness overrule his common sense.

At the lane that led down to the mill, he paused when he heard the sound of chopping in a small wood near the road. It could be Huward. He had no intention of risking a fight with the old bugger. He could well lose, especially if Huward was armed with an axe.

Cautiously, he entered the little wood where he had heard the sound and crept forward to see who it was. A heavy-set figure was swinging his axe with more violence than was necessary: Osbert.

'What are you up to, churl?' Esmon drawled. 'This is not your land, and you have no right to be cutting trees. I shall have to see you fined for your theft.'

'I was sent here by the miller's wife; if you have a complaint, take it to her.'

'Your manner is impudent. Perhaps I should teach you some manners.'

Osbert hefted his axe in his hand and stared at him. 'Keep your hand from your sword, Master. Your father isn't here, and nor are your men-at-arms.'

'Are you threatening me?'

'You are a fool, Esmon. You reckon you can scare me, but it's too late for that. I've lost my Mary, and that was the worst thing that could have happened to me. So now, I ain't scared of anyone, you included. You should be, though!'

Esmon was confused. He took a step back, out of reach of the axe, and he was tempted to draw his sword, but he prudently left it while he tried to learn what Osbert meant. 'I don't know what you're talking about.'

'No? Maybe not. But Sir Richard's man is dead, isn't he? And who was seen doing that? *You!*'

Esmon chuckled. 'That's interesting. So I'll have to enlist the help of my Lord Despenser to avoid the rope, you mean? Or perhaps you mean that I'll have to ask for the support of his friend, the King, to have my sentence quashed and my crime pardoned? You cretin! You have no idea how feeble your threats are to someone as powerful as me! My power is based upon my friends, fool. You grip your axe with care for now, churl, thinking that you are in danger while I'm here, but you're wrong. You need to fear me when I am *not* in view. That's when I will be most danger to you. When I am talking to my friends – or maybe planning your death!'

'You can't scare me.'

'Anyway – where's Wylkyn's body? I don't see it. No body: no murder. No one will convict *me*!'

'No? Not even for the murder of Sir Richard Prouse?' Osbert saw Esmon's face freeze. 'Oh, yes, Master. We all know about Wylkyn, how he brewed things for his Lord. Good, some of them were, others could kill. He was interested in them all, Wylkyn was.'

'Yes, that was why—'

'Why you killed him. Because you stole the poison from his room to kill Sir Richard, and as soon as Wylkyn saw someone had used his potions to murder his master, he ran away. You had to have that castle, though, didn't you? You were in such a hurry, and Sir Richard just wouldn't die. He was prepared to fight, and you couldn't hang around to fight a court case, so you murdered him instead. We all know it, Esmon, and we'll make sure the Coroner does, too.'

Flora was surprised by her mother's apparent lack of concern at Huward's disappearance. She had tried to raise the subject of his not arriving home the night before, but Gilda had ignored her. At the time, Flora had thought that Gilda already knew where he was, that he had gone to an ale-house like the widow's in Murchington, to drink and forget his misery, but then she heard her mother weeping herself to sleep in the bed next to her. Her misery had stilled even Ben's sarcastic whining.

'Do you know where he is?' Flora asked again as they ate their meagre breakfast.

'He'll come back soon enough,' Gilda said. 'He must!'

She looked terrible. Since Mary's death, her face had lost its roundness, and now her features looked haggard, slightly yellow.

Her eyes were red-rimmed and there were blue bruises under them from lack of sleep, while her mouth had lost all colour. Her hands shook slightly as she tried to prepare dough for bread, but she persevered at the task as though it was a means of distracting herself from the end of her world.

Flora left her. Outside, in the sunshine, she felt the sharp, metallic taste of tears welling, but swallowed hard and forced them away. She had to stay strong, both for her mother, and for herself. Her father, her poor, poor father, had broken into pieces like an earthenware jar dropped on stones. Now Mary was dead, he seemed to have collapsed in upon himself.

Turning her face skywards, Flora enjoyed the sun upon her cheeks. It felt as though God Himself was giving her the full impact of His love, a love that could warm the most sorry of humans, and for a while she stood there, basking in it, but the comfort it gave her couldn't last. The loss of her sister, and now the disappearance of her father too, induced a chill in her bones.

She craved the love of her father. He had been at the court yesterday, Flora knew, but he hadn't come back. Flora was worried. She prayed that he hadn't got drunk and fallen into a river or over a cliff. There were so many dangers here, especially for a man who had drunk too much.

The sun was momentarily covered by a cloud, and as it returned again, she opened her eyes. Perhaps Osbert knew where her father had gone? He must have been there at the court, surely; he was one of the court's jury. She could go and ask him. And if there was the slightest sign of sympathy from him, she would throw herself into his arms, and damn the world.

As though the thought was answered by God Himself, she suddenly heard a laugh, and then the regular sound of chopping at wood. That was where Osbert was, in the woods up near the road to Gidleigh's castle.

Inside the house she heard more dry, racking sobs as her mother gave herself up to her misery once more, and that decided her. She had to find her father not only to make sure that he was all right, but also to save her poor mother from this overwhelming despair.

With a determined frown on her face, armed with the logical pretext that she was in fact embarking on a mission for her mother's ease of mind, she set off to follow the sound of axe hewing wood.

In the mill, Ben put his hand on Gilda's. 'It's all right, Mother.'

She snatched hers away. 'All right? When your father has disappeared?'

'But he's not our father, is he?' Ben said slyly. 'I heard you talking to Surval yesterday. All of it.'

'You heard us?' she repeated with a kind of dull sadness.

'So I know Huward isn't our father. I think we could earn more money from our real father, don't you? Leave it to me, Mother. I'll see to it that we're better off now than we have ever been.'

'No! You stay here, don't dare go to him, he'd—'

'What, deny he's my father? I doubt that.'

Coroner Roger led Baldwin and Simon away from the hermit's house. When Simon peered back over his shoulder, he saw that the old man was staring after them still, but as Simon watched, he shook his head and re-entered his house with a slow, despondent gait. The sight gave Simon a pang of remorse. He wished he could like the hermit, but he couldn't. There was something about the man that made him feel wary. Deep in his soul, he loathed murderers and Surval had committed the worst of crimes.

The girl Mary came into his mind. A man like Surval – lonely, miserable, sleeping in a cold hovel, with few comforts of any sort: would it be any surprise if he succumbed to desire for a woman? Especially a young woman, a girl who was fresh, warm, attractive? Surval had done so before, on his own admission – could he have done so again?

He was about to ask Baldwin about the girl's body, when the Coroner spoke.

'These carters here have lost their tongues since I overheard them talking in the tavern.'

He waved a cheerful hand at Alan and Saul, both of whom sat hunched over their reins like men who wanted to ignore those who rode along behind them. Like children, they appeared to think that if they ignored the Coroner, he might disappear.

The Coroner wasn't alone. With him were two servants and a cleric called Arthur, who was there to record the details of his inquests. Simon could not help but notice how well the Coroner got on with his cleric. It was very different from Baldwin and Roger Scut.

'What were they saying?' Baldwin enquired.

'That it was better to leave a murderer and let him go free, rather than capture him. They said this wasn't their vill, after all, and it was nothing to do with them.'

'Do you think they realise that aiding a murderer's escape is a serious offence?' Baldwin asked, and Simon had to look away to hide his smile. He recognised Baldwin's mock-stern voice.

'I doubt it. I don't think they have one good brain between them,' the Coroner said dismissively.

'We couldn't do much to stop him, could we? He caught us,' Alan said sulkily.

'So you admit to seeing the murder? And what happened to the body?'

Alan said, 'We didn't see what happened. They took us away.'

'Where did it happen?' Coroner Roger asked.

'Up on the road on our way here.'

'Your companion's body was found but now it's gone,' Baldwin said. 'So you will have to be arrested and held until we can verify your stories and make sure you'll turn up to the next Keeper's court, and then to the Justices when they eventually get here.'

'But all we did was get attacked and have our stuff stolen! Where's the fairness in that?'

'This has nothing to do with fairness, lad, this is all down to the law,' the Coroner intoned gravely. 'A man was murdered and you were with him. Perhaps *you* two killed him.'

'Christ Jesus!'

'And if you use profane language, you will suffer further,' Baldwin said.

'How much more can we suffer?' Saul demanded bitterly. 'We have been taken and held against our will, left under guard, had our goods ransacked and some of them stolen, been beaten, and now we can't even go to our homes because a Coroner has taken us and wants us to accuse our attacker. Apart from *him* taking *us* prisoner again, maybe ransoming us to the value of all we own, or maybe just killing us, how can things get any worse for us?'

'They could well have been worse,' Baldwin said. 'You have been taken by the King's Keeper and a Coroner. You are witnesses to a crime, not the men who committed it.'

They rode on in silence, creaking and rattling along until they reached the place where the attack had taken place. There the carters sat sullenly, reluctant to speak, while Baldwin and Simon surveyed the land once more.

'Come! Tell us what happened,' Simon said. 'The sooner you get that over with, the sooner you can be away.'

Saul and Alan exchanged a look, and then Saul hawked and spat. 'All right. We were travelling past here, part of a small group on the way to Chagford. We knew that there was a risk that Sir Ralph's men could try to rob us. It's happened to loads of others all the time up here. Not this far north, though. This is right on the South Tawton boundary, and the lord there is quick to take offence on his lands. We thought we were safe enough here.'

'You were caught in the open?' Baldwin said, gazing about him at the hill, the roadway, and then the wall down the slope.

'Yes. The bastards appeared from nowhere, shrieking and howling, riding up along the slope, then spurring their damned horses straight at us, apart from one or two who went behind us. There was nothing we could do. Those who could, whipped up to come down here, but the wall stopped us all. And it was here Wylkyn got it, I reckon.'

'What happened to him? Was he at the front?' Baldwin asked keenly.

'No, he was near the back. Soon as the shouting started, he hurried down to the wall. Most of us just surrendered. After all, this lot were after money, not lives. But we never saw him again, and you say he was found dead.'

'No other man tried to protect his cart?' Baldwin pressed him.

Saul looked at Alan.

It was Alan who responded. 'Some did, yes, but they had their weapons knocked away.'

'I see. What then?'

'It was—'

'Alan!' Saul rasped.

Simon moved languidly, a hand grasping Saul's tunic and pulling. With a short squeak, Saul fell from the cart. In a moment he was up, hot indignation making him blind to the Bailiff's position. He made to try to punch Simon, but the Bailiff knocked his fist wide, yanked at his arm and pulled him backwards. His forearm went about Saul's throat and he said mildly, 'If you dare try anything else, I'll have you imprisoned for assault on a Stannary Bailiff while he's trying to do his duty. Understand?'

Saul nodded, his anger dissipating quickly as he struggled to breathe. Simon released him and turned back to Alan. ' "It was", you were going to say?'

'Sir Ralph's son Esmon led the men,' Alan said after throwing an anguished look at Saul. 'He hared off after Wylkyn, and caught up with us all further on. If anyone killed Wylkyn, it was him. He had blood on his face and tunic.'

'What then?'

'They took us to the castle, where they demanded money and goods before leaving us locked overnight in a grotty little room near the gatehouse.'

'The body, though: did they drag it behind them, throw it onto a cart – what?' Baldwin demanded. Piers had said the body had been left, but he could have lied.

'No. We didn't see it.'

'But the body has disappeared?' Coroner Roger said. 'Who could have taken it?'

'I was hoping that one of these could tell us,' Baldwin admitted. 'But they seem to have little idea. No more than you or I.'

'Hmm.' The Coroner's face was bleak. 'I have had too much experience of fools trying to conceal bodies in the last few years.'

'Well, let us see if even now we can't find his resting place,' Baldwin said firmly.

Chapter Twenty-Seven

Flora was about to call to Osbert when she saw the figure ahead.
With a small gasp of relief, for she had been pushing through
these woods for a while without seeing any sign of him, she
stepped forward into a clearing.

Instantly she saw her mistake. It wasn't Os, it was Esmon, and
as soon as she stepped out into the open, he turned and saw her.

'Ah – you've saved me a journey!' he said. 'I was just coming
to see you.'

'What did you want with me?'

Esmon grinned crookedly, and she felt a stab at her heart as he
said, 'I was hoping to talk to you for a time. How are you since
your sister's death?'

Flora cast a look behind her. There were too many brambles for
her to escape quickly, for her long skirts would snag and tangle in
the thorns. There was no sign of Os, either. Suddenly Flora felt
very lonely – and threatened – a feeling which grew as Esmon
took another step or two towards her.

'Flora, I was very sorry that your sister died.'

She looked at him, but now there was a faint narrowing of her
eyes. There had been an odd tone to his voice. 'We all were,' she
said quietly, her head averted.

'Yes, but she was so . . .'

Flora was anxious and took a step away from Esmon.

'Don't be scared, maid,' he said soothingly.

'I have to go.'

'Where?' He saw her confusion. 'Come, maid, let me calm
you. Why don't we sit down here?'

'After you tried to rape me?'

'I?'

'On your horse. Thank God your father protected me!'

'Oh, that!' he grinned. 'That wasn't meant to scare you, it was only a little fun! Did I scare you? Come here, let me calm you. I wouldn't want to hurt you, maid.'

Flora retreated slowly as he advanced, but now she felt a tree at her back.

'Please, Flora, give me your hand that I might kiss it.'

'Leave me! Please, just *leave* me!' she burst out. All her fears and sorrow seemed to rip from her breast, and she felt sick and dizzy, as though she was about to faint. There was a real sense of nausea, but then it went. He reached out to her, and she saw his hand hovering as though to grab at her breast, and that was enough. There was an explosion of fury in her mind, and she ran at him, screaming, beating at his face and chest with her clenched fists in futile rage.

He caught her wrists, raised her arms easily, and gazed down the length of her body. 'Christ Jesus, but you're lovely, aren't you?'

That was when she shrieked, a high, thin, keening noise like a rabbit in a trap. She jabbed with a knee, but he dodged, and she caught only his thigh. She felt Esmon forcing her to her knees, she was being pulled over his leg, she couldn't stay upright, she was held only by his hands on her wrists and he was setting her down. Then she grew aware of a man in among the trees. As Esmon gave a low chuckle, she saw a face: it was Os, and as she cast him a look, she saw Os step forward, an axe in his hands.

'Os, Os – help me!' she screamed.

'What do you want now, peasant?' Esmon demanded, angry at being discovered, and jerking Flora to her feet again. 'I was here first.'

'I'm here last,' Os said firmly. He set his feet a shoulder's width apart and hefted his axe. 'She doesn't want you here. Leave her.'

'I'll stand or go by my own will, not by your leave!'

'I'll say no more. Go.'

Flora was reluctant to speak. It was against her natural instinct to try to talk to Esmon. He was son to a knight, one of the most powerful men in the country, and as such he was fearsome enough, but with his propensity for violence and rape, Flora found it hard to say anything in his presence. 'Please . . .' she began, but the two men ignored her.

'Leave her,' Os said again, gripping his axe more firmly.

'Go from here, peasant, before I teach you not to be insubordinate in front of your master,' Esmon responded, but he was hampered by his grip on Flora. He let one of her arms go, trying to grab at his sword, but he was unbalanced and Flora tried to dart away, almost pulling him over. 'Keep still, bitch!'

Suddenly Os lifted the axe and sprang forward. It was so quick that Flora scarcely had time to open her mouth to take a swift intake of breath, and then she saw that he had moved to Esmon's side, and as the knight's son reached for his sword, the flat of the axe-head slapped his hand aside, giving a harsh, cracking noise in the stillness of the woods. Instantly Esmon gave a muffled cry, falling back and releasing Flora. She stumbled and fell on her arse.

Esmon could scarcely believe the pain. 'You bastard! You'll pay for this!'

Os said nothing, but slid his hand along the axe-haft, raising it ready to strike. There was no compunction in his eyes, only determination.

'Sweet Jesus!' Esmon sobbed, cradling his hand at his breast. The breath was rasping in his throat. 'This will cost you your life, churl! I'll not see you live after this! You think you can attack me? I'll soon be back, and I'll bring men!'

Osbert eyed him without speaking. It was as though all his contempt for Esmon and Esmon's family was concentrated in that one brief glance; as though a lifetime's loathing and hatred were comingled and, under his glance, Esmon felt devastated. Never in his life had he experienced such withering disgust. He felt like a worm or a slug being surveyed by a gardener.

'Bring as many as you want.'

Flora watched in horror and despair as Esmon turned and made his way from the clearing, nursing his hand tenderly as though every step cost him a sharp agony.

'Os, you have to get away, as far away as you can!'

'Where would I go?'

'I don't know, but as soon as he gets back to the castle, he'll tell his father, and they'll come to kill you. You don't want that, do you?'

'I'll go nowhere.'

'What of his father?'

'I don't fear him.'

'He'll have you killed!'

Osbert didn't answer. He still held his axe, but now he glanced at it as though scarcely recognising what it was, and then he let it fall to the ground. He stood with his fists clenching and unclenching, his jaw set, his eyes flitting everywhere. When she lifted her hand to touch his face, he gave a loud groan and reached for it, taking it and raising it to his mouth. His other arm encircled her waist, and he kissed her warmly, and she responded with all of her heart.

There had been nothing to learn in the greasy turf by the wall where the two carters confirmed that the miner had lain after the attack, although as Simon and Baldwin had already observed, the blood more than adequately confirmed that. Neither carter was comfortable about accusing the killer, but that was unnecessary now. Baldwin was interested more in where the body had been taken than in interrogating the two.

'Leave them for now, Coroner. If we can find this corpse and learn why someone should conceal it, perhaps that will prove who killed him.'

'You speak for yourself, Sir Baldwin,' Coroner Roger stated with gruff amusement. I need the evidence of these two idiots.'

'If you ask them to give their evidence in court, all that you shall have is two men standing before a strong lord and making an accusation. If we can find the body, we shall have a more compelling reason for his arrest.'

'And I can take him to Lydford,' Simon nodded, 'to the gaol where he belongs. At least we can make sure that he pays compensation for his crime, if we can show he was guilty of this murder.'

Coroner Roger shrugged. 'Very well. What of these two?'

Baldwin eyed them. They were an unprepossessing pair, the older man with a perpetually running nose, the younger with the scrawny appearance of a starved cockerel. 'You two can go to the inn we passed on the way here. If you aren't there when we get back, I shall order your arrest and shall have you fined. Is that clear?'

'Oh, aye, Master Knight,' Saul sniffed, adding with heavy irony, 'if we do anything, like trying to save ourselves from being murdered, then you'll see us thrown into the good Bailiff's gaol, where we'll most likely die from starvation. Oh, I thank you, Master. It's good to know we'll be treated so well.'

'Be off with you, and don't decide to run away!' Baldwin said sternly. 'Go!'

'And bear in mind,' the Coroner said with a grim smile, 'that my two servants are with you. They won't let you out of their sight.'

Simon grinned as the two carters grumbled to themselves, eyeing the Coroner's guards without enthusiasm, snapping their reins and lumbering away. Baldwin was smiling too, and Simon could tell his friend was tickled by them. Often Baldwin would have a curious, or so it seemed to most others, affection for the peasants with whom he came into contact, and Simon could see that these two had delighted him, the younger because of his apparent fear, starting at every noise, while the older man was so stolid and unimpressed with the rank and importance of the men who held him here. His sole apparent concern was his cold and how much longer it would last.

As the sound of the horses rattling on their way gradually faded into the distance, Simon stared after them. He was struck with a sudden sense of foreboding; a black mood swept over him, as though the devil had sent a grim presentiment of doom through his soul, but then he blinked, and in a moment it was gone.

'Come along, Simon!' Baldwin called, and he followed his friend to the wall. Even as he did so, he couldn't help but cast a glance over his shoulder, and as he caught sight of the two carts, the sense of foreboding returned.

Esmon seethed with anger, even as his fist throbbed with pain. How dare a mere churl like Osbert attack him – *him!* – the son of a knight, a man of status and fortune. It was incomprehensible. That sort of behaviour led to insurrection and mutiny. He wouldn't stand for it . . . he *couldn't* stand for it.

Leaning against a tree, he saw one of his men at the entrance to the mill's lane. The man grinned and called out: 'Master, the monk escaped last night.'

'How on—'

'Your father's gone to the moor to seek him with many men, but there's been a draw-latch at work in a farm north of here. Food taken.'

Esmon chewed his lip. He first of all wanted to make Os pay for his attack. His hand still hurt and his soul smarted at the insult to his dignity, but he knew he must also try to capture the priest if he could. 'How could he have escaped? This is pathetic! It will bring ridicule upon our heads if it gets out that a cretin of a priest can escape from our gaol! God in Heaven! I suppose we must try to find him.' But if Mark was robbing farms northwards, Esmon could ride out east first and teach Os to attack him. He was itching for revenge.

'Find Brian! Fetch men and horses and have the men arm themselves!' he bellowed.

His man gave a short nod and went to obey his commands. Meanwhile Esmon stood looking up at the castle's keep. He should warn his father what he intended, but since the girl's death his old man had indeed grown old. No longer the cour- ageous man of war, he was now apparently shrunken in mind

and in spirit. Look at the way he'd stopped Esmon from taking
Flora before. Sir Ralph had no right to prevent him from raping
her – other than the customary right of ownership, of course.
She was one of his serfs. It was probably merely the possessive
streak in him. Well, Esmon had had enough of his caprices.
Esmon wanted her, and he'd have her, just as soon as he'd dealt
with Osbert. That son of an adder deserved death for standing in
his way, and what he'd worked so hard to earn, Esmon would be
pleased to deliver.

The man-at-arms was soon back with five more, and Esmon,
wincing, clambered atop his mount. 'Follow me!' he roared,
thrusting his hand beneath his armpit to protect it, snatching at
his reins, and cantering off along the lane to where he had met
Osbert. However, when he reached the clearing, there was no sign
of Osbert, but for the axe which still lay on the ground. Gesturing
to it, Esmon ordered one of the men to collect it, and then led the
way back along the lane to another track. He went into it, scarcely
aware of the men behind him. This way led more directly to
Osbert's house, he knew, and he was keen to get to him. The mad
toad's spawn would surely be walking up this lane, or perhaps he
was already at his home. He could have gone straight there after
the altercation at the clearing, filled with terror and remorse at his
action. Perhaps that was why he'd dropped his axe, because he
was so petrified with horror at his actions?

Somehow that didn't ring true. Esmon had seen terror before in
his life. He had killed enough men, had seen the wakening shock
in their eyes as they saw their fate in Esmon's face, had seen the
intelligence fade from their faces as his sword took their lives, the
way that their bodies either slumped quickly, or began their jigging
dance as the nerves fought for life, had heard enough death rattles,
could recognise fear when he saw it. There was nothing remotely
like fear in Osbert's face when he had confronted Esmon. Only
hard, uncompromising hatred.

It was that memory which made him slow in his onward rush.
There should have been some misgivings about attacking the son
of a knight. It was appalling that a mere churl could think of

lifting a weapon against a man like Esmon, and yet this fellow had done just that.

If it had been another man, one of the wandering tinkers who occasionally passed through here, he wouldn't have been so shocked, because you expected stupid, antisocial behaviour from foreigners, but to see Osbert turn on him was like seeing a favourite mastiff snap at him. It was so incongruous, it was shocking. Osbert was usually so subservient, he could be embarrassing for it was shameful to see such an ox of a man so easily cowed. Something seemed to have made him forget his usual fear of Esmon and his father.

The girl!

Esmon's twisted into a grimace. Of course, that was the reason! Osbert wanted to get into Flora's skirts as much as Esmon himself did – no, more, since he was prepared to risk his life by threatening Esmon and attacking him. Esmon wouldn't endanger *his* life or his livelihood in order to enjoy a tumble even with so sweet a wench as Flora. No, she was not worth risking a life over.

There was a faint thickening in the air ahead and Esmon felt his belly tighten. He recognised that sight: dust raised by men on the track in front of him. He raised his good hand and peered ahead. Here, he and his men were beneath some great trees, oaks and elms, and he felt secure enough. Those ahead would be unlikely to see his own company's dust for the tree trunks, whereas he was looking northwards away from the sun, and the mist showed as an opacity against the woods further in the distance. Above the jangling of steel and puffing of the mounts, he was sure that he could discern the slow rumble and squeak of carts coming closer.

He had no need to speak to his men. They all knew how to operate effectively; they'd been on too many *chevauchées* together not to realise that this was potential spoil. As he made a hand signal, he knew it was redundant. None of them was watching him, they were all slipping to the sides of the path and waiting.

As the first horse appeared, with the bent figure of Saul jogging on the cart, Esmon's men leaped forward, but they had not reckoned on the panic of the horse pulling Saul. Startled, it reared and jumped up in the traces, slipped sideways and blocked the way. Esmon's men were ready to thunder off along the lane and capture any other folk behind Saul, but the kicking, bucking pony effectively prevented them, and Esmon could only watch as Alan took one look at him, then sprang from his seat and pelted away up the lane.

'What is this?' demanded one of Coroner Roger's men. 'Who are you?'

'Shut up and keep still or you'll have a quarrel in your guts,' Brian shouted. True to his word, he had his crossbow ready in his hand. The two men obeyed, sitting without speaking, but showing their contempt for Esmon and his men by refusing to look them in the eyes.

Esmon had to wait, swearing volubly, while Saul tried to calm his beast and stood at last at its head patting it ungently while one of Esmon's men galloped off after Alan.

'So, master merchant. I hope you have enjoyed a successful fair at Chagford. I'd be upset if all I won today for this trouble was a few coins and your wineskin.'

'I don't have any wine,' Saul said gloomily, wiping his nose on his sleeve.

'Perhaps your friends do?' Esmon said, looking at the two men on horseback who had been with Saul and Alan.

'These aren't friends of mine. They're the Coroner's men,' Saul said, and there was an unmistakable leer in his face as he looked up at Esmon. 'Doubt he'll be best pleased when he hears you've caught two of his men.'

Esmon swallowed his immediate reply. It was tempting to simply draw his sword and sweep off Saul's head, but that wouldn't help matters now. He glanced at the two guards. They looked furious, but entirely unworried about their fate. They knew that the servants of a Coroner were safe from the most unruly and wayward of the King's subjects. Even an outlaw must respect the power of the King's Coroner, and only the suicidal would harm them.

'Let's hope that my man catches your companion then, eh, carter?' Esmon hissed at Saul. 'If he does, it would be sad to think of the accidents that could befall a little group like yours, out on the open roads, wouldn't it?'

Saul looked up at him, suddenly worried. It was clear that Esmon was in a killing mood, and Saul suddenly realised that he and Alan were the only men nearby who could identify Esmon as being responsible for the murder of Wylkyn.

Alan was a friend, and he had escaped from Esmon's men before now, if he was to be believed. He should be able to make his way to safety. Saul's only concern was whether Alan would bother to find help to come and rescue him.

'Well?' Esmon demanded as the one-man posse returned.

'He went in among the woods up ahead. I lost him. He got away.'

'You fool, you toad's ass! He might get off and find help!' Esmon spat.

'Help? Where from?'

Esmon stared at the man and would have spoken, but Saul sniffed once and then responded slowly, 'From the Coroner, the Stannary Bailiff and the King's Keeper. They're all a short ride up from here.'

Chapter Twenty-Eight

Simon was still thinking of the two carters as he dropped from his horse and slipped in a pile of horse's muck. He had to catch hold of the cantle of his saddle to stop himself falling, and glared at the other two, who were laughing at his antics.

'Are we going to hunt for this body or not?'

Baldwin was smiling broadly as he swung his leg over his horse's broad rump. 'No. We are going to seek signs that might indicate who could have taken the body.'

'Most impressive,' the Coroner grunted. He spurred his horse towards the wall. 'Except the poor bastard was killed some days ago now. All traces will have been eradicated – if there ever were any!'

'Yes, well, any that remain might survive another few moments,' Baldwin said mildly, adding more curtly, 'provided a clumsy Coroner does not trample them before anyone has an opportunity to seek them out!'

Coroner Roger's face flushed momentarily, for he was unused to being commanded by others, but he saw the merit in Baldwin's words and urged his horse a little further away, leaving it tied with Simon and Baldwin's own.

Baldwin had seen his quick anger, and regretted his words. He had liked the Coroner ever since first meeting him over a year ago, and respected his judgements. Baldwin would have to make some form of compensation later, he decided. For now, he stood with his hands on his hips at the point where the body was supposed to have fallen.

'We were here only a day ago,' Simon objected. 'What will we see now? I thought we were only coming here to show it to the Coroner.'

'We were, but there is something about this . . .' Baldwin broke off, then looked back towards Gidleigh. 'No signs that way, nor northwards nor west. There is only one more direction.'

He went to the wall which had sheltered the boy Henry while he guarded the corpse, sprang lightly over it, and disappeared.

Simon and the Coroner exchanged a look. 'I don't know what he hopes to find either,' Simon shrugged, but he followed Baldwin while the Coroner stayed with their horses.

Baldwin pushed his way through the undergrowth until he came to a little-used path which could have been made by sheep or deer, but which Simon guessed had been man-made, from the width. Furze and ferns had grown stunted and unhealthy for about a yard, which could mean packhorses also used the track.

They carried on silently down the hill, until they came to a deep depression. There, in the bottom, they saw a dead calf.

'A lime-pit?' Simon asked.

'Yes. A place to throw dead and diseased animals to dispose of them cleanly,' Baldwin said pensively. He gazed into the hole, then glanced about him. A few tens of yards away was a pile of stones. Baldwin glanced back at the pit, then stared at the ground. He crouched and peered at some leaves and twigs, then rose and walked to the stones. Before he reached it, he bent over and once more gazed down. Then, nodding to himself, he beckoned Simon.

'What?' Simon asked.

'See that?'

All about, the grass was still slightly damp from the dew, but in this area it had dried. As Simon crouched, he saw that the grasses had been bent, as though a weight had been settled upon them. He glanced up at Baldwin, then back to the ground. It was almost as though someone had swept the grass here in a thick swathe – and then bisected it with a second, narrower sweep near the top, making the shape of a crude cross.

'What do you think of that?' Baldwin asked with satisfaction.

'Very impressive. What about the lime-pit? Shall we order it to be emptied?'

Baldwin said nothing, but smiled enigmatically, then made his way back to the Coroner. There he stood on top of the wall, arms on hips, gazing about him. 'Yes, this is a good spot for an ambush. Plenty of open ground up there, for a small force to use to manoeuvre. They could swing down and take a group of travellers in flank. They would cause mayhem with men unused to war. I can see it now.'

'Wouldn't it be easier to spring a trap in the lane?' Coroner Roger asked. He had joined them and now stood behind Simon, staring at the wall.

'You have experience of war as well, Coroner. What would be the difficulty in a narrow lane?'

'Oh, the narrowness, of course. You'd not be able to sweep past them so easily.'

'That, I think, is the reasoning behind this spot,' Baldwin said. 'It offered a better chance of capturing all the travellers. In a lane, some at the rear must inevitably escape, or at least evade pursuit for some while, making the whole exercise more protracted, while here, the entire group could be rounded up in the open like so many sheep. All those who sought to escape would find themselves rushing away from the men attacking them, and what would they find?'

Simon glanced at the Coroner, who stood with a sour expression on his face as he nodded. 'This damned wall.'

'Yes, if you look up there in the grass, you'll find hoofprints, like ten or twelve men at arms in a line, before they turned and charged down the slope. The carters couldn't turn to the rear because the attackers had hurried around behind them and cut off retreat. They couldn't go forward because there would be bound to be a man or two there as soon as the trap was sprung, and they couldn't go up the hill because that'd be the direction the main force was coming at them from. No, the only way they could go was down the hill, and they'd end up here.'

'As neat a trap as any I have seen.'

Baldwin nodded. 'And one which speaks of a commander's ability.'

'As does the ruthlessness,' the Coroner commented.

'Yes. Sir Ralph's whelp has much to explain.'

'If it *was* him,' the Coroner said.

'Wylkyn had been a member of Sir Richard Prouse's household,' Simon explained. 'And it seems Wylkyn bolted soon after Sir Richard died.'

Baldwin nodded. 'Why should this man decide to leave what must have been a comfortable life in order to have a rough existence on the moors?'

The Coroner grunted. 'He stole something?'

Baldwin shook his head. 'If Wylkyn was a thief, he would have avoided this area. What on earth would have compelled him to return to the place where he committed his crime?'

'Don't expect me to solve a riddle like that,' the Coroner smiled. 'I only deal in the facts, and all I know right now is that this man was killed.'

Baldwin told the Coroner about Wylkyn's store of herbs and potions. 'Wylkyn aided his master by acting as physician to him. In a room at the castle, there are many plants which could cause death. I think Sir Richard took to his bed because of his gout, but once there, someone poisoned him. Perhaps it was the very medicine he used to reduce the pain in his foot, I don't know, but I believe that if Sir Ralph and his son thought Wylkyn had willingly poisoned his master, they would seek to punish him. Kill one noble and you threaten all.'

'Punish him by slaughtering him out here,' the Coroner muttered. 'It would make sense.'

'As would someone else killing Sir Richard with Wylkyn's potions,' Baldwin said. 'The other possibility is that Sir Ralph or his son killed Sir Richard, and Wylkyn got to know about it, and then fled before they could kill him too. They caught him, however, and killed him here to silence him.'

'Who would have taken away his body, though?' Simon asked. 'That's the thing that confuses me. Execute him, that I can understand – but why not hide the corpse immediately? Why do it later? Most knights like Sir Ralph or Esmon would leave the corpse hanging about as a sign to their enemies or other potential thieves. 'Take my property, and this is what'll happen to you!' is more their kind of approach, I'd have thought.'

'Like riding down the Bailiff investigating a miner's murder. Blatant and threatening,' Baldwin agreed. 'If we assume that this Wylkyn had done something to upset Sir Ralph, he would have stayed hidden away on the moors, surely. He wouldn't approach here. Yet if this ambush was conducted because they knew that Wylkyn *was* here, then . . .' He stopped, shaking his head. 'This tale makes no sense. I must think about it.'

'There's one thing that appears consistent,' Coroner Roger said. 'There is flagrant robbery on the King's highways about here. We ought to speak to Sir Ralph and make sure he realises that he'll have to pay if we learn he was involved.'

Os kissed her once more as they parted, then he walked back to the clearing where he had dropped his axe. He was still sorry that Mary was dead – he'd miss her all his life, probably – but in her place, he had found Flora, and she was all a man could want, as well as adoring him. He would be churlish indeed if he didn't reciprocate her love.

They had left the clearing and gone to a deserted charcoal-burner's hut deep in the woods, where they had made their vows, and then they had lain together, sealing their contract in the oldest way possible. Now he knew he would live with her, Os was more than content: he was the happiest man alive.

Which made him more than a little concerned when he thought about how he had spoken to Esmon. It was lucky that Os had been born a freeman. If he wished, he could run away with Flora, take her to a town far from here where they could start afresh. Os was strong and willing to work and there was always a living to be earned by someone like that.

A peasant who bolted could always be chased and brought back, but Os was safe, all because he was born illegitimate. Any illegitimate offspring *could* have been born to a freeman, which meant that all bastards had to be assumed to be free. Everyone in the vill had a fair guess that Os was actually the son of Sir Ralph, not that the knight would ever admit the fact, so no one ever dared to suggest that he might be a peasant's son anyway. He was safe from that.

His axe was gone. There was nothing there. He frowned, searching along from the tree where he'd been working to the farthest edge of the clearing, but there was no sign of his axe, only a heavy stirring of the grass where many horses appeared to have trampled.

'What have you lost?'

'Ben!' he burst out, startled. 'Where did you spring from?'

'Oh, don't mind me. What's gone?'

'I left an axe here.' He couldn't help but feel a more kindly attitude to Ben. He had disliked the boy for a long time, but felt he ought to make the effort to be friendly to him now that he was a brother-in-law.

'Forgot it in your rush, did you?'

'What do you mean?'

'I saw you with Flora.'

Os reddened. 'I'm sorry. We were going to . . .'

Ben sniffed and waved a hand. 'I don't want to know the details. I saw you watching one sister in the river, and now you've shafted another.'

'Oh, you won't lose your sister.'

'I didn't mean I would. I meant you would. Do you know who is Flora's father? No? I didn't think so!'

'Huward, of course, your own father.'

Ben smiled maliciously. 'No. Our father is Sir Ralph of Wonson. The same father as you.'

The small cavalcade rode to the inn and left their horses with the ostler at the gate. Gladly they entered the hall, roaring for ale and wine as they passed under the lintel, but when they reached the fire, the host scurried in looking worried.

'Master Knight, I'm right sorry to—'

'Drinks, Host! Excuses later,' Coroner Roger stated firmly.

'This man, though,' the landlord said, wringing his hands.

'What man?' Simon said sharply. Glancing about him, he saw no sign of Alan and Saul and suddenly he recalled his anxiety watching them ride away. 'The two carters, where are they?'

Baldwin gave a most uncharacteristic curse and clenched his fist. 'By God's vengeance, if he's killed them as well, I'll have Esmon's head.'

The bedraggled and damp figure of Alan was soon with them, sitting near the fire so that his damp woollen clothing gave off the odour of wet dogs. His eyes were hunted; he jumped at every sound. Once the fire crackled, and although he was staring at it, he lurched to his feet and stared fearfully over his shoulder.

'Sit, boy! Tell us what happened to you. Where's your companion?' Coroner Roger rumbled.

'It was Esmon again. We were riding back, taking the little lane that comes from Throwleigh, and we met him with a small company. They got Saul, but his horse blocked the road, so I jumped off and bolted like a rabbit. One of them came after me, so I ducked into the woods to get away. He couldn't follow me when the undergrowth got too thick.'

'This is an outrage!' Coroner Roger said with slow menace. 'What of my men?'

'They were with him. I suppose they were taken as well.'

'They were taken as well, were they?' Coroner Roger repeated. His voice swelled and grew as he absorbed this news. 'Taken as well. The servants of a King's Coroner were captured and taken by a feckless, *witless boy no better than the son of an Exmouth whore AND A BRETON PIRATE*!'

Simon shot him a look. Coroner Roger had always been a calm man, sometimes dry to the point of cynicism, at other occasions caustic, especially when discussing his wife (when she was not present), but Simon now, for the first time, was seeing his friend angry, and the sight was impressive.

The Coroner was not tall, and although he was comfortably padded, his constant travel all over the wilds of Devonshire had kept his body firm and muscled. Now he appeared to expand like an enraged cock-bird when its feathers are ruffled. Sir Roger's chest swelled, his face hardened, his eyes grew flinty and unblinking, his normally smiling mouth became a thin bloodless gash in his blanched visage, and his whole body appeared to still, as though he was so furious his entire energy must be constrained by the focus of his anger.

'Coroner,' Simon said hesitantly. 'Don't worry, we'll get the men back for you.'

'Get them back? I'll say we'll get them back! And not by paying some ransom to a Godless, thieving, renegade knight whose only means of income is the robbing of his neighbours,' Coroner Roger declared at the top of his voice. 'That miserable dog's *turd*! I'll cut out his heart and lungs and *feed them to the hogs*! I'll *hamstring* the bugger! Aye, I'll—'

'You will sit, Coroner, and calm yourself,' Baldwin said soothingly, taking the sputtering man by the elbow, 'so that we can plan how to bring about the release of your men.'

'Release? We'll release them by pulling down his damned castle! You've heard the evidence against this knight and his mewling kitten, haven't you? This fellow here,' Coroner Roger said, grabbing Alan's shirt-front, 'says Esmon, Sir Ralph's son, captured my men, don't you?'

'Yes, sir!' Alan squeaked with alarm.

'And he led the gang who killed Wylkyn.'

'Yes!'

'Who killed Wylkyn? Esmon! Who took all the men from the convoy back to the castle?'

'Esmon.'

'Did he release you?'

'Yes . . .'

'But?' Coroner Roger snarled.

'He demanded ransom from all of us.'

Coroner Roger met Sir Baldwin's gaze. 'Sir Baldwin. You are Keeper of the King's Peace, with authority to pursue felons with the *posse comitatus*. I here declare that I believe Esmon, son of Sir Ralph of Gidleigh Castle, has feloniously captured, ransomed and murdered travellers on the King's highway. I accuse him of seizing the servants of a King's Coroner, and of taking them against their will to his castle. I demand that the posse be raised to force him to submit to the law.'

Baldwin nodded, concealing his true feelings. His belly was in a turmoil, and it was more because his hands would otherwise tremble like a drunkard's that he kept one thumb hooked into his belt, the other fist resting upon his sword's hilt. 'I have never before been asked to assault a noble knight in his own castle.'

'I doubt you have ever before heard of such a series of felonies committed by one man,' Coroner Roger grated.

Baldwin nodded. He looked across at Simon, for perhaps the first time since his appointment as Keeper, doubting his own judgement. No coward, still Baldwin would prefer to avoid being forced to arrest a man so powerful as Sir Ralph or his son, but the accusations made by Alan were uncompromising. The decision was fearsome, yet he knew what he should do, no matter that it might mean his own destruction.

That was all that was uppermost in his mind, he suddenly realised in disgust. Here he was, one of a small number of men who had survived the atrocious destruction of the Knights Templar, who now trembled on the brink of a decision that could save future travellers simply because it meant that he could endanger his own position! If more people had refused to consider their own safety, he knew, his companions from the Templar Order would yet live. Fewer perhaps would have been crippled by the brutal tortures meted out to them in order to force them to confess to ludicrous accusations.

If he arrested Sir Ralph and his son, they must accuse him of crimes against them, crimes which might well be upheld by their powerful friends the Despensers, the King's own friends. If Baldwin set his face against Sir Ralph and Esmon, his future must be endangered, and not only his own: his wife's happiness depended upon him, his daughter's safety too. He had to gamble with their lives.

He knew what he must do before all these thoughts had passed through his mind.

'I shall not assault his castle until I have spoken myself to Sir Ralph and heard his response to these accusations.' He cut off the Coroner's interruption before Roger could draw breath. 'In the meantime, you will sit here, Coroner, with your clerk, and write down all the accusations, the reason why we believe Sir Ralph is guilty, and his son, and when you have done so, you shall send messengers to South Tawton and to Chagford to ask for their help.'

'I will come with you,' Simon said.

'I would prefer you to wait here for my return,' Baldwin said with a pale smile.

'Perhaps, but I'll not leave Hugh in that nest of vipers if I can get him out.'

Chapter Twenty-Nine

When Esmon returned, he dropped from his horse and saw to it that Saul and the other two men were installed in the room off the gatehouse where the carters had been incarcerated the previous week. Once they were safely locked away, he sent a man to fetch him a jug of strong wine while he seated himself near the stable.

His father was going to be livid when he heard about this. He was angry enough when Esmon had killed Wylkyn, but that had almost been a relief after his earlier enervation. It was all since the death of the wench from the mill. Mary's murder had torn the soul from his father, as though Sir Ralph himself felt guilt . . .

Esmon slowly came upright. *Of course! That was it!* That was why he had been so pathetic and feeble ever since; *that* was why he had tried to prevent Esmon from catching young Flora afterwards! Sir Ralph was consumed by guilt, having made his use of the young stale and then killed her in a fit of fury. It was little wonder that he was so upset. No wonder he was keen to see the priest convicted, too! That would protect him.

Well, if he wanted to have people forget his crime, that was one thing. For Esmon, his father's crimes were of no concern. Perhaps his own behaviour might reflect badly, but that was nothing for him to worry about. While they had their friends the Despensers, they were safe from all but a random arrow!

It was infuriating that he'd missed Osbert, though. The bastard should have been back at his home, but when Esmon had reached the place there was no sign of the poxed badger's cub. It was all in stillness, without even a faint spark in the hearth to show that anyone had ever lived there. Osbert had escaped him for now, but he couldn't run away for ever. Esmon would catch him, and when he did, he'd make that whoreson regret his little outburst.

Esmon could move the fingers of his hand, and he was reasonably confident that the bones weren't broken as he'd originally feared, but the bruising would be appalling, of that he was sure.

It was curious. Esmon still had that feeling of lust for the girl, but it was subsumed now by his hatred of Osbert. If he could but ravish Flora, it would give him the additional satisfaction of ruining Osbert's life. He was sure that was the meaning behind the odd look in Osbert's eyes as he protected Flora. Osbert loved her and wanted her for himself.

He sipped at his wine. It was fortunate, perhaps, that his father wasn't here. Apparently he had ridden off some little while before, heading towards Chagford. No one seemed to know why he had gone there, except one of the servants had overheard a messenger saying that Surval wanted to see him. Curious, Esmon thought to himself, sipping at more wine. Was his old man going off his head?

If he was, that would be no bad thing. Esmon could have him locked up in the castle, somewhere nice and quiet, away from others, and Esmon could come into his inheritance.

That was how the idea was planted: a random feeling of contempt for his father's apparent collapse after the death of his wench. That very collapse was a sign of mental feebleness, proof that Sir Ralph was no longer capable of running the vill and the castle.

Esmon was capable. More than that, he had the men to succeed. With Brian and the others, he could hold both castle and vill, and if it appeared that there were richer pickings elsewhere, why, Esmon and his men could move on. This place held no real significance for him. His father had jealously desired it for years, but that was nothing to Esmon. He wanted a bigger, better place than a small rural castle.

It was a foolish dream, though, he told himself. Simple plans always looked simple until put into action, and his father wasn't truly mad. Just a bit enfeebled for some reason.

'So?' asked a small, quiet voice at the back of his mind. 'If he recovers, you could release him then, couldn't you?'

All he would need was a strong-minded clerk or lawyer to

declare that his father was mad, and he could take over the place. Get his mother out, install himself in the great chair before the hearth, and enjoy the life of the free.

His father would be insane with anger. Perhaps it would stir him from his lethargic mood. Since Mary's death he'd been in a stupor.

Scut, said that quiet voice. *There* was a man whose integrity was negotiable.

No! It was mad even to think of such a thing. Quite out of the question. But he could, he supposed, sound out Brian. See what the leader of his men reckoned. And then maybe it wouldn't hurt to talk to Scut. See what the clerk had to say about such an idea. He could ask Scut to look at his hand, then spring the question.

He drained his cup, flexed his hand a few times to test his fingers, and then nodded, satisfied, and walked out to find Roger Scut.

When the door suddenly opened, Surval didn't bother to turn from his contemplation of the cross before him.

'So you came at last.'

'What do you want, old man? Your messenger asked me to come – why?'

Surval crossed himself as he rose to his feet. 'Yes, I am old. And so are you, my Lord. Look at us both: there are almost a hundred years between us. But I declare that there are also differences between us. I have learned by my mistakes; you have not.'

'Ah yes?' Sir Ralph curled his lip as he approached the fire. He didn't sit, but stood with his back to the wall, the safest position for a man on his own in unwelcoming territory. 'What lessons do you have to give me?'

'You are a fornicator.'

'Many are,' Sir Ralph laughed. 'You have no balls. That's not my fault.'

'I choose not to use them.'

'But you have in the past, though, haven't you?' Sir Ralph sneered.

'I saw the miller last night.'

'So? What's it to do with me? He's just a serf. Where is he?'

'I do not know. Perhaps on his way to Exeter to find a new life; perhaps he is going to the coast to board a ship.'

'It'd be better if he does,' Sir Ralph muttered, relaxing slightly.

'All your fine clothes: velvet hose, crimson tunic, bright cloak of fur-trimmed wool, a man of power and authority – and you start at the slightest noise. You should copy me, my Lord,' Surval jeered. 'Join me here in my little chapel and help me serve the poor travellers you once fleeced.'

'You mock me, hermit!'

'Keep your hand from your sword, my Lord. I wouldn't want you to have another death on your conscience.'

'What does that mean?'

'We both know, don't we? Wylkyn had to die because he found out the truth.'

'You *pathetic* little man, you know nothing!'

Surval smiled coldly. 'Calm your ire, Sir Knight. You have much to mend, and little time to do it in.'

Sir Ralph had pulled his sword half from the scabbard, and now he thrust it back home with a muffled curse and sat down. 'What am I to mend?'

'You are sinful, Knight! You should be on your knees begging God's forgiveness, not ranting at me, a mere humble spirit whose sole duty is to see God's will done.'

'Mere humble spirit, my arse! You were a priest who had a good position in the world, who could have been a great magnate in the Church, but no! You had a woman, didn't you? And you killed her.'

'Yes, and there isn't a day I don't sit here and plead with God to take me to Him so that I might see her again and beg for her forgiveness,' Surval said, casting a longing look at his little altar. 'If I could, I should depart this miserable life this moment, and thank my executioner.'

'You ask me to murder you?'

'No, I ask you to make good the sins you have committed. I am here, wallowing in guilt and yet trying to make amends. You, though, you sit in your fine castle and think so little of others that you see them slaughtered to save your name and conceal your guilt.'

'I have nothing to be ashamed of.'

'Your guilt will result in the ruination of your family. Your children will die, Knight.'

'What do you mean?'

'Gilda told me of your crimes against Huward. You have ruined him utterly.'

Sir Ralph felt a sudden shock of weakness attack him. For a while he sat silently, scarcely breathing, merely listening to the blood hammering in his ears, and then he faced Surval once more, but all the boldness was gone from him. In its place was a quiet alarm, like a man who can see a runaway cart heading towards him in a dark alley, but who knows there is no escape.

'Yes,' Surval said quietly. 'Huward knows how you cuckolded him!'

'How could he have learned?'

'Your wife told him. She is, I fear, horrified at what you have done.'

'She will learn to be silent!' Sir Ralph said with a flare of his passion. 'Christ! The bitch knew what she was doing.'

'Of course. You have stolen his life, Sir Ralph.'

'Sweet Jesus! By God's own pains, he could . . .' Sir Ralph felt fear like a fist clench about his heart, and he thought he must die, but the sensation only lasted a moment, and then his sight cleared and he found himself staring at Surval. 'He might kill them!'

'Brother, I do not know,' Surval said.

'You bastard! You keep me here talking while he's planning their death? You delay me . . . I shall return, and when I do, you shall have cause to regret your part in all this, you bastard whoreson!'

Surval set his jaw. 'You would insult our own mother, brother? Begone from here, and I pray that you save their lives, but don't look to return here unless you can be thankful to our blessed mother, *and* thank me for warning you!'

* * *

Baldwin and Simon soon reached the castle.

To Simon's eyes it was curious. For the first time since they had seen it, the place seemed quiet, as if there had been a death and a thrill of horror had affected all the men inside. For once there was no one at the gate itself, and the two passed straight through and into the main court. There they waited, Simon feeling that something was terribly wrong.

It was a relief, when he glanced over towards the hall, to see Hugh walking out with Thomas behind him. Simon and Baldwin crossed to meet them.

'How's the head, Hugh?' Simon asked.

'I'm all right,' Hugh said gruffly. It wasn't exactly true, because he still had a powerful headache, which he was attempting to cure with Sir Ralph's best strong wine, but the wine itself was making him more comfortable. 'Just a bit tired.'

'He's been sleeping all day,' Thomas grumbled behind him.

'Not all day. I spoke to that fat fool of a clerk, didn't I?'

'Much good it did.'

'It did some good,' Hugh declared firmly. He was quiet a moment, and when Simon followed his gaze, he saw Roger Scut appear in a doorway near the gate. Simon glanced back at Hugh, who was assuming once more his customary glower. 'Don't like him.'

'What did you learn from him?' Simon asked.

'He was at the prison, looking at where the monk was kept.'

'Looking at it?' Baldwin said.

'He had a candle, but he dropped it when he heard us.'

Simon turned back, but Roger Scut had already disappeared. 'And? I assume there's something you're bursting to tell us.'

Hugh made a play of drinking his cup of wine, belched softly, and yawned. 'Only one thing . . .'

'The monk was set loose on purpose,' Thomas said, his eyes on Baldwin.

'Show us.'

Hugh and Thomas led the way to the trap door, and stood watching while Simon and Baldwin crouched, peering.

'Certainly it doesn't look as though it's been forced,' Simon admitted.

'No. This bolt fits neatly into the staple in the floor,' Baldwin said, drawing the bolt back and forth a few times. 'And it moves silently, too. No one would hear it opening. Only the prisoner.'

'In which case, who released him? Could it have been Scut?'

Baldwin rocked back on his heels. 'Possibly, but why? What motive could he have, other than, perhaps, to save the life of another cleric? Yet why should he do that? He did more than anyone else to see Mark installed here in the first place.'

'I don't think so, Sir Baldwin!'

The pained tone made Baldwin almost topple over with surprise, but when he righted himself, he found that he was peering up into the nostrils of Roger Scut.

Simon stood. 'It was perfectly obvious you wanted him out of the way. You gave him no support in the court, did you? You could have demanded that Sir Ralph release Mark into your custody on behalf of Bishop Walter, but you let Sir Ralph shove him down into this noisome pit instead. Hardly the action of a man supporting his friend.'

'That may be how you perceived it, Sir Bailiff, but really! Can you think so ill of a priest like me that you'd believe me capable of such an act? Of course I didn't intend to see my friend Mark suffer.'

'Incarceration here would lead to suffering enough,' Baldwin observed.

Roger Scut held out his hands and smiled gently. 'I felt that it could do no harm for Mark to be safely out of the way of others.'

'Like who?' Simon demanded curtly.

Roger Scut withdrew his hands and folded his arms. He had been trying to decide what to say to these two since he had come back, and now he took a deep breath. It was sad to think of that little chapel. All his hopes had been built upon that since his first arrival here and his meeting with Esmon, but there was nothing more to be done. He must extricate himself from this mess as soon as possible.

At first it had all seemed so perfect. Esmon had approached him during that first visit to the chapel, and they had spoken afterwards, with Sir Ralph, of the problems of land ownership and managing the peasants, explaining – as if Roger needed to be told! – how troublesome peasants could be. Better, they said, if they could have an ally in the chapel who could keep them informed. More than that, as Esmon indicated, they might be able to use their friends at court to assist clerics who were useful to them. A cleric at the chapel who helped keep the villeins subservient might soon be offered a more prestigious post in London or Winchester, for example.

Not that Roger was foolish enough to jump at the offer. No, he smiled at first and shrugged, gave noncommittal grunts and yawns as though this was the sort of offer he received each day, and not the kind of thing he had prayed for over long years of obscurity and relative poverty.

It was the final demand he was waiting for, and it took little time to arrive. They wanted him to spy on Sir Baldwin and Simon Puttock. That was easy enough. In fact, he simply told them at every opportunity that Sir Baldwin was a rather uncouth and ignorant buffoon. He disliked Sir Baldwin because Sir Baldwin disliked him, and making the Keeper out to be a fool suited his own prejudice, while the Bailiff he knew was quite astute. That was why he told Esmon, when the fellow asked about Puttock, that the Bailiff was deeply insulted by the harm done to one of his miners. Bailiff Puttock would not rest easy, he said, until he had the murderer hanging from the nearest oak.

Roger Scut had reinforced that message only the day before. The memory made him feel queasy now. At the time he hadn't heard about the near-fatal accident which had happened to the Bailiff's servant. If he had, he might have been a little more circumspect.

He might not be the most intelligent of logicians, but he was able to see a picture when it was laid before him, and it was clear to him that his comments on Bailiff Puttock had led to a murderous attack on him.

And now this! Esmon's outrageous suggestion! That he should agree to Esmon's proposition that his father was incapable, incompetent, and a threat to the security of the manor! Roger Scut could not possibly agree to such a flagrant fraud. What if he was found out? No matter what he said to Esmon and Sir Ralph about Sir Baldwin's intelligence, no matter what he said to himself in the dark hours about how stupid the knight was, how much more perspicacious Roger himself was, how much better ordered he would have the Keeper's court if he had a free rein compared with the slapdash fool, there was no denying that Sir Baldwin had a certain animal cunning. He was quite politically astute, and plain lucky. Going against him was not an attractive proposition.

No. Even before this had been suggested, when Roger had realised what Esmon had tried to do to Simon Puttock, he had decided that his intention to ally himself with the family was wrong and dangerous. He had come to the conclusion that he should change horses, support Baldwin, ensure the safe release of Mark, and guard and guide him to the safety of the Bishop's court. Except his decision had not been blessed with success.

All was going wrong. All his plans were unravelled, and he could see only disaster awaiting him as he surveyed the knight in the stable.

'Sir Baldwin, I am pleased to confess that I have been guilty of a dreadful error. I . . . well, I came to think that Mark could perhaps have been guilty of the crime of which he was accused. It's hard to get that sort of idea out of one's head: that a monk could indeed have slaughtered his woman with their illegitimate child in her womb. Awful, terrible, a truly grievous sin, a . . .'

'Stuff the pretence, priest. It doesn't impress us,' Simon growled.

'It's no pretence! Bailiff, I mean this.'

'Good. Get on with your story.'

Roger Scut turned from him and gazed down his nose at Baldwin. 'So, Sir Knight, in the court I was truly shocked. Nay, devastated. To think that a brother monk could be responsible for so heinous a crime tore at my very soul and rendered me speechless. That was why I was incapable of supporting my poor friend. However, I now realise my error and wish to see my young friend saved. Apart from anything else, I do not believe in his guilt. It is incomprehensible. A priest in Holy Orders murdering a woman – and child? No! Assuredly, no man like Mark could do such a thing.'

'What were you doing here, priest? You were found here by my man. Why?'

'I wanted to see how he could have escaped from this hideous place. I thought that he might have been released.'

'Rather than merely sprouting wings and flying away?' Simon scoffed. 'Of course he was released.'

'But by whom?' Baldwin murmured. 'That's the question to which we must seek an answer.'

'I do not know.'

Simon was gazing down into the cell as Baldwin spoke. 'There's a candle in there. Did they leave that for Mark to read by?'

'No, the priest dropped it. He was looking down into the cell when we found him,' Hugh said. He slurped a little more wine, aware that his head was growing lighter, but he didn't care right now. He was feeling a great deal better, and that was all that mattered.

'You were looking to see who might have released the monk, then?' Simon said. He climbed down the ladder and retrieved the candle. 'This is probably the foulest gaol I've seen. It's even worse than my own in Lydford. At least that is a decent size, but this! It's tiny!'

He felt something under his boot as he was about to return to the ladder. Glancing down, he moved the stones and pebbles on the floor with his boot's toe. Then he frowned and bent to look more closely.

'What is it, Simon?' Baldwin asked.

'Probably nothing,' Simon said. It was a lump of stone or something, encased in leather. An odd decoration for a cell like this – in fact, Simon reckoned it an odd enough thing for anywhere. He picked it up and carried it up the ladder. 'Look.'

Baldwin took it and weighed it in his hand. 'I think, Roger, that you should tell us all you know about Mark's escape last night.'

'Hmm?'

'This is one of your weights to hold down rolls, is it not? I have never seen another man with such a trinket. Why did you bring it last night – to brain the poor fool who languished in here?'

Roger Scut took a deep sigh and walked to a barrel, resting his ample buttocks on it. 'If you must know, it was in order to overpower any guard.'

'*You* sought to get him out?' Simon expostulated.

'I don't think he committed this grave act,' Roger Scut said simply. 'And I thought that if he stayed in here, he would surely die. It seemed better to me that he should be aided in his escape so that the good Bishop could test his case in the Bishop's own court.'

'What did you find here?' Baldwin asked, touching Simon's arm to keep him quiet.

'There was no guard. I was pleased, naturally, because I hate the thought of violence, and I feared having to strike down an innocent who was merely serving his master's will. Yes, that was a relief. I reached the door and pulled the lock and opened it wide, calling to Mark, but there was no one there. I had my candle with me, and held it in one hand while I held the trap open with the other, and peered inside, thinking that the lad must have collapsed in fear and exhaustion, but there was no sign of him, and when I leaned in to make sure, my weight fell from my hand. Trying to hold that and the candle in one fist was too much. I heard it plop into the dirt, but I was reluctant to go down the ladder and resolved to return today. As your man saw,' he added, giving Hugh a baleful glance.

'Have you any idea who could have released Mark?'

'Yes. I think it was Sir Ralph's son, Esmon. The fellow knew that his father would be enraged to hear that Mark had escaped, and would seek him with a fury unsurpassed by the hounds of Hell. Esmon sought to ensure that his father would kill Mark for escaping his cell, and to do so, Esmon made certain that Mark was released. Whether it was Esmon himself or one of his many disreputable men who let Mark out, I do not know.'

'You are sure of this?' Baldwin asked.

'As sure as I can be without hearing Esmon confess, yes.' Roger Scut looked out at the doorway and dropped his voice. 'Do you know what he has done now? He asked me a little while ago whether I would help him to depose his father. I truly believe that lad has no conception of good and evil. He asked me to write a letter confirming that Sir Ralph was too ancient and infirm to be able to continue as Lord of Gidleigh. As though I should do any such thing!'

Baldwin glanced at Simon. He doubted the entire truth of Roger Scut's comments, although their general thrust he thought was probably accurate enough. 'As though,' he repeated drily.

Roger had the grace to look away.

'Do you know what *I* think, Scut?' Baldwin asked. 'I think you came here wanting to brain a guard and release Mark.'

'Yes.'

'Because you thought that then he would be hunted down and killed. You knew Sir Ralph would slaughter him under any pretext. The Bishop would punish Sir Ralph, but so what? You would be here to take over the chapel and all its revenues.'

'Nonsense, that had—'

'You actively sought the death of Mark to fill your own pocket.'

Roger shook his head, but his voice was quieter, as though he scarcely dared deny the charge. 'No, I don't know what you're talking about.'

Simon had listened with contempt. Now he deliberately turned his back on the monk and ignored him. 'Hugh, this Esmon has captured more men today. He took a carter and two of Coroner Roger's men captive. Did you see them arrive, or hear them?'

'I heard someone – over in the gatehouse area.'

'That is where Sir Ralph and his son tend to keep their prisoners ready for ransom,' Roger Scut said helpfully.

'Show me where this room is,' Simon said, speaking to Hugh.

Chapter Thirty

Osbert sat in the shelter of Piers's barn and wrapped his arms about himself. It was not cold, but the ideas that milled in his brain were stifling him, and he felt as though his head were about to explode with the things that evil shit Ben had told him with such amused glee in his voice. Truly, Ben was foul. He deserved to be murdered. It was said that a man's evil could be reflected in his sons, that a man who was sexually incontinent could give birth to a leper, and if that was so, all the sins of Sir Ralph had been stored and concentrated in Ben's voice. He enjoyed using his snake's charm and insinuations to bedevil others.

There were so many things Os wanted to do but he felt enfeebled. As soon as Ben had told him, he had wanted to go to Flora and apologise, to cradle her in his arms. More, he wanted to lie with her, feel her naked body next to his, make love to her like a man should – except he couldn't, not now! Christ Jesus, not ever!

His desires were impossible. Cursed. He must accept that. If he couldn't, he might go mad. God would see to it. For a man like Os to touch Flora with thoughts of passion was *obscene*! She was his *sister*!

He wanted to go to the castle and tear it apart stone by stone; he wanted to feel Sir Ralph's flesh beneath his hands and rend his body to wolf-bait; he wanted to stamp all over Esmon's corpse; he wanted to stab and slash at them just as Esmon had stabbed and slashed at Wylkyn. He wanted to kill, and go on killing, to destroy this terrible injustice. The first woman he had loved was dead, buried and rotting; her sister, whom he now adored in Mary's place, whom he felt the duty to protect with his life, was now ineradicably removed from him. He could no more hope to be her husband than he might hope to marry the Queen. She was removed from him, and with her removal, it felt as though his heart had been plucked from his breast. Life held no pleasure. All that remained was hard, cruel toil, made the more painful by the constant presence of Flora.

'They've gone. Buggered off, the lot of them.' Piers entered, threw his stick against the wall, and crouched leaning with his back against the stone wall. 'But Esmon'll be back. You know that. He'll return, and when he does, he'll want your head.'

'He can have it. What is there for me now?'

Piers shrugged. 'I don't know what your problem is, other than the obvious little things, like trying to kill Sir Ralph's son. Now, if I'd done that, I'd be guilty of *petit treason* and I'd get killed, but you won't. You're safe – you're a freeman. All you have to worry about is getting away from here before Esmon catches you. At least right now, with a murderous monk on the road, you should be safe enough. People have more to worry about than a miserable-looking miller's helper. Unless you meet said monk, of course,' he added thoughtfully.

'I love Flora.'

'Hmm. That's not a huge problem,' Piers said, head cocked on one side. 'What does she think about it?'

'She feels the same. Promised to marry me.'

Piers nodded his head slowly. 'Right. So she loves you too, but you feel bad? Not good? Not glad?'

'I can't do it. I can't ask her to marry me.'

'I . . . You don't have much, no, but you'd make her a good enough husband, wouldn't you? You're not cruel or stupid – at least, I wouldn't have said so until just now. What's the matter?'

Osbert sat back, curled his arms about his legs and rested his chin on his knees. He remained there for some while, staring into the distance, and then gave Piers a disconcertingly straight stare. 'You mean you don't know?'

Piers held his hands out, palms up. 'Don't know what?'

'My mother. She was never ashamed of me, of my bastardy.

She always said, any man born like me shouldn't regret his birth. The fact was, I was free, after all.'

Piers shrugged. He knew the rule of the law: a freeman who fathered a son conferred his freedom on the child, and a bastard must be assumed to be free. 'So?'

'Ben told me. I always loved Mary, and then, when she was gone, I fell in love with Flora. At least Ben saved us.'

'What?' Piers asked, confused.

'I never knew my father. Mother always said it was because he'd married some prune-faced whore.'

'Yes, well. These things happen,' Piers said.

'I always wondered why Mother didn't tell me who it was. I thought it was because she was ashamed. Didn't want to tell my father that she'd given birth.'

'It's common enough.'

'You don't understand, do you?'

Piers didn't, nor did he particularly care. He had spent the whole day riding about the countryside seeking Mark, and now he was going to help Osbert escape, a man who had hurt his master's son. It didn't bear thinking about. 'Neither of us have time for this, Os. Come on.' He was brushing the twigs and straws from his backside when he heard the steps outside. Slow, thoughtful steps, Piers considered, not the sharp, swift footfalls of a man who rushed to a barn with a sword in his hand ready to kill or capture the men inside. Rather they were the reluctant steps of a man who was setting off on a long journey without knowing his destination.

Peering around the doorframe, Piers saw a familiar shape. 'Oh, thank God!'

Osbert was not of a mood to notice a newcomer. 'After he'd shoved his pork sword into my mother and got her with child, he fell in love properly.'

'He married,' Piers said without thinking, and opened his mouth to welcome his new guest, when Osbert spoke again.

'No. The bastard fell in love with Huward's wife. All those children of the miller's? They're Sir Ralph's. Mary, Flora, Ben, and me too. We're all Sir Ralph's children.'

Hearing the sharp intake of breath, he looked up, just in time to see the ravaged face of Huward at the doorway.

'I thought you'd soon be here.'

Esmon stood with a pair of his men-at-arms behind him in the main gatehouse guard room. His hand was still painful, but he found that clenching and unclenching it eased the pain a little, and he was sure that it would only marginally limit his ability to fight if he was forced to draw his sword. Not that there should be any need for that, he thought as he observed Roger Scut at the back of the little band. 'What, a wounded servant, two watchmen, a cleric, a Keeper and a Bailiff? All to come and speak to me? This is quite a party. What do you want? More wine?'

Simon smiled calmly. 'You have a reputation, Master Esmon. Men say that you raid and kill on the moors.'

'Who accuses me? I'll show my innocence,' Esmon said off-handedly.

'You will learn at the next county court. You will be attached.'

'By you, Bailiff? Oh, I don't think you have the power.'

'I think I do, and so does the Coroner and this good Keeper. And since the murder concerns a man going about his business on the moors, a man who mined tin, I have every right to arrest you now and take you to my own court.'

'I don't think I'll submit to that. And what would you want to achieve, anyway? I am a friend of the Despensers. Touch me, and you'll regret it! Copy that Keeper. He seems content to maintain his dignity with silence. Perhaps you should learn from him, Bailiff.'

Baldwin looked up at that. 'You think I was keeping quiet? I was only waiting to hear what the good Bailiff had to say.'

'You've heard him.'

'And I say that you are to be arrested and will be judged by me in my court for breaking the King's Peace, robbing and ransoming to the detriment of the King's subjects.'

'What, nothing of murder?' Esmon sneered.

'That was a crime committed outside my jurisdiction, but the good Bailiff has accused you already.'

'So do you intend to steal me away even now?' Esmon demanded, and his anger was unfeigned. These people had come here and taken advantage of his father's hospitality, and now they dared to accuse him! It was against all the rules of chivalry to behave so rudely. 'I suppose you would like me to put on sackcloth and ashes?'

'No, but I would like to hear you apologise for trying to ride me down in the road,' Simon said.

'What?'

'It was you who rode at me and struck my servant here instead because he tried to save me.'

'I was riding on a road – if your servant got in my way, that's not my concern.'

Baldwin, who was watching Simon, saw the Bailiff's smile subtly alter. Now only Simon's bottom teeth showed, and that, as Baldwin knew, was an infallible sign that Simon's temper was about to snap. He interrupted quickly. 'Esmon, you knocked Hugh here aside and could have killed him. If it was an accident, it should be no trouble to apologise.'

'I certainly think it was a shame I hit *him*,' Esmon said, eyeing Simon with cold anger.

'Good,' Baldwin said hastily. 'And now we can see the carter and Coroner Roger's men released.'

'No. They were found near a farmhouse where someone had robbed a woman. Until my father speaks to them and determines their innocence or guilt, they have to remain here, I fear.'

'They shall be released,' Simon said, slapping his sword hilt. Baldwin caught his elbow to stop him marching forward.

'They stay here, Bailiff, and they'll only be released when my father says so,' Esmon replied. 'I don't know why you think you can claim authority over my father's court, but he takes such arrogance badly.'

Baldwin heard a noise, and glancing over his shoulder, saw more men walking in through the doorway and fanning out to encircle Simon and him. 'So you refuse?'

'Certainly I do. These three were found near a theft. What would you do, Keeper? Let them run wild?'

'Will you surrender to our safekeeping for the murder of the man Wylkyn?'

A woman's voice called sharply, 'What is all this about?'

Esmon could have sworn aloud. 'Mother, please leave us.'

'I asked what this was all about. Why are our guests in here surrounded like felons?'

'These guests, as you call them, want to arrest me.'

'Because of Wylkyn?' Lady Annicia walked in like a lady, but her deportment was not quite as smooth as when she was completely sober. Baldwin could smell the wine on her breath. She glanced at Baldwin and Simon with a perturbed frown. 'He was a terrible man, though. He killed Sir Richard Prouse, you know, and then he drew a knife against poor Esmon too. Last week he tried to hurt my son when he met him on the road, and Esmon defended himself. That is all.'

'It would be, perhaps, if Esmon had not led a raiding party to rob the carters and kill Wylkyn, and it would be easier to believe if the body of Wylkyn hadn't disappeared afterwards,' Simon said. His attention was still fixed on Esmon, keeping an eye on the youth's hands in case he tried to draw a sword.

'I would like to offer you wine, will you come to the hall?' Lady Annicia said. 'I am sure that we can discuss this more sensibly without the need for raised voices.'

'Not until we have seen the men being held,' Baldwin said firmly. 'My Lady, please command your men to open that door.'

'Very well.'

'Mother, I . . .'

'Esmon, you may go to the hall and arrange for wine to be served while we await your father's return.'

'I . . .'

'Go. *Now!*'

He reluctantly submitted and pushed his way through all the men in the room. Outside, he let out his breath in an angry gust. It was infuriating that she had arrived just then. There was no telling what she might do to calm the Bailiff. Esmon had hoped that he might be able to taunt the man into an indiscreet action, pulling a knife or sword. With all the men there, he wouldn't have got two feet before falling under all their blows, and the rest would have been cowed and fearful after such an outburst, but now he didn't know what would happen.

Huward entered the barn, his attention fixed on Osbert with an expression that made Os shiver as though someone had walked over his grave. It was a dead face, as though Huward had already lost his soul and was staring into the pit of Hell.

'Huward, I'm sorry, I didn't realise you were there.'

Standing a little inside the doorway, Huward showed no emotion. He didn't speak; he couldn't. The discovery of his wife's deceit and disloyalty had snapped something inside him. It felt as though his entire life had been a sham. He had believed in his wife, in her love, in her devotion – and in his children. To learn that the children might not be his own, that was too much to bear. Although he had spent the night with Surval trying to come to grips with this, to see how he could rebuild his life and make peace with his wife, the more he considered how she had lied to him over the years, the more he felt that he couldn't go back.

This conclusion he had reached as he walked about during the morning after leaving Surval at dawn. He had not been hungry, and the idea of food made him feel physically sick. Perhaps he could have gone back to his mill, confronted his wife, demanded to know if it were true – but no. It could serve no useful purpose. All it could do was harm the memory of his Mary and hurt poor Flora. Ben would survive, and Gilda would probably be granted a pension from Sir Ralph, the *bastard*! No, Flora didn't deserve to be hurt. And she might still be his own daughter. Gilda couldn't know which was Sir Ralph's and which was Huward's child.

All had been a little early, he recalled for the thousandth time. All had been delivered two to three weeks before their usual term. Did that mean he had been cuckolded perfectly and that all were Sir Ralph's? That thought was like a screw tightening about his forehead, squeezing and making his brain work more slowly.

He had come here to see Piers to tell him that he would leave the area and seek his fortune in another town, because at least that way his remaining daughter might not learn and have to suffer the shame of being pointed at by all the other folk. She might still be his daughter. Ben, he cared less for. The boy had been a pleasing son until he changed a year or more ago, and since then he had grown sharp, bitter, unkind. Perhaps he would improve in later years, if Huward wasn't here.

But Os's words showed he was already too late. He wanted to save the family shame, but the whole vill knew. Os knew, Piers knew, and in a vill like this that meant surely everyone must soon know. There was no escape, only scandal and utter disgrace.

In his breast he felt the welling horror of dishonour. His heart seemed to harden to stone, a massy object in a body now suddenly emptied of all emotion other than all-consuming grief.

'Huward, old friend, I am so sorry you had to learn like this,' Piers was saying, and more in the same vein, but Huward, when he looked at him, wondered only whether Piers had cuckolded him too.

There were some husbands who happily sold their wives as whores, he knew, but that was whoring with the husband's consent, to help provide for a family in sore straits, like during the famine years. But his wife had never mentioned spreading herself for the knight. She'd probably done it for all the men in the Hundred. If she'd betrayed him with one man, why not a thousand? He could never trust her again.

'Do you want some food, Huward? Ale?'

'Leave me *alone*!' he suddenly roared as Piers put a hand to his shoulder. The miller lifted his arm and knocked the Reeve's arm away. It had felt like a snake's bite. Loathsome, then poisonous. It was repellent, this mental venom. There was no one, no man he could trust in the whole vill.

'Huward, I . . .'

'Leave me. Leave me to die. I want nothing more from this place!'

Piers felt as though his heart must rip apart with compassion as he stood in the doorway and watched Huward lumbering down the road towards his home. 'Huward,' he said again, but it was just a whisper. He couldn't do anything. There was nothing any man could do to protect Huward. His life was ruined.

'Sweet Mother of God!' Osbert said, and covered his face with his hands. 'He's dead, already dead. Did you see his face? Jesus, save us all! My father has much to answer for!'

'He has much to answer for,' Piers repeated in agreement.

Sir Ralph found the place lying peaceful and calm as the sun dipped down behind the hills. He tied his horse's reins to a sapling and entered with a feeling of trepidation, wondering whether Huward would be there. If he was, Sir Ralph was not sure how he might react.

It was hard. If he could have stopped himself, if Gilda could have, he would. Until he met her, he had enjoyed many of the women in the area, for they had no clerk to help them bring a suit against their legal owner, and when he wanted to slake his lusts, he could do so with almost any of them, but then he had grown to know Gilda, and that woman had turned his heart and stopped his whoring. He had watched Gilda grow to maturity, and he had been besotted.

She had been utterly different. Long-legged, tall, elegant as a young filly, and with a spark in her eye, she had attracted all the men for miles around. He had known that he must possess her, and she was nothing loath. They had begun meeting, and remained lucky, for she had not succumbed to pregnancy, but they couldn't continue for ever and Annicia would have been very difficult if she had learned that he was whoring about so near to their home, so Sir Ralph had hit upon the scheme of making his mistress legitimate in his own way. He couldn't marry her himself, but he could share her.

The idea was marvellous in its simplicity. He had often noticed the miller watching her with more than a little interest. A man notices another's lustful glances at his woman. At first she had declared her reluctance, but she couldn't live in the castle with him. Something must be done, and at least Sir Ralph could make her life easier than for most other women. One day, Sir Ralph broached the subject with Huward and told him that he thought she would accept him, saying that Sir Ralph himself would offer a sizeable dowry, and Huward had been embarrassingly grateful.

It had led to problems. She had been furious at first, demanding to know what he meant by giving her away to someone she found tedious, but eventually she agreed to follow his plan. The row had been furious like a summer fire on the moors, but when it burned out, they both enjoyed the slow making up.

For the next seventeen years, that was that. His daughters and son were born, and he and Gilda enjoyed their illicit liaison at every opportunity. Huward was delighted to have been told by his master to marry the most attractive wench in the vill, and she grew to agree that Sir Ralph's choice had been good. Huward was a good man, a kind and never overbearing father, a diligent worker, and an undemanding lover. He never had any clue that he was being cuckolded.

Now all that was gone. All was at risk. Annicia was furious. Well, it was no surprise, but he had to confess the reason for his misery over Mary's death. Annicia had accused him of being Mary's lover and getting her pregnant. That accusation was so repugnant that Sir Ralph retaliated by confessing his affair with Gilda.

Poor Mary. She had been the image of her mother. Tall and slender as a willow-wand, soft, gentle, kind even to that half-brained cretin Sampson. And now no more. Gone, like a dandelion clock in a gust. It felt as though a part of him had been destroyed, like a slow stab-wound in his belly, a raking agony that wouldn't mend.

All this passed through his mind as he bent beneath the lintel and glanced inside. There he saw Ben sitting at a bench with a large pitcher of ale before him. The boy stood, uncomfortable in the presence of the Knight, shooting a look at his mother, who sat near the hearth on a stool, watching the flames.

'You, boy – out!'

Ben curled his lip, and Sir Ralph could have sworn he heard an oath, but then he sauntered from the place.

'Gilda? Are you all right?' he asked softly.

She looked across the room at him. Her face was ravaged, her eyes dull, all light dimmed. Where once she had been taut and firm, now she was a haggard bag of flesh that sagged. 'So you came at last.'

'I wanted to come before, but how could I while he was here? He's gone?'

'He didn't come back here after your court. What did you do, taunt him with the facts of my infidelity? Did you say to him how good I was in bed for you, like some whore from the stews?'

'Nothing, I swear it! I told him nothing at all.'

She sighed, a sound that shuddered like a sob, and picked up ash, letting it trickle through her fingers. 'I don't care. If he knows and comes back and kills me, it doesn't matter. There is nothing for me to live for now. He will call me whore, reject my children, and maybe sell me to his friends to make their sport as they will. What is there for me? Ashes and dust. That's all we all win in the end, isn't it? I should never have married him – he deserved better.'

'Don't speak like this, my love, my darling. You are my only love, is there nothing I can—'

'Keep away from me! This is all your doing! You wanted me although you were to marry that cold bitch for her lands, and to possess me, to make me whore for you, you gave me to another, so we could cuckold him – a good, kind man who didn't deserve it, just so you could enjoy yourself with me.'

'My love . . .'

'Don't call me that! I'm not your love. I'm just your serf – your slave. You owned me, but then you made a gift of me to another so that you could come and possess me again. You let another man protect your children, feed them, clothe them, never knowing that they were as cuckoos in his nest. And now my Mary is dead, all because of our deceits.'

'It was the only thing we could do,' he said. 'What else could we have done? If we hadn't, we would never have given birth to her.'

She shuddered again. 'Better we hadn't. I wish we hadn't because losing her is so . . . so . . .'

'We shall find her murderer and see him hang. You will feel better when you see him hanging from my oak tree.'

'You would swear to do that for me? No matter who the murderer is?' she said quickly, a light flashing in her eye.

'As soon as I catch that shitty-trousered priest, I'll—'

'Not *him*,' she said scornfully. 'The man who killed her was your son. Your precious Esmon, the foul degenerate.'

'No, it wasn't him.'

'He was there, wasn't he? My son saw him in the lane, just after he saw you.'

Ralph was silent. It was the one clue he had hoped would not be discovered, the fact that Esmon had been there that day. The terrible gnawing fear began to scratch and scrabble at his bowels. He had lost Mary, he *couldn't* lose Esmon too. 'You must take my word. He is innocent of this.'

'It's one of the few crimes which are not his responsibility, then,' she spat. 'Ask him what he was doing there. Just ask him!'

'I don't have to,' Sir Ralph said miserably. 'He was trying to find Wylkyn, to kill him.'

Chapter Thirty-One

Baldwin was surprised when Lady Annicia took him and Simon out of the hall and into the solar behind. She graciously motioned to them to take seats, but waved the watchmen out, along with Hugh. Roger Scut hung around as though in two minds whether he was invited to join them, and she stood surveying him for a long moment, before finally shrugging her assent to his remaining. However, when she saw that Hugh too had stayed, planted stolidly next to Simon, her expression hardened, although she made no comment.

'So, Lordings, you want these men released. Why should I do so?'

'They are innocent travellers, my Lady,' Baldwin said. He was a little confused by the way that this woman had taken control, but foremost in his mind was the desire to remove the captured men, as well as Simon, Hugh, the watchmen, and himself, from the castle. A castle was always a dangerous place for strangers, but this one, so Baldwin reckoned, was worse than most. The men-at-arms were too surly, and the whole place seemed to be ready to explode into violence and mutiny at any moment:

'The men who are held are guilty of no crime, and were captured on the road while on the King's business. Coroner Roger de Gidleigh had ordered the carter to our inn to wait for us, and he was on his way there under guard from two of the Coroner's own men. These are the fellows you hold. Are they to be ransomed to the King himself?'

'That would be the act of a felon.'

'I know.'

'I shall see them released,' she said coquettishly, 'on the understanding that any charges you might have brought against my son are forgotten. Esmon is a little wilful sometimes, but he is a good child, and I wouldn't want to see him troubled by the threat of a court.'

Simon took an angry breath. 'You wouldn't want him . . . Your son tried to kill me, Lady, and if my servant hadn't risked his own life, I might well be dead! My man Hugh threw himself between me and your son and saved my life.'

'I am sure it was an accident. He will apologise.'

Simon cast a look at Hugh. 'I require no apology, but my servant will need a physician's aid when he gets to his home and I doubt that he could afford the services of a good man. Your son must pay for that. Shall we say fifty shillings?'

'Fifty . . .' the Lady Annicia was astonished to hear so high a sum suggested, but she recovered herself quickly. 'I am sure that my son will be happy to pay. An accident like this is always unfortunate, and we must make sure that your fellow is as well looked after as he can be. Although,' she added with a venomous look at the broadly grinning Hugh, 'I cannot imagine that the physician in his vill would warrant such a price for his skills. I did nurse him myself, you know, and I think he has waxed well on our best wine all day.'

Simon saw Hugh's glee and gave a slow nod. 'I think that will be adequate compensation, Lady.'

'So we can forget all matters which affect my son?'

Baldwin slowly shook his head, watching her all the while. Annicia had the uncomfortable sensation that she was being studied by a serious-minded lawyer. His dark eyes had, she thought, a certain air of reptilian disinterest, just like so many lawyers. 'Your son is accused of murder on the King's highway while trying to capture and rob travellers on their way to Chagford Fair. He will have to stand in court on that charge.'

'He is so accused?' Annicia asked softly. 'And where is the corpse? I had not heard that there was one.'

'I believe I know where it is.'

'But I fear I do not understand,' she said with a smile that failed to conceal her cold determination. 'Do you mean to tell me that my son is to be accused of killing a man when there is no body, no proof of the wounds that killed him, no presentment of Englishry, nothing? I had thought that no body meant no case.'

Baldwin smiled, and once more she was reminded of a reptile: like a snake, he appeared not to blink. 'We shall find the body, madam. And when we do, your son will be arrested on my order as Keeper of the King's Peace.'

She was about to answer, when there came a rattling of hooves on the cobbles outside. Immediately there was shouting and roaring, with one voice calling more clearly than all the others: 'In God's name, all men here, now! There's a fire!'

Simon ran to the door and stared out. 'It's your husband, madam.'

'Fire! Fire at the mill! Every man, bring buckets, help to put it out!'

'I suppose you should go with him,' she said with a strange inflexion in her voice.

Baldwin looked at her. 'Yes, my Lady, but while we are gone, you must ensure that the prisoners are sent on their way to meet with the Coroner. You shall do this?'

'Yes.' She saw his sceptical expression. 'I swear it. You disbelieve me?'

'Not at all, Lady,' he said courteously. The shouting outside was louder, and he heard horses being gathered. 'We must go.'

Baldwin and Simon ran down to the court and Simon had to snatch the reins of his mount from one over-enthusiastic man-at-arms who had mounted it already. As the Bailiff took the beast back, Baldwin smiled at the expression of outrage on his face.

Then they were riding out through the gates and he had no more time to think about anything else as he saw the towering column of flame where the mill had lain.

Sir Ralph had left the place sunk in gloom. Gilda's pain and grief were too hard to bear. Even when he protested, 'I loved her as well,' it made no difference. She wanted revenge against someone, anyone, who could have been responsible for the murder of her child.

'It was that monk, Gilda. He was up there with her. Everyone saw him,' Sir Ralph said. 'Why should *my* lad kill her?'

'He knew you loved her, didn't he?' Gilda was screaming into his face, all rational thought gone as she rose to her feet, lurching towards him, her face streaming with tears. Her terrible desolation made her grasp at any explanation. She hated and feared Esmon, and that convinced her that he was the killer of her daughter. 'He thought you wanted her for yourself, I expect, so he murdered her, just so that you couldn't ever learn what he'd done! He killed her to stop you from raping her too! Her! Your own daughter! How does that make you feel, Sir Knight?'

He retreated from her. 'No, no, Esmon's not so cruel. He couldn't have done that,' but he knew that his protestations were useless. There could be no doubt in any man's mind that Esmon was perfectly capable of the crime.

'It wasn't him,' he said once more. 'He wasn't up there. He couldn't have been.' Yet he knew Esmon *had* been there. He could have ridden past, just as Sir Ralph himself had; he might have seen Mary weeping, just as Sir Ralph had, and could have decided to take her there and then – afterwards breaking her neck. Perhaps it was only a short while after Sir Ralph had been there, a few moments after, while she was still alone.

'It couldn't have been him,' he said more firmly. No. Esmon was a wild boy, certainly, and he was a warrior, but he didn't murder women for no reason. He wouldn't have gone to those extremes to conceal his rape of a peasant; a slave.

Yet once Gilda had voiced it, Sir Ralph was haunted by the idea. He had seen his son when the red mist of rage came over him like a veil of blood, when he would snatch at any weapon to hand.

And then Sir Ralph realised that Mary herself might have goaded him. She could have chided him, telling him to leave her, questioning his chivalry. She was capable of that. And then he could have struck at her in a rage, finally breaking her neck to silence her.

Gilda was rocking back and forth, weeping and calling on God to avenge her poor daughter. A part of Sir Ralph wanted to go to her and comfort her, but he was overwhelmed by the loss of Mary, her accusations against Esmon – and his own newly fired doubts about his son.

When he heard a sound at the door and looked up to see Flora, it was a relief. 'Child, see to your mother. She is uneasy.' He fiddled with his purse, rooted out a coin and was about to give it to her when he felt a pang of shame. It felt as though he was paying a whore. He thrust the coin into her hand as he left the mill, glad to be leaving such a gloom-filled, wretched hovel. Outside, he grabbed his reins and launched himself into his horse's saddle, turning and staring back at the house, wondering what had happened to the miller, why Huward had disappeared so precipitately. He clapped spurs to his beast and swept off up the roadway, but soon he slowed to a trot.

Huward knew. If he could, the big man would surely try to take revenge on Sir Ralph. That's what any man would do – kill the rival who had systematically cuckolded him over many years. It was insane of Annicia to have told him, but when Sir Ralph recalled her pained expression when he admitted Mary was his own child, he could not find it in his heart to blame her. She had been as badly hurt as Huward. So many years, and now all was coming back to destroy him. All he had done, he had done for love – but now all loathed him.

He glanced back at the mill, mouthing a curse at the foolishness of women, but when he saw the smoke and the tongues of fire licking at the building, his anger was forgotten.

Ben watched the knight canter away towards the castle with as much relief as Sir Ralph felt in escaping the place. For Ben it had been a shock to see the knight's horse out at the front of the mill. He didn't understand what he could be doing here at first, because Sir Ralph's visits had grown more infrequent over the years. He remembered the knight dropping in quite often when he was younger, and being sent out to mind the chickens or to fetch water, while his mother entertained him, but in recent times Sir Ralph avoided the place. Ben wondered whether his chat with Elias in the tavern might have reached Sir Ralph's ears.

'Well, Mother, and how was the great man today?' he asked breezily, entering the mill and seeing his mother and Flora at the edge of the hearth.

'Can't you be kind for once?' Flora demanded. 'She's upset again.'

'Yes, well, she's been upset since dear sainted Mary passed on, hasn't she?'

'We've all been sad since then.'

'Except some of us realised that life had to go on,' he said. 'There's no point whingeing about her dying now. It's too late.'

'How can you be so callous about our sister? She was your sister too, wasn't she?'

Ben smiled and walked to the ale barrel.

'So you have nothing to say?' Flora shouted. 'Your sister's lying in her grave, and you just reach for the next ale, is that it?'

'Haven't you told her yet, Mother?' he said, glancing at Gilda.

She sat huddled within Flora's arms, but when he spoke, his contempt made her recoil as though he had hit at her.

Flora hugged her tightly, alarmed to see the tears springing from Gilda's eyes once more, but to her consternation, the woman pushed her away. 'Leave me alone!'

'I see you haven't,' Ben observed.

'Leave us alone!' she sobbed again. 'Why do you want to taunt Flora too?'

'Our mother wasn't quite the upright woman she should have been, you know,' he said relentlessly.

'Few can reach your heights, I suppose,' Flora said witheringly.

'I use the whores when I can, but I'm not married,' he said simply.

Flora opened her mouth, but then a horrible doubt assailed her and she looked at Gilda. Her mother was sitting quite still now, eyes firmly closed against the horror of her own son's insults. 'Mother?'

'Why do you think Father has disappeared?' Ben went on relentlessly. 'Because he learned the truth about our mother – that she has been fucking Sir Ralph all the time she was married to him. I say "Father", but perhaps "fool and cuckold" is fairer. Don't you think so, Mother? "Cuckold" is so much more accurate than a silly term like "Father", don't you think?'

'Don't be so stupid, Ben,' Flora said scathingly. 'You don't know what you're on about, does he, Mother? It's nonsense, isn't it? Mother? Please, tell me it's not true!' Seeing the woman sitting with eyes still firmly closed as though in denial that this conversation was going on around her, she thought Gilda looked more like a carven figure than her real, flesh and blood parent.

She only turned away when she heard her father's voice in the doorway. 'Yes, deny it, woman, if you can!'

Huward was a different man from he who had left this home the day before. Since leaving, he had found that the whole foundation of his life was a lie. The love he thought he possessed from his wife was nothing. She had all the while been slaking her lubricious appetites with another man – and not just any man, but the man who owned Huward, the mill, everything! It was the most hurtful betrayal he could conceive.

'Deny it, you bitch!' His voice was slurred. He had more words he wanted to use – angry, bitter words that would lash at her like whips – but he couldn't get them out. They stuck in his throat as though the barbs he intended for Gilda were choking him.

Ben walked to him wearing a sly grin. 'So, Father, and how are you today? Drunk, I see. Perhaps I should buy you a pot of ale now, to recompense you for all your efforts over the years!'

Huward looked at him wildly. This lad, this *monster*, was taunting him, and suddenly Huward saw the remainder of his life clearly. All men must scorn him: the fool, the butt of jokes, while this boy, the fellow he had thought was his own flesh and blood, laughed at him and lived at Sir Ralph's expense, deriding the peasant who had thought he was his parent. Gilda would live with him, no doubt, in luxury, while he, Huward, shivered in the cold of a loveless old age.

It was impossible to live like that, dishonoured for ever. He couldn't do it; he wouldn't do it.

He clenched his fist before Ben could see the quick change in his eyes, and swung it upwards. There was a crack as his knuckles slammed into the point of Ben's chin and the slight figure lifted from the ground before hurtling back to crash down on the floor.

'*Father!*' Flora screamed, and ran to Ben's side.

Huward paid her no attention. He walked over to his wife and stared down at her with eyes filled with despair. Unbunching his fist, he swung his hand at her and heard, rather than felt, the impact. Gilda's head snapped back as though her neck was broken, and she was flung to the ground where she lay, a trickle of blood leaking from her mouth, her eyes now wide with shock and pain. A faint mewling sound came from her.

Ignoring Flora's squeals of panic and horror, Huward stalked across the room to the lamps and oil. He filled a lamp, walked to the hearth, lit it, and threw it at the doorway. Instantly the cheap pottery smashed and blue flames chased across the floor.

'Father! Please don't kill us. Don't kill me!' Flora begged. She watched the flames licking at a length of material dangling from a table, then smoking and flickering as they continued the dance upwards. Smoke was already coiling about the room as Huward flung a pot of oil at the machinery that had been his life and preoccupation for so many years. He moved like a man in a nightmare, his eyes wild.

'Father!'

The tide of oil was almost at Ben's legs. She grabbed at his tunic, weeping with the effort, dragging him along, only to find her retreat blocked by more flames. There was a slight crackling sound, a flare of noise, and then a foul stench, and Flora turned to see that her mother's head had been engulfed by flames. Gilda was standing, beating at her head, trying to scream, but all that came from her mouth were hoarse, masculine roars as she inhaled the fires that tormented her. Huward was near her, the pot of oil in his hands. He had tipped it over her, and now he stood as though compelled to witness his wife's death.

Flora screamed high and mad. She felt as though her jaw must break from her face, her mouth opened so wide in mortal horror. Giving dry, wracking sobs, she tore her skirts from her legs and ran to her mother. She raised the cloth to beat at the flames that were consuming her mother's face and shoulders, but then felt the dreadful grip of her father. He pulled her away, turned her and peered into her face, and she saw that he was quite mad. It was as though he was looking into her soul to see if there was any part of her that was in truth his.

She wanted to tell him that she was entirely his, she had never been another man's. Sir Ralph was nothing to her, even if his seed had given her life; the only father she had known was Huward. And then there was another deep roar of pain from Gilda, and Flora shuddered and shrieked, high and desperate, and in that moment she saw her father's eyes die, as if he had seen that even Flora, his little Flora, had deserted him.

Flora felt her shoulder released and knew what was to happen. She closed her eyes, waiting for the punch that would finish this hideous scene and give her peace, but nothing happened. When she opened her eyes, he was gone.

Fire was leaping up at the inner walls, washing over the wooden machinery like fingers of liquid death, and all about her was a whistling and bubbling as the conflagration took hold. She went to her mother and tried to pull her dead weight to the door, ignoring the flames that seared her legs.

Chapter Thirty-Two

Huward stood in the cover of the trees and stared back at the destruction of all that he had loved and considered most important in the world. His mill had been his pride, his family had been his joy. Now the building was smoking like a charcoal-burner's stack, thick coils of smoke seeping out of gaps in the thatch and from windows like poisonous grey snakes seeking the daylight.

He was still there when Sir Ralph galloped back to the burning building leaping from his horse and running towards the doorway. Other men appeared, but Huward paid them no attention. He was watching the knight, the man who had caused this destruction.

Sir Ralph shouted something; Huward couldn't hear him over the din of the fire. It sounded almost as though the flames were mocking the knight and him together, laughing at them. Men went to Sir Ralph's side, staring inside, but then Sir Ralph gave a loud cry and pointed. The others grabbed at him, but he slipped away, ducked beneath the flaming timber of the doorway, and was inside. As others scooped water from the river and threw it over the flames, in at the door, over the roof, everywhere, Huward saw one man turn and see him. It was the Bailiff.

Huward moved away. He had done enough. Now he had just one more task to fulfil before he could find peace.

Simon was in two minds whether to go and try to catch up with Huward, but there was someone trapped inside the mill, and he was sure that his duty lay in saving life rather than chasing after the miller. He pulled off his coat as he ran to the river, and threw himself in, making sure that the coat was well soaked. Running back, he draped the coat over his head and plunged inside the mill.

It was hard to see anything. The smoke from the damp thatch was as thick and viscous as oil. Simon stared about him, choking on the harsh fumes. Thinking he saw movement, he walked cautiously towards it, but when he reached the place, he realised it was the dancing flames on a burning timber. Gazing about him again, he saw something else, and was convinced it must be a man. He ran to the figure, and saw that it was Sir Ralph, dragging someone else. Simon took his arm and tried to help him, but then he found himself being overwhelmed by an increasing lassitude, and he couldn't quite recall where the door was. He coughed, and then realised that the acrid stuff had risen up into his nose and was searing his nostrils.

A strong hand gripped his shoulder; it was Baldwin. His old friend tore the coat from Simon's head and threw it away. Then he reached forward, picked up the body from Sir Ralph, placed it over his shoulder and pulled Simon out of that house of horror. Only when he was outside did Simon realise that he had kept hold of Sir Ralph and hauled him out too.

'Thank—' he began, and then submitted to a paroxysm of coughing and retching, feeling the cool grass and stones on his face as he sprawled, incapable of moving.

Huward marched through the woods. As he went, he tugged at his thin leather belt; it would serve his purpose. When he heard running steps, he paid them no heed, but then he saw who it was, and he stopped.

For his part, Mark didn't realise who he had blundered into until he was a scant few feet from Huward, and then his face blanched and he stood like one petrified. He had no idea what to say. There was nothing he *could* say to the man who only yesterday had been demanding his execution for the murder of his daughter. He opened his mouth, but no words came. In preference he would have resorted to flight, but he couldn't. He felt like his feet had taken root with the trees in the dark soil.

Huward broke the silence with a sob. 'Dead. All dead!'

'Who is?' Mark stuttered. In truth, Huward looked as though

he had died and gone to Hell. His face was scorched on the left cheek, his hair seared away, and his eyes were quite mad.

'All. Gilda, Ben, Flora – all dead. All burned. I did it – I had to. Sir Ralph made me. He made me a fool and murderer. He used me and my wife, like he uses everyone. So I've stopped their pain and suffering. My poor Gilda! My poor Flora! Why do I still love them? How can I? They aren't mine, they're *his*!'

'His?' Mark watched as Huward slowly moved away, still muttering heedlessly about his family, and then Mark heard the shouts and saw the smoke. A chill in his heart, he crept towards the edge of the trees and peered out at the scene before him.

In front of the burning mill were some men sprawled on the grass. Mark could see that the Keeper was coughing and staring at the house, his beard singed on one side, while at his feet the Bailiff was being attended by his servant. Sir Ralph sat with his head resting on his hands and gazing at the mill with a kind of disbelieving horror, while at his side, Ben lay like one dead, his upper body covered in a blackened and filthy shirt, his hair all but gone, his hands terribly burned. While Mark watched, he saw Osbert emerging from the mill, a body over his back. Os lurched away from the building, depositing the figure on the ground, and then submitted to a racking cough. The body squirmed. It was Flora, and as her burned flesh touched the ground, she started to wail, long and mournfully. As the Keeper ordered men to her, she gave a sudden cough and, turning over, vomited over the grass. Piers was at her side and mopped at her face with a damp cloth from a bucket.

If he could, Mark would have gone to Flora immediately to pray and ease her pain, but he couldn't. Any of the men there might kill him on sight. No, it was better that he should get away from here. Leave this place of murder and rapine, go to the Bishop's palace and try to find some peace.

They had given up the battle – that much was obvious. The place was an inferno, and the odd bucket or two of water could do nothing to assuage the fearsome hunger of the flames. The fire must be left to burn itself out.

He walked back the way he had come, going quietly as a deer to avoid being heard, but there was no one around. Any men in the area would be at the mill, trying to save what they could. He could breathe more easily, secure in the knowledge that the disaster at the mill had distracted any thought of pursuit of him.

Carrying on, he upset a blackbird, which suddenly flew off, moving close to the ground and crying its warning as it went.

All at once, as the noise faded, Mark became aware that this was a very quiet part of the wood. There seemed to be no animals, no birdsong, no scuttling of mouse feet, nothing. It was disconcerting. Yet there was still the slow creak of boughs rubbing against each other in the wind, a languid, relaxing sound in the peace. He stood still a moment, enjoying the silence, and then a drip or two of rain pattered on his shoulder, except he noticed that it smelled like urine.

When he looked up to see where the drops came from, he saw the body of Huward, dangling from a high branch, his belt suspending him by the neck.

Baldwin had brought a wineskin with him when he left the castle, and now he sent a man to fetch it from his horse. He was weak and dizzy after the strain of trying to hold his breath as long as possible in that terrible place, and he was not as young as he had once been, so lifting and carrying even so slight a body as Ben's had torn something in his back and strained his upper belly. As he moved his shoulders and tentatively flexed muscles, he had to give a wry grin. Once he would have been able to dart in, bring out the girl, then run back in and save another.

The man returned with the skin. Baldwin took a mouthful and swilled it around his teeth, swallowing gratefully before offering it to Simon. The Bailiff was kneeling now, groggy as a fighter who had been felled once too often, spitting the sour flavour of vomit from his mouth. Seeing the skin he took it greedily, gulping at it until Baldwin had to wrench it away.

While Simon groaned and smacked his lips, Baldwin went to the girl and Sir Ralph. Flora was alive – but only just. She looked as though she was sorry not to have been left in the house. Her eyes were open, but she was lying on her back and staring up at the darkening sky. She didn't flinch even when a great roaring crash came from the mill as the machinery collapsed, bringing down the whole roof with it. Sparks gleamed and flew up as the smoke gushed, and then there was a great howl as flames sped to feed upon the fresh timbers. Now the heat was astonishing, with orange-red lighting the whole area, and flames leaping towards the heavens.

'Will you not drink a little, maid?' he asked. 'A sip of wine might clear your mouth of the fumes.'

'I'm not thirsty,' she said.

It was true. Although the whole of her body felt burned, she was content to lie here on the damp grass, uncaring of what the future might bring. It didn't matter. Her soul felt empty. All her family was gone. If her father was ever to return, she would be filled with fear, not love. There was no one, no one at all, who could fill the terrible void that had opened in her life tonight.

Hands lifted her and carried her gently to a horse. There she was placed into the arms of another man, who she soon realised was Sir Ralph, and the horse set off slowly for the castle.

In the past, Flora had always felt a sense of dread when she had passed beneath the gateway, but this time, there was nothing, except the gradual awakening of pain from the dreadful burns on her thighs and face.

And the awareness of the silent sobs of the knight who held her so softly and yet so well.

He was still there as night came on fully.

It took him an age to get the body down. He was unused to clambering up trees, but he must reach out along that branch and slash away at the leather, slowly sawing with his little blunt eating knife until at last there was a short ripping noise and the badly cured leather gave way.

Huward fell silently, and somehow Mark thought that was wrong. A man dropping so far, at least ten feet, should at least gasp or wail, but this body simply disappeared from view and landed on the grass and leaves. When Mark looked down, the bloated face and curiously bloodshot eyes met his accusingly.

It took some while to climb back down, and then Mark was startled to hear Surval's voice.

'Be gracious to him. He was a good man,' the hermit said.

'I never heard a bad word about him.'

'No. I think that was what he feared most,' Surval said contemplatively. 'The idea that all the men he knew in the vill might begin to think of him as a figure of ridicule. He was a kind fellow, but proud, and the idea of losing any respect from the folk here was too appalling for him.'

'He has killed them all, hasn't he? He said something about Sir Ralph.'

Surval gave him a sombre look. 'What would you have done?' he said. 'Huward learned that Sir Ralph fathered all the children: Ben, Flora and Mary were his, not Huward's.'

'He told you all this?'

'And more.'

Mark nodded. He was setting out the body as neatly as he could, trying not to look into Huward's eyes. Huward's hands he crossed over his breast, and then those terrible eyes were closed. Mark bent his head and said a long prayer over the dead man, pleading for Jesus's intervention, asking St Mary to protect Huward's soul and give him her compassion. It seemed ironic to be pleading with her when the whole cycle of death and horror had started with her namesake's murder.

Surval was uncompromising. 'I liked him, but he committed suicide.'

'He did so while he was temporarily mad. That wasn't his fault. Just as,' Mark added, rising to his feet, 'the murder of his family wasn't his fault either. That was down to Sir Ralph.'

Suddenly, as he stood gazing about him, the full horror of Surval's words struck at him, and he uttered a faint gasp as he tottered on legs suddenly powerless to support him. He closed his eyes as the terrible truth was revealed.

'Christ in Heaven!'

'Boy? What is it?' Surval demanded. He had crossed to Mark's side and now he leaned on his staff and peered at the young man, but Mark was incapable of responding.

If it was true that Sir Ralph was the father of the children of Huward's family, then Mark had been sleeping with his own sister! Half-sister, perhaps, but that was no defence. Worse – he had made her pregnant!

'Oh God!'

'You sound petrified, boy,' Surval said quietly. 'What is this – has something alarmed you?'

'You know, don't you?' Mark croaked.

'Perhaps.' Surval lowered his head. 'There is a family resemblance. But remember, vengeance is the Lord's, not ours.'

Mark didn't agree. Standing and staring down at the corpse, he was aware of a revulsion so complete, so all-enveloping, that it made him feel quite weak. Sir Ralph – he was the man responsible for all this misery.

Sir Ralph! He had condemned Mark to Hell, for unknowingly, Mark had committed the sin of incest, but his own ignorance was no excuse. All so that Sir Ralph could slake his carnal lusts with a woman other than his wife. Mark could comprehend a man's desire for a woman, but to have cuckolded a man to this extent, leaving so many souls to perish, that was appalling! Sir Ralph had ruined so many by his thoughtless satisfaction of his desires.

Mark felt sick. He couldn't meet Surval's eyes. Instead he found his gaze passing down his body toward his own cods, staring at his groin with loathing. There, there was the root of all man's sin, he felt. Sex. It had led Sir Ralph to Gilda and then he himself to Mary, poor, beautiful Mary. 'Christ!' At least she had died without knowing the depth of her sins. She didn't have to live with her guilt as Mark would.

Even the sin of self-murder was better than this self-hatred. How could any man live with the weight of this crime burdening him?

'What are you thinking, lad? That Sir Ralph is deserving of death? Leave him for the moment. Come with me to my home and I'll give you a safe bed for the night. Tomorrow I can tell the Coroner about this man's body. Meantime, you can escape. You don't want to be found, do you?'

'Thank you, no. I have to make my way to the Bishop's palace. There's nothing for me here,' Mark said sadly. 'I shouldn't have waited around so long. I should have gone this morning.'

Surval nodded twice with deliberate emphasis. 'If you're sure, fine. But leave vengeance to God. He's better placed to determine guilt than we are.'

'I want to go and pray at my chapel first, though.'

'There's nothing there, lad. It was burned by the vill,' Surval said sympathetically.

So even that had been taken from him. Everything had gone. His soul was tormented by his crime against God's law of incest, his woman was dead and his living was gone; his chapel, which should have been a holy refuge, was destroyed, and now Huward's family was dead, all killed because of Sir Ralph's adultery. Mark knew his thoughts were not rational, knew that he was being less than sensible, but could do nothing about it.

He bade Surval farewell and walked from that grim, desolate place. He knew what he must do: he would go to his burned chapel and pray at the ruined altar, pleading for all those poor souls – Mary, Huward, Gilda, Flora, Ben and Wylkyn. That would take him until the night was at its deepest and darkest, and then he could go to the castle. Nobody would expect him there. He could enter by the fence, the same way he had got out of the place last night.

He had to get back in if he was to kill Sir Ralph.

Baldwin tried hard to refuse Sir Ralph's hospitality, but he did feel as weak as a newborn lamb after his exertions in the fire, and Simon was worse. They had little choice but to accept the man's offer.

As soon as they all arrived the men began bawling for wine and food, and Baldwin was happy enough to sit at a table and gulp at the pot of wine set in front of him while others cared for the wounded. In a change of role that he would have found amusing, were the circumstances less serious, he saw that the still pale-faced Hugh had returned to his duties and was now serving his paler-faced master.

Simon was not looking well, and occasionally gave a dry, hacking cough, but Baldwin was comfortably sure that he would recover. He was younger than Baldwin, and had not been exposed to the fire or smoke for long. The knight watched Hugh fussing over his master with a fond smile. Their companionship, which always appeared to be based upon mutual antipathy, sullen disagreement and regular arguments, was as strong as that which any master could enjoy with a servant.

That was the way of a man's life, though. Service was the basic fact of life, no matter who the man was, and from service grew respect and even, sometimes, love. It took love for a man to risk his own life in saving his master's, as Hugh had when he thrust Simon from the path of that fool Esmon.

Esmon. He had not arrived at the fire, and now, as Baldwin glanced about the room, he could see no sign of the lad. Surely he should be here with his men, but for some reason he was not. The noise in here was deafening, and on a whim, Baldwin got up and walked out to the court.

It was a clear night. The great burning torches that were set near the stables and the gatehouse failed to dim the light from the stars overhead. Baldwin looked up and marvelled once more at their beauty. There was a strange sweep to them, as though God had painted them in a great arc just to demonstrate that He had no need of symmetry in His Heaven. Occasional wisps of cloud floated past slowly, like blue and grey ships of silk, each apparently lighted from within by a flame of white purity.

'Beautiful,' he murmured to himself.

A man-at-arms nearby glanced up. 'It's only clouds.'

'The banal only ever see the banal,' Baldwin said.

'Eh?'

Baldwin was already walking across the yard. The door to the makeshift prison by the gate was wide open, showing the empty room beyond. Sensing a man nearby, he spun on his heel, a hand going to his sword, but it was only Roger Scut.

'They've all gone,' Roger Scut said. 'She released them as soon as you'd left the place.'

'That's good.'

'You don't like me, do you?'

Baldwin surveyed him frankly. Scut was peering at him along his nose once more. It made Baldwin want to break it for him. 'I think you are an arrogant fool, without compassion, and so keen to satisfy your own greed that you'd hurt any other man without counting the cost.'

Roger Scut blinked. He had not expected such abuse. 'Do you always speak to priests with so little respect, or do you reserve your bile for me alone?'

'Have you seen Esmon?' Baldwin rapped out, ignoring the question.

'Why do you ask me?'

'I am not talking to you for the joy of it, Scut. Have you seen him or not?'

'Not recently,' Roger Scut said truthfully. He had not seen Esmon since Baldwin had questioned him at the trap door to the cell.

'Fine,' Baldwin said and was about to leave him when a thought struck him. 'Your leather-covered weight that Simon found at the cell. You said that the cell was already empty when you got to it, and that there was no guard? Of course not. He would have raised the alarm. So who could have released the monk before you reached there?'

'Anyone, so far as I know. I was in the hall and went out when all seemed quiet.'

'So most of Sir Ralph's men were asleep in the hall, I assume?'

'Oh, yes. Only a few guards were not there, the men on the walls.'

'But Sir Ralph and his wife sleep in the solar?'

'Yes.'

'What of Esmon?'

'He remains in the hall at night. He was there and spoke to his father. Sir Ralph couldn't sleep and left to get some air. Apparently he hasn't slept well since the girl died.'

'You saw him leave?'

'Yes. He was soon back. Why?'

Baldwin nodded. That, he felt sure, answered the question about who had released Mark from captivity, if it did not explain why. And then the inspiration struck him.

'My God!' he exclaimed. '*That* is what it was: he had to make sure Mark got out so that he could be hunted down. Sir Ralph thought he wouldn't be able to get away, so he made Mark get out, threatening to kill him if he did not, purely so that the dogs could be set upon him again and he could be killed.'

'You are talking nonsense!' Roger argued. 'Why – Sir Ralph had him put in the gaol! What on earth would he want to set him loose for?'

'Go to the hall, priest,' Baldwin said coldly. 'You are as foul as him. You planned to see this poor devil run down. Yes, and you hoped he might be captured and executed. Then you could take responsibility for his little church and demand to retain it. Why would you want to live in a miserable place like this, though? It is rural, far from any town. Surely you would hate it?'

'And so I would. I never intended living here for long,' Roger Scut said, but he felt stung enough to add, 'Look, Sir Knight, I admit I was wrong. I was offered the inducement of the living of the place as well as being introduced to the Despensers. You know what that means? It means the support of the King, in effect. Me! I could have gone wherever I wanted, with their support.'

'But? I assume that there is a "but"?'

'I realised that I was being foolish. I saw that it would be better by far for me to take Mark back to Exeter with me. I went to his cell, and found it unguarded, the hatch open, and the prisoner released. I looked about the castle for a while, but in the dark I feared that I should only alert other guards to his disappearance so I returned to my bed, and that was that. Yes, I did desire his chapel, but no, I am not evil enough to have seen it through. Especially when I realised that Sir Ralph actively sought Mark's death. That would have been quite wrong.'

Baldwin eyed him with contempt. 'I think Esmon said enough to make you realise that he was more unbalanced than you had realised. You told us how he suggested you should support his bid to depose his father. That scared you, didn't it? Until then you were prepared to sacrifice Mark just for your own greed!'

Baldwin stopped. He had to take a deep breath to control the shaking rage that was overtaking him. This man was the same as the clerks in France who were prepared to see the destruction of the Knights Templar, to see religious men tortured and consumed in the flames, just because it suited the purpose of their masters at the time.

'Scut, if I can, I shall ruin you. I shall not permit you to clerk for me again. You are evil and repellent.'

Chapter Thirty-Three

Mark shivered with fear as he looked at the fence. It was a scant fifteen yards from him, and he could see a place where the stakes were rough and notched. Even he should be able to climb up and over the top.

It was a terrifying prospect. He knew that as he crossed the wide strip of bare grass to the wall, he would be in full view of anyone on top of the wall or the keep, especially in this bright moon- and starlight. It might not be a full moon, but the light it gave was nonetheless clear for that and Mark fancied he would be able to see a mouse scurrying across the expanse.

'Please God, give me strength,' he prayed. The place was still. Occasional bursts of laughter came from the hall, but that was all. The guards appeared to be elsewhere again, just as they had been last night when he escaped the place.

Only one day ago. And now he was desperate to get back in, to avenge Huward and his family, to avenge so many deaths. He would wait here until much later, when even the guards would be nodding at their posts, and then he would slip inside, and if he could, he would strike one blow at Sir Ralph that would forever end his raping and murdering.

After all, Sir Ralph had destroyed Mark's own life. He had made a filthy criminal of him. Mark was polluted, and all because of his damned father.

Baldwin walked away from his conversation with the cleric with a deep sense of disgust. It was hideous to think of a man of God willingly lying to put a comrade into danger, just to satisfy his own lust for wealth and property. There were many clerks and monks who would be pleased to emulate Roger Scut, Baldwin knew. Since the Pope had moved to Avignon to escape the risk of living with the outraged Roman populace, the Church was filled with men who were actively seeking to enrich themselves.

He walked about the yard and spoke to the gatekeeper, asking whether he had seen Esmon.

'He's in the buttery, I think. Haven't you bothered to look there?'

Baldwin bit back the response that was on the tip of his tongue. As a knight, he was unused to being answered in so rude a manner. It was enough to make him grab a sword and teach a lesson in manners but he thought better of it.

He walked to the buttery in a contemplative mood. This castle felt as though it was about to burst into flames like Huward's mill. Men of all stations were sullen, responded badly to commands, and were slow to obey. It had all the atmosphere of a place that was expecting the figurehead to disappear at any time soon. Baldwin had seen it in other places over the years. When a warrior-group was about to change their leader, there was a period of anticipation and fear beforehand. Pretenders to the power would jostle and bicker for position in the affections of the rank and file men, and as the leader became gradually divorced from them, the men would imperceptibly change their allegiances until the new leader felt his time was ripe.

That was the impression Baldwin got, even in his exhausted state. This castle was shortly to change hands again. Sir Ralph was to be replaced, and by whom else than his own son? There was nothing so potent as the disloyalty of a son who craved power.

The buttery was a smallish room for so large a hall. A broad plank had been set upon two barrels, and Ralph's son Esmon stood at it, sipping meditatively from a pot of wine. As his eyes lit upon Baldwin, his face lost all mobility. Baldwin had found a frozen man once, up on a high mountain pass while he was travelling on behalf of his Order. The body had a curious potency about it, as though at any time when he warmed, he might leap into life. Baldwin knew that the same was true for Esmon.

'May I join you?' he asked.

'You want wine? You should have asked a servant to draw some for you,' Esmon replied insolently.

'You should remember your manners, young sir. The castle is not yet yours.'

'What does that mean?'

Baldwin was too tired to bother to explain. 'You killed the miner Wylkyn. Where were you when the girl Mary was murdered?'

'I was out. Why, do you seek to accuse me of another murder?'

'I seek only to learn who killed the girl – and to discover where the body of the miner has been hidden.'

'I have no idea where his corpse is buried.'

'Buried?'

'How else could it have been hidden?'

'A good question,' Baldwin said. He saw no reason to let Esmon know that he was sure he already knew where the body lay. 'You haven't answered my question: where were you when the girl died?'

'I was hunting with Father. We told you.'

'And then you came back here together, you said.'

'Aha. Yes, well, that wasn't quite true. He left before me. I waited a while before setting off. I was helping some friends empty a wineskin.'

'Where did he go?'

Esmon smiled. 'Out on the road where that poor girl was found.'

Baldwin felt physically sick. This boy was deliberately pushing his father forward as the primary suspect. 'You mean he might have passed that road?'

Esmon seemed to lose interest in the matter. He sipped more wine and stared at the wall. 'Don't take my word for it. Ask Elias, the ploughman. He must have seen my father. And the serf Osbert.'

'I have – and yes, they did see him. They also saw *you*, at the bottom of the lane.'

'I didn't ride along that lane,' Esmon said immediately. 'I came up from the tavern. I was there with some of the men, emptying the skin. If you've been told I was on Deave Lane, then whoever said that was lying. And one other thing: you don't like me. I don't care – but I shall own this castle one day, and when I do, I shall be a powerful man in my own right. Don't try to thwart me, Sir Baldwin. I could be a bad enemy.'

Baldwin let his amusement show. 'You try to threaten me? You, a mere child, seek to scare me? I suppose you think that your friends the Despensers will come and save you from any man who dares to stand in your way?'

His laughter stopped and he stepped forward. 'Remember this, boy. I have been a knight for many years, and I have killed many men, but always in fair combat. I have never needed a party behind me to attack a poor miner on a moorland road. That is the act of a coward.'

He left Esmon, seething with anger that the younger man should have dared to threaten him again, but as he entered the hall, he found his mood changing. He saw Simon and Hugh sitting side by side on benches, both drinking happily enough and joining in with the chorus of a bawdy song sung by a very drunk man-at-arms.

Baldwin sat with them, regretting now, as he glanced about him, that he had roused Esmon to anger. A man like him could be a dangerous adversary in a place like this, filled with his own paid men. Any one of the men in this hall could be watching him even now with a speculative eye, waiting until he was asleep so that he could slip a knife in between Baldwin's shoulder-blades.

A cheery thought. He leaned back against the wall, fixing the men in the room with a suspicious glower, but saw no shame or quick embarrassment. Whoever might have been told to kill him was a good actor – or perhaps no one *had* been told. Maybe he was simply paranoid, seeing enemies wherever he looked, or maybe he was being sensible. He should stay awake all night just in case, to guard himself and the others.

It was no good. His tiredness was overwhelming. He allowed his eyes to close for just a moment's peace. Surely that could not be dangerous. Perhaps he could catnap as he used to when he was a young warrior in Acre. Then he could sleep for a half hour and wake refreshed and ready for guard duty. Yes, he would close his eyes for a while, he thought. It could do no harm . . .

He slept like a man who was practising for death.

It was with a great shock of alarm that he awoke. Like a man who has been startled to full wakefulness in an instant, he jerked upright.

The fire in the middle of the floor was still glowing gently. No one had thought to douse it overnight. Often they would not bother in a great hall like this; there were so many men asleep in here, servants and men-at-arms, that any hazard should be minimal. Now the glowing embers were gleaming.

Baldwin heard a creak, and he turned to the heavy tapestries along the wall, but then he heard another creak. It came from the screens, and he listened carefully. All through the room there were loud snores and grunts and whistles from men who had eaten and drunk too much before collapsing where they sat or lay. Snuffing the air, Baldwin was sure that he must be the only man in the room who was not inebriated. The odour of sour breath reeking with wine and ale was pervasive, and he wrinkled his nose in disgust, but as he did so, he caught a whiff of clean, fresh air.

Rising quickly, he rested his hand on his sword and stepped quietly to the screens. Peering around the frame, he looked at the main doors in the cross passage. The door to the court was slightly open, squeaking gently on its hinges, and Baldwin, having convinced himself that there was no assassin concealed there, went to the door. He opened it and took a deep breath of the clean night air. From the sky, he thought that it was the very last hours of the night. In the morning he would regret this, he told himself. He would be all the more tired for having woken in the middle of the night.

As he shut the door quietly and made his way back to the hall, he had no idea how accurate his forecast was to prove.

True to his gloomy prediction, he woke late, with eyes gritty and his senses dulled from the unwarranted disturbance during the night. He was snappish to Hugh and Simon, both of whom appeared to have thrived on their excesses of the night before. It was a rare occurrence for Simon to be so happy and refreshed after drinking; if Simon were to wake so cheerfully every morning, Baldwin would probably have murdered him by now.

'Come on, Baldwin. Time we were up.'

'Leave me in peace,' he groaned. The room had not yet woken and men lay snoring all about. Most were the castle's servants, but there were some eleven men-at-arms as well, lying in one corner all together, as though they were huddled for security away from the rest of the castle's staff. One man was stirring.

'We have to get a move on.'

'There's no hurry.'

'You've forgotten?'

'Forgotten what?'

'Baldwin, wake up, in God's name! The Coroner, remember? He's collecting the posse of the county to come here.'

'My God!'

'I thought that might stir you,' Simon said with grim satisfaction. 'He'll more than likely think we're being held hostage for ransom. We should collect ourselves and leave before things get out of hand.'

Baldwin nodded and dressed himself as swiftly as he could. His sword he hung on his belt, and with the comfortable weight dangling at his hip he immediately felt much stronger and safer. It was curious, this sense of power and authority that a mere hunk of steel could confer. Baldwin knew that his was an awesome weapon, capable of removing a man's head in one blow, but that did not alter the fact that here, in this castle, with so many men-at-arms in the pay of Sir Ralph and his son, he was not safe. Any feeling of security that he won by donning his belt was false. Safety lay outside, with Coroner Roger and the men he was gathering.

Hugh had already collected up their small packs and stood with them bound to the long staff he always carried, their weight carefully balanced to be comfortable on his shoulder. He paid no attention to the men all about them, but stood chewing his inner lip like a man who was deep in thought. At least he was no longer suffering from the after-effects of Esmon's attack.

'We had best leave now,' Simon said. He had the same lack of faith in their host. 'We can break our fast at the inn with the Coroner.'

'That suits me very well,' Baldwin said, but even as he and Simon made to walk to the door, Esmon entered. Baldwin saw Hugh's eyes narrow, and his stance subtly alter, as though he was ready to strike at the knight's son.

'You aren't leaving us already, my lords? Food is on the way, and you would be better served by eating your fill first.'

'We are seeking your father to thank him for his hospitality,' Baldwin said.

'He is in the solar. Would you wish me to call him for you?'

'No. No, there's no need to wake him,' Simon said hurriedly.

'But you must see him before you leave. Wait until you have broken your fast, for then he shall be risen and ready to wish you Godspeed,' Esmon said, smiling coldly. 'You will be safe here,' he added.

There was little that Simon and Baldwin could do in the face of his polite insistence. Explaining the reason for their departure would hardly be courteous, Baldwin thought, and yet waiting until the *posse comitatus* arrived was scarcely a better option. They must simply eat quickly, and be gone.

With that resolve, he returned with Simon and Hugh to their bench and waited, but Baldwin noticed that Hugh carefully removed their packs from his staff and set the length of timber well within his reach.

Before very long, servants arrived in the hall and they began to set out the trestles and place the long board tables on top, giving three long rows perpendicular to the great table on the dais where Sir Ralph would sit with his family. Men brought in cloths which they draped over the tables, then more men appeared with bread trenchers. A panter went to the Lord's table and set out his knives, while another, little more than a boy, took up a bowl and towel and stood waiting, and the steward stood and watched them all with a serious expression on his face, as though daring them to misbehave in his master's hall. Baldwin was sure that he spent much of his time glaring at the men-at-arms in the corner. They were still all there, standing or sitting, laughing at jokes, a few playing dice.

Obviously feeling that it was no good and must be given up as a bad job, the steward shook his head in apparent disgust, and then twitched aside the tapestry that covered the door to the solar, opening the door and disappearing. A few moments later, he reappeared in the hall, and walked to the corner of the table. There he nodded to a lad who waited at the door to the screens, and Simon saw him walk out.

This was a part of the routine of the place, he knew. The boy would go to the little bell out at the doorway and strike it to call all the servants in to eat or serve. There were always shifts of servants at halls like this one. One group would eat while the other served them, and then there would be a change so that the servers could themselves eat. All perfectly normal, and Simon paid little attention as the bell was sounded and all the men from the castle came in. They went to their places as though all the seats were already allotted, a fact borne out by the way three men stood muttering darkly on seeing Baldwin, Simon and Hugh sitting.

There was one other man whom Simon could not help but hear. He was an older man, thin and unwell in appearance, as though he had suffered from a fever recently, and he was glowering at his neighbours.

'It was my old dad's, that knife. One of you thieving bastards has it, and you can just give it me back. Think it's a sodding joke, don't you?'

'Come on, it's just fallen from your belt somewhere. You'll find it soon enough.'

'It was on my belt last night when I went to sleep. Think I've lost my mind because of a bit of a cold? I can remember where I put it: same as always, right by my hand in case any of those mad

buggers over there decide to try something,' he said, throwing a
ferocious scowl towards the men-at-arms.

'Well, it's not there now.'

'Maybe one of them took it off you?' another man laughed, but
Simon paid them little attention as he smelled the scent of fresh
baked bread and heard the welcoming sound of ale pouring into
jugs. His mouth filled with saliva and he gazed hopefully at the
door to the screens.

Baldwin was more interested in the door to the solar. Now that
all his men were in the room, he was sure that the knight would
soon arrive, and sure enough, when all the benches and stools
were filled, the steward returned to the door, moving the tapestry
once more, and tapped on it. Shortly afterwards, Ben and Flora
entered, Flora as pale as a sheet of vellum where her face was not
burned. The left side of her face was a weeping, raw wound, and
she moved slowly as though in great sadness and pain. At her side
was Ben, but the lad had lost his strutting mien. His hair was all
but burned away, and there was a great sore on the point of his
skull, while his cheeks were cracked and bleeding. He moved as
though terrified that he would attract attention to himself, as if he
could trust no one. Perhaps, Baldwin thought, someone who had
seen his own father try to murder him, would be marked forever
afterwards with that kind of fear.

The steward led them to the side of the main table and seated
them with great care, setting a jug of wine before Flora and
selecting an apple from a pile for her. Ben sat shivering, hardly
even glancing at the food set out before him.

A moment or two later, the room fell silent as Sir Ralph
appeared with his wife at his side. They walked in regally, Sir
Ralph nodding to his steward, and allowing a momentary annoyance to pass over his face as a man-at-arms gave a shout of
delight on seeing how the dice had fallen. Others in the room
shushed the man, but he growled, staring down any of the servants
who met his gaze. When he was satisfied that he had cowed all, he
deliberately sat with his back to Sir Ralph.

The Lord threw a bitter glance at his son, but Esmon affected not to notice. Baldwin, looking at the stiffness in Sir Ralph's back, was convinced that he would make his son pay for the man's rudeness later.

There was a breeze in the room. The tapestries behind Sir Ralph rippled occasionally, while Baldwin was aware that sometimes a candle or two would smoke and gutter at the same time, although he gave little thought to the matter. He was too busy keeping his eyes on the men-at-arms.

They had no respect for Sir Ralph, that was quite evident. Their noise was unmannerly, as though they no longer cared about how the master of the castle might view their rudeness.

Sir Ralph was chewing his food stolidly but by the fact that he spoke not at all and never once so much as glanced towards the disruptive men, Baldwin was convinced that he was more angry than anyone would have guessed.

It was all too common now, because of the number of men who must be hired for money rather than for their loyalty, for mutinies to take place. Mercenaries were everywhere. It was the greed for personal wealth that led to it, Baldwin thought. In his day, men knew their rank, but now ploughmen were demanding more money than they had received the last year, and so were masons, shepherds and others, as though they had a right to more. It was sheer lunacy.

Baldwin remained true to the old ways. His men were all loyal and deserving of his trust because they had been with his family for many years. Some castles he knew had been built specifically to take note of the unruly mob who were supposed to be the armed guards of the castle's Lord. Instead of sharing a building with their leader, he was segregated in order that he could protect himself and his family in a separate chamber, just in case his men proved disloyal. Such was the case here, Baldwin told himself, glancing back at the strong door to the solar block. Sir Ralph and his wife retired into that separate area where they could at least bolt the door to protect themselves from unruly men-at-arms. It was a dreadful comment on the way that things had changed since the turn of the century.

He frowned a moment. And then his eyes focused. The men here were uncaring for the honour and position of their own master. Unless they were intending to leave immediately, perhaps they had some idea of deposing Sir Ralph: that was what Roger Scut had implied, wasn't it? That Esmon was planning to overthrow his father and install himself in Sir Ralph's place?

What better way to achieve that aim than by murdering Sir Ralph, Baldwin thought, using an assassin, like the Hashishim. Someone like that would wait for a signal. He glanced carefully at the men all about, wondering whether any might be about to shout or whistle for an accomplice to attack. Or perhaps not. Men would be most relaxed after a meal, he reasoned. Perhaps the signal was merely the end of eating.

But there *was* a ritual that signalled the end of the meal, he realised, remembering the meals he had eaten here before.

With that thought, he stood. Aware that he was being watched by all eyes, he edged his way behind the men seated at his table, until he reached the dais. There he bowed slightly to Sir Ralph, who kept a wary eye on him as though expecting Sir Baldwin to leap upon him. The steward appeared to hold the same doubts, and made as though to block Baldwin's path, but then events suddenly moved so swiftly that Baldwin could only recall what happened when he later spoke to Simon.

First, Sir Ralph held up his hand to his steward, but then he stood. He set his own hand on his sword, ready to pull it out. Roger Scut, sitting nearby, immediately stood and began to speak the Grace. Instantly the tapestries exploded: two, which had been joined to seal a gap, billowing out and exposing the grim, white features of Mark. He held a long dagger in his hand, and with fearful but determined eyes, he launched himself at Sir Ralph.

The knight was concentrating on Baldwin, but some instinct made him turn his head just as Baldwin grabbed his own sword. It came out in a sweep of flashing blue, the peacock-coloured blade hissing as it slithered from the scabbard, and then Baldwin beat at Mark's dagger hand, severing it cleanly at the elbow. It fell to the floor still holding the blade.

Only then did he see that Mark's other hand gripped a small eating knife, and this was aimed at Sir Ralph's throat. Unheeding of his lost fist, Mark pressed on, and Baldwin turned his sword. With scarcely any effort, his blade sank into Mark's breast, the priest's onward rush forcing himself onto it like a wild hog spitted upon a lance.

Sir Ralph was retreating to give himself fighting room, his own sword out now, but seeing that Mark was beyond further attack, he spun round as though expecting another from the men in the corner. None of them had moved, however, as though the action was as much of a surprise to them as to all the others in the room. Sir Ralph stood and waited, daring them to make a move. For a short while all was quiet but for the choking and bubbling that came from Mark, and then gradually the men at the table shrugged and turned away.

'Let me get to him!' Roger Scut demanded, his face white with shock. Baldwin's sword had come within a few inches of his own head and the sharp sound of that blade slicing through the air and then thwacking through Mark's arm had almost made him empty his bowels. It was with relief that he realised his habit was not bespattered with faeces.

Roger Scut was full of mixed emotions. He had automatically risen to come and help this man before he died, for Roger took his duties seriously when they directly affected a soul, especially when that man was a cleric. Now, he felt his heart twist as he looked on the ruin of the man he had wanted to die so that he could take his chapel. Now it was that Roger felt the full shame and dishonour of his actions.

Mark turned and met Roger's stare unflinchingly, and Roger felt as though Jesus Himself had stabbed him with a look; but where he would have expected hatred or scorn, all he saw was gratitude.

'Please . . . my confession . . .'

Roger knelt quickly at his side. He gripped Mark's remaining hand and bent his head in prayer. Behind him he heard Sir Ralph hawk and spit. Then he spoke, and Mark had to work to keep his eyes shut as he prayed, trying to ignore the venom in the knight's voice.

'Yes, you look after him!' Sir Ralph sneered. 'You damned monks always stick together, don't you! You stopped him from being executed for one murder, and because of your stupid actions, he was able to come here today and nearly kill me. Murderous traitor! Evil degenerate! Well, he's done now! Let the bastard die slowly, so he can feel the weight of his treachery!'

Chapter Thirty-Four

Having spoken, Sir Ralph stormed from the room up to his solar, his wife joining him. Baldwin remained where he was, his sword still ready, flashing blue and red in the light.

There was no need to fear more violence. He could see that the men at the tables were surprised at the suddenness of the attack and the speed of Mark's defeat. Taking up a fallen towel, Baldwin carefully cleaned the blood from his blade, then wiped it on his tunic to dry it off. Satisfied, he thrust it home into his scabbard, and he would have left to rejoin Simon and Hugh, except something in the dying man's eyes made him remain.

'Must tell you . . . It was him . . . made Huward kill his family . . .'

'What do you mean?'

'His wife . . . Gilda was Sir Ralph's . . . whore. All children, Sir Ralph's. None Huward's.' He coughed up a ball of bloody phlegm. 'Huward dead. Hanged himself in a tree.'

'Where?'

'Hill behind mill . . . not far . . .'

Baldwin nodded. 'Mary. Did you kill her?'

'Hit her. Not hard. Loved her.'

'Did you break her neck?' Simon asked.

'Punched. Just once.'

'You swear you did not break her neck?' Baldwin pressed.

'Yes. Told you . . . I loved her. Went back later . . . wanted to make up. She was dead. All that blood. Knew I'd be accused. Ran away.'

'So she did not collapse and lose her child while you were there?'

'She was well when I left . . . My poor Mary.'

'Did you see anyone else who could have killed her? Anyone at all, from after you left her to when you found her dead?' Baldwin had to know.

Mark winced, both eyes snapping shut with a sudden pain. He raised an arm to wipe his face, but it was his stump. His face seemed to tear with loss, with the realisation that he was dying. He sobbed silently a moment, then breathed, 'Sir Ralph.'

'Is that why you wanted to kill him? You thought he was the murderer?'

The man was fading fast now. A quivering as though he was terribly frozen was causing his limbs to shudder and one heel was knocking a staccato rhythm on the dais's floor. His face was a deathly pale, his eyes wide with knowledge of his impending doom. Roger Scut murmured that he should conserve his breath to confess his sins, but he continued weakly.

'No more . . . All done. Sir Ralph was father of Mary . . . father of me too . . . Incest . . . Ruined . . . me . . .'

'By God's love,' Roger Scut muttered under his breath, and then swiftly began the process of the Seven Interrogations, his guilt making him careful and precise. Mark choked and answered as he could, but Baldwin could only feel relief that he was able to respond to the last and relax on hearing the *viaticum*. It would have been a terrible weight for Baldwin to bear, had Mark not received the promise of God's forgiveness.

'Sweet Jesus!' Baldwin stood, his head bowed, staring at the boy as his lifeblood drained, forming a puddle which surrounded his head like a red halo. 'He wanted to murder Sir Ralph because Sir Ralph was his father.'

'That's hardly the best excuse for murder!'

'This is no laughing matter, Simon!' Baldwin burst out. 'That boy discovered that the girl he loved was his sister; *he had got his own sister with child without knowing it!* An incest! Is it any wonder his mind was turned?'

'You mean Mary was Sir Ralph's child as well?'

'Exactly – and I *killed* him,' Baldwin said. He suddenly felt the appalling weight of his action 'That boy was forced into crimes because of Sir Ralph's offences, Simon – not because of his own sins. Oh God! What have I done? I killed him for *that*? I should have killed Sir Ralph!'

'You prevented a murder,' Simon said steadily.

'By committing an injustice! And that's worse than a mere crime!' Baldwin hissed.

Coroner Roger was at the tavern when the men started to arrive. Those from Chagford were first, led by a Reeve, John. All were grim-faced at the thought of the work they must do today, but shouldered poles with their billhooks rammed hard onto the ends. Some self-consciously carried swords which their forefathers had passed down over long years, but the Coroner was happier to see that many of them bore bows and quivers full of arrows. If this day was to end in a battle, the more archers the better, and since King Edward I's day, every vill had men trained with long bows.

Next were the men from South Tawton with a trained Squire, Master Hector, who had seen battles, and whom Coroner Roger felt he could trust. That was a relief, for so often there were knaves and fools sent when a posse was commanded to ride.

Aye, it was all too common that you'd end up with the dullest slugs in the county when you had to catch someone, when what you needed were the strongest men both in the arm and in the head, the Coroner told himself, running an eye over the men gathered in the roadway in front of the inn. At least this lot seemed intelligent enough, and most were experienced in fighting. If they hadn't been in tussles in the wars with or against the King, and God knew, few enough men in the realm had avoided any fighting in the last few years, then they had been involved in scrapes with the bands of cudgel-men, the *trail bastons* who were still such a pest.

He didn't like to admit the fact even to himself, but Coroner Roger was anxious. Sir Baldwin and Master Puttock were both capable fighters; Roger had seen Sir Baldwin last year fighting a powerful opponent and slaying him, and he knew Simon was a doughty ally. If they had been set upon, they would have given a good account of themselves – of that he was quite certain.

The question was, had they been given a chance to defend themselves? Coroner Roger knew that they had left this place yesterday afternoon, intending to rescue the Coroner's two men and Saul, and the three had returned safe and well, if grumbling bitterly, and said that the Keeper and his friend were still at the castle. There had been news of a fire, too, but no sign of Baldwin or Simon. It was a known fact that Sir Ralph and his son were capable of taking hostages and ransoming them. If that was what they intended with Baldwin and Simon, Coroner Roger would soon show them the error of their ways.

Although he had never seen the need to broadcast his affection, Roger was fond of both men, and the thought that they might be held in a grotty cell without food was disquieting. Still worse was the thought that they might even now be in peril of their lives. What Sir Ralph could be holding them for, Coroner Roger had no idea, and he didn't care. If they were being held, he would have them released. If he was to act swiftly, he could come to the castle and surprise the men guarding it. Then he could take the place quickly with a minimum of bloodshed.

The Coroner sat with the Squire and the Reeve, and debated with them the best means of gaining access to the castle. None of them knew it well, but the Squire had passed by it a few times, and the Reeve had once gone there with a message.

'Sir Richard never had the money to properly guard it and the perimeter is largely a wooden palisade at the rear, dug into the wall.' The Reeve was a sharp-eyed man with the dark, weather-beaten features of a farmer. Although his waist spoke of his prosperity, the green tunic he wore was faded, and his leather belt was straining as though he had not bought new clothes for many years. He had a quick mind, and spoke with decision about matters he understood.

'How clear are the approaches?' Coroner Roger asked. They were using sticks to mark out the land in the dirt at their feet.

'Not very. There are trees on the hillside behind here, but there is a broad expanse leading to the walls which is still clear. If the guards are attentive, it'll be a hard fight to break in over the wall. If they aren't, it'd be quite easy to get in.'

'What about the front?' asked Squire Hubert, a heavy-shouldered man in his early twenties with a narrow, regular face and light hair. His eyes were a startling blue, and when they fixed upon the Coroner, Roger had the uncomfortable impression that he was being interrogated. Squire Hubert sat quietly for the most part, deferring to Coroner Roger, but he was clearly a trained warrior. Younger than the other two men, he yet had experience of three wars and had managed men in battle. He was no strategist, he said, but if he was told what he must do, he would achieve his objectives.

'Clear. There's roads coming in from the north here, from the east here, and the south too. We could ride to the gate, but then we'd be standing out in the open with arrows and all sorts being thrown at us. Not a nice prospect.'

'But if we had a small party at the rear, while more go to the front as though to storm, and then pull back as though defeated, the guards might all go to the front, leaving the rear walls clear to be scaled. If need be, we can deal with any individual guards who remain.'

Coroner Roger nodded. 'That makes most sense. We have to rescue my friends and end this family's reign of fear.'

'We've heard about their depredations for too long,' the Reeve said. 'No one wanted to accuse the new Lord of Gidleigh, though. Bastard! I can't guess how much he and his son have extorted from people passing by.'

'You say he killed this miner?' Squire Hector asked. 'Do you know of any others he might have murdered?'

'Not at present, but the main thing is, we have to remove the threat before any others meet the same fate,' the Coroner said. 'Especially my two friends.'

'In which case, we should hurry,' Squire Hubert said. The sun was rising in the sky. 'We want to get there before the day is far advanced.'

Their plan was soon agreed. They had almost seventy men, which the Coroner and the Squire both felt was adequate. As they rode, Coroner Roger and the Squire discussed tactics. 'I'll take twenty-odd to the gate,' Coroner Roger said. 'You take the rest to the rear.'

'Good!' Squire Hubert said. His voice was warm and enthusiastic. 'The Reeve and I shall get in while you are making some little noise, then rush the garrison.'

'And open the gates so that we may enter,' Coroner Roger reminded him. 'But be careful that you don't visit death on my friends.'

'One dark man with a beard that covers only the point of his jaw, wearing a crimson tunic; the other a taller man, thicker in the belly, and wearing a tatty green coat and worn boots.'

'For God's sake, don't tell him I said that!' Coroner Roger said lightly, but in his heart all he could see was a castle in flames, and the bodies of his friends lying in the dirt, trampled by maddened horses and terrified men.

Baldwin left the hall and stood outside in the yard. He was there some while later when Simon walked out.

'Baldwin, we have to try to get out of here before Coroner Roger arrives.'

'Yes, you're right, I know,' Baldwin said, but Simon could see that his mind was elsewhere.

'The boy ran at Sir Ralph. There was nothing else you could do.'

'I could have used the flat of my blade to turn his knives. There was no need to kill him. I am an experienced fighter – and him? He was a monk, in Christ's name!'

As he spoke, there was a gruff clearing of a throat behind them, and they turned to find Sir Ralph in the doorway to his hall. Seeing that he had their attention, he walked slowly towards them.

'My Lords, I have to thank you for . . . Sir Baldwin, I owe you my life.'

'You do. Undeservedly.'

'Perhaps. But I shall try to meet your expectations of me,' Sir Ralph said, a little stiffly, for he had not expected Baldwin to meet him with such discourtesy.

'My expectations? I doubt that, Sir Ralph! All this mayhem – it's all your fault, isn't it?'

The other knight lifted his head with a faint renewal of his past haughtiness. 'Me? Why should it be my fault?'

'Because you are the father of all the sins here, that's why! Do you realise who that boy was, whom I have just executed for you?'

'The monk? I . . . I don't understand.'

'Don't you? Yet he was your flesh and blood, Sir Ralph. He was your son!'

'No,' Sir Ralph scoffed. 'He can't have been. I never saw him before he arrived here.'

'Call Scut here. Let's see what he can tell us.'

Roger arrived a few moments later, wiping his hands free of Mark's blood. 'What is it?' he demanded pettishly. 'I have work to attend to, laying out that poor boy.'

'That boy,' Sir Ralph said. 'Where was he from?'

'Axminster. The poor fellow was born to a mother without a father. He was one of those taken into the cathedral by Bishop Walter some years ago.'

'Axminster?' Sir Ralph said.

'Did you know a woman there?' Baldwin pressed him.

'Well, I did, yes, but surely she would have let me know if I had . . .' Sir Ralph closed his mouth. He had met a widow there, it was true, and for a month he had stayed with her, but Mark couldn't be his son. It was impossible. 'No, he's no relation of mine. His blood is not mine.'

'He thought he was your son,' Baldwin said.

'It is true, Sir Ralph,' Roger Scut said. 'He confessed as much to me.'

'And you didn't see fit to tell *me*!' Sir Ralph snarled. 'Why was that?'

'I didn't think he could have been telling the truth. It sounded like a pleasing excuse, a way of escaping your anger, nothing more.'

'And you saw a means of acquiring another chapel for no effort,' Sir Baldwin said with poisonous sweetness. 'You couldn't tell Sir Ralph that this boy was his own son, could you? If Sir Ralph knew that, he would move Heaven and earth to protect his son and leave him there in his chapel, where Sir Ralph could meet him often.'

'Oh, nonsense!' Roger said nervously.

Suddenly Sir Ralph's forearm was across Roger Scut's windpipe. 'Is it true?' he demanded through gritted teeth. 'Did you conceal my paternity from me to enrich your purse? If you did, as there's a God in Heaven, I'll cut out your heart and feed it to the pigs, Master Priest!'

'I have done nothing of the sort!' Roger Scut squeaked. He couldn't swallow now, and the pain was increasing.

'Leave him, Sir Ralph! You can't evade your guilt and sins by attacking another.'

'Get off me!'

Simon was about to take hold of Sir Ralph's arm to release Roger Scut – with a degree of reluctance, admittedly – when there came another interruption. At the gate, a man on the wall cried out to the gatekeeper. 'Shut the gates, and do it quick!'

Hearing the shout, Brian came out from the buttery where he had been enjoying his morning whet with another man-at-arms. 'What is it?'

'Men. Looks like twenty or so, marching here with a man leading them on horseback.'

Baldwin and Simon exchanged a glance.

'What's all this about?' Sir Ralph asked distractedly. 'Who can they be?'

'It is the Coroner, I expect,' Baldwin said soothingly. 'He was expecting Simon and me last night, and when we didn't turn up, I suppose he grew concerned.'

'And since I am such a foul brigand, he assumed I'd have imprisoned you and tried to persuade you to give me all your fortune?' Sir Ralph said caustically.

'Sir Ralph, you can't let these two go.' It was Brian of Doncaster. He had strolled over to them, his hands in his belt.

'Don't tell me what I can do with guests in my own castle.'

'I have to. You would risk my life and the lives of my men if you opened that gate. The Coroner isn't here for these men only, is he? He's here because of the raiding and the murder of Wylkyn. I can't have you opening the gates and surrendering the place. You do that, you'll put all our necks in the noose.'

'Open the gate!' Sir Ralph roared. 'You: Keeper! Open the gate, I said. Slide back the bars.'

The gatekeeper smiled and nodded, but then looked at Brian, who shook his head and said, 'It stays barred until I say it can open.'

Chapter Thirty-Five

The Coroner wasn't surprised to find the gates closed to him. This was the home of a felon and brigand, and any large force must make him seek safety first, rather than risking an invasion.

'Wait here,' he commanded. Thomas and Godwen were with him as his Lieutenants, and both nodded. He rode to the gate and bellowed in his loudest voice, 'Open this gate in the name of the King!'

'Who demands it?'

A face had appeared on the wall near the gate itself, and Coroner Roger directed his attention to the man. 'Are you Sir Ralph?'

'No, I'm his Constable. Who are you? What do you want here?'

'I am the King's Coroner, and I want to talk to your master about the murder of Wylkyn the miner, and about the arrest and imprisonment of my own servants.'

'Wylkyn died trying to attack Sir Ralph's son Esmon, and as for your servants, there had been a theft in the area. It was our duty to preserve the King's Peace, and we arrested them in good faith. Now if you intend to hold an inquest into the death of the miner, tell us when and where and my master will attend, but we will not throw open the gates to everyone who demands it at the head of a small host.'

'You will open this gate in the King's name, or you will be kept inside to starve.'

'You can sit there outside as long as you want, friend, but we have plenty of stores here. Now leave the gate unless you want an arrow to speed you on your way!'

'You dare to threaten a Coroner? Fetch out your master, you brigand!'

'Call me a brigand?' Brian called sharply, and snatched up a crossbow. He aimed it at Coroner Roger. 'You will not speak to Sir Ralph while you wait there at his gate like a thief! What, do you want to take his castle for yourself? Get away before I loose this bolt!'

'I shall not go until I speak to the master of the castle!'

'He orders me to hold you away. Would you have me break my master's lawful command? Go!'

It didn't occur to Coroner Roger that he was speaking to a mutineer, so he was in two minds. There was no clamour of fighting from the rear of the castle as yet, and he would have expected some noise by now. If he remained, he was sure that he would soon be punctured by the man's bolt, but if he left, it could mean that the men attempting to scale the walls might be seen and slaughtered.

'Very well, I shall go. But first, ask your Lord to come here. I want to speak to him about the inquest.'

'You aren't listening, are you? I told you, he said I was to come up here and hold you away. He won't come.'

'What of his son? Is Esmon in the castle?'

'Old man, I am growing bored with your questions. Go back to your tavern and wait. We'll send for you when my master wants to speak with you.'

'I shall, but first—'

Brian heard it a moment before Coroner Roger, and he whirled around, frowning. There had been a cry of pain; only quiet, but it sounded like the call of a man who was suddenly struck down. Brian had been a warrior too long to mistake the noise.

The Keeper and his Bailiff friend were still down there in the yard with two men guarding each, while Sir Ralph was a short way away with another three men about him. None of them had broken free, so far as Brian could see. No, the call came from somewhere else. In the hall, he knew, Esmon was sitting with a crossbow pointing at his breast. There was no sign that he had escaped.

Brian turned back to the Coroner, but there was a niggling doubt in his mind. This little uprising of his had been thought out long ago, but now he had implemented it, he was nervous. It had seemed the ideal time to take over the castle, when he heard that there was a small band arriving to question Sir Ralph, because it gave Brian and his men the excuse to kill Sir Ralph and Esmon while blaming the attackers. Brian and his men would swear that they had turned to support the Coroner's men, and had had to kill Sir Ralph and Esmon because they refused to put up their weapons. Easy. And while the Coroner investigated, Brian and his men could have it away on their feet with any of Sir Ralph's plate and money they could lay their hands on. There was little need to fear a small local force such as the one which the Coroner had brought. In Brian's band there were men who had killed and fought in battles up and down the kingdom.

Yet there was something amiss. A man had cried out. Where, and who was it?

Lady Annicia retired to her solar with Flora as soon as Mark fell. The sight of Sir Baldwin swiping the clerk's hand off, the blood fountaining from the stump spattering the tables, made the Lady curl her lip in distaste, but she saw that Flora was close to fainting.

'Come, child!' she said, leading Flora from the room and through into the solar.

Ben had leaped to his feet, and now he stayed at the back of the hall staring about him at the clerk, Sir Baldwin and the other men as though expecting to be run through himself at any moment. He scarcely glanced at his sister as Lady Annicia gently pulled Flora after her.

'Thank you, my Lady,' Flora stammered as they went into the little downstairs chamber.

'You have had to cope with enough already,' Lady Annicia said coldly. 'Your house, your father, and now this.'

'Why should he want to kill Sir Ralph?'

'Come, dear. Call him by the correct title: "Father".'

Flora closed her eyes and hung her head. She had hoped that there would be no need to talk about that. 'I am sorry.'

'It's not your fault, child. It's my husband and your mother we must blame, if anyone.'

'I had no idea.'

'Of course. At least he kept it quiet,' Lady Annicia said, pouring wine.

They had said nothing after that. Both had plenty to occupy their minds. While Flora wept silently, in memory of Huward and her mother, both dead, Annicia was musing on the shame that her husband's affairs had heaped upon her. It was not pleasant. There were all too many catty wives in the shire who would be delighted to bruit news abroad of Sir Ralph's womanising. They would say that it was no surprise he sought younger flesh when the alternative was an ugly old bitch like his wife. She knew how women of her class would turn on any other who had shown a chink in her armour. Draining her cup, she poured more wine.

When the shouting started outside, she did little more than glance up, but when the man entered her solar, she stood with quivering outrage. 'What do you think you are doing in here?'

To her astonishment, he drew his knife and pointed it at her. 'Keeping you quiet, Lady. Make a squeak and I'll use this to mark your face for ever. Be still and sit silent. All right?'

Astonished, she flopped into her chair and gazed at Flora as though this too was her fault. It felt as though everything was going wrong. Flora was her husband's, not hers; the justifiable vengeance on that miner had brought her son, apparently, into danger – and now there was this man . . .

'I know you. You're one of Brian's men.'

'Quiet.'

She knew him. That could only mean one thing: treachery. Lady Annicia shot a look at Flora, but she obviously didn't understand what was happening. Lady Annicia sipped reflectively at her wine, and then poured more.

'You want some?' she asked him, motioning towards her drink and taking hold of the heavy pewter jug.

'You can't get me drunk!' he said sneeringly.

Without pausing to think, she continued the movement. It sent the wine from her cup dashing into the guard's eyes. He raised his hands to protect his face, and as he did so, the Lady leaped at him, knocking his knife-hand away with her cup, then swinging the jug with all her weight and malice. The almost full jug connected with a dull, echoing crack, and then she was lifting it again and bringing it down with both hands. It hit the man between his ear and temple, and he fell like a pole-axed ox, suddenly collapsing vertically.

She stood, panting slightly, watching for any movement. His knife was on the floor, and she put her foot on it. At the same time she noticed the blood welling from a gash on the side of his skull, and the twitching in his hands and feet. He looked as though he would never rise again. To be safe, she brought it down once more, with full force, and then crouched and took his knife. Because she was practical, she thrust it into his breast to make sure of him. There was surprisingly little blood, she thought.

'Come!' she said to Flora, and went to the door.

The lock opened quietly enough, and she peered through the tapestries, which had been pulled aside. In the room beyond she could see Ben and Esmon sitting side by side, a guard holding a crossbow standing with his back to her. Esmon, her Esmon, looked merely enraged, but Ben was listless, as though he expected or even welcomed death. Beyond the two were many of the castle's servants, held in a corner of the room by two men armed with swords. She gauged the distance. It was at least six yards between her and the bowman, and the high table was in the way. She wasn't sure if she could get to him.

She threw open the door with a scream, and hurried out, the jug still in her hand. 'Rape! Rape! He's tried to rape me!'

The guard turned, his mouth wide open. For an instant his task was forgotten, and she saw that Ben too was gaping at her, but her son, her lovely Esmon, was not so stupid, and he was already at the guard. There was a confused grapple, and then Annicia saw that the whole of the man's head appeared to explode. Shards of something flew from the crown of his skull, warm stuff spattered her face and hair, and the crossbow's bolt struck the timbers of the ceiling, penetrating and staying in the wood while the guard, already dead, toppled slowly and then fell.

In the corner, the other guards tried to hold the servants back, but they were forced to cover their prisoners while keeping an eye on Esmon, who had now taken the bowman's sword. Facing the threat from Esmon as well as all the servants, the two guards exchanged a glance, and then bolted for the door.

'Mother, you stay in here!' Esmon called, and ran after them. Ben watched him, but was incapable of movement. He sat like one already slain. His fear petrified him and made him remain in his seat. Even as Esmon snatched up his own sword from the doorway where the guard had made him set it, as he struggled and hauled the bowstring back until it caught on the nut, Ben could not move. When Esmon had the bow cocked, he went back to the guard's body and found the small pouch filled with steel-tipped bolts. He took a handful, placed one in the groove of the crossbow and went to the door. Outside, he saw the men guarding his father.

With a shout, he ran down the steps to the yard, bow in one hand, sword in the other. A guard by his father's side realised something was wrong and turned. Esmon gave an incoherent roar and pointed the crossbow at him. He fired, still running, and saw the bolt fly, true to his aim, through the man's throat. A red mist burst from the man, and he grabbed at his neck, gurgling as he started to drown in his own blood. Then Esmon was on the next guard.

He saw Baldwin move as soon as the first guard fell, thrashing as he tried to breathe. Another guard had turned to face Esmon, and Baldwin took his arm, spun him around, and hurled him into a third. He dropped to the dying guard and took his knife, whirling as a guard tried to stab at his back; he leaped back, and the sword whistled near his breast, and then he closed swiftly. The man tried to reverse the action of his sword, but he was too slow and Baldwin was already slashing upwards with his knife, inside the man's ribcage, a ferocious glare on his face as the blade sheared through the man's viscera, his blood drenching Baldwin's hand.

There was a crack behind him, and when he turned, he saw a guard on the ground, his face bloody where Hugh's staff had cracked full-force into his nose, but then he saw that more men were pouring from the gatehouse towards them. Brian was up on the wall, watching in a fury as he saw his men falling. In his hand was a crossbow, and he raised it. Baldwin took a deep breath, convinced that the bolt would strike him, but the machine wasn't pointing at him. The string thrummed, and Baldwin saw the blur as the steel-tipped death flew through the air.

It hit Esmon on his left shoulder as he was lifting his sword to parry a heavy blow. Its massy weight smashed through his bones, locking his arm and shoulder in place, and with the impact, shards of bone exploded onwards, splinters tearing through his lungs and slicing through veins. He knew he was dying as soon as he felt the terrible shock of the impact, and when he looked down and saw the bolt's wooden shaft protruding from his shoulder, he gave a bellow of fury and rage, like a bear tired of the baiting, and hurled himself onwards, determined to kill as many of his enemies as he could before he died.

'Sir Ralph!' Baldwin said. 'Come with us!'

'My son!'

'Leave him – he's dead.'

'No! He can't be!' Sir Ralph cried. 'Esmon!'

'That's your man, Sir Ralph, *he's* your enemy!' Baldwin shouted, pointing to Brian, who was desperately trying to recock the crossbow. 'Do you want to die here, now, or come to safety and kill your son's murderer? Will you avenge Esmon's death or wail and gnash your teeth until you're killed in your turn?'

He grabbed Sir Ralph's shoulder and half dragged the man back towards the keep. 'Come on!'

Simon was fighting another man, and he heard Baldwin's cry even as he saw Hugh manoeuvring behind his opponent. There was a loud crack, and the man disappeared. 'Hugh!'

'Sir Baldwin's over there,' Hugh pointed, and Simon nodded, running after them.

* * *

Coroner Roger saw the way that Brian turned, shouted, and then took aim. There was nothing he could do to stop the man firing, and he glared at his men. Two of them had strung bows, and he shouted, all but unintelligibly, that they must fire on Brian. In a couple of moments the bows were in action and two yard-long arrows sped to him.

Brian was fortunate. In the moment that the arrows were fired he had loosed his second bolt at Esmon, missing as Esmon avoided a sword thrust, and before they struck, he bent to reach for a fresh bolt. One arrow thumped into the stone of the wall behind him, and he ducked a little lower as the second hurtled past him.

At his side, the gate's watchman muttered, 'Fuck! These bastards are getting serious!'

Brian chuckled. The blood was singing in his veins, and he felt more alive than he had done in weeks. 'Make sure the gate stays barred,' he grinned and dropped down the ladder to the yard.

Esmon was dying. He rested on his sword, the point sitting on the ground, panting while two men watched him warily. They were trained fighters. Seeing he was soon to die anyway, they saw no point in risking their own lives while he still had a spark of energy left. They would move in when he was past defence.

Brian gave a dry, humourless laugh. He dragged back the string on his bow, set another bolt in the groove, and shot Esmon through the heart.

Baldwin and Simon slammed the door shut. It was made of good, new, light-coloured oak, and the bars too were fresh and clean, as though they had recently been renewed. Simon slid them from their housings in the wall, dragging them across until the timbers fitted into the slots on the opposite wall.

They were in a rib-vaulted cellar with a loop in the east wall that gave a dim illumination to the room. Stairs within the thickness of the wall near the door led upwards, and the four men hurried to climb them as weapons began to hammer on the door.

Upstairs was a smaller chamber. This was about seven yards long, four wide. There was a loop over the barred doorway, a fireplace in the eastern wall with another two loops, and a fourth in the northern wall.

'Rats in a trap,' Baldwin breathed.

'Yes, but we can make their lives difficult,' Simon said, staring about for a weapon which might be dropped on the heads of the men attacking the place.

'There's nothing,' Sir Ralph said. 'I didn't want that rabble having access to too many weapons in case they decided to mutiny.'

'That was wise,' Baldwin said sarcastically. 'Perhaps it would have been wiser still not to allow them into your castle?'

Sir Ralph said nothing. His eyes held a strange kind of wildness which Baldwin had not seen before, but then he had not seen men witness their sons being shot down before them. His heart went out to Sir Ralph. He disliked the man, detested the way he had behaved, and yet he could sympathise with his present appalling situation.

'Where are the women? Your wife and the girl Flora?' Simon asked.

'I don't know. Did the men leave them in the hall?'

'It's possible,' Simon grunted. 'But if they're there, that's where Ben and Esmon were too, so they're probably safe.'

'We won't know until we get out of here,' Baldwin said. He glanced about him. 'And there's no easy escape.'

Simon nodded, and cocked his head. There was a change in the sounds from below. No more thumping, but gleeful roars, as though a new force had broken into the castle's yard.

Chapter Thirty-Six

It was with relief that Coroner Roger heard the sudden bellow from the rear of the castle. Squire Hubert and the Reeve were climbing the walls! The Coroner debated whether to chase around to the back to join them, but the Squire had promised he'd have the gate opened in moments and was true to his word. Soon there was a grating noise as the bars were dragged back, and then the gates opened quietly on their greased hinges. The Coroner spurred his mount inside, Thomas and Godwen at his side, the posse immediately behind them.

The yard looked as though it was filled with corpses. Everywhere was the metallic scent of blood. The Coroner gazed around, urgently seeking a face he knew, and he felt only relief when he realised that nowhere could he see Baldwin or Simon among the dead or wounded.

Ahead there was a fight at the foot of the tower. When the men had clambered over the fence, they had been hidden by the mass of the tower itself, and they had surprised Brian and his men at the foot of the keep.

Coroner Roger roared at his men and, brandishing his sword, cantered to them. He could see Brian, who turned with a look of shock on his face at this new threat, and bellowed to his own men. One fell as Godwen rode over him, but then two men grabbed Godwen's booted foot and pulled him from his mount. Before Coroner Roger could get to him, he heard an almost insane-sounding scream of pure demoniacal rage, and saw Thomas running past him on foot, a heavy war-axe in his left hand, a thick, battered-looking club in his right. With these he flailed about him like a berserker of old, and soon there was a respectful space about him. Godwen was lying still on the ground and Thomas went to him, standing over him with his weapons ready.

The Coroner saw that Brian was being pushed back, but then two of his men appeared from behind, from the stables, and suddenly it was the Coroner's men who were being beaten back. Coroner Roger dropped from his horse to rally the men, running to the front, and arrived in time to see Brian pointing at him. Roger had time to deflect one blow at his head, and then, when he threw a look at Brian again, he saw to his horror that the man had a crossbow in his hands and was aiming it at him.

For the Coroner, time seemed to stand still. The noise of the battle faded and died, and he was aware only of the point of the bolt that was aiming at his body. Men about him screamed and shouted, stabbed, slashed, moved forward and back, lifted their arms, and then themselves fell, and Coroner Roger knew nothing of them. The sounds were faded and dulled as though heard from an immense distance, while all he could hear was the blood hammering in his veins like an enormous drum. He could think of nothing but his wife, whom he adored, whom he would have wanted to see just once more, and yet whom he must never see again. That thought was hideously painful, as though the quarrel's dart had already punctured his breast. She was his lover, but more than that, she was his very best friend.

Then the door to the keep was pulled wide, and Sir Ralph stood in the doorway for an instant, before running straight at Brian, roaring '*TRAITOR! TRAITOR!*'

His onward rush took him through the first group of men, and he was almost at Brian's back in the time that it took Brian to glance over his shoulder. Seeing his peril, he ducked, and the crossbow was pointed away. Suddenly Coroner Roger was aware that he had been holding his breath, and he exhaled, light-headed. Then he felt his senses renew as he caught sight of Baldwin and Simon leaving the door to the keep. They ran out and joined Sir Ralph in attacking Brian's men in flank, and that turned the course of the battle.

Brian and his men had been pushed back until now he was at the hall's entrance with the last few of his men. There was a scuffle there, and Roger saw Sir Ralph trying to clamber up the steps to reach Brian, but then he saw that dreadful crossbow rise, saw Brian take a casual aim – from that distance, a matter of feet, he could not miss – and fire.

The bolt struck Sir Ralph in the forehead, and the Coroner saw his head jerk as though struck by a hammer. Even as Sir Ralph's body hesitated, Coroner Roger knew he was dead. No man could survive a wound like that. Then Sir Ralph fell backwards down the steps and lay at the foot of them, a crumpled body with all life gone, and then Brian was in the hall, the door slammed firmly shut in the face of the attackers.

'Aha! Coroner. We thought you might have forgotten us,' Baldwin gasped.

'You thought I'd forgotten *you*? When I'd promised you a good meal last night, I knew you had to be ill or detained, when you never arrived. A trencherman like you, missing a free meal!'

Baldwin could laugh now. The relief of surviving made him feel an excess of delight that rushed through his veins and into his head, almost like sex. He gave a great sigh. 'I am glad you have so little understanding of my appetites.'

'Ha! You think so?' said the Coroner, and hiccupped.

He stumbled, a hand grabbing for Baldwin, catching him by the shoulder. Baldwin smiled still more broadly, thinking merely that his friend had stubbed his boot or tripped on a cobble, but then the Coroner coughed, and a little gobbet of blood spattered on Baldwin's tunic. Coroner Roger was gazing up at Baldwin's face with an expression of confusion, and then a frown passed over his features. That was when the knight saw the point of the crossbow bolt protruding from Coroner Roger's breast.

'Christ Jesus!' he murmured, and it was almost a sob. The Coroner was now feebly trying to stay on his feet, but his legs would not support him. Baldwin tried to smile at him, but he had a great choking lump in his throat, and the words would not come for a moment.

At the hall, Baldwin saw a movement in the great window. Brian must be standing on a table to fire through it. 'Look out! 'Ware the crossbow in the window, there,' he roared, before carrying Coroner Roger into the protection of the keep.

Flora and Lady Annicia remained in the relative safety of the solar block with Ben. Lady Annicia had been in the hall when Brian leaped in through the door with his remaining companions, slamming and barring the door to the hall. She had been going to ask about her husband when she saw the expression on Brian's face. There was a feral brutality there; this man was going to die, and like a badger caught in a narrow alley, he was turning at bay ready to slaughter as many others as he could.

She slammed shut the door to the solar, shoving the first of the heavy bolts across before Brian could reach her. Then the other two bolts, one at the top, one at the bottom. The oak timbers of the door were sound enough to hold any man at bay for an age. Without an axe, he could do little more than hurl abuse through it. There was one loud thud, and she guessed that it was a crossbow bolt slamming into it, but the point failed to penetrate the inch-thick wood.

There was a slight gap between door and frame, and from this she could see Brian stacking one table upon another, then peering through the window and firing. Suddenly the shouting outside grew louder, and she wondered what was going on. Lady Annicia was worried. She hoped that her husband and son were still alive and well, but she had seen nothing of either. Similarly, she had seen nothing of the other men. Where were her own servants – the grooms, gardeners, steward and others?

At a fresh outburst of noise, she peeped through the door crack again, in time to see a howling flurry of arrows fly through the window. All was quiet for a while, and then there was a sudden shout of pain. One of the men had been pinned to the floor by an arrow, the fletchings still quivering, protruding from his calf.

'We can't stay here,' she said under her breath, 'but there's no other way out.'

'We can't get out from above?' Flora asked.

She shook her head. All the windows were barred. Ben sat on a chair, his face a mass of weeping burns, and he began to chuckle. 'Father will save us. He won't let us come to any harm. Father? Dad? Help!'

'Shut up, fool,' Lady Annicia snarled. Ben took hold of her shoulder. Before she knew what was happening, his fist struck her chin, and she tumbled down, stunned. She saw, as if through a misted glass, Ben swing his fist into Flora's face; the girl was knocked off her stool by the force of the blow. Ben went to the door, unbolted it and pulled it open.

'Dad! Father, I'm here!' he called, heaving the door wide and pelting into the room. As he did so, there was a noise like a flock of geese flying through the air, and a cloud of arrows appeared. Ben was struck, in the throat, the breast and legs. Then, still upright, he began to shriek, a hideous scream like a rabbit in a fox's mouth.

'Kill him!' Brian ordered, and Ben's cry was cut off as a sword whistled in an arc. With a thump, it sliced through his neck and his head flew off. It was then that Lady Annicia fainted.

Baldwin had gently set Coroner Roger on the ground, and he lay still, his fingers clasping Baldwin's shoulder. 'Old friend, hold on. Please, hold on.'

He went out to the yard again. Brian and his men were being forced to keep their heads down, because a group of six archers were up on the walls, shooting down through the window. In a corner, near the door to the hall, Baldwin saw Hubert, and he ran to the Squire.

'We shall have to storm it,' Hubert said. 'We can't break in from here, the door's too thick, but if we bring the ladders here, we can set them against the window and climb in there.'

'It would be too dangerous,' Baldwin reckoned. 'They have crossbows in there, and they could cut you to pieces as you tried to lack through the bars and squirm between them.'

'What else can we do? Fire the place and drive them out?'

Baldwin looked at the hall, remembering the horror on the face of Flora as she awoke after the fire last night. 'Only if there's no other way.'

Simon joined them, fingering his blade with a black expression. 'He's dead. The Coroner's dead.'

There was a roar from the hall, then they heard Brian's voice.

'You! Coroner! Can you hear me?'

'The Coroner's not here,' Squire Hubert said, but Baldwin put his hand on Hubert's forearm.

'I am here – the Keeper. Will you surrender to us?'

'Set us free and we'll go. There's no need for more bloodshed.'

'You have to surrender unconditionally.'

'We won't. We have two hostages here, Lady Annicia and a girl . . .'

'Shit!' Simon muttered. 'That must be Flora.'

'. . . but they won't be hurt if you let us have free passage from here.'

'No!' Baldwin shouted. 'You must surrender unconditionally.'

'We won't. If you don't want these women to die, you'll have to set us loose. We want all your men away from the door. Any more arrows coming into the hall will hit the women first. They are in the room without cover.'

'It's true, Sir Baldwin! He has us sitting in the middle of the floor.'

'Lady Annicia, are you harmed?' Baldwin called, muttering under his breath, 'Damn! If we let them go, we'll never catch them again.'

'No. Not yet. Not from these men,' came her response.

'Baldwin, you have to agree to let them free if the women are released,' Simon said.

'We can't! He's murdered the Coroner and God knows who else. How can we let him go?'

'Do you want the ladies' blood on your hands?' Squire Hubert demanded. 'Come, we have to let him go, and as soon as he's ridden off, we can attack him.'

'This man is no fool,' Baldwin said. 'Right, Squire, take four men and remove all the horses from the stables. There will be none here when they come out. All of them, mind. I don't want one left. Simon, when he comes out, we can offer him sanctuary, but I won't have him leave this vill without releasing the women.'

'Very well.'

They could see Squire Hubert at the stables. In a moment there was an alarmed neighing, a scattering of hooves, and then a sudden explosion of noise as men bellowed and shouted at the sight of all the castle's horses pelting out of the stables. Some few beasts became lost and milled about the yard, their metal-shod hooves a threat to all the men who approached, but then they realised where the gate was, and there was a clattering as they galloped off, out of the castle and through to the road. Baldwin, glancing quickly after them, saw Squire Hubert and two other men on their own horses rallying them all and keeping them together in a tight pack.

When he looked back, he saw Brian at the window, his face a picture of dismay. That gave Baldwin some satisfaction for a moment, but then came the call once more.

'That was clever, Sir Keeper, but not clever enough! If you want one of these women to live, you'd best decide which is the one worth saving, because one of them is going to get cut into little pieces for what you just did. Tell me which shall live, which shall die. There's no hurry.'

'Burn them out,' Godwen said. 'That's the only way.'

'Don't be mad! That would enrage them further and guarantee that they would kill their hostages,' Baldwin snarled.

'Sir Baldwin. Let me go in!' Osbert had joined the Coroner's men, and he gripped his axe like a man who was desperate to hew at something other than wood. 'She's my sister, Sir Baldwin. Let me get her out.'

'How? If you know of a way inside, tell us!'

Osbert gave a dry smile. 'There's always a back passage. If you can distract them here, at the front of the place, I can get in, if you have a ladder.'

Baldwin gained the impression of great confidence. He nodded slowly, but then he noticed some logs waiting to be cut for timber or firewood, and began to speak to Simon about creating a diversion.

The room felt hot. Brian wiped at his face with his sleeve, listening intently. He had two hostages and he was keen to lose neither, but he didn't expect that he would be permitted to live. The expression on Sir Baldwin's face had told him that. There was a rage that was near to madness in the knight's eyes and Brian was quite sure that he would be executed before he could find a mount. Especially now the bastard had loosed all the animals from the stables.

Flora and Annicia sat mute. Both had the look of women who scarcely cared now whether they might live or die. Flora's bodice was drenched in blood from her brother's death. She had gone to him as soon as his head began to bounce, and cradled his body with the blood pumping obscenely from the severed neck. Annicia was little better. She had heard that her only son and her husband had been slaughtered by this man, and now she was numb to any fresh pain. There was nothing left.

They were no risk, Brian thought contemptuously. But others were. Nobody would be of a mind to commit arson here, yet there was too much silence for them not to be plotting. He had to know what Sir Baldwin and the other attackers intended. It was maddening, this uncertainty. Surely there must be a sign or noise of some sort soon. Surprise, that was what a leader of men always sought, and no doubt that was what the Keeper was planning, but Brian hoped that the knight would hurry up. The waiting was a terrible strain. His nerves were already frayed, and the idea that after so much thought and planning, his attempt at taking over the place was all to cock, was truly infuriating.

He slammed a fist into a table top, making it jump, and as it settled, he thought he heard something. A quiet, scraping noise that came from the back of the hall, maybe up in the solar.

Then there was a crash at the main door, and the whole hall seemed to shake with the impact. The bars across the door jumped in their seats, and one of Brian's men let out a nervous cry. It would have affected their morale, but another man let out a fart, and that had the opposite impact. Men laughed, tested their blades, shifted their jacks about their shoulders, and faced the direction of the threat.

Brian himself stood at the front. There was another thundering noise like a massive hammer, and the timbers of the door could be heard to strain. Brian was uncertain whether to wait here or go to the women and hold a knife to their throats. That way, any man entering the hall would see him, and surely understand the message: 'Set us loose or both die.'

A third shattering blow hit the door, and this time the entire door frame seemed to move. The bars moved in their sockets and creaked, and Brian went to the women, pulling out his knife as he went.

But the tapestries moved as though in a gust of wind. For a second he hesitated, and as a fourth shock swept through the hall, the tapestries were suddenly swept aside, and in rushed three armed men.

Chapter Thirty-Seven

It was the garderobe that gave them access. Os, like many others, had collected the box filled with wood ash from beneath the seat of the little room fitted on the outer wall of the solar. The room was shingled, and it took Os only a few minutes, once he had manhandled the ladder into place, to remove some of the thin chestnut tiles and open the roof. From then, he could climb in, axe held ready, and wait for Baldwin and Simon to join him.

Simon felt as though there was a thrilling in his veins, as if a thousand thousand birds were beating their wings along each of his limbs, the soft fluttering heightening all his senses, making his ears hear with greater sensitivity, making his eyes see more clearly, making his brain operate at twice its normal speed.

It was only the three of them. Baldwin wanted the rest of the men to grab the largest baulk of timber and pound at the door. That would distract Brian and his men. Meanwhile, the three would enter by the garderobe, hurry downstairs, and attack from inside. Osbert's task was to get to the door and break or remove the bars so that all the others could pile inside. Baldwin and Simon would hold off the others so he could do so. They had crept down the stairs, soon reaching the lower chamber. There they found the guard whom Lady Annicia had killed. The door beyond was open, and they stood a moment listening. Then, on Baldwin's count of three, they thrust the curtains aside and ran in.

Brian was in the middle of the floor. He saw Baldwin and turned to face him with a snarl on his face, still holding his crossbow. Osbert saw it, but ignored the danger. He ran straight on, past Brian, who turned to try to fire at him, but he was too slow, and the bolt went wide, punching a neat hole in the plaster of the wall. Then Osbert was at Brian's men. His axe rose and swept around. Blood flew in gouts, and then he was at the bars.

The men tried to stop him. He had shattered the skull of one, who fell instantly. A second had a vast gouge in his shoulder, which had a flap of skin that flopped wildly, but the two last men were unhurt, and even as they reeled from the shock of Osbert's attack, they were preparing to stop him reaching the door, for all could see his intention.

It was Simon who now flew at them. While Os thumped into the door at full speed and began to drag at the timbers, Simon arrived behind them with a scream so intense, so visceral, that one man shrieked in response. Both turned to fight him, forgetting for a moment the threat that Os posed. He pulled the first bar fully back, reached for the second and hauled, but the thing was stuck fast. It wouldn't move. The pressure from outside had pinned the wood in the stone slot, and he couldn't make it shift. He cursed, sweat pouring from his brow, and then punched it with main force. In his fist he felt a bone crunch and break, and then the bar moved, just a little, and he could slide it back.

The door slammed open, knocking Os from his feet, and in rushed the force, led by the Reeve of Chagford and Hugh. The two men fighting with Simon were despatched, and then Osbert could go to Flora. She sat in her chair, and he picked her up, unheeding of the pain in his hand, and carried her outside.

Baldwin had gone straight to Brian. He must reach the felon before he could kill the women. Brian had the crossbow in his hand, but it was useless now, so much sinew and wood. He had no time to reload and fire. Instead he swung it upwards, blocking Baldwin's first blow. Baldwin slipped down and stabbed, but the blade went wide, knocked aside by the crossbow. It was only when Baldwin pushed forward and tried to get inside Brian's reach, that he nicked Brian. He felt the blade grate on bone as he darted forward, and although Brian said nothing, Baldwin could see how his mouth became set. Baldwin had hurt him.

The bow was hurled at his head, and he must duck, and in the same moment Brian dragged out his sword and a dagger. Now he crouched, the knife forward, the sword held back for a swift riposte. Baldwin had no second weapon, and he paced forward slowly, warily watching Brian's eyes, aware of the entire man, not only one hand or weapon, but the complete fighter. He saw a certain tension in Brian's calves, and took a quick breath. Then Brian launched his attack.

He was good. His sword whirled high, and his dagger was almost an invisible blur underneath, the blow shielded and hidden by the greater threat of the sword, and Baldwin must retreat, blocking both with speed, only to see that both were only the first part of an attack. Now the dagger slid sideways as if to eviscerate Baldwin, and as he countered that, he realised that the sword was slicing towards his throat. He parried, then tried to regain the initiative by turning his blade and thrusting forward, but before he could complete the movement, he saw the dagger moving in once more. He sucked in his breath, curved his body away from the glistening, grey metal, and felt it slash at his belly, the pain non-existent, the only sensation that of a faint dragging of skin with a dullness afterwards.

He would need another new tunic, he thought to himself inconsequentially, and then had to duck as Brian's sword whirled past his skull. The dagger was there again, under his eyes, and he must move back again.

And then he saw it. Brian was confident of his victory. Baldwin must seem so old, so slow, Brian knew he could kill him. The blades flashed again and Baldwin gave way again, giving the impression of feebleness, watching carefully. Yes, there it was again: the shift of balance and quick change of foot. It was very quick, very assured, but it was a weakness.

The sword darted at his belly, the dagger behind and above, so that it could stab behind the false threat of the sword, but then he moved his feet just before lunging, and Baldwin had him. He grabbed Brian's sword hand with his left, pushed, crouched, and kicked as hard as he could on Brian's knee. There was a satisfying crunch, a high scream of pain, and Brian fell.

Baldwin stood over him, kicked him in the belly as he tried to stand, and then stabbed down once with his sword.

'That is for Coroner Roger!'

The next morning was bright and clean, as though nothing foul or unpleasant could exist beneath the clear blue sky. When Simon rose, he could see not a single cloud to mar the perfection. The view was delightful, all the more so because he felt, if a little stiff, at least unmarked.

Hugh was at the trough in the courtyard when Simon left the inn, morosely washing a linen shirt. 'Look at this! Torn, and the blood is all over it. I'll never get it clean.'

'Is that yours, Hugh? I didn't think you were hurt,' Simon said with some alarm. He had shown his man no sympathy after the fighting. His attention had been concentrated on Baldwin, who was bleeding slowly from a long scratch in his belly.

'No, it's not the shirt I was wearing yesterday,' Hugh said glumly. 'It's much better than that, it's the one the gatekeeper was wearing. He won't need it again.'

'No,' Simon said distastefully. There was an old tradition of taking a dead man's clothes. It was perfectly in order, but Simon would have hated to feel the shirt of a dead man against his own flesh. 'Have you seen anyone else yet?'

'No. Think they're all still drunk,' Hugh said censoriously. 'Not good to drink so much after something like that.'

It was true. The men had all sunk to the ground in exhaustion after the battle. None of Brian's men were left alive to trouble the area, and the attacking force was utterly spent from danger, from terror and from exertion. It was a long while before Baldwin could command them to begin to haul all the bodies into the yard. One pile was formed of Brian and his men, the other of the men who had helped destroy them, and when all was done, Simon himself had gone to the church next door, and asked the priest to come and attend to the dying as well as the dead. He had been reluctant, apparently convinced that a band of marauding outlaws had descended upon his vill and intended making off with all his silver.

In the end, Simon gave up and sent for Roger Scut. In minutes the rotund figure appeared. He had been locked in the room in the gatehouse, and now he gazed along the length of his nose like a prelate who was trying to elevate his nostrils above the stench of the common folk, but then he saw the dead bodies and crossed himself. He then earned Simon's undying respect by demanding to know where the wounded were, and before anything else he went to them, attempting, as best he could in his clumsy manner, to ease their pain.

They hadn't been able to bury anyone. That would be the responsibility of the vill's folk later, but Baldwin had been very insistent that Coroner Roger's body should be taken away from the place. It was brought to the inn, and lay in a cool storeroom even now. Baldwin had taken on the role of Coroner, and recorded the details of the action with the help of Roger's own clerk. There had been much else to clear and mend, and it had taken some time to track down the vill's peasants and organise them into labour squads, removing the bodies from the yard when Roger Scut told them that they could.

Simon stretched. His left shoulder was painful where someone had clubbed him and his foot was intensely painful where he had strained the tendons, but bearing in mind how close he had come to being stabbed or shot, he felt he had escaped lightly.

'Hugh . . .'

'Sir?'

'When we get home, remind me to give you five marks.'

'Five?' Hugh stared with his face quite blank for a moment. Then he sniffed, glanced up at the sun, and returned to his scrubbing. 'That's good. I can buy my wife a shirt.'

More than just a damned shirt, Simon thought. Five marks was probably more money than he had ever before possessed. 'And Hugh, if you don't want to come to Dartmouth, I'll understand. You can stay at Lydford and look after things there.'

'You mean that?'

'I wouldn't have said so otherwise,' Simon said heavily. It would be a hard parting. Hugh had saved Simon from harm on several occasions, and although he was undoubtedly the surliest bugger of a servant whom Simon had ever met, he was still a companion of many years, and losing him would be a wrench.

He turned on his heel to walk away, but stopped when he heard the quiet reply.

'Sir? Thank you, sir. My wife, she'll be pleased.'

Later in the morning, Baldwin made his way back to the castle. From the very beginning he had thought it a tinderbox of *petit treason* and mutiny, but the knowledge that he had been proved correct gave him no satisfaction.

At the gate, he saw Sampson and Surval. The fool was fearful, gazing about him with wide, scared eyes, but Surval met Baldwin's eyes with a steady gaze. 'I heard that the Coroner died yesterday. Is that right?'

'I am sorry to say that yes, it is.'

'You sound as though you mean that, Sir Knight.'

'I do. He was a good man and a good friend.'

'Rare to hear someone say that about a Coroner.'

'Roger was a rare man.'

Surval nodded thoughtfully. 'Sir Baldwin, I have a mind to help you.'

'That would be kind. How, though?'

'You were seeking the body of Wylkyn. We can tell you where it is.'

'That is curious. I found his body out on the moors, lying under a pile of rocks near a lime pit – is that what you were going to tell me?'

'Yes.' Surval frowned. 'You found Wylkyn yourself?'

'It was not difficult,' Baldwin said. 'Especially when I saw that there was a lime pit not far away. I think Esmon killed Wylkyn, and later decided to have the evidence of his murder removed. If it were not for the mutiny here, I should have sent for the body before now.'

'Why should he do that – hide the body there?'

'I believe he had convinced himself that he was justified in executing Wylkyn, because the fellow had murdered his own

master, Sir Richard Prouse. That sort of killing, to a man like
Esmon, would be intolerable. He thought an attack on one knight
was the same as an attack on the whole class of knights. So he
killed Wylkyn – and left the body where it lay. It was carrion, not
to be given the dignity of a burial.'

'But then he had it moved?'

'Yes. He must have realised that the discovery of a corpse
could be at best an embarrassment to him. So he had a change of
mind and arranged to have it destroyed. No doubt he ordered that
the body should be taken to the lime pit and disposed of.'

'You think so?' The hermit began to look edgy.

'I do not come to accuse,' Baldwin told him. 'The body was
carried to the pit, but then it was taken away again, by two men.
It was put in a field and covered in stones to protect it from wild
animals. And I shall tell you this: the men who took Wylkyn
there not only buried him with compassion and generosity, they
also sought to protect his soul. They crossed his arms over his
breast, then placed a cross on them, and I expect they prayed for
him.'

'How would you reckon all this?'

'I followed their trail. It was easy to follow them to the pit.
Then they picked a resting-place that was not far away. I soon
found him.'

'But the praying?'

'Someone had been there on the morning I visited. There was
the shape of a man lying with his arms outstretched, Surval, in the
dampness of the grass. And you pray on your belly like a saint of
old.'

'That is not proof.'

'Did I say it was?'   •

'Perhaps they didn't believe in Wylkyn's guilt.'

'No,' Baldwin said pensively. 'Perhaps they didn't. And then
again, there are still the questions about the death of Mary. It was
obviously not Mark. Who else could have wanted to kill her?'

Surval looked at him from under beetling brows. He gave a
short sigh. 'I want to help you, Sir Knight. I believe you are a

good man, especially after hearing your words about Wylkyn's body. I was near the road myself that day.'

'Yes saw what happened?' Baldwin said sharply.

'Some of it. I saw Mark argue and then snap. He punched Mary on the shoulder, although not hard enough to hurt her, I'd have thought.'

'Why didn't you tell of this before?' Baldwin asked suspiciously.

'Many have heard of my offence, Sir Baldwin. Would it be safe for me to expose myself to suspicion by revealing to superstitious villeins that I was there? Once a murderer, always a murderer! No, I thought it better to hold my tongue.'

'Even though Mark could have been executed?' Baldwin demanded.

'He was in no danger of that, Sir Baldwin, was he? He was a cleric – but me? No one believes a hermit is genuine. We are all supposed to be fraudsters, lazy vagabonds who have found an easy station.'

'There was every danger!' Baldwin snapped. 'He was accused of being a false monk!'

'I didn't know,' Surval objected. 'Not then. If I had, I would have protected him. I would have told all I knew.'

Baldwin doubted that. Surval had not bothered to go to the court held in the castle, when Mark was accused, but then, he would have assumed that even after a murder, Mark would be protected by his cloth. It was logical. And Surval was speaking sense. His own risk *was* greater than Mark's.

'So what did you see?'

'The whole thing,' Surval said simply. 'I saw Mark strike her, but not cruelly, not too hard. It wasn't like when I hit my woman. That was malicious. My God! I was so evil! How could I have done that to someone I loved?'

'Mark: he hit her?'

'Yes. I saw it. The moment he'd done so, he raised his hands to his face in shame. Mary said nothing, just stared at him in shock. He must have felt awful, because he turned away and started weeping silently, and retching as if he was going to be sick, but instead, he simply ran from the place.'

'And she was all right?'

'Yes. Perfectly all right. She looked upset, but she wasn't in pain or anything. A short time later, Sir Ralph appeared. I had been going to her side, but when I heard his horse, I stopped. He and I did not like each other. He spoke to her, and asked her how she fared. She was fine then. He left a little while later. Then I saw her put her hand on her belly, like any young mother, except there was a look of concern on her face. And she had grown pale, a little odd-looking – as if she felt giddy.'

'What then?'

'I cleared off. I was not of a mood to stand there watching her. I heard a noise, and when I investigated, I found Sampson. He had seen the argument and left just after Mark himself.'

'So Sampson could not have killed her? You saw her alive and then saw him leaving the place?'

'She was alive when Sampson left,' Surval said with certainty.

'Did you see anyone else?'

'No. When I left, I could hear the plough still moving. That was all. I didn't see anyone else.'

'Why did you keep this secret until now, then? There is little in this to help us, and little enough to do you harm!' Baldwin exclaimed. 'This whole matter is ridiculous! Why does no one try to help find the girl's killer?'

'Because it hurts any vill to accept that a man within it could do such a wicked thing.'

There was a curious tone in the hermit's voice. 'What do you mean?' Baldwin asked. 'Do you have any idea who could have done this?'

'I know Elias was in the field with Ben. I also know that no one else passed along the lane after Sir Ralph,' Surval said. 'Later, I saw Ben running down the roadway to get help. Elias remained.'

'So?'

'What if that little slap, the shock of his hand upon her – and, who knows, perhaps the thought that she had lost him? – made poor Mary lose her child? Perhaps she fell to the ground, whimpering and weeping, and Elias found her like that.'

'What if he did?'

'A young girl lying on the ground, the soil about her covered in her blood. It would look as though she had been attacked.'

'Which is surely what Elias thought,' Baldwin agreed.

'Elias feels strongly that women should not be molested. He lost his own daughter because she was raped. She died slowly, because she had been kicked in the belly. Wouldn't he think it kinder to kill her swiftly?'

Baldwin recalled seeing Elias with rabbits, how he stroked them to calm them before speedily breaking their necks. 'So one could say that Mark did, in fact, kill her. If he hadn't hit her and made her collapse, she might still be alive.'

'And this terrible tale might have a different ending.'

'You do not feel that Wylkyn killed his master?'

'No. He would never have harmed Sir Richard. His whole endeavour was to help the poor man with his possets and potions.'

'Then . . .'

'I think Mark was keen to assist his father.'

'Sweet Jesus! You mean this?'

'I was there in the room. Mark was present for much of the time. Anyone could have gone into Wylkyn's room to fetch powders or leaves, Mark the same as anyone. He knew his father was Sir Ralph, and he sought to further my brother's interests. Perhaps he intended to tell Ralph what he had done, and try to claim benefits of some sort. Maybe seek patronage.'

'I find that hard to believe.'

'There is little a man like Mark would not do to improve his prospects, Sir Baldwin. I know that someone like you is immune to the lust of better offices, but for a political monk, what else is there? Especially when he is left in a backwater like this. What is more natural than that he should dream of halls of his own, of power and influence?'

'So Esmon wrongly assumed that Wylkyn must have murdered Sir Richard, and sought to avenge the crime.'

'Exactly.'

'A terrible mess.'

'Life often is, Sir Baldwin.'

'True, my friend.'

'You seem to feel the misery of other people, good sir.'

'There are times,' Baldwin said quietly, 'when I feel that I carry the weight of too many men's sins and grief on my shoulders.'

Chapter Thirty-Eight

He found Simon sitting on a barrel near the mill, disconsolately throwing stones into the mill-leat. 'Roger was a good man.'

'Yes,' Baldwin said. 'I shall take his body to his widow as soon as I can make arrangements.'

Simon nodded and threw another stone into the river. 'It seems as though the whole of my life has been turned upside down in the last few months. First my Lord Abbot's decision that I should move to Dartmouth to live, then the news that my daughter has found herself a lover, and now poor Roger is dead. A friend who died trying to save us.'

'I know. And the hardest knock is that I doubt whether we would have been in any danger if he and his men had not arrived when they did.'

'That did surprise me. What made Brian take over the castle just then?'

'I doubt he would have rebelled if it was not for the show of force at the gate. It made him feel insecure and he chose to protect himself as he knew how – by taking the place. If the rear wall had been secure, he might have held out for weeks.'

'If he'd not bothered to fight, he'd still be alive now, and so would many others. Coroner Roger would only have arrested Sir Ralph and his son.'

'Yes. Instead many died. And we still have an investigation to complete.'

'Wylkyn?'

'Yes. I know where his body lies.'

'Under the pile of stones, of course. Then let's fetch it.'

'We cannot report it to Roger now. There is no one else here to whom we can give it.'

'There is another Coroner who lives in Exeter, isn't there?'

Baldwin sighed. 'Yes. But think of it in this way, Simon. How much easier would it be, should this body be added to the toll from yesterday? Will it help any man to learn that the vill aided the concealment of a body? Or that an old man and a fool hid Wylkyn on the orders of Esmon of Gidleigh?'

'No, of course not. But justice demands something.'

'You talk to me of justice today?'

Simon saw a picture of Roger in his mind's eye, the dark features, the piratical grin, the cynical leer when he doubted a witness's words, and slowly shook his head. 'What do you want to do?'

'Find Piers and Elias and Roger Scut. With them we can fetch the body.'

It took no time to gather the men and soon they were on their way, Hugh leading a small farm cart, Piers and Elias walking alongside, and Roger Scut, Baldwin and Simon on horseback. Their route took them back along the path where the girl had died, and Baldwin asked exactly where she had been found. Elias pointed out the position.

'I see. And you were in that field with Ben?'

'No. That 'un.'

Baldwin stared at the freshly ploughed soil. He could see over the hedge, but no one on the road would have been visible. On the opposite side, a hedge had been recently laid, the long branches set down horizontally and kept in place with pegs and grasses to form a strong, living barrier to the sheep and cattle that would next year graze here. 'That's where Osbert was?'

'Aye.'

Baldwin nodded, but then looked nearer. 'And this must be where Sampson and Surval were.'

Elias shot him a look, but it was Piers who said, 'Surval never told me he was here.'

'Perhaps you forgot to ask him?' Baldwin said mildly, but then he met Elias's look before urging his mount onwards.

At the wall, Hugh let his pony wander without taking the cart from its back. Baldwin and Simon's horses were loosely hobbled so that they could nibble at the grass while the men climbed over the fence and took the track Baldwin had found before.

'Are you sure he's here?' Piers said doubtfully. 'This isn't the easiest place to hide a man, is it?'

'When I was here the other day, I found small drops of blood on the way,' Baldwin said shortly. 'They led me to the pit here, as though someone was going to throw in something, and yet all there was, was a dead calf. Ah yes. There it is.'

They had reached the pit now.

'Maybe someone from the farm put it here?' Piers said helpfully.

'But as I said, there was blood on the way here,' Baldwin said as he led them to the pile of stones. 'And you will find him in there. Please get him out. There should be no need to tell anyone else of this. If we keep silent ourselves, we can remove him, put him with the dead in the churchyard and make an addition to the records to show that Wylkyn died trying to help us storm the castle.'

Roger Scut's head shot up. 'You expect me to add this man's name to the list? I can be no part of that! I should be perjuring myself!'

'Scut, if you do not, I shall tell the Dean about your efforts: seeking to accuse an innocent monk of a murder he didn't commit, releasing him from gaol so that he could be hunted down and killed, and all so that you could take more wealth to yourself. Would you like that?' Baldwin asked with silky sarcasm.

'I didn't release him. Sir Ralph did.'

'But you tried, didn't you?' Simon said. 'And Dean Peter is an old friend of mine and Sir Baldwin's. He would trust us.'

'Very well. I suppose I shall have to agree under the threat of your blackmail,' Roger Scut said with a show of reluctance. 'If that is all . . .'

'No, it is not. You also have a farmer, Jack, whom you have forced to give up lands he himself acquired. You will give them back to him in their entirety.'

'What? I can't do that! What would my other peasants say?'

Baldwin reached out almost lazily, and grabbed a handful of his tunic. He pulled Scut to him. 'Arse that you are, by name and behaviour, I swear this to you: if you do not release Jack from your intolerable service, I shall see you ruined in the Church. You wanted this little chapel so that you could take the money from it, didn't you? Well, if you do not agree to my demand, Scut, I shall make it my job to tell the good Dean that you are so keen on it, and I will ensure, Scut, that you have it and it alone. You will take Mark's place here, without a Lord, now that Sir Ralph is dead, without a patron, and without any income. I can do this, Scut, if you do not release Jack and return to him all the lands you have recently taken from him.'

'I shall release him,' Scut said sulkily. 'Although he is a lazy devil, and why on earth you want to assist someone like that is beyond me.'

Piers gave a cry of revulsion. 'We have him!'

Baldwin released Scut and nodded slowly while the man patted down his habit and tried not to look embarrassed. He walked over with Simon to view the corpse as it was exposed, Baldwin in their wake.

The discovery of the body was no great surprise to Baldwin because he had known that Wylkyn was here as soon as he had come to look at the spot with Simon and the Coroner. He could have kicked himself for not investigating properly on the previous occasion, but then he had not enjoyed the luxury of time, and it was only when he had a little pause for reflection that he had been able to see what he had first missed.

'It is sad to see a man like him brought down,' he observed to Elias.

'At least he died quickly, didn't he?'

'How can you tell?'

'All those wounds.'

'But he could have suffered a great deal while receiving them!'

'Perhaps.'

'Like that poor girl Mary.'

'Her?' Elias nodded sadly. 'Ruined, poor chit.'

'I heard your own daughter was raped.'

'Yes,' he sighed.

'You miss her. She was how old?'

'About fifteen.'

'That must have been a terrible loss to you.'

'It was.'

'And her death was not so kindly as this man's?'

'No. She bled to death, poor child.'

Baldwin drew him away from the others a few paces. 'But Mary was not raped, Elias.'

'So?'

'She willingly gave herself. It was wrong to kill her.'

'Who says I killed her?'

'You found her lying by the way, you saw the blood, and you thought she was dead, so you sent her brother to fetch help. You thought someone had raped and murdered her, just as they killed your own child. Except when you went to her, once Ben was gone, you realised she wasn't dead, but she had collapsed because of the bleeding, just like your girl's.'

'The Coroner reckoned my daughter died because the man kicked her and broke something inside her. There was lots of blood, all running down her thighs and legs. My poor lass. It was terrible!'

'So she was already dead when she was found?' Baldwin asked gently.

'No. It took her an age to die. And when I saw young Mary lying there like that, all the blood down her legs, and all, I thought it was happening all over again.' His eyes were glistening now, and he sniffed as he continued. 'I sat with her, and then I touched her, and her head just flopped down. Her neck was broken.'

'You found her alive, didn't you? You concealed her from Ben's view so you could kill her.'

'No. She was dead already.'

'You took her head and snapped her neck like a rabbit.'

Elias shook his head. '*No*, Sir Baldwin. I swear she was already dead. Ask Surval. He saw me.'

'You saw Surval there? You didn't mention that before.'

'No, well. Not much point telling of others there, is there? It'd only get him fined as well. The vill can do without more fines.'

Baldwin studied him. He hadn't mentioned Surval, so far as he could remember. 'Where was Surval?'

Elias scowled. 'I saw him over there, leaning on that great stick of his, as I came out of the field. He was up beyond Mary's body.'

'So you came out into the road, saw her, sent Ben to fetch help, and sat down patiently to wait?' Baldwin said.

'There's no need for sarcasm. I saw her and shielded Ben from the sight, yes, and then, once he'd gone, I dipped back into the hedge to puke up. It was so like my own little girl's death. I thought Mary had been raped at the time, but now . . . well, I reckon she just lost her child.'

'And then someone broke her neck for her,' Baldwin added sharply.

'Yes. *But not me.*'

When they arrived at the hermit's hut, he was sitting outside, staring at the bridge.

'You have spoken to Elias?' he said.

Baldwin nodded. 'And I believe him.'

'No one believes a hermit, do they?'

'Not always, no. You were the man who killed Mary, weren't you?'

'Why do you think so?'

'Because you were there. We spent so much time thinking that others must be involved, but you were there, and you had the same motive as any others. You wanted to halt her pain, didn't you? Not because you'd seen your daughter die, but because you'd seen your own woman miscarry and bleed to death after you lost control and beat her up. You couldn't bear to see another girl die like that.'

Surval nodded. 'Yes. It's true. But I only killed her to save her pain. That was all. Only to save her pain.'

Simon could see that Baldwin was inclined to believe the old hermit – and yet there was something that tugged at his mind. He remembered hearing something before – something about this hermit.

'What will you do with me?' Surval asked serenely.

Baldwin's voice was tired. 'There have been too many deaths. I do not honestly care what happens to you. I think you meant to do her a service, and for that, perhaps, you should be congratulated.'

'I am grateful, Sir Knight. Not that I can disagree with you, of course.' Surval smiled and leaned back. 'It is a grand day, friends. A beautiful day.'

'It must feel like you're reprieved from a terrible fate,' Simon said without thinking.

'Hmm? Aye, I suppose so.'

'It was a shame that you did not feel it necessary to defend Mark, though.'

'True. But how could I reject other men's accusations against him without betraying my own role?'

'Poor Mark. And he was related to you, we find.'

'Yes. He was my nephew. So many are my nephews or nieces!'

'You once told me you have a child,' Baldwin said.

'You know him – Osbert. He is a good fellow. He doesn't know he is my boy, though. His mother told everyone it was Ralph. I didn't want to get into trouble with the Bishop, and it was all too easy to believe stories about my late, unlamented brother!'

Seeing him sitting back in the sun, absorbing the warmth, Simon suddenly remembered what he had heard and when, and he felt a cold premonition. It was during the ride here from Lydford. They had got lost and had to cross over the bridge, and Osbert, after they met Surval, had mentioned that Sir Richard had disliked the hermit. 'How did you like Sir Richard?' he asked now.

'He was a good enough man.'

'Did he support you and your bridge?'

'Of course. Why shouldn't he?'

Baldwin was watching the Bailiff as though wondering whether he might have been clubbed on the head during the fighting yesterday, but Simon felt like a harrier which sees its fox starting to flag. 'I heard he was trying to throw you off here because he thought you were no more than a felon escaping justice.'

'He had heard of me, I think, from my brother or nephew. They couldn't keep their mouths shut.'

'He died quickly.'

'Fairly, yes.'

'How did he die?'

'He had a seizure. Horrible.'

'You saw him?'

'I was there for much of the time, yes. I wasn't there when he actually expired.'

'No. There was no need, was there?' Simon said. 'Baldwin, we have been very stupid. There was only ever one murderer. The same man killed Sir Richard *and* the girl. Sir Richard because he threatened Surval's home . . .'

'He wanted to report me to the Bishop and have me removed. It wasn't anything to do with me, though. He simply wished to get back at my brother!' Surval looked from one man to the other, and saw incomprehension in their eyes. 'Very well, masters, you don't understand. I'll try to explain. I have a home here, a pleasing house, and I have my own altar, at which I abase myself. It is a part of me, this home. It is all I have now. In some ways, it *is* me! It defines me. My life, my soul, all that I am, is here. And Sir Richard wanted to throw me from the place. He intended sending me back to the Bishop. Not because of anything I had done, but because he thought any man related to my brother must be my brother's ally. Well, I wasn't.'

Baldwin asked, 'How did he know you were brother to Sir Ralph? It was seemingly well enough hidden to others about here?'

Surval gazed at him with surprise. 'We grew up here, and so did Sir Richard; even if he was younger than us, he knew us as close peers as well as neighbours. Our families hunted and dined together. But that meant nothing last year when that damned moneylender died in Exeter.'

He chewed his lip. 'You remember what things were like. The whole country on tenterhooks, armies massing to fight the enemies of the King, the Despensers called back from their exile and pardoned . . . and the Despensers – damn them! – came back and once more had the ear of the King to the detriment of the realm. Well, my brother had thrown in his lot with the Despensers some little while before. But Sir Richard hadn't.

'Sir Richard had borrowed a sum from a moneylender, and when that man was murdered, Sir Richard found people demanding repayment. The debt was taken by the King, and because of Sir Ralph's friendship with the Despensers, they persuaded the King to let my brother take over the castle. Sir Richard fought back in the only way he knew. He employed clerks to argue, he sought another moneylender, and then he tried to slander my brother through me.'

Surval grunted to himself. 'It wasn't the act of a kind or generous soul. He sought to ruin my brother's reputation by first ruining mine. Perhaps once he had removed me, he thought he could slander Ralph and thereby gain a little time to find more money and keep his castle. That it would have destroyed my reputation meant nothing to him.

'I have rebuilt my life here. The thought of leaving – especially in order to satisfy another man's spite against a brother I detest – seemed terribly unfair. So I sought to protect myself.'

'By killing again.' Baldwin's face was set like moorstone.

'Yes. He was going to destroy me, so I sought to destroy him first,' Surval said with a fierce defiance. 'When Sir Richard was forced to take to his bed with his gout, I went to visit the castle. I offered him peace, and tried to reason with him, but he wouldn't listen, and while I was there, I saw Wylkyn mix medicine for his master. When I asked what it was, he told me it was henbane. I knew where Wylkyn kept his stock of herbs, and I looked in there. I confess, I hadn't realised henbane could be used to ease the gout, but when I heard Wylkyn say that, I added more and mixed it with Sir Richard's wine. Within a day he was complaining about his sight and some giddiness. Soon he fell to lethargy, and within a day or two, he was in a delirium, and then he died.' The hermit gave a long sigh.

'You poisoned him over several days?'

'The priest from the church only saw him on the first day or two. After that, the monk from the chapel and I remained with him. We prayed together for his soul.'

'Even though you were killing him?' Simon burst out.

'Bailiff, a man's soul is more important than any petty disputes on earth,' the hermit said sententiously.

'You killed him to keep your place here,' Baldwin stated.

'It is everything to me!'

'What of the girl?' Baldwin asked, a sadness gradually overtaking him on hearing this confession. Surval was clearly an intelligent man, and he had sought to protect himself as best he might, but in so doing he had caused the deaths of too many others: Sir Richard, Mary and Wylkyn at first, but now Mark, Esmon, Sir Ralph, Ben, Huward and all the others, because if he had not committed those first crimes, Sir Ralph's affair might not have become known, his men might not have rebelled, and many would now be alive who had died.

Surval shook his head, staring down at the ground. 'I knew of the affair between Mark and her. Who didn't? In a vill, there are never any secrets. No matter what, lovers will be seen. And these two were. It was terrible. The appalling sin of incest in the first degree.'

'But they had no idea that they were guilty of such a sin!'

'They knew he was a monk, sworn to celibacy,' Surval shot out. 'He was supposed to have dedicated himself to God, but instead he enjoyed the girl's body.'

'She was pregnant,' Simon said quietly.

'I didn't realise that at first, but then she began to moan and cry.'

'In the road? You were there with her?' Baldwin confirmed.

'Yes. I went to speak to her after the others had passed by. She looked unhappy, troubled. Of course, she had just lost her child.'

'The blow,' Baldwin mused.

'Yes, I think her shock and horror at Mark's violence made her miscarry. I tried to soothe her, explained that it was for the best because it was her brother's child, but she wouldn't listen. She screamed at me, really loudly, and I . . . well, I saw that the anguish and morbid terror were gripping her, so I killed her. It was kinder. She was in terrible pain, and bleeding heavily.'

'You murdered her just as you did your own woman.'

'No, Sir Baldwin. I protected her from her shame. Imagine how she could have lived, knowing that her child was repellent to God Himself? It was better to spare her that. I was being kind.'

'And you were willing to allow Mark to hang for your crime.'

'Ach! There was no risk he'd hang. He was young. He could soon rebuild his life. Perhaps he'd be protected by the Bishop. But me, what could I do? If I was accused again, I'd die. This place is all I have. Without it, I *am* dead.'

A week later, Simon and Baldwin returned to Gidleigh with Coroner Roger's body. Baldwin was in a filthy mood, because he had ridden all the way to Exeter with Thomas, delivering Surval to the Bishop, and all during that long journey, Thomas had done nothing but complain about Godwen's behaviour, how he was insulting Thomas's family and Thomas himself, making sneering jibes about Thomas's brother-in-law and others.

'In God's name,' Baldwin exploded after ten miles, 'I begin to wish you had not bothered to save his damned life, if you loathe the man so much!'

Thomas had stared at him, quite appalled. 'Sir Baldwin! You can't choose who should live or die just because you like them or not!'

'I believe you saved him because life without your feuding partner would be insufferable.'

'That is a terrible accusation!' Thomas said with hurt in his voice, and he was silent. Then he flashed a grin at Baldwin. 'Mind, it does add spice to have an enemy!'

Baldwin had given a longsuffering grunt. Now, with Coroner Roger's widow at his side, walking to the church in Gidleigh, he could not recall any humour. It felt as though in the midst of her grief, she had sucked all the levity from people about her. Not surprising, Baldwin told himself; not after the shock of loss which she had suffered.

'He always adored this area,' Roger's widow said. She was a large woman, her face ravaged with tears, and she leaned heavily on her maidservant as she walked behind the sheeted body of her husband.

Simon nodded. 'He was born here, wasn't he?'

'And now he has died here and can be buried here,' she agreed. 'Daft old fool that he was, he'd probably be glad to think that although he lived most of his life in Exeter, he still came back here in the end.'

'I am so sorry,' Baldwin said sincerely. 'If I could have done anything to save him, I would.'

'I know that,' she said.

She moved on behind the body being carried by the four bearers, all of whom were servants from his home in Exeter. The weather was foul, which was nothing new, merely a return to normal conditions, Baldwin thought to himself. Grey skies hurled chilly gobbets of rain like slingshots at the people standing by the grave. It was an old-fashioned grave, like those of many in this area, so that Roger would be buried kneeling as though in prayer. He would have liked that, his wife had said. He had not been as religious as he should have been during life, so it was best that he had a head start in death. Surely a man praying would win God's attention faster than a lazy fool lying on his back.

After the short ceremony, Baldwin and Simon walked together to the entrance of Gidleigh Castle. The gate stood wide still, and servants bustled about as enthusiastically as they ever had.

'You can hardly tell anything happened, can you?' Simon said.

'No. But the memories are here nonetheless,' Baldwin said, tapping his breast.

'You still feel the pain, don't you?'

'Yes. I murdered that poor devil when all he wanted was to stop the pain.'

'He was mad, Baldwin. You wouldn't hesitate if it were a rabid dog, would you?'

'No. Yet Mark's offence was, he wanted to learn more about his real father. Since he had learned who his father was, he wanted to come and be accepted. Instead, he found himself being made the convenient scapegoat of another's crimes.'

'He did hit poor Mary. From what Surval said, he made her miscarry.'

'True – but I doubt he intended to. And I do not think he would have wanted her to lose their child, either. Yet when he saw her dead body, he bolted. He thought his careless blow had killed her, so he hared off in the hope that he could make it to the Bishop's palace where he would be safe. And he would have been, had I not insisted on bringing him back, partly because of Scut and my loathing for him. Only then did he hear of her broken neck and realise he was innocent.'

'You aren't to blame for his death,' Simon tried again.

'I think I am. *I* brought him back here, *I* surrendered him to his father's tender care, *I* had him exposed in court, and *I* actually ended his life.'

'Because he was attempting a murder!'

'The murder of a man who probably deserved it. Some men do, because there is no other means by which their crimes can be resolved or justice dealt. Yet I executed poor Mark, the final terrible act in his pathetic life. And I must carry the guilt of that with me for ever.'

'You should not carry guilt, Sir Knight, but exorcise it,' said a fussy voice.

'Scut. I should have expected you to appear at some point,' Baldwin said, but without warmth.

'People have been coming here to see where the battle was fought,' the cleric said. 'They call it the "Battle of the Mad Monk of Gidleigh" now, and folk have come all the way from Moretonhampstead to see where it took place.'

'You will remain here?' Baldwin asked, a tinge of hopefulness in his voice.

'No, I shall return to Crediton. I wish nothing more to do with this area. I shall return to the church and forget.'

'You are fortunate.'

'What you should do is serve a penance. Travel, Sir Knight! Go on a pilgrimage, to Canterbury or further afield. It would salve your conscience.'

'A pilgrimage – me? Perhaps,' Baldwin smiled.

'How is Flora?' Simon asked.

'Not good. She appears to be suffering a slow, lingering death. She wastes away, but there is no apparent cure, no matter what the leaches prescribe.'

'She has not recovered from her horrors? It is not surprising,' Baldwin said. 'Women are the weaker sex.'

'Weaker be damned,' Scut said with surprising force. 'There's something else at bottom. Can you think of anything that should have upset her so strongly?'

'I heard,' Simon said, 'that she and Osbert were to marry, but he has not spoken to her since the fire.'

'Oh. The oldest reason in the world,' Baldwin sighed. 'I wish we could cure it.'

Roger Scut sniffed and peered along his nose at the stolid figure of Osbert in the distance. 'Leave it to me,' he grunted. 'If he has strung that girl along, I shall put the fear of Hellfire into him!'

Chapter Thirty-Nine

Simon was almost home again. The events of the last days were, happily, beginning to fade as he rode along the ridge that wound its way to the castle and his own home.

'Sir?'

'What, Hugh?'

'Were you serious, like, about me staying on here when you go to Dartmouth?'

'Yes. I don't want to lose you and your support, but I'd rather that than force you so far away.'

'Oh.'

They reached the yard before his house, and Simon dropped thankfully from his mount. He strode into the house. There, in his hall, he saw his daughter and a youth.

'Ah. Um . . . Edith . . .'

'Oh! *Father!*' she cried, and ran into his arms. 'You were gone so long. Do you know Peter? He's apprentice to Master Harold, the merchant. Peter, this is my father.'

'Sir, er, Bailiff, er, er . . .'

Simon was ready to blast the fellow for coming here and upsetting the nature of his homecoming, but then he thought again. The lad was gentle, devoted to Edith, from the way he watched her with a hound's eyes, and if his clothing was anything to go by, his master was wealthy. There were many worse suitors whom Edith could have chosen. He was not, thank God, a priest or an already married man. That was greatly in his favour.

'I am pleased to meet you, and here's my hand on that,' Simon said warmly. 'Please, take a seat and have a little wine. Hugh? *HUGH!* Wine here.'

He settled back in his seat, gratefully accepting the cup that Hugh brought to him, and sighed contentedly. His daughter looked very happy, he thought, glancing at Edith, not that she noticed his look; she had eyes only for her man.

Peter, he mused. The same name as his son. Perhaps there was a sign there. Maybe this Peter was to be trusted as a son. And perhaps, he thought, it was no sign at all but merely the fluke of chance. Someone else favoured that saint's name over all the others.

It would be good to have a son to whom he could speak as an equal, a fellow who would give his daughter a happy home and children, but Simon still felt dubious. This lad was too young. Hell and damnation: Edith was too! She'd been in love with so many others in the last year or two. He watched them covertly. There was something between them, he noted. Edith looked relaxed, and mature. Surprisingly mature.

Perhaps it wasn't so surprising. She was old enough to marry, to bear her own children, to live with her husband. Simon was the one who was confused about his age and position. He saw a middle-aged man in the mirror, but still felt young. And now, after the case of the mad monk at Gidleigh, he was still more confused. Giving Hugh the freedom to stay with his wife was not something he regretted, but it was a grim thought that he would have to live without Hugh when he moved with his wife to Dartmouth.

Dartmouth! He pursed his lips. That would be a while now. The Abbot wouldn't mind, because any churchman's first responsibility had to be to the cure of souls, but Simon did not look forward to telling his master that he would be grateful for a little time free so that he could make a penitential journey. Simon would still move to Dartmouth, but Abbot Robert must allow him to go on pilgrimage first.

The idea of travelling to Spain was daunting, but curiously attractive too. He had heard much of the countries over the sea from Baldwin, and there was a tingling delight at the thought of going and seeing them. It was alarming and exciting all at once.

And he certainly owed thanks to God. He and Baldwin had been in danger too many times over the last year. It was time to give thanks.

His soul needed cleansing. He would go with Baldwin on the long journey to Spain. And while he was gone, he thought, surreptitiously eyeing his daughter and Peter once more, perhaps this fellow's father would take care of his daughter. Hugh would remain and protect the house and Simon's wife until Simon's return.

His wife. Right now he was more scared of telling his wife this news than he ever had been during the battle at the castle.

Roger Scut grunted with the effort as he lifted one end of the long plank into place in the socket of the wall. It fitted, he thought, and went to the other end, raising that too. Balancing it on his shoulder, he started up the ladder to set it into the corresponding socket on the opposite wall, but as he climbed, the angle of the ladder made the plank move. It teetered and dropped, all but pulling him from the ladder.

He let his end fall and stood on the ladder without speaking. If he had opened his mouth, he knew that only expletives would have erupted from it. Better by far to remain silent. Only when his temper had returned to an even level did he sniff, clear his throat, and climb back down to the ground.

'Master cleric! Would you like some help?'

'Osbert, if I could fall on my knees and shower your feet with kisses, I would do so for that offer, but I fear my knees are a little barked and my back is twisted. If I fell to my knees, I might not be able to rise again.'

Osbert grinned. He had a slash in his flank where a man-at-arms had thrust at him after he opened the door to the hall, but it was healing nicely, according to his physician.

'I can at least hold one end of the plank up there.'

With his help Roger Scut soon had the timber up. This was the first piece of the roof, the long plank that rested on the two highest points of the walls, and against which he could start to position the roof trusses. 'That's better!' he approved, hands on his hips, when he was once more on the ground and could look up at the new timber.

'You're sure the walls will take the weight again? The fire was fierce here.'

'With God's support, this little house will remain secure,' Roger Scut said with a confidence he did not feel. 'May I offer you some bread and cheese? I have ale, too.'

Osbert nodded at the mention of ale, and the two men went to the monk's little shelter, a rude dwelling built of branches and twigs with mud caking the gaps to make it windproof. There had been much rain in the last few days, and Osbert knew Scut was having to replenish the mud daily.

'Now!' the monk said, leaning back against a post when he had set out all his food and a jug of ale. 'Tell me all. How is your wife?'

Osbert smiled shyly. 'She is well, I thank you. Her face is healing, and Lady Annicia has promised us the mill when it is completed. I hope to be able to finish the roof next week.'

Roger Scut nodded, outwardly content, although in reality he was burning with jealousy. It had taken him so long to clear all the debris from the chapel, and all the effort had been his own. Others were not keen to see the little building restored. They preferred to think of it as defiled.

'If you wanted,' Os said haltingly, 'I think I could persuade some men to help you.'

'There is no need. They think this place is evil, but it's not true. This is a house of God. With care and love, it can rise again. Especially if the monk who lives here can prove himself to the community.'

'Will you remain?'

'Come, Os! I married you, what more do you want from me!' Scut laughed.

Osbert gave a fleeting smile. He had married Flora at the first opportunity.

After the attack on the castle, he had left the place and gone back to his old home. The news that Ben had given him, that

Huward had been a cuckold and Flora was likely Sir Ralph's and not the miller's, had struck him dumb with horror. He had wanted her so badly. After discovering the power of his love for her, after wanting her sister for so long, learning that he was prevented by that most simple barrier from ever marrying her had all but destroyed him.

And then, soon after the battle at the castle, this same Scut had hurried to his home and berated him for being so feeble-minded that he couldn't see that he himself looked in no way like Sir Ralph. It wasn't something he'd have thought of.

As soon as the news had sunk in, he had dropped his tools and sped to the castle, where Flora had been living as maid to Lady Annicia. Scut had followed him, and with the priest at his side, he had stated his desire to marry Flora. Then, when he had fallen silent, he had stood gazing at her with mingled dread, at the thought of a refusal, and expectation. He was sure she wouldn't refuse him. And at last, when she dropped her eyes and told him in front of the witnesses that she was pleased to marry him now, he had felt as though his breast would burst for sheer joy.

'I am the happiest man in the world, monk.'

Roger Scut paused. He had been gulping a mazer of ale, and now he slowly lowered the cup. It was automatic. He couldn't help but gaze down his nose at the lad, the great, lumbering oaf, who sat with that beatific smile all but splitting his head in two. His mouth opened to let slip a scathing comment, but he closed his mouth and instead, smiled in return. It was not his place to be contemptuous of peasants. He had no right.

That point had been made abundantly clear when he had met the representative of the Bishop. It was Peter Clifford, the Dean of Crediton, who appeared at the castle a day or two after Sir Baldwin himself had gone, and held a meeting with Roger. It had not been a pleasant meeting. Much of Roger Scut's behaviour was known to the Dean, and Roger had not been able to deny the main thrust of the accusation, which was that he had been seeking to win money to the detriment of his holy duties. It would have to cease.

'It is over, Dean,' Roger had said. 'I will not forget the lessons which I have learned here. In future, I shall be humble *and* obedient. Trust me, I do not intend ever trying to seek preferment. Rather, I would take a small church far from anywhere and live the quiet life of the recluse.'

The Dean had smiled at that. A thin, calculating smile, and at the sight of it, Roger Scut had felt his cods freeze.

'Very well. But there is no need to find a church, when we have a chapel that needs repairing. See to that, and we shall be pleased enough. Let the rebuilding be your penance for your pride and greed. And when it is done, we shall consider where you may best serve the Church.'

Os was finished. He had to go to the castle now to speak to the carpenter and Lady Annicia's steward about the timbers he needed for the mill, and he rose and gave a fond farewell to the priest. For him, Roger Scut was a generous, kindly man who deserved respect.

It was odd. Roger felt quite warm inside as Os left. It was as though a man's wholehearted respect was enough in itself to cheer him. A curious thought. He went back to his chapel and stared up at the single beam. It was good to see the beginning of his efforts. Next he must set the roof trusses in place, each leaning at opposite sides of the main beam, and begin the laborious task of nailing each rafter in place. Someone else must bind the thatch.

So much labour. He had already ripped his tunic in three places, and there was no bath here. If he wished to clean himself, he must mortify his flesh in the freezing stream. Yet oddly enough, there was something about this place, something that had struck a chord in his breast . . .

Hearing a mew, he bent and picked up his kitten. Os had brought it a week ago. Strange, he'd never owned a pet, but this small, frail-feeling creature was oddly comforting.

In fact, if he wasn't ever allowed back to Crediton . . . he wasn't sure that he'd care.

* * *

Thomas sat in the alehouse feeling pleased with life. His arm still smarted from a long raking cut that had opened it almost to the elbow from the wrist, and there was a startlingly bright coloured bruise on his flank where a cudgel had connected during the battle at Gidleigh Castle, but apart from that he felt well enough.

As his ale arrived, he saw that another figure had appeared in the doorway – Godwen. This was the first time he'd seen him since the attack on the castle. Godwen had been badly pounded, even with Thomas guarding him, and he'd been taken to the Lady Annicia's hall to be rested and nursed while Thomas had gone off to Crediton with messages for the Dean, and had been kept there. Other, unwounded messengers had been sent back.

Slowly, Godwen walked down the steps towards Thomas.

'You want to sit?' Thomas said.

'Yes. Thanks.'

It was rare indeed to see Godwen short of a sharp comment or patronising remark, and Thomas felt his eyes widen. 'Fancy a drink?' he asked gruffly.

'Thanks.'

Thomas hailed the woman who owned the place and sat back, carefully avoiding Godwen's red-rimmed eye. They had been friends for a little while, it was true, but their families had been on terms of near-hostility for many years; and then when Thomas was successful in his wooing of Bea, he had fallen out with Godwen. Shortly afterwards, Godwen had married another girl – as though to show that he was perfectly capable of winning whichever woman he wished, but the marriage was not a success. His Jen was a lively, attractive woman, but Godwen had always wanted Bea, and that was that. It was the end of their friendship.

'I heard,' Godwen said, grimly staring into his cup. 'The Keeper told me today. You saved my life.'

Thomas shrugged his shoulders. If asked, he couldn't have explained why he had leaped into the fray to rescue Godwen from those mercenaries, but there was a vague anger at the prospect that his own personal enemy, whose enmity had been forged in the hot fire of his youth, should be taken away by someone who had never even so much as thumbed his nose at Godwen before. That was unbearable. Even Godwen deserved to die at the hand of someone who truly hated him, rather than someone who simply saw him as an irritating obstacle.

'Thank you.'

'No matter.'

'It is to me.'

'Forget it,' Thomas said. He lifted his cup and took a long draught.

His offhand manner irked Godwen. 'There's no need to be so ungracious. You jumped in there, when I'd been knocked down, and stood over me. You could have been shot . . . anything. I appreciate it, I tell you!'

'It was nothing.'

'You just can't bear me thanking you, can you?' Godwen hissed. 'You great dough-laden tub of lard, why can't I just say thanks?'

Thomas slowly turned to peer at him. 'Tub of what?'

'You heard me. God's faith! You are intolerable.'

'At least I don't try long words and such to confuse folk.'

'Aha! Yes, lack of education is a virtue in your family, isn't it?'

'There's nothing wrong with my family.'

'No, nothing that a dose of rat poison wouldn't cure.'

'And how is the lovely Jen?' Thomas jeered. He couldn't help it. It was the effect of sitting next to this man. 'By Christ's wounds, I wish I'd left you to be trampled. It's all you're good for, anyway. Useless barrel of shit.'

'You call me a barrel of shit?'

'Well, tell me if I'm wrong, but I think you'd have to be a barrel. Shit on its own wouldn't stand so tall,' Thomas explained politely.

Godwen's face blanched. He snapped his head to Thomas, winced and hissed as a pain shot through his temples, and jerked a thumb at the door. 'Right, let's go out now, then, and talk about this with steel!'

'I'm not fighting *you*!'

'Aha! Scared of me, are you?'

'No. But I fear what the Keeper would say if he came here and learned we'd been fighting.'

'Oh, it's only fear of losing some blood, is it? If you're scared, leave your dagger here, and we'll fight bare-handed. I could whip you with a hand bound behind my back!'

'You?' Thomas leered, slowly letting his gaze travel the length of Godwen's body.

Godwen stood, tottered, grabbed at the table, then spat, 'Now. Outside, you bastard!'

Thomas rose. As soon as he did so, the pain stabbed at his flank again, and it was with a hand resting on his bruised and broken ribs that he followed Godwen. The rest of the ale-house, nothing loath, went too.

In later years, men still talked about that fight. The way that Godwen threw the first punch, missed, and almost fell on his face; how Thomas aimed a kick at his arse as he passed, slipped in a pat of dog turd, and fell to sit in it. With a roar, he was up again, and then moaning, grabbed at his side. By then Godwen was back, and he ran at Thomas. The other man moved away, but not quickly enough, and Godwen caught his bad side with a flailing fist, which made Thomas give a bellow of rage and agony, while Godwen himself was little better pleased, since he had jarred his own badly damaged shoulder.

That was the extent of the battle. Both withdrew, their honour proven, if not entirely to either man's satisfaction. Both limping, they returned to their drinks. Studiously avoiding each other's faces, they drained their ale. This time Godwen replenished their drinks, and while neither spoke, there was a curious expression on both faces. Later, when Baldwin questioned the alewife, she said that it was as though the natural balance of their humours had been restored. The two had been extremely uncomfortable with their imposed status as lifesaver and man owing gratitude.

'I shall speak to them and tell them never to brawl in public,' Baldwin said. He was preparing to go on his pilgrimage, and he didn't want the trouble of this silly fight. It was beneath him.

'I wouldn't if I was you,' the alewife said sagely.

'Why not?'

'They're back to normal now. They'll snarl and bicker like two tomcats, but when all's said and done, they're happy again. Just leave them be.'

'But shouldn't I make Godwen prove his gratitude?' Baldwin wondered.

If he had asked Thomas, he would have had a speedy reply. Both men wanted what they already had. The certainty of a local enemy. It was so much easier than an uncertain one.

Sir Baldwin patted his servant on the back as he glanced about the room for the last time. 'Take good care of them, Edgar. I won't be gone that long.'

'No? Travelling from here to Spain?' his servant scoffed. 'I only fear that you'll come upon footpads or felons on the way, without me to guard you.'

'There will be plenty of other travellers, I have no doubt.'

'Perhaps. So long as none of them are more dangerous than others we have known.'

Baldwin smiled and pulled on a heavy riding cloak, as his wife entered the room.

'My love! Please be careful,' Jeanne cried.

'It would be worse if I were travelling alone, but with Simon, I am bound to be safe. Anyway, we shall have many companions. The road to Santiago is filled with pilgrims.'

'Then farewell, my love. Return to us soon,' she said.

He grabbed her and hugged her closely. She was brought up to be restrained and not show her emotions, but he could see the tears trembling on her eyelids, and he loved her for not making a show at his departure. 'I love you,' he whispered. 'I shall be back soon.'

'I love you too,' she said. 'And don't delay. Are you sure there's nothing else you can do to exorcise this demon?'

'No, my love, nothing else. I have killed an innocent. My pilgrimage, I hope, will wash away that guilt.'

'And if it doesn't?'

'Why then, my Lady, I shall return here to you and live disgracefully for the rest of my days,' he said lightly before he hugged her again. 'But I will come back safely, and I shall be freed from this sense of sin, I swear,' he added.

There. It was over.

The funerals of her husband and her beloved child had originally taken place only a couple of days after the mutiny, but now, after some negotiation and the promise of funds, the two had been disinterred and reburied up near the altar in the church.

As she sat, Annicia was aware of the people coming and going about her. Many came to offer her their condolences once again, for they sought to remain on friendly terms with the attractive widow of Gidleigh. She possessed good lands, several herds and flocks, and was rumoured to be rich enough to benefit any new husband.

The priest himself, a pompous, self-important little twerp, twittered about her, his hands fluttering, nervous in the presence of his Lady, but she gave him short shrift and at last she was alone in the great room.

Rising, she felt slightly giddy. At once there was a steadying hand on her arm, and she smiled at Flora without speaking. She was growing fond of her husband's daughter. There was no doubt in her mind that Flora was his child: Flora's eyes, her brow, her lips, all were too much like Sir Ralph's. For his sake if for no other, she was pleased to see Flora so happy in her wedlock. It was good to see so cheery a wife.

Leaving Flora, she walked slowly to the front of the church and stood staring down at the new slabs set into the ground at her feet. There were three in a line, each equidistant from the altar. Although she couldn't read, she was perfectly well aware that the central one was Esmon's, because she had insisted that he should be there, right next to his father. On his other side lay Sir Ralph, and her eyes rested on his slab a moment, without reverence or respect, but with a certain friendship. After all, she had been married to him for some while.

No, her attention was divided equally between the only two men she had ever really loved. Esmon lay there in the middle of the floor, and next to him was his father, Sir Richard Prouse, once the elegant, suave master of Gidleigh – murdered, or so she had thought, by Wylkyn.

'God forgive me!' she said quietly. 'I truly believed he was the murderer, or I should never have persuaded my son to kill him.'

Of course, she now knew that Wylkyn was innocent of the crime. But that was not her fault. It was the only obvious conclusion at the time.

She was sorry that an innocent man was dead, but she felt no remorse, only sadness for the two men she had loved and lost: her lover, Sir Richard Prouse, and her son by him, Esmon. They were all that mattered to her.

Final Note

I should now confess that the whole of this story is based on the poor man who came to be known as 'The Mad Monk': Robert de Middelcote, who lived and served in the chapel not far from Gidleigh. Like Mark, he too had a girlfriend, he too had her conceive, and he too ran from the area. His crime was that he punched his woman in the belly and killed their child in her womb on 28 March 1328.

His tale then diverged from Mark's, because he escaped all the way to the outskirts of Exeter, to Haldon Hill, where he was captured. The records show that he was hauled off to the Bishop's court, but sadly the result of the action has been lost.

We do know what happened to his chapel, though. It was demolished, the stones taken away, and a new chapel built nearer Gidleigh. This new one was consecrated in 1332. We cannot be certain where the old chapel was, so I have made a guess for the purposes of this book. Some people do reckon to be able to point to the old one. If you want to find it, I suggest you try walking over the land from Gidleigh towards Moortown. It should be along that old footpath somewhere.

But I warn you, when I mention that Mark is disgusted by all the mud, I am not joking. This is about the wettest footpath on the eastern section of the moor!

Michael Jecks

Now you can buy any of these other bestselling books by **Michael Jecks** from your bookshop or *direct from his publisher*.

FREE P&P AND UK DELIVERY
(Overseas and Ireland £3.50 per book)

The Sticklepath Strangler	£6.99
The Tournament of Blood	£6.99
The Traitor of St Giles	£6.99
The Boy-Bishop's Glovemaker	£6.99
Belladonna at Belstone	£6.99
Squire Throwleigh's Heir	£6.99
The Leper's Return	£6.99
The Abbot's Gibbet	£6.99
The Crediton Killings	£6.99
A Moorland Hanging	£6.99
The Merchant's Partner	£6.99
The Last Templar	£6.99

TO ORDER SIMPLY CALL THIS NUMBER

01235 400 414

or visit our website: www.madaboutbooks.com

Prices and availability subject to change without notice.